INSATIABLE

DOUBLEDAY

New York London Toronto

Sydney Auckland

ALSO BY MARNE DAVIS KELLOGG

Tramp

Nothing But Gossip

Birthday Party

INSATIABLE

A Novel

MARNE DAVIS

KELLOGG

PUBLISHED BY DOUBLEDAY
a division of Random House, Inc.
1540 Broadway, New York, New York 10036

DOUBLEDAY and the portrayal of an anchor with a dolphin are
trademarks of Doubleday, a division of Random House, Inc.

Book design by Dana Leigh Treglia

Library of Congress Cataloging-in-Publication Data

Kellogg, Marne Davis.
Insatiable / by Marne Davis Kellogg.— 1st ed.
p.   cm.
1. Women painters—Fiction.   I. Title.
PS3561.E39253 I57 2001
813'.54—dc21
00-057005

ISBN 0-385-49578-1

1   3   5   7   9   10   8   6   4   2

For my husband Peter, the love of my life.

In memory of our Gussie.

And for Madeline K. Albright,
with admiration and gratitude
for her service and leadership.

PROLOGUE

*T*his was the last time I would drive it, this meandering, meaningless rural stretch of state highway 301 between Emporia and Jarrett, and the last time I'd visit the "death house," as they like to call it in their overblown testosterone way. It's full of show-off bruisers in Sam Browne belts who will, by God, show us today just how tough they are when they stick a needle in her tender arm, and kill my Madam.

I wiggled into the plush car seat and adjusted the little pillow, trying to find some comfort—I'm quite certain at least two of my disks have ruptured, which has resulted in a whole new program of medications: In addition to my allergy pills, I'm now forced to take four or five anti-inflammatories every morning, which makes it necessary for me to chew up an equal number of antacids, and I won't even begin to tell you the hell that plays with my systems, if you know what I mean. Maybe when all this is over, I'll go see a physician. When all this is over, I'll have time to do a lot of things, but there'll be no joy in their doing.

I pulled out of town and pointed the rented Taurus due north. As I gained speed down the lonesome highway in the midday heat—I-95 would have been quicker, but there was really no hurry—the sun broke through the trees and burned through the side window and, for a second, reflected off my watch into the rearview mirror, blinding me the way Ryder McCormick's good eye did the last time I saw him, when it twinkled with such triumphant evil as the verdict was read. Oh, Lord, I shuddered. The triumph of evil. And all the while his glass eye remained dark, unfeeling, solid, as cruel and implacable as Darth Vader's mask.

The quiet, Southern Virginia farmland flowed by and I watched the trial again, as I did every day in my mind's eye, trying to figure out how he got away with it.

No one stood up for her at the trial, or at the sentencing hearing. No one but me, and who am I? No one but the butler. Ryder had worn an eye-patch throughout the entire three-month ordeal, lest a single juror forget for a single moment that he was half blind. A half blind man who had cared for his invalid and dying wife. Not just any dying wife, mind you, but Mary Anne Schlumbacher McCormick, a delightful, wealthy, brilliant—let me say it again—*invalid,* who had only weeks at the most to live, anyway. The prosecution claimed that my Madam, wild with jealousy, had cold-bloodedly and maliciously shot Mrs. McCormick in the head and dumped her out of her wheelchair into the lake. Madam and I knew it was a lie. I had served them tea that afternoon out on the dock at Mrs. McCormick's farm, and Madam and I had left together. I'd been with her the whole time. Well, just about the whole time.

"We'd both become afraid of Jackie," Ryder mewled about Madam from the stand. He had worn the same clothes to court every day—a rumpled sport coat with a buttoned cardigan vest and a *knit tie.* The sight almost made me laugh out loud. Ryder McCormick, the biggest sartorial snob on the face of the earth, in a cardigan vest and a knit tie? Please. "She was stalking us. My wife was terrified, and I know the fear intensified her illness. The doctor said she had only weeks, maybe just days, to live. And then, to come home and find her floating in the lake, her wheelchair overturned on the dock. She was as frail as a dove. Oh,

God, my beloved, beloved Mary Anne . . ." Then Ryder fell apart. It went beyond losing his composure, he just flat out burst into tears and blubbered like a big baby. And the judge called a recess. What absolute crap.

GREENSVILLE CORRECTIONAL FACILITY, the sign read. SLOW TO 5 MPH. DIM LIGHTS. STOP.

"This'll be your last visit." The guard checked my driver's license and one of his sidekicks frisked me while another guided a German Shepherd through my car.

"Next to the last," I said.

"You coming back tonight?"

I nodded.

He breathed out hard and shook his head. What more could he say? "You're clear to enter, Mr. Weatherby-Smythe. Follow the road to the first right, through the gates. The guard there will tell you how to proceed. Welcome to Greensville."

He'd recited the same instructions every day for four days, ever since they'd moved her down from the women's prison in Fluvanna for her execution.

Madam had never looked or acted afraid. I could not imagine what she was made of that gave her such strength, beyond her adoration of the Blessed Virgin. But you'd think, even with that, she'd give up a tear or two.

The door of the visiting room opened with a slow click and she shuffled in wearing her orange jumpsuit and white Keds scuffs, her wrists caught at her waist with a heavy shackle belt that rubbed them raw, her ankles encircled with bruising steel cuffs that were joined with a short link of chain. The light shone off her hair as off wet coal, and her hooded dark blue eyes gazed at me peacefully. She held a thick manila envelope in her hands and waited patiently while one of the burly female guards removed the shackles. Then she sat down across the table and lit a cigarette. "How are the dogs?"

"Fine, Madam. As naughty as ever." My jaunty answer was hollow. I struggled not to cry.

Madam smiled and handed the envelope to the heavy-girthed matron, who outweighed me two-to-one. Her only weapon, beyond arms and legs as thick as tree trunks, was a small solar-powered microphone clipped to her shirt collar. She opened the envelope and riffled through the pages, looking for contraband, before putting them back in and passing the packet to me.

"You don't need to look at those now, Nigel," Madam said. "Just some last minute papers. But, listen to me, my darling friend . . ." She gave me a look so drenched in love and kindness, I could feel my heart begin to swell with tears. My chest tightened and I couldn't breathe. Her voice was calm. "That envelope also contains my will, and I've left everything to you. You'll be able to live very comfortably."

What fun was the money without her? The brown paper felt like ashes in my hands.

"Do you promise you'll come tonight?"

I nodded.

"You'll bury me at the farm?"

"Yes, Madam," I whispered.

"You'll stay at the farm forever?"

"I promise."

She stood and ground out her cigarette and focused her eyes on mine. The matron re-hitched the chains.

"I love you, Nigel."

"I love you with all my heart, Madam."

Now I am going to tell you my story, straight out. I won't pull any punches and I don't care if you believe any of it or not.

1

THREE YEARS EARLIER

"Who was that?" Madam's voice came around the corner from her dressing room and sounded hopeful. God knows, we could use a little joy around this house at the moment.

I hung up the phone.

I lacked both the heart and the guts to tell her it was the bank. My pay check had bounced. Again. What some would call my spinelessness, but which I preferred to regard as amenability, has ceased to concern me. I am what I am. And, in fact, I think it is this ability to be amenable, my willingness to play second fiddle, to hold the towel for the victor or the vanquished, to soldier on—loyal, steadfast, and true—that makes me a good servant. Perhaps even a great one. "Wrong number," I answered.

It was a perfect country morning. Sunlight filtered through the lacy branches of the dense hardwoods that towered over the house and down the hill. The trees were now mostly bare after a spectacular Virginia autumn and gave a glimpse of the clear, sharp sky. The sun had forced a velvety mist from the heavy dew that blanketed the fields overnight, and in the woods beyond, where the ground was wet and cobwebby, thick with fallen leaves. All the night creatures had retired, leaving only an occasional red fox scurrying home to its den, turning his turf over to the few remaining songbirds and our herd of pet white-tailed deer. The mist was bright and patchy. It danced over the meadow and flirted with the trees before vanishing into thin air. Sometimes, especially on silent mornings such as this, I found our forest as magical as that of Titania and Oberon, where little was what it seemed.

Much like our illusory life, filled with phonies of little substance, pursued by others who would go to any extent to join this fake, glittery world. A world where people appear to have unlimited time, money, and happiness. A world of danger and hidden traps . . . of silly, vain, reckless flatterers. A world of sophisticated fools. But, I mused—enjoying the moment of quiet as I gathered up Madam's breakfast tray—they were *our* fools and their vanity paid our bills. So who was I to judge? And frankly, today, with our finances in the state they're in, we could use another fool or two.

I watched three of the white-tails—a young stag with furry antlers just budding from his head and two wide-eyed does—tentatively enter the meadow, their black noses shiny, ears and tails twitching, their footprints as distinctive in the dew as if it were snow.

"The deer are here," I said.

"I can't imagine what they think they're going to find to eat until that hay's delivered—they've already inhaled every leaf on the property. Did you get a good price on it?"

"Pretty fair." See what I mean? We're down to worrying about the price of hay.

It had been a rough few months. Madam's mother had died and—in a letter delivered from her lawyers the day after her death—informed Madam that her mother had left the bulk of her estate, which consisted primarily of her gigantic, demented, and wildly overvalued paintings, to the Museum of Modern Art in New York City. This upset Madam so much she locked herself in her room for two days and refused to attend her own mother's funeral, a massive blow-out at the Musée d'Orsay. I went, just so I could report the details, in case she asked. Which she did the minute I returned to the Place Vauban apartment where her mother had lived and painted for forty years, and where Madam had grown up, the only child of Constanza di Fidelio, one of the Twentieth Century's most famous painters, and her late husband, Rubirosa.

Constanza was a raving mad, lunatic bitch. She had been cruel and jealous, and, in most people's opinions, maybe even borderline psychotic. She ran her studio like an old-fashioned opium den where any and every mind-altering substance known to mankind was not only available, but bountiful. People came and went around the clock, eating, sleeping, and fornicating whenever and wherever the urge overtook them. For my Madam, it must have been like growing up in Bedlam, so I didn't find it at all surprising that now, as an equally famous, much-in-demand portrait artist, she was a little off-beam, a little cockeyed herself. Who wouldn't be, under the circumstances? And me? I loved her in spite of, because of, her vulnerabilities.

We'd been back stateside, at Madam's small farm in Middleburg, Virginia for several weeks, struggling to keep up appearances. She'd counted on more from her mother, but actually, to tell the truth, I myself wasn't a bit surprised at the mean-spirited inheritance: the Paris studio and a handful of minor works, which—if Madam sold them judiciously—could help bridge the span between what she made and what she spent.

The few works Constanza had previously given her daughter as gifts during their occasional periods of reconciliation, and that hung in our house—the *Zodiacs*, twelve separate works that when hung together theoretically made up a single piece, although I personally could never figure them out, and *Andromeda*, a gigantic, ochre-colored mess—were copies. Fakes. Madam had sold the originals before they'd even made it through the front door, spending the money on mortgage payments and gardenias.

We'd been living without a net for quite a while. What we needed was a rich man. She kept herself in tip-top shape but who's kidding who: time was running out.

"I'll be out in the studio, Nigel," she said, entering the bedroom in her work uniform: a loose linen shirt over a Lycra body-stocking—today's was black—and soft leather ballet slippers.

Madam is what we refer to in England as an "exotic," with looks that teetered just on this side of good, a coin-toss that had landed in her favor. Her coal-black hair that, but for chance, could have been drab and coarse, was instead thick and wavy, and today, instead of being pulled tightly into a chignon and hidden under a cluster of gardenias, it tumbled in a ponytail mid-way down her back. And her eyes—wide, unreadable, so dark a blue they were almost black—were heavily hooded and slightly tilted. With five seconds more or less gestation, they could have been heavy, lethargic, froggy eyes. Instead, they shone with intelligence and always glittered just a little on this side of danger. Her mouth, full-lipped, always ready to laugh or cry, would have been wrecked by a set of perfect teeth and we would have been robbed of her slightly gap-toothed smile. She was as lush and volatile and alluring as a gypsy.

I've never been too clear on where her father, Rubirosa, who died when she was a child, came from. Some days he was portrayed as an Argentinean playboy, others as a Mexican freedom fighter, and still others as a Philippine lumber baron. Whatever he was, he was swarthy and there had been a good deal of money involved. Now all gone, of course, pissed out the window into the Place Vauban by Constanza's stream of needy lovers.

Little wonder that Madam herself was a keg of nitro that pulsed like an African drum. She was wild and unpredictable, funny and charming, morose and maudlin, bold and direct, timid and withdrawn. The only qualities she had not inherited from her mother, as far as I could tell, were cruelty and vindictiveness. In fact, she was just the opposite: Madam was way too easily manipulated, she had far too much need to be liked and far too little confidence in her own strengths. In my opinion, she was a perfect candidate for Multiple Personality Disorder, but, according to my *Family Medical Reference Guide*, which I kept with me at all times, she did not exhibit any of the symptoms—fragmentation, delusions, detachment, and so forth. Not yet, anyhow. As it was, she could have been the poster girl for Bipolar Disorder, complete Manic-

Depressive lunacy, but of course when she went for her annual physical, she was as normal as pie. I think a little Lithium would have helped her a lot, but then, again, it probably would have stolen her talent. So I kept my mouth shut and soldiered on, ready as always to catch her at the fall.

She had been born in France, named Jacqueline in honor of Jacqueline Bouvier Kennedy (later Onassis), and educated from the seventh grade on in America, at an exclusive girls' boarding school in Virginia. So when she was in America, she was American. In France, French. In Bolivia, Bolivian. And so forth. Of everywhere, and yet, nowhere. A true exotic.

An exotic with all the good humor of a bear with sore toenails. My Madam, who could charm the birds out of the trees if she wanted to, had—as I mentioned—been in a ghastly mood since her mother died and left all her money to the museum. This bad humor was exacerbated by the fact that Madam was locked into a sick affair with a rogue named Ryder McCormick, one of her own late mother's long-time lovers. Ever since Madam entered puberty, there had been an unrelenting sexual undercurrent between them—dark and forbidden—never satisfied, never consummated until those final, endless days of Constanza's life when, as she lay on her deathbed, eaten alive by lung cancer, contorted with pain and unable to move, her lover and her daughter surrendered to their passion, fucking each other insatiably right outside her door.

Ryder McCormick, with his bloody good looks and that bloody glass eye that glittered as hard and cold as ice, was bad news. His charm and manners were polished and flawless. He was elegant, graceful, overpowering, and had the sort of domineering effect on men and women that dared them to challenge him because he had no money of his own. He was a sycophant and he was the first to admit it—proud of the fact that he had always been a kept man.

But no matter how great and long-awaited the sex between them was, something much darker lurked beneath the surface. Some element of Ryder's personality enabled him to gain a malignant, almost Rasputin-like power over certain people. Constanza had been unable, or at least unwilling, to stand up to him. He had dominated her in a way that demeaned and degraded her and now that mantle had slid as silently and invisibly as toxic fog from mother to daughter. Madam had willingly surrendered the keys to her psyche, unwittingly invited him to come in and become her jailer. And now, barring some cataclysm or catastrophe, it looked as though there would be no escape.

Well, be that as it may, no matter how horrible or wrong it was, it was also none of my knitting. My opinion had not been solicited, and even if it had, I wouldn't have offered it. Madam's frequent trysts with Ryder inevitably left her feeling angry, betrayed, empty, guilty, and wanting more. I knew. I was always there for the stormy aftermath—a depth of damage and frustration that exceeded the perennial and pathetic humiliation of the single woman in love with the married man. She careened like a caged canary between the warpath and the love nest. I was the one who jollied her up, playing a few hands of gin or having a cocktail with her in the library while we watched *Biography*. But her need for him sat there in the room with us.

I prayed for relief.

"And who's *this?*" She stopped at the window and frowned, her fists jammed onto her hips. The Yorkies started barking like lunatics.

A dull gray sedan approached down the long gravel driveway. I'd watched enough American television to know no one you ever want to see arrives in a gray sedan. A man and a woman got out.

"I'll send them away."

There would be no joy in Middleburg today.

2

*I*s Jacqueline di Fidelio home?" asked the man, who wore a non-descript dark suit. His brown hair was close-clipped and a small scab had formed on his chin where he'd cut himself shaving. A wall-eyed distortion of my face reflected back at me in his dark glasses, which I assumed he'd left on to avoid eye contact and intimidate me in case I made any trouble, which I could have assured him right there on the spot, I would in no way do. Not me.

He and the woman held up wallets displaying official identifications, which I scrutinized. Agent Romano with the Federal Bureau of Investigation and Agent Collier with the Internal Revenue Service.

"Please come in. I'll inquire if Madam is available."

My paycheck has bounced and now if Madam is about to be arrested and incarcerated, I thought as I ascended the stairs, one heavy, deliberate step at a time—which, for someone as diminutive and happy as I, was a skill achieved only with years and years of assiduous daily practice—what will I do?

In butler school, my lack of "deliberateness," my inability to proceed with purposeful dignity, was what kept me back a year. I had too much joie de vivre, I was too much a terrier to trudge naturally. It had to be browbeaten out of me. I had to be cowed into submission, thudded on the head with a club like a lumbering, dumb beast. Finally, the overtly stated fact that if I did not get with the program, I would not receive my certificate from Lady Atchley's School—my absolute last chance if I were to avoid going to work for my parole officer's uncle at his trash collecting business—terrified me to such an extent I immediately wiped the smile off my face and settled properly into the traces. The thought of spending the rest of my life bouncing through Birmingham's potholed streets as I clutched the slimy handrails of one of those reeking, smoke-belching garbage trucks wearing filthy coveralls and a wide, thick leather belt cinched tight enough to keep my kidneys from rupturing straight out of my body when I picked up heavy barrels of week-old festering chicken parts and dirty diapers, was so indescribably execrable, it scared the wits right out of me. For the rest of my term at Lady Atchley's, I became as dull and invisible as the rest of my butler mates, to whom being unnoticeable came naturally.

So if these government people were looking for trouble, they were barking up the wrong tree. Life's underbelly has never been my cup of tea.

Under their cold, imperturbable eyes, my heart and my feet turned to lead. It was all I could do to drag them up the stairs. It was a natural trudge. Lady Atchley would have been proud.

"I'd sure love to have a butler," the IRS woman said to her colleague. She was a strawberry-blonde and her voice reminded me of one of Madam's clients, an especially tiresome woman who lived in Ft. Myers, Florida who spoke in a flat Minnesota monotone. I suspected she had to have even the most basic jokes explained to her in excruciating detail and then she would still not get them.

It may seem to you I am too judgmental, maybe you even find me bitchy, but the fact of the matter is, I'm a pretty good judge of character and I like to make snap evaluations and then see if I'm right, which I generally am. Besides, in the evenings, when it's just Madam and me in the library for cocktails, she asks what I think, and my observations usually are good for a laugh or two, if nothing more. Sometimes it's enough to get us all the way through dinner.

The government people were what I call the new kind of humans. They had the hard, bony, scary look of forty-year-olds who work out everyday and have no body fat. Who take their children from all-day daycare to evening-care at the health club while they work out and count it as quality family-time because they're in the next room and not wearing their business clothes. These were the kinds of people who frightened me most, because they were jealous, they had *attitudes,* they hated rich people, and worst of all, they had *power.* They could destroy our lives without even the smallest backward glance and feel totally justified in whatever actions they took, because they truly believed that somewhere, somehow, we *deserved* it.

They'd settled in the sunroom on white wicker armchairs with bright yellow chintz cushions. Large windows opened out onto the field, which had turned sharp and clear with no remnants of the early morning's gentle mist. I poured cups of coffee and set a plate of bite-sized sticky orange rolls on the square glass coffee table among the stacks of thick, glossy art books.

"Thank you, Nigel," Madam said. Her face had gone pale and in spite of the fact that she was over six-feet tall, six-one-and-a-half to be exact, she looked diminutive and defenseless. She could be shockingly meek, a real turn-tail artist—and she had that look about her now. But then again, it could all change like lightning and she could detonate like a hydrogen bomb. Madam was as unstable as Uranium-238, and you never really knew what you were going to get until it was too late. Right now, I could see she was stalled, casting back and forth between attacker and victim, aggressor and defender. I was afraid that if she didn't pull herself together and just act like a normal, intelligent human being, we'd sink without bubbles into the swampy oblivion of the broke and broken, which I've spent my entire life trying to swim clear of.

The Internal Revenue Service was nothing to mess around with— especially when you were in Madam's perpetually precarious position with them—and everyone in the room knew it.

I pulled the French doors closed with great showy ceremony, just as Madam likes it done when there are visitors we're not too sure of, or who we know will be impressed by such Hollywood-style folderol—we're very into the theatrical around this household—and prayed we were on the right track.

Then I tiptoed around the living room sofa and sat quietly in a small chair next to the matching pair of doors I'd left open at the far end. I was quiet as a mouse. What would she do without me?

3

FBI Agent Romero spoke first. "Miss di Fidelio," he began in a warm and ingratiating way. "I assume you're familiar with the March 18, 1990, Gardner Museum robbery in Boston in which thirteen paintings, worth approximately two hundred and fifty million dollars, were stolen. I assume you also know none of those works has been recovered."

Madam regarded him through a cloud of exhaled smoke. "Everyone knows about the missing Gardner works. I hope you don't think I took them." She joked to no effect. Her hand trembled slightly as she took another drag on her cigarette.

"Do you know an international art dealer named Armand Weil?"

"Of course. He's the most powerful dealer in the world. Everyone knows Armand Weil. You don't think *he* stole them?"

"We have reason to believe Mr. Weil is in possession of a number of these stolen works, in particular the big four." The agent withdrew a folded paper from the breast pocket of his jacket. *"The Concert* by Vermeer; two Rembrandts: *Lady and Gentleman in Black* and *Storm on the Sea of Galilee,* and an Edward Manet called *Chez Tortoni."*

"That's the most ridiculous thing I've ever heard," Madam laughed. "I don't know where you get your information, but I can tell you right now, Armand wouldn't be involved in anything like that. He'd be out of business in no time if he were dealing in stolen or counterfeit pieces. It would destroy his reputation." She sipped her coffee and—now that she realized they were there about business other than her back taxes—placed the cup steadily back on its saucer and patted the large ottoman beside her for the dogs to come up.

"You're right, Miss di Fidelio." Romero was sitting on the edge of his chair with his feet spread and firmly planted, and now he leaned forward and laid his forearms across his knees. He clasped his hands together and then spread them, extending his palms toward her in a conciliatory way. "Mr. Weil is a very powerful person, so we don't want to make a premature or wrong move against him. But, not only do we suspect that he has possession of these works, we also have reason to believe he is the biggest art thief in the world."

Madam was caught totally off-guard. "Are you *crazy?* Armand Weil stealing works of art? What are you all smoking for breakfast over there at the FBI? Besides, since when is the FBI interested in stolen art? You don't track it, you don't have any numbers on it."

"We have changed our priorities since the insurance industry started putting pressure on Congress."

"Typical," Madam huffed. "Besides, so what? The Gardner works weren't insured in the first place."

Ignoring her attitude, Agent Romero continued tonelessly. "Since that robbery, museums and collectors have changed their policies drastically. Consequently, many more claims are being made against the insurance companies. We're here to ask you to help us confirm whether or not Mr. Weil has the four Gardner paintings, or if he has knowledge of their whereabouts. And then, if he does have possession, to help return them to their rightful owner."

"You want me to spy on him to help out the insurance companies?" She shook her head adamantly. "No way. It would put me out of business. I'm an upstanding American citizen and I believe in doing whatever I can to help my government, but I won't spy on a colleague who I know has absolutely nothing to do with your problem. I'm sorry, but you've wasted your time coming out here."

"Well," Romero started. "We aren't exactly asking you to spy. We'd like you to consider—"

"I don't think I've made myself very clear."

Uh oh. Warning bells started going off in my head. I had a very bad feeling about this. Her tone had changed. This was not a good time to have a fit of pique, a show of grandeur.

"What kind of person do you think I am that I would do such a thing? I don't think you understand how I make my living." Her voice became arrogant. "I paint people's portraits. Important people, rich people. Leaders. I go all over the world and I live with them. In their homes, their villas, their chalets, on their yachts. I'm one of the most sought-after portraitists in the world, not simply because I do a good job—lots of artists have talent—but because I keep my mouth shut. I'm discreet. So now, here you come, asking me to pass on information about someone who could ruin my career? I wouldn't even begin to consider doing something like that."

I jumped to my feet and entered the sunroom just as Madam rose from her chair, darkening the space around her and towering over her visitors like an angry Athena.

So what if she was more gifted and more temperamental in her field than Maria Callas had been in hers, Jacqueline di Fidelio could be her own worst enemy. Long on fantasy, short on reality. Or to paraphrase the words of the immortal Michael Bennett from *A Chorus Line:* Talent: Ten. Judgment: Three.

The dogs jumped to the floor and shot under the sofa.

"I'd like you to leave."

"But Miss di Fidelio—"

"Now."

"I'd like to explain . . ." He implored, to deaf ears.

"More coffee, sir?"

"Not *now*, Nigel." She had ended up in front of the fake *Andromeda*—an oversized mess of chromium oxide green, Mars yellow, and the full spectrum of ochres: from Oxford to Roman, from flesh to burnt—which made it appear as though a cataclysm of galactic goo had shot out of her head.

"Let's cut to the chase, Miss di Fidelio, and clear up the picture for you a little." Agent Collier, the tight-lipped, strawberry-blonde—I told you she was trouble, I knew it the moment I laid eyes on her—ignored the theatrics and snapped open her briefcase. She withdrew a sheet of paper, which she offered with a long-fingered, bloodless hand across the table to Madam, who looked down her nose at the official document as if it were written in Mandarin and folded her arms across her chest, refusing to accept it.

Unperturbed, Agent Collier laid the paper on the coffee table and continued. "As of eight o'clock this morning, you owed $658,774 and change—and growing—in past-due taxes, penalties, and interest to the people of the United States of America—those self-same 'people' of whom you claim to be so proud a part. Now," she clipped the case closed, "we are prepared to make you a one-time-only offer: You help us retrieve these, and any other, stolen paintings you come across in your dealings with Mr. Weil, or we take everything you own. You have five minutes to decide. Starting now." Collier looked at her watch and appeared to push a little button as if it were a stop-watch.

"You can't just . . ." Madam said.

"We can and we have," Collier retorted, cool and steady. She'd played this scene hundreds of times. "You may be a world-famous artist, Ms. di Fidelio, but as far as I'm concerned, you're nothing but a spoiled, caught, tax-cheat and criminal. We have authorization documents signed by the director of the Internal Revenue Service. The padlocks and the red stickers are in the trunk of the car. We're ready to go."

"Padlocks?" Madam shrieked. "Are you kidding? Nigel, *do* something."

Oh, Lord. We're really in it this time. Madam ran from the room.

"I'll talk to her, miss." I picked up the piece of paper. "I'm sure there won't be any problem at all."

"I'm sure you're right."

After they were gone, I noticed they'd never touched the orange rolls or coffee, another one of their stupid little power moves.

At the far end of the meadow, a wisp of smoke curled up from the stone chimney of Madam's studio, and I knew that Ryder had arrived and was waiting for her. The dogs and I watched silently through the sunroom windows as Madam marched toward him, crossing the field swiftly on her long legs, propelled by her anger.

4

CHRISTMASTIME

I can't wait to get off this floating litter box," I said to one of the Yorkies.

We'd been on Mrs. Payne's mega-yacht, the *Kiss-Kiss,* a 230 foot-long Ecco ocean liner, for three weeks, two of them enduring a stomach-lurching float from Marbella, Spain, to Palm Beach, Florida. For the last week, we'd been anchored in crystal clear waters doing a slow bob-and-roll two miles offshore from one of America's most exclusive clubs, or at any rate, one of its most expensive, Conrad Robertson's Sol d'Oro, while Madam finished Mrs. Payne's portrait.

I was killing time until the mid-morning coffee hour by sitting at Madam's dressing table, trying on her jewelry—all of it dramatically oversized. They're such skillful knock-offs of hammered Lalaounis chokers and cuffs and Bulgari-style emerald and ruby necklaces and earrings that only the designers themselves could tell the difference. The pieces were part of Madam's Amazonian stagecraft, so audacious that no one would have the nerve to think they weren't the real thing. Even the ropes of sixteen-millimeter black pearls looked as if they had been scooped up from Java's ocean floor, instead of a table at a Madison Avenue boutique's half-off clearance sale.

The dogs watched me from their favorite spot, the middle of the bed pillows. I sprayed on a little Opium perfume from an antique Lalique crystal atomizer engraved with a maiden in a transparent gown with a bow in her hair and a bouquet of lilies of the valley in her hand, dipping her toe into a pool while birds watched from a tree. For just the briefest moment I considered pocketing it. But instead, I admired myself in the bank of three mirrors atop the classically curved table. I glittered like a maharaja.

Just because I'm a perfectionist and have always had a somewhat delicate physiognomy, lots of people think I'm gay. But I'm not. I might have thought I was for a while when I was younger, until I found myself incarcerated for being an accomplice to grand theft, of which, I admit, I was guilty. But all I was, was the safe-cracker. I didn't even have a gun. That ungodly prison experience made me swear off almost all sex of any kind, almost forever. Basically, I'm sexless. I do admit to occasional urges of one kind or another every so often, but I seldom give in to them because I know how quickly they can get out of hand. I'm truly very happy living vicariously. The fast lane was simply too fast for me.

I gazed longingly toward the distant coastline. There were people having fun over there on terra firma. A voyage on the *Kiss-Kiss* was reported to be fun as well, when there were other guests; it could accommodate eight couples in unimaginable comfort. But for three interminable weeks it had been just Lynette Payne, Madam, and me. And the crew, of course. It was a big ship and the days were long.

The boat itself was magnificent, if boats were your thing. It was blindingly white, with ribbons of dark-tinted windows along two of the four decks. And since there were no guests on this particular cruise, she carried a skeleton crew of seventeen, a distinct society unto itself; those who see nothing yet see everything, who hear nothing yet hear everything. They were highly skilled and elegantly deferential, but, behind the scenes, they had their own quirks and power struggles. It was an exclusive close-knit world, this cadre of professionals who made their living in service on private yachts.

The crew was divided into four sovereign nations—bridge, galley, above decks/housekeeping, and spa—each with its own emperor who ferociously protected his turf while respecting the others'.

Up on the bridge, after a week of floating at anchor, the all-Norwegian crew was bored out of their minds. They had electronics and navigation systems more sophisticated than many countries' navies and all they were being used for was video war games. The captain, a dashing Nordic god in snow-white tropicals—crisp white shirt with golden epaulets and starched and creased Bermuda shorts—worked on his tan. He spent most of each day reclined in a lounge chair on the pilot's deck, sipping iced tea or non-alcoholic beer and leaving his first officer in charge as de facto captain. The first officer spent his days twirling about in the captain's high chair, taking infrequent looks through the binoculars and surfing the net, searching for a ship he could command himself. The engine room chief had become so immersed in Patrick O'Brien's nautical mysteries, he had trouble differentiating fantasy from reality; and the radio man/navigator, the youngest of the group, had taken up an email correspondence with a Danish cyber pornography queen. The Norwegians kept completely to themselves, like identical quadruplets who didn't need anyone else. Every afternoon, they played basketball one-on-one for an hour on the foredeck, and while they didn't mind an audience, they never invited anyone else to join in.

The galley—which gleamed like a stainless steel operating room— was under the iron-fisted control of Paul Bernard, a temperamental five-star chef stolen from a three-star Michelin kitchen in Paris. He had a staff of five: two frightened sous-chefs; an overly sensitive master *patissier* who burst into tears regularly over the fact that everybody was always on a diet or off sugar or only wanted vanilla ice cream with fudge sauce, and two beautiful Dutch scullery-girls, Hilda and Heidi, who were like flashes of sunshine in a concentration camp when they weren't being reprimanded by Chef Paul. There was always a crisis in the galley. The atmosphere was so poisonous it upset my stomach, but the meals they produced three, and often four times a day were sumptuous, and when Chef was invited out to say hello at the end of dinner, he always put on a fresh smock, accepted the compliments, and smiled graciously. Mrs. Payne, who had never visited the galley, had no idea of the terror that lurked just behind that swinging door. Just as she had no idea that every cruise began with a completely new kitchen staff because the scuttlebutt in the culinary world was to avoid Chef Paul and the *Kiss-Kiss* if you possibly could.

The decks were under the command of a megalomaniacal, pint-sized majordomo in a cheap toupee, Fernando, whose demeanor was proper, tight-lipped and, when in the presence of his employer or her guests, verging on obsequious, a quality wholly redeemed and balanced by his outrageous, below-decks sense of humor. Fernando's frequent asides while we were serving meals or cocktails were so unexpected, acerbic, and on-target, I'd actually had to leave the room a time or two to compose myself. This was his first, and last, cruise on the *Kiss-Kiss*. He had accepted a position with a divorced Fortune 500 CEO in Connecticut.

"I start after the first of the year. He works twenty hours a day—never home. Entertains only occasionally. He has no wife. He has no children. He has no boats," he told me, his Italian accent lyrical. "Never again. Mrs. Payne has cured me of working for women. She is a pig, always touching me, petting me like one of her cats. It is disgusting."

Fernando and I usually got together in the evenings after our ladies had retired, and sipped a neat single malt while we tried to beat one another at gin rummy. Unfortunately, we were equally accomplished cheaters.

Fernando's wife Elena was his chief housekeeper, who also doubled as the ship's nurse, even though I know a thousand times more about medicine than she does. Her three maids kept the eight master suites, main saloons, dining room, library, game parlor, and fantail sparkling.

Finally, Mrs. Payne's personal trainer/masseur, Lars, and his beautician/wife, Sherree, completed the crew. Sherree gave free manicures, pedicures, and facials to the staff when she wasn't working on Mrs. Payne or working out with Lars.

There were four jet skis and a trap and skeet range for guests to enjoy, and, in case of disaster at sea, four twenty-five-foot-long, ocean-worthy, capsize-proof lifeboats, each equipped with a three-hundred horsepower diesel inboard engine, a satellite phone, and enough food, water, and medical supplies for twelve to survive comfortably for several weeks.

There was also a launch used to ferry guests, supplies, daily mail, and overnight packages back and forth to shore.

The outdoor cushions were Mediterranean blue with white piping. All the awnings were yellow. It was an outrageously luxurious craft, the kind of boat featured in *Architectural Digest* or *Town & Country* articles written to make life for those on-board look enviably grand.

How deceiving looks can be.

5

My system, always iffy at best, had been in an uproar the whole time we'd been at sea. I'd been dreadfully nauseous and then developed an alarmingly red and painful rash behind my ears and around the base of my skull. Fortunately, after checking in my doctor book—I cannot tell you how many times this book has saved me in the nick of time from becoming truly, truly ill—and confirming by the charts that I did not have ABNORMAL SKIN PIGMENTATION: *Have some areas of your skin become much paler or darker than usual?* (I think that means more brown than red.) Or PSORIASIS: *Do you have one or more red patches covered with silvery-white, flaking skin?* (My rash was more red than white.) Or RUBELLA: *Is there an abnormal swelling down the sides of the back of your neck or at the base of your skull?* (The answer to this was yes, but I didn't seem to have more than the slightly elevated fever which I almost always have. My mother finally tossed in the towel on trying to figure out my higher-than-normal temperature.) Or PITYRIA-SIS ROSEA: *Do you have several oval, red, flaky patches on your chest, back or abdomen?* (Still confined generally to my neck.) However, there was a good chance it was RINGWORM: *Do you have one or more red, scaly patches spreading out in a ring?*

Where on earth would I get *ringworm?* Mrs. Payne's godawful cats, that's where. Oh Lord, I hate cats.

Finally, tonight, Mrs. Payne would give the party everyone in Palm Beach considered the Christmas season opener and we'd get off this big tin can once and for all.

As I looked around the cabin, making sure all was properly tidied, I prayed Madam wouldn't accept another client on a boat. I knew we were in desperate need of money, but with all the names on her waiting list, I wished she hadn't accepted the commission from Mrs. Payne.

"Mrs. Payne travels in a crowd that isn't really ours," I'd explained to Fernando one evening, trying to distract him from snookering me in another round of gin. I'd already lost three dollars.

"Oh? And your crowd is?" He discarded the King of Spades.

"Older, quieter, more discreet. Mrs. Payne's friends flash their money around. The *Kiss-Kiss* is a perfect example," I sniffed, as though I were a social arbiter from Mayfair instead of a sewer rat from Birmingham. "This is the world of conspicuous collectors and consumers, who acquire *objets,* art, jewelry, and furniture at public auction. They want the world to know what they've just bought, instead of making their acquisitions quietly and unobtrusively through private brokers."

"Is that so?" said Fernando.

"Or," I continued, "to keep to the nautical theme, ours is the Criss-Craft, not the mega-yacht, world." I picked up the King and accidentally discarded the Jack. Hell.

"I see." Fernando picked up the Jack and smiled over his hand at me like a cat. Dammit. He knew I'd messed up. "Tell me, has the sad reality dawned on you, sir, that your world is the one doing the selling of the family treasures? Because they haven't accomplished anything since their grandfathers set them up? And hers is the one doing the buying? What a cruel world it is. *Gin!*"

Not that Fernando really bought the argument he was peddling. He just reveled in the art of the trump, no matter the context. Fernando followed Elena around in his white gloves, lips pressed shut and nostrils flared, always looking for trouble.

I'm just the opposite. I'm always looking for sunshine. One evening as the stars were just beginning to appear I told him I thought the crew's quarters were lovely.

"God save me from provincials." He rolled his eyes.

"Very lovely, in fact. And, just so you know, I'm not a provincial. I'm an Englishman."

The crew's quarters, down at the water-line, were well-above par, with a good-sized staff kitchen and sitting room with a game table, comfortable armchairs for reading, satellite television, and a large video library. There was also a well-equipped fitness room just for the crew. Private cabins with private baths, good beds, and nice linens. Mine even had a small sitting room.

"I've had the opportunity to make a thorough study of staff accommodations over the last few years," I said. "And I've come to a few conclusions."

"I'm breathless with anticipation."

"Good. That's what I hoped you would say. While Americans have no sense of how to handle their servants, they are, generally speaking, far and away the best to work for, precisely because they don't know how to behave and are ridiculously guilty at having servants at all. And, generally speaking—if one can remain flexible, maintain a sense of humor, and appreciate spontaneity—which I personally consider nothing more than outrageous self-indulgence—the best of the Americans to work for are the Texans. Naturally there are exceptions. Present circumstances for instance."

"She makes me shudder," Fernando said.

"I think the worst to work for are probably Middle Easterners and Saudis. They treat their servants like slaves."

"Well, they are slaves."

"When Madam and I went to Qadoor to do the emir's portrait, thank God she had the foresight to tell them I was her doctor and had to live in a room that connected to hers. If she'd said I was her butler or valet, I would've ended up sleeping on the floor of one of those un-air-conditioned, flea-infested, common rooms with the rest of the wretches who go to work hiding their stink beneath those long robes with the fouled hems."

"Nigel, that's enough," Fernando laughed. "I get the picture."

I knew he wanted me to keep going. "I know they have social and religious rules about never touching someone's left hand because it is used for personal business. Well, if you want to know what *I* think: Never touch any of them anywhere. Their bathrooms are indescribable. I would rather die than use one. You cannot imagine the state my bowels were in when we returned from that particular junket."

"That, I don't want to hear about," Fernando said.

"Oh, look, there's the Pegasus."

The little enameled clock on the bed table said ten forty-five. I pulled off the last of the jewels—a diamond ear clip with a bird's-egg-sized, blood-red ruby pendant—dropped it in its velvet sack, and tucked it gently among a stack of scarves in Madam's suitcase, a large, worn, Louis Vuitton affair she had taken from her dead mother's closet. I suppose the ancient valise served its purpose, because in a business like Madam's, it does not pay to look more prosperous than your clients, but it does not pay to look less well-bred, either.

I have a brand new Samsonite. With wheels. I don't need to impress anybody.

I looked in the mirror to make sure my tropical attire was properly squared away—short white jacket squared-up and brushed clean, black trousers properly creased, shoes gleaming, white shirt still unwrinkled, and tie clean-up to my neck and straight down. My hair was cleanly parted, hands were scrubbed and nails tidily clipped, with no breakfast eggs or bits of toast lingering about my lips. I tore open two antacid tablets, and in spite of their binding properties, crunched them up and swallowed, gagging through their chalky taste, then took an allergy pill to guard against the cats. I stepped out onto the passageway where the light Florida breeze was soft and sweet against my delicate English skin.

6

"When can I see it?" Lynette Payne pleaded. "I don't want to have to wait until tonight."

"Ten more minutes," Madam told her, hands and body in constant motion as she worked to complete the portrait. In her sizzling-red, full-length body-stocking and no shirt, she looked like a ballerina warming up for the *Firebird*. Perspiration dampened her neck and her fingernails were rimmed black with paint. "Maybe fifteen."

Lynette posed, as she had for three hours every morning, in a voluminous, salmon satin, strapless ball gown. She kept a large hand mirror tucked behind her and every few minutes would pull it out and smile—a pursed, little curve of her lips—at herself. She sat unflinchingly, her back ramrod-straight, on a Louis XIV settee in front of a roaring fire, which Fernando stoked-up every twenty minutes while the ship's industrial air-conditioning system kept the saloon at a comfortable seventy-two degrees.

Above the antique mantel intricately carved with a Bourbon coat of arms and French flora and fauna, hung Renoir's *Matin de Juin,* an ethereal picture of a Parisian flower market whose baskets of poppies matched Lynette's gown.

Mozart played in the background while Fernando and I unobtrusively arranged a late morning snack on a sideboard at the far end of the room.

"I don't think I'll ever get over how perfectly the flowers in the painting match the color of Mrs. Payne's dress," I remarked. Madam and I were very suspicious of the painting's authenticity. I remembered when Mrs. Payne had purchased it at a high-profile auction in London, but even so, experts can be (and occasionally are) duped. The provenance declared the work's pedigree to be indisputable, and she'd paid a record price, more than 18 million dollars, beating out a Japanese industrialist. The story made front page news in the art world.

Fernando raised his eyebrows. "Certainly this is not the first time you've noticed."

I smiled. I was going to miss Fernando. "You don't think it's a fake, do you?" I asked guilelessly.

"It's always been in the hands of private collectors. Who the hell knows where *Matin de Juin* came from or how many of them there are?"

It was truly one of Renoir's most beautiful and rarely-seen works. After a few brief hours of notoriety at the auction, it had vanished again from public sight and took up its place in the main saloon of the *Kiss-Kiss,* becoming, in essence, nothing more than an accessory to Mrs. Payne's Michael Casey ballgown.

"The dress is beautiful," I said, trying to keep things on a positive note.

"On someone half her age."

The gown and both paintings—the portrait and the Renoir—with their peachy-salmon tones, provided the anchors for the theme of this year's Christmas decor. It would have been unthinkable to Lynette not to have a Christmas theme—"Christmas evidently not being theme enough in itself," Fernando had observed—and with the color scheme well-specified in a series of phone calls and one site visit, a florist and his two assistants had come out from a shop in Palm Beach and, working through the night, had decorated the ship in shell pink and shimmering silver.

"I wouldn't be surprised to see the Easter bunny come hippety-hop through the door instead of Santa Claus," Fernando muttered. Then he laid a cloth across his arm, turned to his employer, pulled a little camera out of his pocket, and snapped her picture.

"Oh!" she exclaimed, startled by the flash. "You scared me, Fernando."

"I'm sorry, Madam," he said. "You and your girls look so pretty, I wanted a snapshot of my own. I am going to miss you so much."

Get the shovel. He would go to any length.

Okay. So wouldn't we all?

The "girls" to whom he referred were six snowy-white, caterwauling Persian cats who rubbed and preened and played and scratched among the folds of her skirt and jumped in and out of her lap and tiptoed across the back of the priceless settee, stretching and digging their vicious little claws into its champagne silk damask. This was almost worse than the constant mewling and hissing during the entire goddamned trip. You could hear the fragile old threads pop and shred all the way across the room.

"Fernando," Lynette whined into her mirror. "I'm going to miss you and Elena. I think I'll die. Jackie, do you think my lipstick needs touching up?"

"No," Madam answered, but Lynette dug a tube of lipstick out of her lap anyway and added another coat.

"I don't see why you're leaving me, Fernando. I don't like the new couple." She turned her head this way and that, admiring her reflection. "Jackie, do you really think these colors were the right choice? Not too orangey?"

"The colors are perfect. You look absolutely stunning."

"Give the new couple a chance, Mrs. Payne," Fernando told her. "You'll like them very much. I spoke with him on the phone a few minutes ago, and they have Villa Lynetta completely ready for your arrival tomorrow. You'll have a wonderful Christmas there. Look at all the friends who are joining you, and you yourself told me you're never as happy anywhere as you are at Casa di Campo."

"But I want *you!*"

Fernando's cringe was imperceptible to all but me. "You know if it were only me I would stay, Mrs. Payne. It's breaking my heart, too, but . . ." he shrugged. ". . . what can I do? Elena's health can't take the traveling."

"You don't love me anymore," Lynette pouted. Into the mirror.

In her mid-to-late sixties, Lynette Payne was incapable of an honest look in that mirror, and to make matters worse, she never had anyone around her who had the nerve to tell her to take off the blinders. For starters there was her hair; most of it had been dead for at least six years. It was so over-processed with bleach, it lay lifelessly down her back like some kind of old, dead animal. It didn't move.

"I can either tell her how wrecked it is," Sherree, the beautician, told me one night over a Drambuie on the staff deck, "or I can just keep doing what she wants and keep my job. Lars and I like this life, and Mrs. Payne likes her hair. Do you think I want her to go around looking the way she does? Look at her make-up. She hasn't changed it since she was twenty. But if she's happy, I'm happy."

Lynette's face and neck had the smoothest skin money could buy, except that she had bought them a little too frequently, rushing into the surgeon's suite at the slightest wrinkle, and now there was a tautness to her skin that made it cleave too closely to her bones and shine like a porcelain mask. Her eyes were wide open and shocked-looking. She had dieted to the point of anorexia, but in spite of that, and the daily workouts and semi-weekly massages with Lars, her body remained big-boned and crude, more farmhand than princess. She'd fixed everything that was fixable, but she could not accept that she was aging.

"What do you mean, 'aging'?" Fernando asked in disgust. "She has *aged.* Sixty-five-year-old skin is not nice to look at, I don't care what kind of shape she's in."

He was quite right, of course, I thought, as I watched her pose on the settee. A solid roll of mottled skin drooped over the top of her evening gown, all the way around her back, from armpit to armpit, and gathered in small stacks like ruched silk behind her elbows.

7

*S*top fidgeting, Lynette," Madam warned. "I'm at the most crucial part." Then, almost as an aside to herself, she murmured, "I really think this is the best work I've ever done. I'm so happy."

This was not an entirely true statement, but it was an artist's fairly harmless and regular comment designed to heighten the subject's excitement and level of trust.

People love to name-drop schools of painting to show just how sophisticated they are—Romanticism, Purism, Impressionism, Classicism, Realism, Neo-Classical Realism, Modernism, Post-Modernism, Cubism, and so forth.

Madam has developed her own school, which she gives name to privately, but would never share with a client: Reality-Impressionism.

Reality-Impressionism is the cornerstone of Jacqueline di Fidelio's success. The reality is that she makes her living painting portraits, and if she wants the demand for her talent to continue, so she can continue to collect her stratospheric, six-figure fees, then, bottom-line: None of her subjects have flaws. They are as pure as if the sun had turned pink, or in this case, peach.

I walked behind the easel to refill Madam's glass with what looked like water but was, in fact, iced vodka and stared at the large canvas. What I saw was a full-body portrait of an aristocratic and delicately-boned woman with a lively countenance, settled lushly in palatial surroundings. The subject sat turned slightly to her right, her back straight and trim, an interested and affectionate expression on her face, as though she were listening to you speak and it was the most fascinating conversation she'd ever had. She held a delicate coffee cup and saucer in her hands—which served to draw the eye to the rings that adorned slim, pale fingers—as if she were engaging in an after-dinner chat and was so engrossed she had completely forgotten to take a sip. The cats snuggled benignly around her. The fireplace and the Renoir made as perfect a background as could ever have been conceived, and the overall effect was one of noblesse and splendor. Madam's wily talent never failed to amaze me: Lynette Hammond Payne looked like the Breck Girl of 1956, as dewy and luscious as a Gainsborough virgin.

Lynette sighed. Her face clouded. "I don't see why, if Nigel can see it, I can't."

"I promise you I did not look, Mrs. Payne," I teased and rejoined Fernando. She gave us both her flirty "naughty-boy" look, the same one she gave to all the "boys," servants or not. It was really sad.

"Five more minutes." Jackie was ticking the final glistening dew drops onto the pearls, and spots of fire onto the diamonds. She rubbed her arm across her face. "Tell me about the party."

"I've *told* you about the party a hundred times," Lynette grumped.

I knew Madam like a book, and I knew she was getting anxious. She was trying to delay the inevitable. The moment when she would have to show her work to the client, when everything hung in the balance. And her heart had already begun to hammer with dread. She tensed-up her shoulders and rotated her neck, trying to relax.

"Go through the whole guest list one last time and when you're done, I will be, too. There must have been some overnight changes. Divorces? Reconciliations? Marriages, births, deaths? Sex-change operations?"

Lynette twittered girlishly and stretched her hands, making the light flash on her shiny, melon-colored nails which she kept filed to sharp, little kitty-cat points.

I know I've been hard on Lynette, but there's more: besides her delusional vanity, I also found her to be an empty, shallow, broken-hearted soul. Pathetic, even. One of the heiresses to the Hammond Oil Company fortune, she had hit the super-big jackpot in her marriage to the now-late Mr. Payne, who invented some obscure widget that no computer could survive without. She could buy just about anything or anyone, but she had no friends. The closest thing she had to one at the moment was Madam, and Lynette was paying her a hundred and fifty-thousand dollars to be her friend, to like her. Sitting for a portrait is grueling and now about all Lynette wanted to do was throw a big temper tantrum, but she also wanted Madam to keep liking her. In fact she was desperate for her to keep liking her.

"Let me see." She cast her eyes to the ceiling Fragonard had painted for one of Madame du Barry's sitting rooms. "Who should I start with? Did I tell you that Conrad is bringing Princess May? And Princess Margaret will be here. And Betty Shelley. She just called yesterday to say she's bringing *all three* Mitchell girls. Can you imagine?"

"Where are their husbands?" Madam's pretense at curiosity was wearing thin.

"Oh, those boys all work. Mr. Schweitzer's running his banks; Mr. Merano is running his oil company, and Prince Vassar, of course, is learning to run Russia on the chance they decide to return to the monarchy. And that darling young Aursburg couple—did you know, he works, too? Some Internet record company in Germany. It used to be all the royals did was cruise around and make their money by showing up at parties. But almost all the younger ones work these days."

"Unlike most of the people we know," Fernando teased, "who have way too much time on their hands. A job wouldn't hurt them a bit."

Lynette blushed. "You are naughty, naughty 'Nando. Hand me that cat." He obliged and she held it up in front of her face, "Kiss, kiss, kiss," she cooed, and then continued. "The regular Palm Beach crowd is coming, I'm not going to name all of them again. Also, Julianne Knight called this a.m. and said she and David are going to be able to make it after all. Dominick Dunne—I've always wanted him to include one of my parties in his books, don't you think that would be fun?—But I don't think our crowd's quite racy enough. My brother and sisters, of course. If I didn't invite them, it wouldn't be worth the trouble they'd cause."

"Your family is pretty interesting. What is it you call your father?"

"If I have to hear about those self-indulgent, middle-aged brats again, I think I'll scream," Fernando whispered.

"You mean Daddy Rex? The old honey's too creaky and frail to travel anymore, he just stays on the ranch, but Junior's coming. He'll probably bring some whore, as usual. Probably two of them. And my younger sister Patty will be here—if she can tear herself away from her workout schedule for an hour—and you know my middle sister, Bianca, and her husband, Charles. Did you know she's just been made vice-chairman at MOMA? Well, of course you did, they're doing that retrospective of your mother. Cameron and Jilly Ernst are coming. Do you know, she's fifty years old and they just had a baby? All surrogated, naturally. But it's completely theirs—his sperm and her egg."

"Yes." Madam took her smallest brush and applied the *coup de maître,* the gift of life to Lynette's eyes. "I understand the poor little thing's three months old and she's only spent two weeks with it, so far."

"He wanted it. Not her." She tossed this off as though that explained everything and made it okay.

"Virtually no moral compass," Fernando whispered. "Connecticut will be like heaven to us."

"Who else?" Jackie asked.

"Armand Weil."

That's why we're here. How silly of me not to mention it before. Madam's target, the international art dealer whom the IRS suspected of stealing the Gardner Museum paintings, one of the world's most eligible and elusive bachelors, Armand Weil would be attending, as he did every Hammond family event to which he was invited. The Hammonds collected at the highest level and were among his most valued clients. He had personally assembled their original collection, one of the world's finest, and now served as its de facto curator, in charge of keeping it always at the forefront.

"He's such a dreamboat, it's too bad all he cares about is work. And guess who called this morning?"

"I can't," Jackie said. "Not if I'm going to finish. You have to tell me."

"Ryder and Mary Ann McCormick will be here! I am just tickled! Now, Jackie dear, speaking of Ryder McCormick, you and I have spent so much time together I feel like we're sisters, and I was wondering, can I ask you a personal question?"

"Certainly." Jackie was hidden by the canvas and Lynette couldn't see a smirk touch her lips. I remained inscrutable, of course. Well, my lips might have tightened slightly with distaste. Or was it disapproval? It couldn't have been jealousy. No, I would have to say, honestly, it was anger. Madam should have a fabulous man. A man who cherished her, who brought out the best in her, who would maybe even marry her. A man like Armand—she could snatch him away from his work if she wanted to, just like that.

"Are you having an affair with Ryder?" Lynette Payne asked.

"What planet has she just dropped in from?" I asked Fernando as I carried the champagne bucket to the sideboard.

"Come on, Lynette," Madam smiled around the canvas. "What do you really want to know?"

A crimson flush crawled up Lynette's neck. "If you consider him to be your own private property or if he's available. He's so divinely attractive. And face it, he's much closer to my age than yours."

Madam laid her brush carefully on the paint tray and wiped her hands on a towel, indicating that the session was over. She stepped back and examined her work. "We're all available," she answered, pulling the band out of her hair and shaking it free. "And when he sees you in that dress tonight, I'm afraid I'm going to end up out in the cold."

Out in the cold along with Ryder's wife, the lovely, wheel-chair-bound Mary Anne Schlumbacher. One never truly knows what goes on behind closed doors, so who's to say if she and Ryder were happy or not? They had been married for almost ten years, and to all appearances he was a moderately attentive husband. I imagined that Ryder was free to do whatever he wanted, with whomever he wanted, within carefully prescribed and well-defined boundaries.

The way they'd purchased the farm next door to ours is a perfect example of the arrangement. Mary Anne knew where Madam lived, just as she must have been aware that almost every morning and every afternoon her husband climbed on his large chestnut hunter, jumped a couple of fences, and tied up at the little studio at the far end of our field. Just as she was no doubt aware that several times a year he had flown to Paris and tied himself up at Madam's mother's studio. I had absolutely no idea what he provided his wife that would compensate for such flagrant infidelity, unless she were simply another willing victim of his domineering personality. Or maybe she just plain loved him, even though he was nothing more than a dissipated bum with a fabulous old body.

Oh, yes. I'll admit, the man could turn my head, as well. He was too handsome for anybody's good. I think it was the glass eye.

Poor Mary Anne, stuck in that chair with God-knows-what disease. I'd checked The Book extensively and was fairly certain it was some sort of arthritis, but whether it was Infectious, Osteo-, or Rheumatoid, without additional information I couldn't be sure.

"Would you like to see your portrait?" Jackie asked.

"Yes!" Lynette brushed the cats to the floor and, with a rustle of satin, joined Jackie in front of the painting. The air sizzled with excitement. Her eyes filled with tears. "I've never looked so beautiful," she exclaimed.

Quite so. I popped the cork and filled their flutes with Dom Pérignon.

8

After Fernando and I served the ladies a lunch of seared red snapper with lemon and capers, baby asparagus with Hollandaise, and a chilled bottle of velvety Chateau Puligny Montrachet, Madam spent the afternoon resting in her cabin, while I did the same in mine, fighting off a slight fever. Oh Lord, deliver me from this boat. She rang for me at four-thirty, after her workout.

The dogs' little black eyes twinkled at me from the deep pillows on her bed and their little tails batted the covers.

"Did you have a good workout?" I asked. She regularly did thirty minutes on the treadmill, fifteen more on the StairMaster, and then another quarter-hour of free weights.

"First rate. I'm going to miss the view from this gym. I was thinking, what if we moved my workout equipment into the sun room?"

"Good idea." I flipped the switch on the countertop espresso machine.

"Then I had a massage and a nap, and now I'm ready to rock and roll. So, you think I should wear the pewter lamé?" She held up the long-sleeved, feather-light dress in front of the mirror. Her face looked calmer this evening, as it always did when she'd finished a commission. As if she'd had a good night's sleep. Hopefully, this meant smoother waters were headed our way. "I was thinking more along the lines of the short black silk."

"Packed." I poured two capfuls of citrus-scented bath gel under the raging spigot. According to the publicity brochure, the lemon-lime botanical aromas would give her "a luxurious, uncommon sense of well-being and energy." "Besides, all the ladies will be wearing short black silk, or beaded jackets over short black silk. I was thinking what would look best in *W,* and I think you in the pewter in front of that salmon in the portrait will be stunning."

I turned my back and poured the now-finished shots of espresso into a blender as she slid beneath the fragrant bubbles.

"You're the boss," Madam said. "I trust your taste much more than mine." She unscrewed the top from a heavy glass jar that sat on the side of the tub and smeared a heavy mask of Italian mud on her face, then placed cucumber slices on her eyes. "I hate to admit it, but I'm nervous about tonight."

"Nervous?"

She nodded her head. "I'm nervous about Armand. Of all the people they could have ordered me to spy on, they would pick Armand. He's always turned me to jelly."

"More than Mr. McCormick?" I tried to keep the hope out of my voice.

"It's totally different. There's something about Armand. He's so settled and distinguished. And I've never heard him gossiped about at all, have you? But he must have a couple of mistresses stashed here and there."

"Naturally, Madam, he's a Frenchman."

"You don't think he's gay, do you?" Madam turned on the hot water spigot and plumped up the bubbles.

"Most assuredly not."

"Are you sorry we don't live like this, Nigel?"

"Like what?" I measured out a heaping tablespoon of cocoa.

"You know. With a big yacht and our own plane. Cooks and maids. Houses everywhere."

"Heavens, no. I am particularly thankful you do *not* have a big yacht." Madam laughed. She knew how dreadfully ill I'd been since we left Spain.

"How long have you worked for me, Nigel?"

"Ten years, Madam."

"Ten years?" She lifted one of the cucumber slices and looked at me with one of her cobra eyes. "Really? Good grief. Seems like ten days."

How it happened was, I was fresh from prison and had just received my hard-earned diploma from Lady Atchley's butler school when a friend of mine, a jewel thief, asked me to help rob a country house.

"I've had it from the cook's cousin," he'd told me, "that the lord and lady are occupied in the summer house for four hours every day, from ten-to-two, sitting for their portrait."

The household staff was taking advantage of the time to lounge about, and basically left the main house unattended. "The safe is old. For someone of your talents, it'll be like opening a jam jar."

I went so far as to accompany him to the village to reconnoiter, and as it was, the next day an article appeared in the local paper about the artist who was doing the lord and lady's portrait. She looked nice, a young woman just getting started in her career, and I made a snap decision at that moment to change my life. I put a letter in the mail to her at the manor house, making up my background, giving a number of false references, and saying I was looking for a new position, available immediately. And, I continued, since I didn't want my current employer to know what I was doing, if she were interested to please contact me through the local pub.

She was probably only twenty-nine or thirty, naively trusting as only an artist can be, and she didn't know a person could be so cheeky as to actually make up references. For my part, I was sincere in my desire to change. We were a match made in heaven. I was so grateful to her for taking me in that I hadn't looked at another safe since.

So, I thought, as she stepped into the shower to scrub off the mask and wash her hair, and I dropped a scoop of vanilla ice cream into the cooled espresso and chocolate and turned on the motor, am I sorry we live the way we do? Only slightly. I would like an airplane, a nice little jet, and perhaps a house in Barbados, because I suspect I have the beginnings of arthritis from the rainy winters in Virginia. But between the loft in New York City and the studio in Paris, and Effie and Scully, the housekeeper and gardener I was already responsible for in Virginia, would I like more staff? More responsibility? Never.

"Are you all right, Nigel?" Steam billowed forth as Madam stepped from the shower and gathered a fluffy Pratesi bathsheet around her. "You seem awfully quiet."

"I haven't wanted to mention it, but could you just take a quick peek at this rash on my neck? I'm afraid I've picked up a spot of ringworm from the cats."

"Ringworm? Let me see. Turn around in the light."

"Don't touch it, Madam." I jumped away. "Ringworm can be terribly contagious."

"Be still. Let me look." She turned me toward the light and leaned down to examine my neck. Then she started to laugh. "You are such a case sometimes, Nigel. I can't believe it. Ringworm! Your imagination is fantastic."

Stung, I stepped away. "I'm sorry to have troubled you."

"No, no. Don't be hurt! You do have a rash, darling, and it's a doozie. But I promise you, it's not ringworm."

"What then?"

"It's the patches."

Oh, Lord. I'd stuck on so many seasickness patches that I'd burned off almost all the skin behind my ears. I do admit I can be something of an alarmist, but better safe than sorry, I always say.

"Oh, thanks be to God."

"Amen. Are you still planning to take the dogs and the luggage over now, before the party?"

I nodded.

"Why not just take it all when we leave? I hate for you to make an extra trip."

"Everything's already loaded on the launch. It gets too confusing with the dogs and the guests, and I want us to be able to leave cleanly whenever you're ready."

"I really appreciate it, Nigel. You take beautiful care of me."

"It's my pleasure, Madam. Well," I tidied up the counter, "if that's all, I'll be on my way."

"I'll see you at the party." Madam gulped down her espresso shake and slipped into her terry robe.

9

*L*ynette had hired extra launches to shuttle her guests back and forth from the Sol d'Oro Club pier, and finally, as the party was starting to fill up, I saw Armand Weil step onto the *Kiss-Kiss*'s marina/swimming platform and enter the ship at water-level. The new arrivals passed along the tied-up jet skis, and made their way up the winding stairs to the main deck, where Lynette greeted them and Fernando handed them the cocktails they had ordered by radio on the way over.

"Just wait till you see the portrait, Armand," Lynette said. "It's her best work. I'm telling you, Jackie is a genius."

"I'm looking forward to it." Armand accepted a glass of white wine, excused himself, and stepped out onto the crowded fantail. He spotted Madam along the opposite rail and headed in her direction.

While I knew the pewter lamé gown and the gardenias in her hair were the right choice artistically, I hadn't counted on how she would look in the golden twilight when she got up close to Armand Weil. She looked almost naked, sculpted in precious metal, her body skimmed with silver leaf.

Now, this is the kind of man Madam needs, I thought. Elegant, sleek, sophisticated, impeccably trim in his black faille Armani dinner jacket. He was divine—all that money and power. And his French accent? Irresistible. Every word becomes an invitation. And furthermore, unlike Ryder—who had the sexual control, discrimination, and morals of a dog—Armand Weil was a first class gentleman. A real man.

He was formidable, two or three inches taller than Madam, making him about six-four or five, a man who could block the sun. His stature was enhanced by an almost Prussian precision—nothing wasted, no move, no time. His clothes were cut with no room to spare. His shirt collar was snug to his throat, and the cuffs, caught with gleaming cabochon links, left exactly enough room for comfortable movement around his narrow wrists. His nails were clipped short and buffed. His color implied approximately twelve minutes a day in the tanning bed. The crisp points of a white handkerchief were visible from his breast pocket. His face could just as easily have been a boxer's as a banker's. There were scars and imperfections, graying hair parted slightly off-center, a well-barbered mustache, even white teeth, and behind his horn-rimmed glasses, an aggressive expression in his eyes that said he lived his life on the offensive. This was a born conqueror, a man who kept his sense of humor out of the boardroom.

Madam removed a very dry, straight-up vodka martini from my tray and offered it to him. "This is much more fun than white wine," she said.

He accepted the drink and kissed her on both cheeks, his mustache brushing her skin. "You have read my mind, chérie. I understand congratulations are in order. Lynette says you're a genius."

It made me weak-kneed to watch them, the way they devoured each other. A tape of their conversation as they exchanged pleasantries would reveal nothing more than an exchange of words, but the electricity was apparent in their every glance and gesture.

"Where have you been?" Armand asked lightly. "You are the woman I have looked for my entire life."

Madam laughed.

Unfortunately, just as it was getting good, their exchange was interrupted by the raucous arrival of Lynette's younger brother, Junior Hammond, who burst onto the deck like an elephant with what appeared to be a hooker on each arm. Junior was morbidly obese, and tonight looked like Orson Welles playing Big Daddy in his white linen suit and white beaver cowboy hat, which he now pulled off his head and spun out over the ocean like a Frisbee. He then pulled two silver-plated six-shooters out of the holsters on his bulbous hips and, with a rebel yell, unloaded them into the fancy Stetson.

"God *Damn,* I like to do that," Junior declared loudly.

The girls in the sequined dresses squealed and hugged, and he swatted their bottoms and then the three of them went indoors.

Conversation resumed as if nothing at all had happened. No one ever fooled themselves about a Hammond invitation, it always came with good news and bad news. The good news was the Dom Pérignon and Beluga caviar; the bad news was the Hammonds.

"Have you been contacted about any of the Gardner works?" Madam asked Armand.

"Naturally, many times. Why? Have you?"

"Yes, interestingly." She leaned back and rested her elbows on the rail, turning the front of the pewter gown into a silvery shield. "A client told me he would be willing to pay fifty million for the Vermeer. No questions asked."

"I know people who would pay more than that. What is it you want to know?" Armand asked. The sun had reached its lowest point on the horizon and now cut into his eyes. They were as blue and direct as Kashmir sapphires.

"You hear more than I do. If you can find the painting, I'm willing to pay a significant reward."

"How significant?"

"Five million," Madam answered.

I almost choked on my throat lozenge. She couldn't afford five cents for a reward.

"Must be a big client," Armand said.

"The biggest. I'll do anything to keep him happy."

"You aren't thinking of becoming a dealer are you? Going into competition with me? You must know everyone in the world is on the lookout for those works."

"I know. And, no, I'm not going into competition with you, Armand. I've simply gotten myself into a little bit of a mess and finding the Vermeer would make everything right."

"If I hear anything, I'll let you know, then you can race me."

"Don't tease me." Madam stepped away from the rail. "I mean it. It's serious."

Armand's expression was curious and cool, revealing nothing. "You look so tragic, *Jacqueline.*" He laid his hand gently on her arm. "It's only a painting. It will turn up."

"There you are, Jackie!" Lynette materialized through the throng. Lord, I couldn't wait to get away from that woman. "You promised to stay by me. You're the guest of honor and everyone's simply mad to see you. Come with me, both of you. Suzy Menzes has just arrived and wants to snap our picture." Lynette tucked one arm into each of theirs and led them inside to stand in front of the fire, alongside the portrait. Flashbulbs popped, followed by polite applause, and then Lynette was surrounded by friends, leaving Madam and Armand alone again.

"You handle all this extremely well," he said. "One second a star and the next abandoned to let your patron accept congratulations for your work."

"It's how I make my living. I like it."

"Look out," Fernando whispered in my ear. "Here they come."

Oh, damn. It was Ryder pushing Mary Anne's wheelchair through the door. I rushed over to intercept them. "Good evening, Mr. and Mrs. McCormick. Champagne?"

"Hello, Nigel." Ryder was as tall as Armand and wore his dark hair slicked back from a receding hairline. His single-buttoned dinner jacket had been perfectly fitted onto his wide-shouldered, trim-waisted body. His eyes were a clear, sky blue.

I say "eyes," but in truth, as you know, only one of them was real. The other had been lost when he and one of his wives, I don't know which one, had a fight on a chair lift in Aspen, and she stabbed him in the face with one of her ski poles. As the story goes, when she wounded him, he was in such searing pain that he fought back furiously, instinctively, as one would, and she accidentally fell off the lift at its highest point, plummeting onto a steep, rocky hill-side and breaking her neck. She died instantly. Some say their marriage was on the rocks already and she stabbed him in an effort to defend herself as he was trying to throw her off the lift. Nevertheless, the coroner's inquest came up empty-handed and charges were never filed. Ryder was the sort of man always rumored about. There was always a sense of mystery and intrigue about him. And he always managed to land on his feet.

His face was strong-jawed, evenly tanned. "Champagne, darling?"

"Please," Mary Anne answered.

"How was the float from Spain, Nigel?"

"Excellent, sir, thank you." I handed Mary Anne a flute. Her hands looked as delicate as butterfly wings, almost transparent. Whatever she suffered from, it was definitely getting worse. Parkinson's? Multiple sclerosis? Muscular dystrophy?

"I'll have a martini, please," Ryder said.

"Excellent."

I moved toward the bar and Lynette slid in on them like the smiling serpent in the Garden of Eden.

"I especially like the way you've included the Renoir in the painting," Armand said. "Your colors are exquisite."

"Thanks. It's what she wanted. I'm pleased with how it turned out."

"You know, Jacqueline, I look at the skill and beauty of your work," he mused. "How you paint your subjects as they would like to see themselves. And even though the paintings are sublime and stately, they cannot hide a wildness in you. I feel it as strongly as I feel your presence here beside me."

Madam laughed and took a cigarette from a silver cup set on a side table. "Heavens, Armand, I'm not as complicated as all that."

"But you are." Armand held his lighter for her. "I know more about you than you think. Remember, I knew your mother."

Her gaze was direct, laughing. "We all knew my mother. She could be a monster."

"Then why do you pursue an affair with the monster's monster, Ryder McCormick? He belongs on the trash heap of her history, not yours. Look at him. What can he possibly offer you?"

"I'm not really sure." Madam shrugged and blew smoke at the ceiling. She never looked at Ryder when he was with his wife, and it was because of the guilt. Mary Anne was a woman she respected, and, I suppose, Madam thought that if she didn't look at her, then she did not exist. Whenever they were forced to greet one another, Madam was cordial and abrupt and excused herself quickly. Mary Anne, who had a wisdom that can come only from suffering, looked at her with understanding, which only intensified Madam's shame and denial.

"You need a man, Jacqueline." Armand moved closer to her, their bodies almost touching. "Someone who can bring you love and passion and security, who understands your world. Not a dissipated hanger-on who exerts some sort of sick control over you."

"Are you offering yourself? You're just as married as Ryder."

"You mean to my work? Yes, it's true. She is my mistress and wife, and her demands are constant. But I'll tell you, you are the only woman for whom I would leave her."

"If I had a dollar for every man who's said that to me, I'd be as rich as you are."

"But I mean it." Armand moved closer. His lips were close to her ear—two friends sharing a secret. "Someday I hope you will let me show you."

Suddenly there was a startling crash of breaking glass, and I realized I'd become so caught up in Armand's words, I'd let my tray tip; a half-dozen empty flutes had simply slid off onto the floor. Oh, Lord.

10

I didn't see either one of them for a while after that. I wandered the room, picking up on bits of gossip here and there.

Conrad and Princess May looked to be very, very tight with one another, trading intimate looks and what I believe were keys. I knew she was staying at Sol d'Oro, once a society matron's fairy-tale ocean front palazzo and now Mr. Robertson's private club.

"I'll be expecting you," he said.

"No, darling," the Princess purred. "I'll be expecting *you.*"

Unfortunately, my good breeding and Lady Atchley's stern warnings Never To Linger forced me to move on.

Lynette had cornered Dominick Dunne, who was slightly arched over a sofa back while she pressed in on him. He stared up at her, unblinking, through his thick, round glasses.

"Everyone has been absolutely terrified since the robbery," she was saying. "I mean, can you imagine? Gagged and tied up in their own closet? *Pistol-whipped?* Sam had a lump on his head the size of a goose-egg. I mean, the robber just plain conked him!"

"Really." Mr. Dunne was not even slightly interested. "I heard the whole thing was an insurance scam perpetrated by Sam himself to cover his Merrill Lynch margin accounts."

"Oh, you are as much a scamp as everyone says," Lynette scolded. "Cross my heart. You just don't expect such a thing to happen at a place like Le Ventage, it's supposed to be so exclusive. But since it's not ex-actly a private club, more a real estate development, they really can't control who they let in. I was thinking: Wouldn't it be the perfect setting for a murder? Right up your alley."

"Well . . ."

"I have a beautiful, beautiful house there that sits empty eleven months a year—the staff's on year-round except for Fernando and my maid—and you'd be welcome to use it. Live there for as long as you like. I only come to the desert for January so I wouldn't be in your way at all. What do you think?"

"I think I need some air," Mr. Dunne said. "Excuse me." He took off through the door and joined the Mitchell girls, who had huddled to-gether, happy for an occasion to catch up.

Shortly thereafter, the party started to break up as a number of the more respectable guests began leaving for dry land.

Lord Brocklehurst's brother, who had been three-sheets-to-the-wind when he'd arrived and was now totally gone, began to play the piano and mutilate Elton John songs while one of Junior Hammond's floozies tried to sing along. Junior and the other girl were nowhere in sight.

I went below to make sure, for the last time, that all was ready for our departure—you never know when a missing earring will turn up un-der a table skirt or a favorite book left hidden beneath a newspaper.

When I reached the door of her suite, I could hear Madam and Ry-der going at it like banshees. I listened until I could tell the moment of truth was approaching, as certain and imminent as "We Have Ignition" at Cape Canaveral.

I threw open the door. "Oh, goodness. I'm so terribly sorry. I had no idea you were in here."

They looked at me wild-eyed, gasping for breath. Nirvana snatched from their hands. Madam's hair and makeup were an absolute mess.

"Jesus Christ!" Ryder roared, as one of Madam's legs dropped to the floor from his waist. "Haven't you ever heard of knocking?"

"I'm terribly, terribly sorry, sir." As I closed the door behind me, I could hear her laughing uproariously and Ryder saying furiously, "I don't know why you put up with that idiot. He's no more a butler than I am. He's a menace."

Takes one to know one.

Finally, it was time to go. I'd said my goodbyes to Fernando and the rest of the crew earlier in the evening. Fernando and I exchanged small gifts—I gave him an engraved sterling silver shot glass from Tiffany for his beloved single malt, and he gave me a leather passport wallet with my initials, all delivered courtesy of the daily mail launch. We promised to stay in touch. I had his new number in Connecticut. He, Elena, and I—taken by what? I don't know, silliness, the effusion of our friendship, the excitement of the party, living in a world of privilege, surrounded by unlimited money, none of it ours, the Christmas spirit—decided we would meet to celebrate being on dry land with dinner at Le Cirque 2000 after they got settled.

"I don't care if it takes all our savings," he said. "It'll be worth every penny."

"Couldn't agree more, my friend," I laughed and shook his hand. We both knew we would no more spend the money to have dinner at Le Cirque 2000 than we would fly to the moon. "Merry Christmas."

I made sure to pass through the main saloon to bid the portrait adieu, knowing I'd never see it again. That was one thing about Madam's works, we always have to leave them behind, and even if I wasn't sad to leave the boat, I would miss the painting. It was a show-stopper and in the now-quiet, overblown room, it looked like it wanted to come with me. "Good-bye, old girl," I said, then descended to the lower deck and boarded the launch. Something wasn't quite right. But I couldn't think what it was.

"I'm going to miss you so much." Lynette kissed Madam on each cheek and hugged her, tears running down her face. She looked old and haggard. "It's going to be so quiet without you and your precious dogs."

We were the last to leave. The giant yacht was silent.

"I can't thank you enough for the painting," she wept. "I've never looked so beautiful in my life. It's as though you saw right through me and touched my inner self."

"I just painted what I saw," Jackie answered, removing herself carefully from Lynette's clinging embrace. "I think it's the best work I've ever done."

"When will we see each other? Can you have lunch next week? Do you want to come to Casa for Christmas? I've got plenty of room . . ."

"We're going home first thing in the morning," Madam told her firmly. "But we'll catch up soon. Thank you so much for all your hospitality, Lynette. Yours were truly the most pleasant sessions I've ever had."

She reached down, and I took her hand to help her into the little speed boat. As soon as she was aboard, the mate cast-off, the captain turned up the throttle, and we powered away from the *Kiss-Kiss*. Moments later, Lynette appeared up on the fantail, silhouetted in the shimmering moonlight, and waved until the yacht became a twinkling spot on the horizon.

"The Renoir," I stuttered under my breath. "It wasn't there."

"Pardon?" Madam asked.

"It wasn't there."

But my words were drowned out with first the sight and then the sound of a shattering explosion. The *Kiss-Kiss* disappeared into an immense ball of fire, as violently as if an atomic bomb had been detonated. Flaming shards flew high into the sky as the conflagration grew and the roar thundered across the water. It reminded me of films I'd seen of nuclear tests in Nevada in the nineteen fifties when the ground began to move toward the observers in waves and everyone watched paralyzed in open-mouthed horror, their brains unable to comprehend what their eyes were seeing. The burning water moved out in circles that extinguished themselves before they reached us as we sped toward shore.

11

*T*he flames painted our faces with the most delicate subtlety, turning us into survivors in a Cecil B. DeMille epic. I wondered whether Madam had seen her masterpiece, its canvas still wet, sail into the sky like a burning raft.

Then I thought, thank God I'd taken the dogs over earlier, because if they'd been with us, either they would have slowed down our departure and we would have been blown to smithereens along with everybody and everything on the *Kiss-Kiss,* or if we'd already been on the launch, the explosion would have scared them to death.

Funny the things that go through your mind when disaster strikes. It took me another split second to realize that there had been lots of people on that ship, my friends, and they'd all just been killed.

The captain pulled back on the power and grabbed his radio microphone. "Mayday. Mayday. Mayday. This is the Payne charter launch. Palm Beach Coast Guard come in, please."

"Payne charter, this is Palm Beach Coast Guard. State your location and the nature of your emergency," a disembodied voice came back.

"I am one mile due east of Sol d'Oro. My lat. and long. are two-six-four-two by zero-eight-zero-tick-zero-zero-tick-zero-zero." He spoke the abbreviated lingo with the speed of a teletype machine. "The super-yacht *Kiss-Kiss* has just exploded approximately one mile due east of my position."

"We are underway Payne charter." A Klaxon alarm blared in the background over the speaker. "Please repeat your location and the nature of your distress."

The mate handed us each a life jacket while the captain repeated the information calmly and succinctly.

"Roger, Payne launch. How many s.o.b.?" He turned to me and my mind was blank. I stared at him stupidly.

"How many people were onboard?" he demanded.

"Let me think," I floundered, trying to name them all in my head. "Altogether there were seventeen of them so, yes, seventeen in crew."

"Don't forget Lynette," Madam added. Her voice was incredulous, scolding. "My God, Nigel, it was her boat."

"I'm, I'm sorry," I stuttered. "Mrs. Payne. Eighteen."

"Eighteen on the *Kiss-Kiss*," the man spoke into the mike. "Four on the launch. We are uninjured."

And then the unimaginable happened: *The captain turned the boat around.* "I'm returning to check for survivors." He announced over the microphone.

"Roger."

We slammed over the water at full throttle, heading straight for the flames.

"Are you all right, Madam?" I called over the roaring engine.

She was leaning out over the side of the launch, squinting into the wind. Tears streamed straight back from her eyes into her hair, a hank of which had pulled loose and flew out in a long, dark banner. She looked over at me, her expression bewildered and horrified. She nodded. "You?"

"Perfectly." I held on tight, sure the wild ride was going to crack all of my teeth right in two and afraid of what we might find. Why didn't the captain just leave it to the professionals?

What we found was nothing but tiny bits of unrecognizable debris. The ship had vanished. The people were gone. Vaporized, I supposed. The fires had even burned themselves out by the time we got there. The mind-numbing shock I felt was indescribable. I put my arm around Madam's trembling shoulders and hugged her close as we headed toward shore. She seemed almost catatonic.

A small but growing crowd, including one police detective, a handful of uniformed officers, five television crews, and the usual rag-tag assembly of paparazzi who inhabit Palm Beach for the winter greeted us when we finally arrived at the Sol d'Oro dock just after midnight. The lights on the television cameras turned the balmy Palm Beach darkness into a harsh halogen glare that assaulted our eyes and made us squint unbecomingly. I watched the jostling group of newsmongers absorb Madam into their midst like a Venus's-flytrap engulfing a juicy new bug. They were all shouting questions at the same time.

"Jackie, who was onboard?"

"Do you think it was a bomb or a gas leak?"

"How much was the ship worth?"

"Look over here Jackie!"

"Jackie! Who all was at the party tonight? Did Lynette Payne have any enemies? Jackie!"

"Jackie just let me get one shot!"

"Conrad! Look this way!" And so forth. It was a terrifying and out-of-control situation, verging on becoming a mob scene.

Finally the police formed a barrier of sorts between Madam and Conrad Robertson and the wolf pack. Conrad placed a tartan blanket over Madam's shoulders and drew her to him as he guided her gently along the walk to the house. It struck me then that they were the same height. Her evening sandals dangled from her hand.

"Miss di Fidelio." The detective walked beside her. At least I assumed he was a detective, he'd flashed a badge and had on a suit. "I'd like to ask you a few questions."

"Not now," Conrad snapped. "Can't you see she's in shock?"

"It'll just take a few minutes." The man tagged along doggedly. "Now's the time she'll remember the most. It's important, sir."

All Madam could do was shake her head. She had yet to speak a word since our arrival.

I, of course, followed with the hand luggage. Why would anyone give a thought to the butler who had come just as close to death as the mistress? Whose clothes were just as soaked? Who had to stop and put down the bags twice to deal with attacks of chills and sneezing? Whose heart was beating so fast, fibrillation and cardiac arrest were no doubt imminent? If I fell over dead right here on the spot, I can promise you, no one would have noticed until it was far too late. I would suffer massive brain damage at the very least.

If you expect to be pampered, service is not the life for you.

Conrad directed the press to stay outside on the porch, where a young man in a white jacket had already set up a table with a silver urn of hot coffee, a linen-covered tray of fresh buttery scones, and two bottles of Corvoisier VSOP to smooth any ruffled feathers the reporters might have as a result of their exclusion, and escorted Madam and the police inspector into the main living room. Its wall of oceanfront French doors showed a black Atlantic beyond, punctuated by pinpoints of light caused by the distant cluster of search-and-rescue boats where the explosion had occurred. The rest of Conrad's houseguests, all couples who had attended the party, had assembled and were anxious to do whatever they could for Madam. The mood was extremely grave, no remnant remained of Lynette's jolly kickoff of the Christmas season. A second detective arrived, and after he had received quick whispered instructions from the first, they both began to circulate among the guests and question each one briefly, taking copious notes.

A man, presumably Conrad Robertson's, a very proper fellow in an immaculate charcoal suit with a white bar towel draped over his left arm, stood at the ready to bring my Madam anything she wanted.

"Whiskey, neat," I told him. She had taken a seat by the fire and kept the blanket close around her.

The room was surprisingly quiet. No one knew exactly what to do. They wanted to help, but were unsure exactly how to approach the survivor of a disaster, so they talked to each other and kept an eerily calm distance from Madam, obviously working studiously not to stare at her.

"Do you want me to stay?" I whispered.

"No. I'm fine." She looked up at me, eyes dark and filled with tears. "So many people, Nigel. I just can't believe it."

My throat had tightened. I nodded mutely.

She tossed off the whiskey and held her glass out for a refill. "Do you really think it could have been on purpose? That somebody put a bomb on there?"

"I don't know. Until the newsmen asked that question, it had never entered my mind."

She was halfway through her second whiskey when the senior detective stepped forward. "Miss di Fidelio, I'm Sergeant Marisco. Do you think we could go into the next room and talk privately? I know you've been through a lot but it'll only take a couple of minutes. What you saw and heard are essential—you're the only eyewitness we've got."

See what I mean? It doesn't occur to people that we servants see or hear anything. Sooner or later he'd figure out that I was there, too, and come knocking at my door. But the truth was, I couldn't remember much of anything, just the flames and the other-worldly, far-away noise.

"Of course. You go on, Nigel. I'll call you if I need anything." She got to her feet, leaving her shoes and the blanket behind, and accompanied him onto the sun porch.

I went up the back stairs to my room. I was overwhelmingly sad.

Once I'd poured myself three fingers of brandy and checked The Book under CHILBLAINS—no definition available, but I was fairly certain I was suffering from them, whatever they were—I changed into dry clothes and descended to the staff kitchen, where one of the girls handed me another good-sized brandy and a mug of steaming tomato soup laced with a little sherry and sprinkled with buttery croutons.

"Thank you, miss." I didn't know which to gulp first, but started with the hot soup to warm myself up. It was the best soup I'd ever tasted and I told her so.

It hadn't seemed possible for her to look more fair, but when she smiled, the room filled with warmth. For a second, she seemed so freshly innocent, exactly like the kitchen girls on the ship, Hilda and Heidi, that I couldn't bear to look at her. "Thank you, sir. I made it myself." She held up a Campbell's soup can and gave a small self-deprecating smile, then offered soberly, "I'm so sorry about what happened tonight. Are you all right?"

I shrugged.

"I heard there was a crew of seventeen. Were they all your friends?"

"A few of them," I answered, not wanting to talk. "What's your name?"

"Ruthie O'Connor, sir. And yours?"

"Weatherby-Smythe. Nigel Weatherby-Smythe," I answered and then sneezed uncontrollably.

"Oh, Mr. Weatherby-Smythe." She raced to my side and put her hand on my arm. "I'm afraid you've taken a terrible chill. Oh, my goodness, and look at your neck. It's raw, don't you want me to put some salve on it?"

"No, no. It's nothing." I patted her hand. "I'm perfectly fine. Just a small sunburn."

Damned if I would tell her it was from seasickness patches. Didn't want her to think I was some sort of weak sister.

And then I burst into tears. My friend Fernando was gone. The explosion would not leave my eyes. Eighteen people, all dead. Up in flames. Poof. Gone from the face of the earth.

The detective finally got around to questioning me after two o'clock, but by then I was so exhausted, all I could do was mumble. Finally, he left, and I took an Ambien and went to bed.

12

The next morning the explosion of the *Kiss-Kiss* was the lead story on CNN and made the front page of practically every newspaper in the world. Was it sabotage? A gas leak? Lynette and the entire Hammond Family—an extremely litigious group, notorious for their internecine feuds—and their powerful friends, created an array of juicy news possibilities as rich as the subjects themselves: If it was a bomb, they were all potential targets *and* possible suspects. If it was an accident, there were an unlimited number of dramatic survivor and close-call, "That-could-have-been-me," stories.

"How do you feel this morning? You've lost your sister and escaped the blast. Do you think it was an accident or sabotage?" a television reporter shouted across a boxwood divider at Junior Hammond whom he'd tracked down having breakfast by himself on the outdoor terrace at the Four Seasons.

"I feel terrible, you stupid bastard," Junior answered. His Churchillian jowls shook like pudding beneath a gray beaver Stetson identical to the one he'd shot holes in off the stern of the ship, and he pulled his silver-plated six-shooters out of his jacket pockets and cocked them just as the hotel security guards grabbed the astonished reporter and his cameraman and threw them off the property.

Paparazzi were everywhere. They had multiplied a hundredfold overnight, materializing out of thin air, flooding the airport and all the luxury hotel lobbies. They swarmed around the gates and private docks of the waterfront estates, especially Sol d'Oro, with their three-foot-long Dr. Seuss-like telephoto lenses, waiting for a glimpse of Madam or one of the other guests.

Detective Marisco returned at ten o'clock with a bomb expert and questioned Madam and me again in the sitting room of Madam's suite, which was banked with white lilacs. Snow-white, handkerchief linen drapes fluttered gently in the ocean breeze.

"Did Mrs. Payne have any enemies? Did any of the crew appear disgruntled? Try to remember exactly what area of the ship blew up first. Where did you see the first spark of flame? How fast did it spread? You said the chef was unpopular, just how unpopular? You said the butler was leaving. Can you think of anyone who would want you dead?"

"*Me?*" she asked. "No." The thought hadn't occurred to her, but now that the seed had been planted, it took quick root, fueled by Madam's paranoid fantasies. Her mind spun through the possibilities. "No," she said again. "At least I hope not. People like me, at least they say they do. They like my work. I have to think this was an accident."

All I could think about was the missing Renoir, and keeping my mouth shut about it was the hardest thing I'd ever done. But I'd not had a chance to discuss it with Madam, and I thought, if she wanted to mention it, she would. It wasn't my place. But—and I know I'm not a detective—it *could* have had something to do with the explosion.

There was nothing more we could add.

"Unless you need me for anything else," Madam told him, "I'd like to go home."

"Are you planning to drive or fly back to Virginia?"

"Drive."

"You might want to wait until tomorrow. Let that mob outside cool off, because I can see them chasing you the whole way. We don't want to have any more accidents."

"All right."

In spite of calls from friends, including Armand and Ryder, with invitations for lunch or tea or dinner, Madam secluded herself in her room among the white lilacs and cried for most of the day as the shock began to wear off.

The next morning, well before dawn, we roared through the gates of Sol d'Oro, catching the dozing paparazzi off-guard, and zoomed onto I-95 heading north at seventy-five miles an hour—Madam at the wheel of her new black Range Rover, darting between semis like John Elway dodging tackles—before they knew what had hit them.

I didn't mind the wild ride. I was accustomed to Madam's driving and had brewed up a little St. John's Wort tea before our departure. My nerves were steady as steel. We stopped at a Starbucks in Daytona just as the sun was breaking the horizon and, in spite of the morning chill, sat on the vast, empty beach and watched the light come across the placid water. We were both exhausted. Neither of us had been able to erase the image of the fireball and the people extinguished by it. The tide was going out and the dogs ran back and forth, barking madly at the docile waves.

"I wonder if it was a family thing," Madam said. Her skin was as translucent as the sand. She wore a long black tunic, dark leggings, and soft J.P. Tod driving shoes. Sitting cross-legged on the beach with the steaming latte cupped in her long fingers, she looked a little like a smoking volcanic rock. "The Hammonds are always making headlines for trying to screw each other."

"I don't know," I shrugged. "I've never met any of them before and I hope I never see any of them again. Personally, I think it was either a complete accident, some sort of gas leak, or it had something to do with the Renoir."

"What about the Renoir?"

"Don't you remember? I told you it was gone."

"What are you talking about?"

"When I walked through the living room just before we left, it wasn't there. It was gone. I told you just before the explosion."

Madam shook her head. "I don't remember that. But even so, to kill all those people over a painting? I hope not. The whole thing makes me sick to my stomach. But you were right, Nigel."

"About what?"

"Not to mention the painting to the police."

The art world is very closed, very tight, a subculture that polices itself. Paintings disappear and reappear with some regularity, and the last thing anyone wants is a bunch of Interpol art and antiquities specialists or insurance investigators digging around in their affairs.

I got to my feet. "We'd better keep moving, we have a long way to go."

We switched places in the middle of South Carolina, and eleven hours after we'd left Palm Beach, I pulled into the driveway in Middleburg. It was twilight, just dark enough for me to see a lamp burning in Madam's studio. The light shone off Ryder's hunter, hitched to the tree by the cottage's little blue door.

"Will you be wanting dinner, Madam?"

"No, thanks, Nigel. Ryder said he was going to bring something."

She slammed the car door and ran down the path.

I fingered the new passport wallet in my pocket—the leather was buttery kid. I'd tucked a little slip of paper with Ruthie O'Connor's phone number into it. Everything just seemed a complete waste.

13

*C*hristmas passed without incident. Ryder had gone to Texas with Mary Anne and the entire Schlumbacher clan, which was a required annual command performance if he were to continue to enjoy the benefits associated with being married to one of the world's richest women. His absence let a breeze of normalcy blow through our little farm, and it seemed to invigorate all of us. I made steamed cider and we strung popcorn and cranberries while the dogs watched like statues, waiting for a broken kernel to fall on the floor.

The whole county was decorated; swags of pine trimmed with fruit and ribbons hung from estate gateposts, and green wreaths appeared on every door. The village of Middleburg looked like a Christmas card with miles of fresh garlands criss-crossing the narrow streets and wreaths trimmed with red bows hanging from the old-fashioned lampposts. On Saturday morning, the county turned out for the Hunt Parade—it takes the horses and the hounds approximately one and a half minutes to go from one end of town to the other and if you turn around to sneeze you miss the whole thing. This is immediately followed by the Christmas parade, a much more lavish affair that displays the town's ambulance and fire trucks from which the firemen throw armloads of candies to the children (I must admit I always grab as much saltwater taffy as I can, sometimes even right out of a child's sticky little paw). The high school band marches and the middle school stilt and unicycle teams proudly show off their skills. Madam goes with friends and I tag along with the dogs and a thermos of hot toddies. The well-dressed crowd is full of cheer, and I saw someone across the street who looked so much like Fernando I almost called out to him, but then he turned and the nose was all wrong.

As she did most years, Madam had Christmas Eve dinner at the Mattingly Farm—a magnificent old hunt-country pile—with the Mattinglys, a magnificent old hunt-country family made up of presidents, senators, and ambassadors, whose horses lived in greater luxury than ninety-nine-point-nine-nine percent of the rest of America and, basically, just about a hundred percent of the rest of the world.

All of the farm buildings, including the stable, where Christmas Eve cocktails were served, were hand-laid field stone. It boasted twelve stalls, six along each side, which housed a dozen premier hunter-jumpers, whose coats glistened and rippled with the celestial sheen that comes only from good breeding and daily massages with precious oils. At the end of that corridor, just beyond a twinkling Christmas tree, were three shower stalls where the beasts were taken to bathe and have a good rub-down after their work-outs. These were the champions of the Orange County Hunt, the most prestigious hunt of the Piedmont Valley, where equestrian competition and Virginia Gentleman bourbon are revered with the same holy esteem as politics and military service—and they were incredibly arrogant, especially for horses.

The Mattinglys had taken Madam to their bosom when she attended boarding school with their daughter, and she had celebrated Christmas Eve with them ever since.

"I wish one of these years you would come with me," she said as she climbed into the Rover. She looked like a Christmas fairy princess in her red velvet gown, with fresh holly sprigs tucked into her chignon.

Starlight sparkled off her hair. "It's always such a beautiful evening. Mass in the living room, cocktails in the barn, and all the family in that big old dining room with all their ancestors all over the walls. Nothing but candlelight. You would love it."

"I'm sure I would, Madam, and please thank them again for including me, but I really prefer sticking to my old Anglican Christmas."

That was only partially true, of course. My mum would forgive me for attending a Catholic mass, but there are not enough antihistamines in the world to get me through cocktails in a barn.

"You could take a Sudafed," she said, reading my mind.

"A horse by any other name is still a horse. Besides, I don't want to leave Tom by himself on Christmas Eve. Call me if you need anything." I would sup, as I had for ten years, with Tom, the butler from the farm down the road, and attend midnight services at the little Episcopal church in Upperville. It would be perfectly fine. I would say prayers for all the departed souls. The *Kiss-Kiss,* Fernando, the explosion . . . when I thought of it at all, some days it seemed a hundred years ago; other days it seemed like a dream, as if none of it had ever happened.

We had heard from Detective Marisco that the *Kiss-Kiss* was almost completely reassembled in an airplane hangar where the Coast Guard, Palm Beach police, and National Transportation Safety Board would continue their investigation. They were treating it as a bombing.

Our life went on.

Because she has lived such a solitary life (aside from the frequent long- and short-term love affairs), Madam has developed a number of creative talents, but cooking was most definitely not among them. To my mind—despite what we so-called experts and pundits say—creativity and cooking never have, and never will, go hand-in-hand. However, in spite of our protestations, Madam always insists upon observing the rituals of Boxing Day—the day after Christmas. According to time-honored English tradition, this was the day when the household staff, which had worked itself to death on Christmas Day, received their one day a year off and gift boxes from their masters—hence, Boxing Day. Today, because most everybody works—masters and servants alike—the servants get more than one day a year off, and everybody celebrates Boxing Day.

Everybody except Madam.

"You really should take the day off, too," I urge.

"Absolutely not. I love doing this and God knows, you all certainly deserve it. Don't worry, it's going to be a lot better this time. I swear to God. I'm doing all Thai-Indochine Colonial Pacific Fusion."

Whatever the hell that was.

Every year, she works slavishly in the kitchen, Frank Sinatra at full blast, preparing an extravaganza for me, the tiresome cook Effie, and Effie's close-mouthed husband Scully, our gardener and general house-man. Every year, we ask her to skip it. Every year, she tries something new. Every year, it's absolutely frightful, totally indigestible, and occasionally even dangerous, such as the time she did wild mushroom every-thing and we all started to go numb and had to rush to the hospital to have our stomachs pumped. Thank God she never stints on the wine. The quality sometimes, but never the quantity.

I chewed up four antacids before slipping into my bottle-green vel-vet dinner jacket and bracing myself for this year's onslaught of culinary torture.

Madam greeted us in the library, red poinsettias tucked gaily into her hair, her beautiful, irregular face shiny and eager. She offered a tray of what appeared to be raw little pot-stickers. "Pop it in all at once," she instructed. Her voice was enthusiastic, hopeful, as it always was at the start of our annual gag-fest.

"How pretty," I lied, ungluing the smallest one from its banana leaf doily and placing it cautiously in my mouth. "What are they?" I bit in.

"Lemon grass, quail egg, and escargot raviolis with Australian Abo-rigine hot pepper sauce. They're supposed to be the hottest peppers in the world. I hope I didn't use too much."

I swallowed and gulped my flute of Veuve-Cliquot. Nonvintage.

The combination of lively French champagne and these miniature, inflammable cannon balls was so powerful, for a few heart-stopping mo-ments I was uncertain if the doughy little bullet ricocheting around my gullet would stay inside and simply scorch me to death, or if it would hurl itself as from a flame-thrower back across the library, crash through the mullioned window, and set fire to the soggy garden.

"Have another," she urged, as I blew my nose and coughed and wheezed uncontrollably, perspiration pouring down my face.

"No more for me, Madam," I was finally able to gasp. "I'm saving room for dinner."

"Roasted wild English partridge, black pudding, and wild mushroom purée!" she declared. There were roses in her cheeks and lights flashing in her eyes.

"I thought you promised no more wild mushrooms."

"These aren't really wild, darling, they're just morels."

"And black pudding," I stated flatly.

Effie and Scully were from Pennsylvania, so they didn't know what black pudding was when it showed up on their plates looking like thick slices of Boston brown bread out of a can, alongside grayish-pink, underdone game bird and a chunky lump of wild morel mushroom death. I personally would rather be dragged around the Roman Coliseum behind a chariot pulled by wild horses than eat one bite of this dinner. Furthermore, I have never known anyone who ate black pudding more than once.

Effie, a very good-hearted soul, was the first to take a bite of it. It was a fairly good-sized forkful and she mushed it around in her mouth before gulping it down with huge mouthfuls of acceptable red burgundy. "What is it?"

Scully stared at his plate and kept his rough hands in his lap. His jaw was set.

"Black pudding!" Madam smiled. "I'm not sure exactly what's in it but the butcher said it was perfect with partridge. What do you think?" She, herself, took a bite. All was quiet for a second or two, and then she shuddered and gagged. "Oh God," she exclaimed. "This is *disgusting.*" Her shoulders heaved, and she spat into her napkin, then drank her entire glass of wine as though it were colored water. "Good God." She poured more wine and drank it, then tore off a chunk of her dinner roll and chewed it up. "That is the most disgusting thing I've ever tasted. What on earth *is* it? Nigel, do you know?"

"I'm not really too sure, Madam."

What black pudding is, although I would never tell it at table, is actually blood pudding. It's pork blood, mixed with hunks of pork fat, shoved into a sausage casing and boiled. It is then sliced and has the texture of a fine, airy blood soufflé. It's something cooked up centuries ago by someone who had absolutely nothing left to eat except a bucket of congealed pig blood left over from the slaughter, a few scraps of fat, and some entrails, which he rinsed out with god-knows-what. Black pudding is right up there with that equally revolting Scottish concoction haggis, whereby they take a sheep's brains and bake them inside its stomach. No wonder they invented scotch.

Madam cleared the plates quickly and then we all had two more glasses of wine and more bread and butter. "We can't have dessert *yet*," she said. "We've only been at the table for ten minutes."

"Yes, we can," the three of us said in unison.

Next up was a Croquembouche, typically a spectacular confection of feather-light puffs filled with either ice cream or whipped cream and glued into an opulent pyramid with crackling burnt sugar. It is a concoction only the most accomplished pastry chef would undertake, and always with a sense of fear and trepidation. And then, only the best of the best would use ice cream as the filling because it is so damnably hard to work with. Whipped cream is much less volatile. Do I need to tell you that Madam chose ice cream? She toiled for five hours, swearing at the ice cream, which melted from both ends of her pastry tube, opening and slamming the freezer door every five seconds, racing back to the stove, trying to keep the finicky sugar at the proper temperature. The kitchen became a sticky sea of burning sugar threads and slippery puddles of cream. But an hour before we were due to present ourselves for cocktails, she finally got it all glued together, and so what if it wasn't a pyramid, more of a football-shaped lump? She got the damned thing done and shoved it into the freezer to try to firm up the ice cream, which had been mostly liquefied by the white-hot sugar and was oozing out of the little pastry puffs.

Do I have to tell you what happened when she opened the freezer door? The platter tipped and the entire thing slid off and crashed onto the floor where it was immediately attacked by the dogs.

"Shit," we heard Madam mutter behind the kitchen door. Then she stuck her head into the dining room. "Let's just move on to the cheese."

The cheese always saves the day, along with another bottle of burgundy, and Madam is such a superb hostess, the Boxing Day horror is fun in spite of everything. We all get roaring drunk and laugh ridiculously and she gives us each gifts she cannot afford. This year she gave me a crystal decanter and six old-fashioned glasses engraved with African wildlife—the perfect thing for the drinks table in my sitting room, although I have virtually no interest in Africa. Every disease known to man has come from there and continues to do so. I was just reading about a new Ugandan strain of viral flu, as if AIDS and Ebola weren't enough. I would rather die than touch a monkey and I would not even begin to consider a visit to Uganda for all the tea in China. And for that matter, I wouldn't visit China, either.

14

NEW YEAR'S EVE

*M*adam and I spent a quiet New Year's Eve together.
Although we are as devoted to each other as brother and sister, she plays her life, her innermost self, very close to the vest, which would surprise those who know her because she gives the impression of being extremely outgoing and forthcoming about every aspect of her existence. By showing what could appear to be everything, she in fact shows nothing.

We were in the library, a wonderfully cozy room, jam-packed with bookcases, paintings, and sculptures. The heavy draperies of the tall Palladian windows were tied back with braided cords, and the dogs were resting on a blue velvet cushion before the fireplace. Madam and I were sipping Manhattans and watching *Biography* reruns on A&E, she curled up on her favorite red paisley sofa with a navy cashmere throw over her legs, working on a Della Robbia needlepoint. I, at the antique Edwardian game table by the windows, fiddled with the same jigsaw puzzle I'd been fiddling with for over a year, a silly thing I thought would turn out to be a mill with some children picking yellow flowers around the pond—the flowers were the killer. They seemed to be everywhere. The picture to guide me was long lost. A nice fire crackled in the hearth. A classic Virginia ice storm raged. Tree branches scrapped the windows like wild animals clawing to get in.

Rembrandt's biography—as if we, in our little household, needed any reminder of how unstable and compromising the life of a portrait artist can be—had just wrapped up and Christina Onassis's had begun, a truly tragic story. Abandoned by her glamorous, silly mother, Christina worshipped her father, who treated her like dirt—teasing and mocking her unmercifully and publicly—because she had been unfortunate enough to inherit his looks. Her handsome older brother had gotten their mother's classic bones and clear eyes. Christina was a scowling little troll whose smile only deformed her more, and as she grew older, her father's abuse became more demeaning and more public and she never recovered from it. We watched her splashing around on her private island, Skorpios, after her whole family was dead: mother, father, brother. She was terribly bloated from liquor and drugs and rich food, and the pain in her eyes could break your heart. She was surrounded by freeloaders who cared virtually nothing about her.

Suddenly, I heard a strange choking kind of noise and realized it was Madam. She was crying. But it was more than crying, it was a moaning, almost a keening sound. The sort of wail you try to swallow but that swallows you instead.

"Madam?" I looked up from my puzzle, my hand full of yellow cardboard flowers. "Are you all right?" I jumped to my feet, but she waved me back to my chair.

"No, no, I'm fine, Nigel. But, my God," she wept. "That poor girl. She had no one to save her, no one to love her. That could have been me."

"Pardon?" My hand had locked like a vise around the puzzle pieces and I could feel them cutting into it. A door was opening and, wherever it led, I didn't want to go through it.

"Nigel, there are so many things you don't know about me. Things I've never told anyone, but dear God, seeing this story . . ." she stopped, wiped the tears from her face, and took a breath. "I know you worry about me because I seem so alone. But I'm not."

I stayed quiet and watched her. She drew her knees to her chest, hugging them to her, tucking herself into a ball.

"I'm sorry, but I don't know what you're talking about."

She stared into the fire.

"Do you know that since I was a little, little girl, whenever my mother's friends came over, she would lock me in the closet?" Her eyes seemed filled with a combination of embarrassment and shame. Pain of disclosure, or humiliation, I don't know which, twisted her face, and she tightened the grip on her legs, hugging them closer. "Can you imagine such a thing? Locking up a three-year-old in the dark? 'You're too ugly for my friends to see you,' she'd say. 'I wish I'd never had you.' And she'd lock me in an empty closet in her bedroom. It was more the size of a cabinet—the door blended with the wall . . . you know I've never told anyone about this before."

But, the flood-gates had opened. She could not stop telling and I could not believe my ears. I wanted to cover them, to not hear her story. We all have stories. I didn't want to hear hers any more than I wanted to tell her mine. Let's just leave it in the past, leave it alone, I wanted to scream, my heart thudding in my chest.

"She'd leave me in there for hours, but it always felt like days. She said if I made any noise, she'd kill me. I was terrified. I knew she meant it. My mother's capacity for violence was unlimited. It was completely black in there, only a thin line of light beneath the door, and the floor was unfinished, full of splinters, sweltering in the summer and freezing in the winter. I had discovered some towels on the shelf, and wrapped myself in them for warmth. Sometimes I couldn't control myself and, well, never mind, the point is that as little as I was—I look back on it now and I can't believe how clever and furtive I became—I quickly learned to protect myself. When she was out, I would throw the towels away and take fresh ones out of her bathroom. I'd hide them back on the shelf and she would blame the maid for stealing. I also hid chocolate."

A log burned through its center and caved into the fire, sending out a comforting, purifying shower of sparks.

"It was true. I was ugly. She said I looked like a frog—just like that poor Onassis girl—and I guess I did. When I was little, maybe three or four, I'd cry until I fell asleep, and when I got a little older I'd pray to God and the Blessed Virgin to save me. Somewhere I'd seen a picture of the Virgin, and the minute I saw it, I knew it had been painted just for me. Her robes were gold and white gossamer, they shimmered as though they were the breath of angels. And her hands reached out—to me. The expression on her face was full of love—for me. Everything about her told me not to worry, she would never let me down or leave me alone. But when you're five years old and imprisoned in a hard, cold cabinet, and you can hear your mother talking and laughing and telling her friends that her daughter has gone out for the afternoon or the night— 'She's such an ugly, boring little frog, I'm glad to have her off my hands for a few hours. It's much more amusing when she's gone.' That was my mother's favorite word: amusing. I think it's the most pretentious word in the English language—sometimes it was hard to believe the Virgin was at hand. Do you understand?"

It was hard for me to speak, I was anguished and heart-broken by what she was telling me and I wanted her to stop. "I'm sorry," was the best I could do.

"No. No." She lit a cigarette and waved the match out before tossing it toward the fire. "Don't be sorry. I'm not telling you this to make you feel sorry for me and I know you're sitting there thinking this will some-how change our life, that I'll wake up one morning and start resenting you or something because you know too much about me, but I promise you, I won't."

She knows me like a book. I fought back tears. I'm a child and a coward. I'm not proud of my lack of courage.

"I'm telling you this so you can understand why I am the way I am. She imprisoned me as a punishment for something I could not control— I came to terms with that years ago. I was a child, none of it was my fault. One day, with only the wisdom a child can have, I realized the joke was on her: She didn't realize she was giving me more than she was tak-ing away. You cannot imagine the power this knowledge gave me. It was then, sitting there in the dark with the presence of our Lady, that I started to see the colors, beautiful, beautiful colors, put together in ways I'd never before seen nor imagined. In my head, my mind's eye, I began to paint. Not my mother's cruel, demonic visions, but magnificent scenes of sunsets and dawns, scenes of hope and majesty. And then it came to me that no matter what my mother said to me or did to me, she could not touch me or hurt me. The Virgin had saved me. I've never been alone again."

Madam smiled. "I don't even hate her anymore, because I realized when I was in my early twenties, I had to make a decision: Did I want to dedicate my life to blaming and hating my mother or did I want to take what I had and get on with it? Did I want to live in the dark or the light? I chose the light and forgave her a long time ago. But I'm not so naïve as to say this did not influence my relationships with people. As you know, I appear to be long on faith in myself and way, way short on faith in others. But the truth is, I'm way short on faith in all of us."

What she'd said—in spite of my reluctance to hear it—answered all those unfathomable questions about why she sometimes acted as she did. Why there had been an endless string of men—charming, talented, wealthy, available men—but never a deep or enduring relationship with a man, or even any close women friends. We were identical in so many ways, like two lost lambs crying in the wilderness for our mothers. Madam's maternal trust had been violated and was irreparable. My beloved mother died when I was in prison and I never got to tell her goodbye. She was lost to me forever.

So what was the explanation for Madam's incomprehensible relationship with Ryder? Was it to punish her mother? A last-ditch search for a father? Or to punish herself? He was so beneath the others she'd had affairs with, there was nothing to recommend him—beyond the animal, of course, and, as we all know, he had animal in spades.

"Well," she said, after I'd remained quiet for maybe longer than I should, "what are you thinking?"

"I was wondering about Ryder," I answered.

"Ummm." Madam tossed the blanket aside, went to the drinks table, and pulled the decanter of Manhattans from its bed of ice. She refilled her glass and then mine. "Ryder. I haven't quite worked that one out myself. I do know I'm starting to get tired of the situation. But on the other hand," she dropped in a fresh cherry and smiled at me, "I'm also looking forward to seeing him tomorrow. I don't know. It's a mess, isn't it?"

I nodded. "If I may," I said, "I don't think he's the man for you."

"I know. I can't figure out what I'm doing with him. He knows me too well. He knows about the closet-prison Mother locked me in. Sometimes he was the one who let me out. Maybe I feel I owe him something because he used to protect me."

"You don't owe him anything."

She looked at her hands. "I know," she whispered. "I don't know what it is with him."

"What about Armand? He adores you and he's one of the few men I've ever thought was telling the truth when he said he'd do anything for you."

She nodded. "He's so close to the real thing, I'm afraid to get in too deep. What if I gave in to him the way I want to, and he turned out to be like all the others?"

"If it were me, I think I would take the risk."

"Besides, he works too hard. His life is his business."

"It's good to have a man who works."

"You know what I mean. I don't think he has the time for real love. I don't think he would ever put love first."

"Would you?"

Madam laughed. "Touché."

The grandfather clock in the hallway chimed midnight. We raised our glasses to each other from our respective perches.

"Happy New Year, Nigel. I feel so much better now that I've told you. Just got rid of it all. This is the right way to begin a new year."

I didn't especially agree. I wished she'd kept it all to herself because, even if she felt better, I would stew about it for days. But it was my job to be gracious. "Happy New Year to you, too, Madam," I said. "Let's have a good one."

15

To celebrate New Year's Day, Madam planned a cozy, low-key luncheon for her and Ryder in her studio, which is, in fact, the most charming little one-bedroom stone cottage I have ever seen outside of the Cotswolds, which I admit I have never visited, but I've seen just as many pictures as anyone. Besides, as an Englishman, I have an innate understanding of such details, even if I am from Birmingham. It had taken me days to pull the luncheon together. Once Effie finished scrubbing and dusting, I set up a table for two in front of the fireplace and laid it with the dearest, antique Madeira cloth I'd ever seen. I had laundered and ironed it myself and the linen was so crisp, you could almost cut your fingers on the edges.

One thing you can count on about married men who are having affairs, especially ones who live in terror of losing their wives: They are desperately guilty about almost everything, so the extremes and excesses they go to to make themselves feel better are extraordinary, even if they're using their sick, wheel-chair-bound wife's dough. For example, Ryder had sent Madam approximately five hundred red roses—isn't it interesting he hadn't figured out yet that all she really likes are gardenias? The place was wall-to-wall in perfect blossoms, which, thankfully, had zero fragrance, otherwise, I could not have considered entering the premises. I'm becoming horribly sensitive to a great many scents. Thankfully gardenia isn't among them.

Interestingly, Armand had sent her a single, small bouquet of lilies of the valley which she had put on her bed table in the main house. *"Ma Jacqueline,"* his note had read. "I have suffered a *coup de foudre* at your hands. May the new year bring us closer in every way. *Je t'aime,* Armand."

I wedged the cocktail tray into the roses at the edge of Madam's desk and quickly checked myself in the mirror. My brownish hair was well-parted and carefully slicked into place, my face was cleanly shaven, and my bright brown eyes clear and shining. My mum would be so proud of me. Out of nowhere, a wave of emotion engulfed me so totally I lost complete control of myself, and for a minute I was afraid I would drown. The tears would not stop. I sat on the sofa and sobbed into my handkerchief. It had been almost fifteen years. When would the pain of losing her heal? The last she knew of me was the shame of my prison sentence. Oh, Lord, how I wish she could see me now.

"Nigel, you are a magician." Madam put her hand on my shoulder, her touch as gentle as a whisper. She had on a plain jersey sheath in a buttery, tawny brown. It was grim and rainy outside, and with the silver and crystal glittering in the firelight, and the gardenias resting in her hair like white velvet birds, she reminded me of an exotic wild cat, ready to pounce on her prey, which, as we know, was due to arrive any minute.

She prowled among the roses without seeming to notice their presence. "Thank you for listening to me last night."

"No thanks are necessary."

"It really helped me see things more clearly, and I've decided I'm going to do it."

"Madam?"

"I'm going to give Ryder an ultimatum, get the year off to a really good, brand new start. He's got to decide. Her or me. I'm not going to live like this anymore, it's wrecking my life."

I kept my mouth firmly shut and tossed a handful of sweet balsam chips on the fire—lovely scent and very good for the sinuses.

"You're right about Armand. Maybe I should give him a chance. He said such nice things to me at Lynette's party, about how I should have a man who appreciates me, who would be proud to be seen with me in public, and I've been thinking about it, and he's right. Not to mention the small deaths I die when I think about Mary Anne. First my mother, now me. I can't even imagine how much she must hate me, and she's such a *nice* person. And she's in a *wheel-chair* for God's sake. If I were her, I'd kill me. Then I'd kill Ryder. He is a complete bastard, isn't he? He's got it made, and I'm sick of it. I mean, look at this." She jabbed her finger at her wrist watch. "The one day he promises to be on time and he's late. What in the hell am I doing with this loser?"

"Would you like a Bloody Mary, Madam?"

"Good idea."

Two strong cocktails and ten cigarettes later, when the thunder clouds over her head had built to monumental proportions, Ryder galloped up to the door, leapt off the chestnut, and swept Madam into his arms. She pushed him away.

"I know you're mad," he said. "But I have a good excuse."

She crossed her arms over her chest and looked at him, unable to conceal her hurt and relief. "What?"

"May I at least come in? It's cold out here."

She stood aside to let him pass and followed him across the oak transom, which he had to stoop slightly to cross without cracking his head.

"Bloody Mary, sir?" I asked.

"Please. That is, if Madam doesn't mind." He placed his riding hat on the chair by the door and shrugged out of his rain gear. Underneath, he was suited up in skin-tight fawn jodhpurs, gleaming black and cordovan boots, a perfectly fitted black jacket—its lapel decked with a tiny French Legion d'Honneur rosette which he had stolen from someone else's coat room at some long-gone dinner party—white shirt, and a yellow tie covered with red horses. He did look smashing.

"Be my guest." Her voice was matter-of-fact.

"Little chilly in here," Ryder said wryly and looked to me for support.

"Let me add a log, sir."

"That's not what I meant." He positioned himself in front of the blaze and rubbed his hands together nervously.

Jackie's portrait of her mother hung over the mantel. It was one of Madam's best works. Today, Constanza seemed particularly full of loathing. I used to think that Madam kept her mother's portrait out of some sense of familial duty; it was, after all, her mother. But today, it occurred to me that Madam had hung it where she could see it regularly to keep herself strong and focused. Or maybe she just didn't see it at all anymore.

"I was going to give you this over lunch, but I can see I'd better give it to you now." Ryder retrieved a black velvet box with a red satin ribbon from his raincoat pocket.

"Jacqueline di Fidelio, will you marry me?"

Oh, for heaven's sakes. Get the bucket. If Madam falls for that old ploy—the common move of a desperate, married man who knows he's on thin ice—she deserves whatever she gets.

She let the ribbon drift to the floor and snapped open the box. A dome-shaped ring with a huge, round, central diamond surrounded by several circles of diamonds in diminishing size sparkled from the velvet cushion. It was impressive, but from my point-of-view there were a few serious problems with this gift. First of all, Ryder was still married. And secondly, this ring, no matter how magnificent, was no engagement ring. It was a *dinner* ring.

He slipped it onto her finger.

"Oh, Ryder," she cried, and threw her arms around him, all backbone out the window. "I love you so much."

"There's my girl." He smoothed her hair, looked at me with his good eye, and winked. It was a paternal, there-there, wink. I wanted to punch him. One of these days, I would.

"So you talked to Mary Anne," Madam said, over the Lobster Thermidor and a crisp Sancerre 1997. "What did she say?"

Ryder swiped his lips with the linen square. "I told her that you are absolutely critical to my life. That I could not live without you. She said she understood."

"Did you ask her for a divorce?"

Ryder held up his hands. "Not so fast, sweetheart. Not so fast. I need to go slowly, but it's not going to be a problem. You just have to trust me and be patient for a little longer. You know, she can't take too many big hits at one time. I mean, I just want a divorce, I don't want to kill her." He laughed and took a manly quaff of wine. "Although I wouldn't especially mind if she died. It certainly would uncomplicate things."

"Don't say that. Not even as a joke." Jackie looked at the ring. "Do you think we could get married next Christmas? In Paris?"

"I don't see why not."

I could see a hundred reasons why not. Did Madam really believe that Mary Anne Schlumbacher McCormick was just going to *hand over* her husband without a fight? And just what, I ask, did Madam think they were going to live on? These were two people with serious overhead. Most of her painting fees were earmarked for the Internal Revenue Service. Ryder's money was not his, it was all his wife's. Had anyone ever heard of the McCormick fortune? Of course not. It was the *Schlumbacher* fortune.

I began to clear the table and accidentally dropped Ryder's cutlery into his lap, staining his jodhpurs with lobster sauce, which made his temper flare, but he kept it under control, evidently sensing that he was on less-than-solid footing and that a fit of pique might push her over the edge, in the wrong direction.

"I'm so terribly sorry, sir," I lied. "Would you like me to douse it with club soda?"

"No. It's fine."

"So when *are* you going to ask her for the divorce?" Madam asked as I placed a chocolate truffle cake on the side table, filled their champagne flutes with pale pink Cristal, and listened expectantly. This was going to be a whopper.

"Well, she's got a series of treatments coming up at the end of the month and they usually knock her out for a few days, so I'd say I'll probably tell her in mid- to late February. Certainly before the MOMA show. How's that?"

I cut into the cake, slicing two wedges with a razor-sharp knife, and served them up.

"Good," said Madam. "That'll be perfect."

I detected a new tone in her voice, a courteous, distant steeliness, and the possibility that she meant what she said this time about his making a choice occurred to me. Go, Madam. She devoured her cake in three fast bites.

"Did I tell you I'm gone from mid-January through February?" she continued lightly.

"No," Ryder responded irritably. He had lost control of the conversation and it aggravated him. "Where will you be?"

"New York."

"Oh? Doing who?"

"You know I never tell you who I'm working on until I'm done. But now, at least you've given me one thing to look forward to about the MOMA show. I've been dreading it, but with this," she cast a look at the ring, "everything will be different."

"Oh?" Ryder held his lighter to her cigarette and then his. "How so?"

"We'll be engaged," she laughed. "We'll have gone public."

"Right."

"I'm going to hold you to this, Ryder."

"Do you want me to swear on a Bible?"

Jackie smiled. "Yes."

Ryder smiled back, wrinkling the scars around his bad eye. The fire-light caught it, turning it slightly milky.

The next day, the federal agents returned. We had just finished breakfast and I was leaving to take the dogs on a long walk when the gray sedan materialized out of the morning fog shortly after eight. I showed them into the sunroom as before but made no offer of coffee or rolls. Madam joined them a few minutes later.

"We understand you made contact with Mr. Weil," Agent Romero said without preamble.

"Yes. I did."

"Did you learn anything about the Vermeer?"

"Yes. I learned he doesn't have it," Madam answered firmly. She seemed resigned to her role as informant. "But I told him I'd be willing to offer a five million dollar reward."

"Where were you planning to get five million dollars?" Agent Collier asked. Her hands were red and coarse, as if she'd been doing too many Christmas dishes. She was impossibly rude.

"I'm sure the insurance company would be happy to pay for the information." The claws began to come out.

Romero stepped in. "Do you have any idea who would have wanted to blow up Mrs. Payne's yacht?"

Madam shook her head. "Not a clue. Don't you have any leads yet?"

Neither agent replied.

"We have a tip that Mr. Weil has the Vermeer in a vault at his house in Aspen. He's giving a party there in March. Get yourself invited."

"Excuse me? How do you propose I do that?"

"You'll think of something." He opened his briefcase, withdrew a large manila envelope, and laid it on the table. "We happened to come across the builder's plans for the place showing the location of the vault and the security system. You'll find them useful in conducting your search. I convinced the director to give you an extension to the end of the quarter, although the penalties and interest will continue to accrue."

"Accrue?"

"Naturally. Don't you open your mail? You get a monthly statement. Your tax bill now totals seven hundred and eighty-three thousand dollars, but I got you ninety days."

Naturally, Madam didn't mention the missing Renoir to the agents. And to tell you the truth, as the whole incident began to fade into the mist, I realized maybe I'd been imagining things. I hadn't actually stopped to make sure the Renoir wasn't there as I'd passed through the saloon, it was just an impression I'd gotten that it was missing. The whole thing was becoming surreal.

16

NEW YORK CITY

We left for New York ten days later. Instead of taking I-95 the whole way, we decided to go through Annapolis, cross the Bay at Sandy Point, and head up the Eastern Shore, catching Highway 13 just south of Wilmington, where the road practically intersects the main, and possibly only, runway at the local airport. The reason we did all this was so we could stop at the diner at the end of the runway for a cup of coffee and a big piece of coconut cream pie. Sounds charming, doesn't it? The highways on the eastern seaboard are a nightmare, and the pie is not worth the extra drive time.

"I'll take it from here." Madam directed me to pull into a rest stop just outside of Newark. Across the water, Manhattan's skyscrapers drifted in and out of the clouds.

"I'll go ahead and walk the dogs now." I pulled on their little sweaters and lifted them to the ground. "It'll just be a minute."

We were in the midst of one of the stormiest winters on record—the whole world had turned gunmetal gray, the sky and the earth were indistinguishable—and while it wasn't snowing at the moment, it was bitterly cold and the wind cut through my Chesterfield as I dragged the little darlings across the icy parking lot to a forlorn patch of brown grass. Then we raced back to the warmth of the car and, after some treats and sips of Evian water, the dogs curled up in the back seat and went back to sleep. I was happy not to have to drive into the city. Every now and then I get a little rattled and find myself heading for the wrong side of the road.

"May I ask you a question, Madam?" I asked as we descended into the Holland Tunnel.

"Of course."

"I've noticed you haven't been wearing Ryder's ring." I tried to keep the hope out of my voice.

"No, and I don't intend to until he asks Mary Anne for a divorce. Besides, can you believe he gave me a *dinner* ring? What does he think, I'm a complete idiot?" She laughed.

"Do you think the ring was Mrs. McCormick's?"

"*What?*"

The devil must have taken over my tongue, because I was fomenting trouble and liking it. "It's terrible of me to say, but do you think it was part of her jewelry collection?"

She whooped with laughter. "You know what? I wouldn't put it past him. I'm starting to see him in a whole new light. Ever since I decided to give him the ultimatum—which I never did do because he promised he would finally get things moving and I know you think it was just another big lie—anyway, since I realized I could make him choose, I realized I could live without him, too." She glanced over at me, the lights of the tunnel flashing on her face. "Do you know what I mean?"

"Perfectly."

"I need to break myself loose, take myself back from him. I was thinking maybe I ought to go to a shrink, but I've spent half my life with shrinks, what more could I possibly learn?"

"Well, have you been telling the psychiatrists the truth? I mean, about everything? Like being locked in the cabinet?"

"Forget it. That's none of their business."

"Well, it could be germane." I tried to keep the sarcasm out of my voice.

"Well, of course it's germane. But I can't be blabbing around stuff like that. Can you imagine if it got out? It'd be on the cover of *People* magazine. I'd be out of business."

Traffic stopped inside the tunnel and we sat in silence looking at the grimy walls and trying not to breathe the fumes too deeply.

"Besides," she said, once the cars started moving again. "I've been thinking a lot about Mary Anne. It's like I'm becoming obsessed with her. I like her. I admire her. She's an absolutely outstanding individual. Look at all the boards she serves on and all the money she gives away. And her art collection? It's one of the finest in the world. Her eye is one of the greatest. She is ten times more substantial as a human being than Ryder."

"Surely you aren't just figuring that out," I offered, but she ignored me.

". . . and I certainly don't want her to suffer any more than she already does, especially because of me. I mean, I go so hot and cold on him. He has this weird power over me when I'm near him, but now that we're headed off to go work again, the glow fades fast. So, I don't know. Should I marry him? Would I marry him? I'm not sure."

We emerged from the tunnel just then, so I couldn't be certain if it was the light or her remarks that dazzled my eyes.

"I'm going to start seeing other men. I've been living like a cloistered nun since Mother died. Just look at this city. Isn't it the best?"

I peeked out the window, but to tell the truth, the only thing worse than my trying to drive in Manhattan was being driven in it by Madam. She ignored virtually everyone and everything, talking the whole time as though she had a chauffeur. Cars screeched all around us. How she'd never killed anyone I'll never know. I'd chewed up three Dramamine tablets since we left Newark. Without water.

"It's full of fabulous men. Well, here we are." She slammed on the brakes in front of our Soho loft building, which had become so chic we now had a doorman, George.

I almost kissed him I was so glad to be out of the car.

It doesn't matter what you think about New York, we all know it has a spectacular American energy all its own. I love London, Paris, San

Francisco, Middleburg. I love every place we live and work, except the boats of course, but New York gets me psyched up like no place else, and once we'd arrived and stowed the car, I was bursting to get out there and be among 'em, as they say, even if there were piles of filthy snow lining the sidewalks and the temperature was insane. Thank the Lord it wasn't so cold that I needed to pull on a surgical mask. I've never been comfortable about breathing through my muffler—I know most people wrap theirs around their face and carry on—but those scarves become absolute *hotbeds* of germs. If you have even the slightest hint of a cold and breathe it into your muffler, well, you're down for the winter. And listen to me: Never, ever, borrow anyone's muffler for any reason.

Madam promptly sequestered herself in her studio and got on the phone with her upcoming clients to reconfirm their schedules. She was here to do two "Captain of Industry" boardroom portraits. Full-body commissions, each costing in excess of one hundred fifty thousand dollars, they would keep us in gardenias, living the life, for a few more months. One of the men, the chairman of Wissoco Industries, Mr. Wiss to be exact, would sit every morning from nine to eleven, and his vice-chairman Mr. Ross, from one to three in the afternoons. Counting all the interruptions for their urgent phone calls and business emergencies, it would take most of the month to complete the paintings. She'd done two lengthy photography sessions with each of them and had tacked the blow-ups onto padded panels in the Middleburg studio. For several days, she'd studied the shots, going over them with a magnifying glass, memorizing every one of their physical characteristics—Mr. Wiss had too much of a belly, which, she explained to me, she would reduce to a respectable girth, befitting a man of his accomplishments and stature. Mr. Ross, the young turk and heir-apparent, had a sallow, lumpy complexion he'd admitted to her he wished were warmer. She'd gotten to know them in such painstaking detail from the photographs—sitting, walking, standing, talking, smiling, laughing, contemplating—that the next day, when Messrs. Wiss and Ross arrived for their respective sittings, they would be like old friends. As the sessions progressed, she would get to know them intimately; everything that went on in their minds and hearts, even a few of their secrets, until they would, in reality, become old friends and it would be the warmth of that familiarity that would finally bring the portraits to life.

I peeked into the studio before I left on my errands. Madam had erected two easels and laid out the photos, sketch pads, charcoal, crayons, and tubes of paint on a long work table. She was beginning to prepare one of the canvases, covering it with a coat of luminous white acrylic. She worked in silence.

Closing the door quietly, I headed down the street to Dean & DeLuca, which I know is an expensive place to do the daily marketing, but I wouldn't have gone there if Madam had specifically told me not to and she hadn't said a word. I set to work provisioning up the apartment— eggs, bacon, sardines, capers, cornichons, Lucca olive oil, two roasted chickens, four cans of fancy albacore tuna, garlic, four heads of butter lettuce, a case of Evian water, and eight different kinds of cheese. Next door I ordered a case each of sauvignon blanc, red burgundy, and champagne. Then I hit the florist.

The loft was large, an entire floor, and so you can imagine it could not have been more different from the cozy little Virginia farmhouse, which could be made to radiate charm with a single vase of freshly cut garden roses placed on the round pedestal table in the entry hall. Instead—with its sixteen-foot ceilings, gigantic windows, high-gloss floors, and hard-edged avant-garde furniture—the loft required arresting, overscale arrangements, birds of paradise and paleonopsis, entire birch trees, and forsythia bushes that cost a fortune.

We settled into our working routine: for Madam an early morning walk followed by the two sittings, a rigorous afternoon workout, and quiet nights when she would very occasionally accept a dinner invitation from a prospective client. A rigid regimen, it was designed to keep her focused on her work, and to my knowledge, she neither saw nor spoke to Ryder or Armand, though they both left frequent messages and sent weekly bouquets, which did wonders for my flower budget. On those nights she did go out, I was seldom still awake when she came in. But one evening I was up particularly late, lying on the puffy yellow-and-fuchsia toile chaise in my sitting room—mine were the only traditional rooms in the place since contemporary furniture disagrees with my

digestion—watching *Law & Order* reruns, and palpating a pain in my abdomen just below my ribcage and slightly to the right—oh, Lord, if I
have gallstones I don't know what I'll do. My grandmother had terrific
bouts with her gallbladder. What a mess it was, too—when Madam
knocked on the door.

"Am I interrupting?" she asked.

"Certainly not." I jumped to my feet and tightened my Burberry robe
around me. If I wasn't better by morning, I'd go for an ultrasound.

"Please don't get up. I'm here to ask a favor." She had just returned
from dinner with Charles and Bianca Roosevelt and was slightly tipsy.
She was wearing a dark Armani pants suit and a long fur coat, which she
shrugged off and tossed onto a side chair. "Do you have any cigarettes?"

"Please." I indicated the Georgian silver box engraved with some
long lost Georgian subject's coat-of-arms, which sat on my coffee table
among a number of other collected treasures and oversized art books.
"Help yourself. May I offer you something to drink? A little cognac?
Fernet-Branca?"

"Fernet-Branca would be just right."

I stepped into my fleece-lined slippers, crossed to the copper-lined
dry sink where I kept my modest bar, and poured out a small snifter for
each of us. It might help my pain. I knew it certainly wouldn't hurt it.

"I thought everything was set for the show," she grimaced as she
took her first sip of the bitter digestif. "But it's not. I need you to go to
Paris and pick up a couple of pieces."

In one week, the Museum of Modern Art, of which Bianca Hammond Roosevelt was vice-chairman of the board, would open a major
retrospective of Constanza di Fidelio. They'd assembled works from museums and private collections all over the world, over one hundred altogether. An international hoard of press and guests would attend the gala.
I didn't see what possible difference two more of her sick paintings
could make, but who am I to question?

"No problem. When do you want me to go?"

"Right away. Tomorrow or the day after."

"Which pieces?"

"*The Gemini.*"

"Oh." I knew them well. The twins. One good, one evil; identical
Day-Glo fluorescent bug-eyed monsters. One blue, orange, and green.

The other, pink, red, and yellow. I didn't know which was supposed to be which, good or evil. In my opinion, they weren't worth the trip.

"I thought they were too delicate to travel," I said.

"I've talked to Claude." Claude LaGallienne owned the Parisian gallery that controlled Constanza's work. "He'll have the last word and, if they can make the trip, he'll crate them. All you have to do is escort them back to the States."

"Are you sure? I don't think they're that great."

"Nigel."

"All right. I'll go as soon as I can."

"Thank you."

After she left, I called to make the necessary arrangements—Air France had space available on their six-thirty the next night—and then snuggled under the down quilt on my little French cherrywood sleigh bed in my soft cotton flannel pajamas; as cozy as a bug in a rug, as my mum liked to say. The fact is, I thought as I drifted off to sleep, French medicine is significantly more advanced than its American counterpart, and if my self-diagnosis turned out to be correct—if, God forbid, this were gallstones—I would be much more comfortable having a French surgeon handle the matter. I'll tell you, that American Hospital in Neuilly is fabulous.

I slept like a baby.

17

"*etit déjuner, Monsieur Smythe?*" the steward asked in a hushed voice. His white jacket was crisp and fresh, and as he spoke, he folded my comforter and stowed it in the large bin behind my seat. Lights along the Irish and British coasts twinkled in and out of the clouds thousands of feet below the window of the Air France jumbo jet.

"*Non, merci,*" I answered. "*Seulement café et fromage, s'il vous plait.*"

By the time I returned from changing out of my warm-ups and splashing water on my face, the first class cabin was coming slowly to life, though the winter sun had scarcely tinted the horizon. The steward had placed a cup of impossibly strong coffee, a large gooey wedge of Camembert, and a crispy baguette on my side table. I ate them slowly, full of sleepy melancholy, and looked out the window as we approached the French coastline.

I can never fly across the Norman cliffs without being filled with emotion. My father died in Operation Overlord, the Invasion of Normandy, in June 1945. It was at Sword Beach, where the English troops came ashore—flatter terrain than Utah or Omaha, but just as deadly. I don't know if he even made it onto land, all I know is that he is buried in the English Military Cemetery in Bayeux. I never even knew him, but whenever I fly across that pastoral part of the world I want to fall out of the plane and float down and cover him with my body.

One autumn, Mum and I did our pilgrimage to Normandy. We were almost the only ones there except for busloads of bored French school children. After visiting Father, we went to the American Cemetery at Omaha Beach, and I was overwhelmed by the tragic grandeur of it. Everything seemed larger than life, scaled for the gods. At one end, a colonnade of pure white marble columns tower dozens of feet into the air and form a mighty semi-circle around a golden statue of a man leaping to the sky, reaching for glory. White marble monoliths rise at either end of the crescent monument, each flanked by an iron urn large enough to contain the Olympic flame. Above each urn, carved into the white stone, is a bas-relief sculpture—so subtle, most people probably don't even notice it. I did.

The sculpture is of a nude young man, physically, in the prime of his life. His body is perfect, his muscles pulse with youthful energy and pride. Astride a magnificent war horse galloping with such ferocious power it would terrify any person in its path, the young man holds a sword over his head, preparing to vanquish his foe. Just as we feel his adrenaline and excitement at the coming battle, we watch a beautiful angel—hovering over him, its robes rippling in the wind, its wings full and perfect in their flight, its expression one of love and peace—lift him from the horse just at that glorious moment of triumphant salvation. I want to believe that this is reality for men who die in battle. I want to believe this is what happened to my dad, and to all the men and women who have literally saved the world.

The countryside, brown in the creaky winter dawn, unrolled dimly beneath us, drawing closer as the big 747 descended to earth at Charles de Gaulle. Once on the ground, I passed easily through customs and ducked into the international lounge for a long, hot shower. Then, completely refreshed, I climbed into a taxi and went directly to La Durée for a creamy cup of café au lait and a warm *pain au chocolat,* the only civilized solution to a dreary winter morning in Paris.

I felt incredibly, unspeakably happy as I sipped my coffee and watched the traffic jam itself into knots around the Madeline. I was thinking about what lay ahead. About the lover I would meet in—I checked my watch—just about the amount of time it would take to walk through the Luxembourg Gardens, cross the river at Pont Voltaire, and cut past Les Invalides to Place Vauban and Constanza's studio, now Madam's. Ours. My stomach churned with anticipation. It had been months since our last tryst, and there was so much I wanted to say. So much I wanted to do.

I paid the bill, pulled on my Chesterfield, grabbed my valise, and, as the city began to come to life, I strode down Rue Royale past the magnificent flower shops that, even at this early hour, already overflowed with tubs of the world's most exotic and beautiful blossoms. I stopped and impulsively bought two dozen ridiculously expensive sunflower-yellow tulips, then moved on.

God, I was so happy. I was the mightiest man in the world, a golden man, reaching for glory.

Twenty minutes later, when I entered the classic Place and saw lights burning in the penthouse studio, I became positively giddy, even a little light-headed. The concierge peeked out of her cell at the gated entrance to the courtyard, saw it was me, and returned to her Gauloise and *Figaro* without even the tiniest greeting or recognition. I didn't mind, I had bigger fish to fry.

I studied myself in the elevator mirror as it bumped up the six long flights. Eyes bright, skin still taut, parted dark hair that wouldn't stay put. I ignored whatever it was lurking there behind my gaze that made me turn away.

The little wrought-iron cage whirred and banged and jolted to a stop. I stepped onto the landing and pressed the brass buzzer. The freshly enameled black door flew open. "I thought you'd never get here," Ryder said frantically and took me in his arms. He had on one of Madam's dresses.

And there I was, like a dog to vomit.

18

*N*ow listen. I said I'd given up *almost* all kinds of sex *almost* forever, but I swear to God—as I've been trying to get, and hopefully have successfully gotten, across—there is something about this man that is irresistible. To everyone. We seldom meet, certainly not since he and Madam became lovers, in spite of his frequent little innuendoes, cash-filled notes, and messages begging me to rendezvous. The fact is, our affair has been going on for years, almost since the day I went to work for Madam and we went to Paris to visit her mother. Our duplicitous treachery has insured our discretion. Well, I say ours, but what I mean is, his. As you know, I am the very soul of discretion; it's my job. But if word ever got out that he liked what he liked, he'd really be in trouble. He'd certainly get that divorce—and no cash settlement—from Mary Anne in nothing flat. Mary Anne was an iron lady on fast wheels, and when she jerked Ryder's chain, he heeled quicker than a kicked dog.

If she found out he liked to dress up, she'd . . . well, I can't even imagine what she'd do. But it wouldn't be amicable, I can tell you that.

"Claude is coming by this afternoon," I said later. It was raining outside. I had on gray flannel slacks, a navy cashmere turtleneck and soft loafers. The tulips, in a large vase in the center of the table, made the kitchen seem sunny in spite of the rain. "I'd like you gone right after you've got things squared away."

"Yes, sir." Ryder bustled barefoot around the kitchen in a flowered silk kimono. A thin gold ID bracelet circled his ankle. He had set the table with a rare Vicky St. Staël breakfast set—paper-thin, deep cranberry-red china covered with gold stars—and was busily flipping crepes, stirring the crab filling, refreshing my champagne, lighting my cigarette.

"And another thing, I want you to break it off with Madam."

He stopped what he was doing. He didn't make a sound.

"If you want her, you can't have me, and vice-versa," I said as matter-of-factly as I could, crushing out my cigarette. Its smoke wound through the flowers. "What in the hell are you trying to prove with all this anyhow?"

"I can't stop," he finally answered. "I have to have her."

"Why?"

"She's mine. I own her."

"She's not yours any more than I am. You can't own people, Ryder."

"She's always been mine. Ever since she was a child."

"I'm warning you, break it off or you'll be sorry." I was glad his back was to me and he couldn't see my hand shake as I began to pick up my coffee cup, thought better of it, and returned it to the saucer. Where was this courage coming from? My resolve surprised me, probably just as much as it did him. "I'll do everything I can to keep you away from her. You're destroying her life."

"Mind your own business."

"Madam is my business. And all the secrets are out. I know everything."

He spun around and his eye burned over at me. "No, you don't."

"I do. She told me everything, even told me about the closet."

"No, goddamn it, she did not. She couldn't have. She would never tell anyone about that. That's *our* secret."

"She did. All of it. Your power is finished, my friend. You're as gutted as a fish, and I'm telling you to leave her alone. I'll block every move you make to see that you do, don't think I won't."

All of a sudden, he picked up the beautiful, delicate plates and slammed them onto the marble drain-board, shattering them. The cutlery clattered onto the hard floor. "Go to hell," he snarled. "You stupid little faggot."

"You'll be sorry for that remark, Ryder," I said, my voice low. I had gotten to my feet and was shaking with fury. "You should be more careful about what you say. Things can come back and get you."

"Don't threaten me." His lips had curled unflatteringly and his good eye had narrowed to a slit while the bad one remained fully open. If I hadn't known him, I might have been afraid, he looked so menacing.

"Get your pants on and get out, you pathetic old queen. Leave the money in the hall," I ordered and left the room. Moments later I heard the door slam.

The truly pathetic, dirty little fact is: In spite of our brave words, neither one of us would say anything to anybody. We were both cowards and had too much to lose. He would lose his wife and all her money if she found out he was what he was. And I ran the risk of losing Madam, who might see my duplicity as disloyalty, who might not believe I would do anything to protect her.

Even at its best, the affair with Ryder had emitted a very disagreeable, unsavory essence, almost like the gagging shock of cod liver oil or curdled milk. I had never been comfortable with it, but sometimes we all get ourselves into situations, relationships, that for one reason or another, are just easier to keep up than to stop. With Ryder, the pleasure was always tawdry and short-lived. Sometimes after it was over, I thought, if I could, I would scrub off all my skin in the shower. If it hadn't been for the fact that he had thought he was tremendously lucky to get me—which was, as much as I hate to admit it, very, very good for my ego—and that he shared his broker's advice with me and gave me enough money to act on it, I would have stopped long ago, well before his affair with Madam. I also hope you don't think I am in the slightest bit proud of myself.

Clearly, Ryder and I would never meet again under these circumstances. I had so many things in my life I was ashamed of, this affair had seemed minor in comparison, but now, as the day passed, I grew so god-damned mad, I wanted to kill him. Regardless of what I said just a moment ago about being too cowardly to bring the affair to light, I knew it would take all my self-control not to give the whole thing away the next time I saw him in public, which, unfortunately, would be very soon. The following week, as a matter of fact, at the MOMA opening. He and I would both be loaded for bear.

I went to work like a maniac, scrubbing every inch of the apartment, eradicating every sign of him, wiping every object, every surface he might have touched in his decades of visits. I threw away every sheet and towel in the place, except brand new ones still in their wrappers. I threw away the clothes he'd worn and the dishes he'd dined from, including those from our still-born brunch, the champagne glasses and the coffee pot. Everything—all down the trash chute. I ransacked Constanza's drawers, ripping to shreds and throwing away every photograph of Ryder I could find. I obliterated, excised, and banished him from Place Vauban. I had declared war. I felt like a Knight Templar in the Crusades, on a mission to save my Madam. Maybe it would be the only worthwhile thing I'd done in my life.

Claude LaGallienne arrived with his assistant promptly at three and commenced, with an air of unassailable, prissy self-importance, to examine the paintings. After a while the cigarette smoke in the living room was so thick that, when I brought him some coffee, made in a new pot, and a plate of chocolates, I opened the windows.

"*Non! Non! Non!*" he thundered. "*Trop froid. Trop fragile. Fermez. Immediatement!*"

The gallery owner was a gigantic Gallic pain-in-the-neck in a gray suit that desperately needed a good cleaning. He stank of body odor and aftershave. I closed the window without comment and returned to my pantry, where I picked up an old Wilbur Smith novel about diamond hunters I'd found. *Trop froid. Trop fragile.* Please. Those paintings were as tough and heartless as Constanza. They'd still be around when we were all long gone.

Two hours later, Monsieur Claude, as he preferred to be called, declared the works travelworthy, and the next morning, he and his limp-wristed assistant returned with two blue-smocked workmen who commenced building the shipping crates under Monsieur Claude's imperious supervision. In my opinion, the crates themselves, meticulously fitted and tightly screwed together, were finer works of art than the paintings.

The entire process took days, and during that time I got myself pulled together after my encounter with Ryder. I walked and walked and walked. The beauty of Paris and the remote, reserved gentility of its inhabitants repositioned me in the universe and brought me peace. I lounged in book stores, lingered in cafés, avoided reality. It was all so bittersweet. I longed for a life of my own, my own home, regular friends, regular family. Like Madam, I ached to belong to someone, to have someone with whom to share it all. I indulged totally in my feelings, a luxury I seldom permit myself to enjoy, and I came up cleansed because I'd looked at my life and realized how fortunate I was. Also, as a sort of side note, no matter what I ate or drank, my gallbladder never flared up once.

I didn't hear from Madam, but if she needed me, I knew she would call. I'd left her daily messages to keep her posted on the progress of the crates. Finally, late in the afternoon of the fourth day, the job was done, and with the gallery's shipping agent and a pair of customs bureaucrats on hand, the giant *Gemini* were swathed in protective bubble wrap and anchored solidly in their eight-by-twelve-foot boxes, which were then screwed tightly shut, affixed with government seals of authentication as well as my own signature on each side, lowered by ropes from the balcony, and loaded into a large van. Ready to make their crossing.

So was I. Five days of introspection is plenty. I couldn't wait to get back to work.

19

We flew through massive North Atlantic winter storms the whole way home, and I was certain we were going to crash or have a mid-air collision. I never worry about crashing when I'm on my way *to* Europe, but flying around the east coast of America scares me to death. Maybe because I'm always seeing news stories that read, "Some telephone company wires were accidentally cut by a construction crew in Scarsdale digging to install new television cable and the whole air traffic control system was down for twenty minutes today."

Lord have mercy.

One time, years ago, when the Vincennes accidentally shot down an Iranian passenger plane, all three hundred people aboard free fell to the earth from a very high altitude. When their bodies were recovered from the Persian Gulf, they were all nude. I remember a television reporter saying, I wonder what all those people were doing naked in that plane? Well, of course, they hadn't been naked at all, the wind had blown off their clothes as they fell, but the thought of being discovered floating starkers in Long Island Sound gives me a nervous breakdown. What happens when you hit the water? All your bones are broken, that's what, because you might as well be running into a slab of concrete. Do you even know it? Or have the extreme altitude and cold and sheer velocity of your fall knocked you unconscious? There are two answers to that: If you're outside the aircraft, there's probably been some sort of explosion and the cabin pressure has been destroyed so you've been shot from the plane like a bullet and most likely knocked out. If you're still in the plane and there's no fire with acrid fumes to render you insensible, then you are fully present for every second of your demise as you fall back to earth, a fall that can take forever—much longer than your life itself. I skip life jacket demonstrations on jetliners because I know they're a complete joke, as evidenced by the Swiss Air crash in Nova Scotia. If it comes down to it, the jackets are really just something to keep the panicked passengers occupied while the plane is hurtling like a meteor toward the ocean's hard, unforgiving surface. Airplanes and meteors have similar flotation capabilities. Theoretically, a modern jetliner *could* bob for a few minutes on the water if it were placed there carefully, like a toy in a bathtub, letting all the passengers scramble out in an orderly fashion along the wings. The only problem with that theory is that a passenger jet is like a giant beer can. Imagine what happens when you put an empty beer can on your driveway and stomp it with your foot. Generally, when a jet hits the water in an emergency crash situation, it's moving at a pretty fast clip and its thin aluminum skin is instantaneously crushed as easily as that can as the craft slams onto the hard water, plunging deep into the icy drink at two or three hundred miles an hour. Now imagine exactly how much help that life jacket would be. Zero. Airlines like their passengers to believe they are actually in flying boats and everything will be fine—they pretend the jackets will save your life, you pretend to believe it. But believe me: If you are heading for the water, kiss yourself goodbye.

Fortunately, five days after I left, I managed to land safely in New York. Thick, heavy snow quickly blanketed the wings of the plane as we rolled to a stop at the gate. Moments after the door was opened, a U.S. Customs Service agent appeared at my seat. "Mr. Nigel Smythe?" he asked.

"Yes. Weatherby-Smythe."

"May I see your passport, please?"

I handed him my green British passport, declaring me a subject of Her Majesty the Queen, and he balanced it on the back of the seat in front of mine, flipped to an empty page, stamped it, and handed it back.

"Pleasant flight?" he asked while I gathered up my gear.

"Very, thanks."

"Welcome to the United States, Mr. Smythe. We'll go out this way."

I followed him down the steps into the swirling snow, and around to the aft cargo hold where four men were muscling the *Gemini*'s large crates off the plane. I authenticated my signature on the various seals and then officially delivered the paintings, along with their accompanying documents, into the care of the exhibition's curator in the presence of two armed guards from the museum. The crates were carefully hoisted into an unmarked truck.

Five minutes later, I joined the taxi queue.

No one greeted me, but then, I hadn't expected anyone to.

My taxi was hot as hell and stank of fried onions.

"Excuse me," I called to the driver as we pulled away from the international terminal. "Would you mind turning down the music?"

He was a black, black man and his eyes, their whites yellow and ridged with lumpy veins, flashed at me angrily in the rearview mirror. "WHAT?" he challenged.

"The music." I pointed at my ears. "Sorry. Too loud."

"WHAT YOU SAY?" He had grabbed his steering wheel tightly in both hands and leaned toward it, toward the mirror, putting his face very close to it. He screamed into the mirror like he wanted to kill me.

It was a nightmare. "I SAID," I finally yelled back, "TURN DOWN THE GODDAMNED MUSIC!"

I swear to God, I thought he was going to pull over to the side of the road and come back there and beat me up. Instead, he slapped his hand so hard on the dashboard it sounded like a gun shot.

"YOU FUCK!" he screamed and then slapped the steering wheel. "YOU FUCK!"

All this time we were careening down the Long Island Expressway through walls of heavy black slush, weaving in and out of traffic and throwing up a wake of crud like a water-skiing boat in Cypress Gardens. I was terrified. But more than terrified, I got mad and lost my temper.

"FUCK YOU!" I screamed back at him. "I'M TURNING YOU IN." Where in the hell was all this anger, not to mention bravery, coming from? I was constantly amazing myself lately. I pulled out my cell phone and started punching in the taxi company phone number posted on his license. Finally, as we hydroplaned through the tollbooth on the Williamsburg Bridge, he jabbed his finger at the stop button on his boom box and it became blessedly silent.

Personally, I think for a fifty-dollar cab ride from Kennedy into lower Manhattan, you should get more than a disgruntled driver who doesn't speak English, and has a homicidal attitude, and a filthy cab. I gave him a minimal tip, slammed the door, and dashed past George into the building before he could curse me further.

The low, relaxing strains of a Brazilian samba and Madam's laughter—party sounds—coming down the stairs from the living room greeted me when I entered the loft, which could only mean that in my absence, Madam had finished the portraits and been paid. In the entry hall, an unfamiliar hat and coat lay on a side chair. I picked up the coat. It was magnificent, black vicuña from Turnbull & Asser, extremely large—wide and short and soft as a baby's cheek—and smelled faintly of Polo aftershave. The hat was silver beaver, a Stetson from Carmichael's Western Wear in Dallas, Texas. These were not Armand Weil's things. The coat would have hung on him like a shroud. Nor, thankfully, were they Ryder's. I recognized them as Junior Hammond's.

Well, I thought as I hung the overcoat in the closet and placed the hat on the rack, let's look on the bright side. At least Junior Hammond is single. And rich. Everything else, starting with his greasy, red-neck obesity, can be fixed. Then, with the dogs spinning about my legs like little black and silvery-gold mops, I went up the back stairs to my quarters for a quick wash. I'd missed the dogs terribly. And they me. When all is said and done, one really doesn't need anything more than a loving dog or two.

Nothing could have prepared me for the scene in the living room. This was not anything I ever could have imagined.

"Nigel," Madam beamed. "You're home!"

"Yes."

It was early evening, and the room was richly textured with light and shadow, dense with candle and fire light. It glowed off the dark plank floors and shone brightly off the hard chrome edges of the spare furniture. Outside the tall windows, Lady Liberty's torch flickered through the snow, and the running lights of a lone tug glowed as it made-way slowly across the harbor.

Madam had on a leopard print body stocking and a black velvet smock. A velvet net covered her chignon, and silver bangles were stacked up each arm. She sat bare-foot and cross-legged on the floor in front of the fire, her elbows on her knees, hands in fists at her chin, staring at Junior across a Scrabble board that teetered on a footstool between them. A cigarette smoldered in a full ashtray beside her. She was rosy-cheeked and bright-eyed, full of life.

Junior was equally ebullient, but whether it was from fun, happiness, or fatness, I could not say. His suit jacket was crumpled into a sloppy ball on a chair and he'd removed his tie and unbuttoned his shirt collar. He looked like the Pillsbury Dough-Boy who'd gotten his apron strings tied tight enough to divide him into two loaves. His belt cut deeply into his waist, placing equal strain on his shirt buttons, zipper, and trouser seams, or, in other words, his heart and abdomen. His pants pockets were stretched so far open they were torn, and the white linings were visible. His face glowed with ruddy splotches of high blood pressure and his eyes bulged from beneath fleshy lids. He was a Strasbourg goose, force-fed corn through a funnel, unable to swallow until he stood up.

Madam had made a platter of tuna fish sandwiches for lunch—their tinny smell permeated the apartment—and they were on their second bottle of Dom Pérignon. Junior cradled a jumbo bag of Lay's sour cream and onion potato chips protectively in his lap. I wondered how long he'd been here and if this were his first visit. There seemed to be a definite, and new, familiarity between them.

Junior Hammond was a man of famously vulgar tastes, accustomed to going out with women to whom he did not speak. He generally preferred them in pairs and seldom knew their names. He carried a big bankroll and paid them off in the limo on the way home, always making sure the driver dropped him off first, and he never invited the girls up. Junior was incapable of a healthy relationship and he knew it. He was as rich as he was fat and he knew, when it came to almost all women, the excess money carried more weight than the excess weight. He made no secret of the fact that his tastes were depraved and he'd never lasted long enough with what he considered a "nice" woman to tell her about, much less ask her to perform, his preferences. It was as though, after a couple of dates, the lady would know something important was missing from his character, sense something even darker and cruder below his surface vulgarity, and come up with a bullet-proof excuse not to see him again. Sitting on the floor playing a board game with Jacqueline di Fidelio was probably the closest he'd ever come to doing something normal with a member of the opposite sex.

She seemed more than happy to be on the receiving end of Junior's childlike adoration. I'd never seen her look so fresh, or so relaxed. She was having fun. That was it. There had been so little fun the last few months, the look of it had become almost foreign. Her eyes, instead of glittering, twinkled. And her smile, instead of the lock-jawed grimace Ryder evinced, touched her whole face. Her laughter burst out spontaneously. I had grown so accustomed to the combat postures she and Ryder provoked in each other that it took me a moment to recognize real pleasure.

All of a sudden, I felt myself getting angry all over again. That bastard, Ryder, took her beauty, and everything else about her, for granted, and tried to grind it all into the ground, using Sigmund Freud as his insidious heel. Correction: *Used* to. I was going to beat that son-of-a-bitch at his own game if it killed me.

A pair of alligator-skin cowboy boots sat on the hearth. I knew they cost about five thousand dollars and my heart soared. Here was one of the richest men in the world, in our house, eating our potato chips and tuna fish and drinking our champagne in front of our fire. And he was single. He could probably pay Madam's back taxes with the change in his pocket.

"Great pleasure to see you, Mr. Hammond," I said as I removed the glistening green bottle from its sterling silver ice bucket and refreshed their glasses.

"Yeah," he grunted and ferociously crammed a handful of chips into his overworked mouth. Junior Hammond needed so badly to prove his masculinity that he was rude to the help.

"Will there be anything else, Madam?" I asked.

"Do you want another sandwich, Junior?" She held out the decimated plate. She'd cut the crusts of the bread, and the edges of the sandwiches had dried out and started to curl. "Actually, I think we have some DoveBars for dessert. Do you want one of those?"

We do? I thought. We've *never* had DoveBars in this house in my life. Death bars is what I call them.

"No, thanks, sugarplum. I'm trying to keep an eye on my weight."

I removed the sandwich platter from her outstretched hand. Far be it for me to encourage his gluttony. The man was a heart-attack waiting to happen.

"Well, maybe I'll have just one."

"I'll have one, too, please, Nigel. I'm glad you're home."

"Thank you, Madam." I made a small bow. "I'm glad to be back."

That was before I saw the kitchen.

20

All my life, I have avoided the use of profanity, except under the most extreme circumstances—such as in the taxi—because to me, it shows a lack of education, articulation, and self-control. However, when I walked into the kitchen, I almost crossed the line for the second time that day. The mess was unimaginable. She left the empty tuna cans on the bread board, letting pungent fishy oil ooze into the grainy wood, but that was nothing compared to the rest of the shambles. I don't think anything had been rinsed, wiped, or thrown away since I'd left. A week's worth of take-out containers, plates with dried food, half-drunk cups of coffee, containers of spoiled cream, and a dozen glasses with the remains of wines and champagnes, all just heaped into the sink and left on the counters. And my beautiful, shiny hardwood floors were dull with dirt and spills.

This was so unlike Madam, I couldn't understand what had gone on.

I knew she'd been working hard all week, but she always worked hard and kept a disciplined schedule. On the other hand, I'd never been away from her for so many days during a commission. I wondered if Junior had been here the whole time I was gone. I supposed this was what it felt like to be a mother, or perhaps, Madam's wife: appalled at the mess, but touched and grateful at the same time. My place was reaffirmed. The entire kitchen would have to be disinfected. Immediately. It's fortunate I've never made time for jet-lag.

I delivered the DoveBars, fixed myself a double espresso, and went to work, casting an occasional eye on the scene in case she needed me.

"You sure seemed happy to see him," Junior Hammond mumbled through a mouthful of ice cream. He shifted his stumpy legs in an effort to rearrange the bulk.

"Well, of course," Madam answered, slightly puzzled. "I *am* happy to see him. Why wouldn't I be?"

"Well, sugar, you know my Daddy Rex, he always taught us, 'never be too good to the Mexicans.' " He squelched down a belch. " 'You give 'em too much and, next thing you know, they start thinking they're your equals, start making demands.' "

Fortunately, I caught the Royal Worcester terrine millimeters before it hit the floor.

"Well," Madam bristled, "I have the opposite philosophy. You can never be too nice to your employees because you never know when the tables will be turned. As fast as you go up? That's how fast you can come down. Besides, I need all the friends I can get."

Precisely. Don't I know it. There I was, a nice young man with a nice mum and a nice little home and, bingo, I find myself in the clink.

"Huh." Junior scratched a kitchen match on the floor, held the flame to a ridiculously thick Cohiba, and puffed it into life. "You do have one hell of a damn good point, especially if you're in the oil business. We're accustomed to big ups and big downs. We're boom and bust people. I just never thought about it in regard to the nigras." His fat lips made sticky, sucking noises on the big cigar. "Daddy Rex—have you ever met him?"

Madam shook her head. She and I were both totally shocked by what he'd just said. "Did you just say *nigras?*"

"Now don't go gettin' all liberal on me, baby girl. I didn't mean any-thing by it. I apologize. It was really just a slip of the tongue." The more he tried to pass off the remark as nothing more than West Texas idiom, the more he could see she wasn't buying it. So he went to work on get-ting sorrier. "I swear to God, I don't think like that and I don't talk like that. *Goddamn,* I don't know why I said it. But come on now, honey, you know what I mean . . ."

"Well, no," Madam replied coldly. "I don't."

"What I meant was *staff* people, people who work for you. Don't make this hard for me, baby girl. You know who I'm talking about. The *help.* That's what I mean to say, the *help.* Hell, I *love* Nigel. I'd hire him away from you if I could."

I almost screamed out loud.

"First of all, even if Nigel were black as night, he'd never be a 'nigra,' and furthermore, he is much more than 'the help,' Junior," she said, clearly struggling to control her temper. "He does work for me, but he's also my friend and companion. It's important you understand that."

"I am so *damned* sorry I said that. I really, really am. It was unforgiv-able. I'm just not *like* that." He slapped his hand on his knee. "I don't know why I'm always screwing things up. Shit," he drawled, sounding as though he were about to cry. "It was just my daddy coming out in me, that old bastard's always getting me in trouble." He blew his nose so loudly, it occurred to me that maybe he really *was* crying. "You know, even though he's my daddy and I love him, he is the meanest mother-fucker on the face of the earth. Meanest sonofabitch I ever knew and you can believe me when I say I've known some sons o' bitches in my day. Mama Lureen used to say he was as heartless as a hungry cobra in a basket of newborn kittens. Now isn't that a picture makes you cringe, a big old snake gobbling up a bunch of helpless little pussy cats? Daddy Rex, he used to do things to my sisters and me when we were kids you wouldn't believe. It's a miracle I even lived past the age of fifteen."

"What are you talking about?"

That's what I wanted to know, I thought as I swabbed the refrig-erator with ammonia, making sure I looked busy in case they glanced over. Whatever his father did to him, in my opinion, it clearly wasn't enough.

"I don't want to talk about that now. It's nothing for polite company, believe me. Just water over the dam. I want you to say you'll forgive me. I want us to be friends. You're the nicest girl I ever knew." He blew his nose again, louder this time. "Please say you'll forgive me. Please."

Madam regarded him. Her lips were locked in a line and an angry flush covered her neck. "I'll forgive you this time, Junior," she said presently. "But believe me, there's no second chance on an attitude like that in this house."

The ice in the champagne bucket rattled as he withdrew the bottle. "Let's have a little more bubbly," Junior said. "We're having too nice a day. I don't want to wreck it. I'm so goddamned sorry."

The Scrabble tiles clicked in the now-quiet room.

"There," Madam said after a while. "That's a word: 'gaff.' Eleven points. I don't know about your father, Junior, but I'm really surprised to think you aren't nice to your household help. I think it's all an act. We don't know each other that well but I'm a pretty good judge of character and I think you hide behind a lot of smoke and mirrors. As a matter of fact, I'd be willing to bet you've been misunderstood pretty much your whole life and there's a little boy in there that's just dying to get out, to be loved, and to love back. You're just like all the rest of us."

Junior grunted again and fiddled with his tiles. Neither one of them spoke for several minutes.

"Yeah, you're probably right. Deep down I'm probably one hell of a nice guy, but we don't put much stock in all that psychology horse-hockey on the ranch. We grew up putting our faith in biscuits and gravy, keeping Mama Lureen in bourbon, and staying a belt length away from Daddy Rex."

"I'll tell you another thing," Madam's voice grew steadily in conviction, the way a person's voice does when they're trying to talk themselves into something. "All your country-boy talk is a big bunch of baloney, too. Hammond Oil is well diversified, well-protected from boom and bust swings in the economy. So don't try to fool me with your aw-shucks, country-bumpkin act. I can spot that stuff a mile away. I can catch you coming around corners quicker than you can grab your hat. Now come on, it's your turn. Play."

Junior coughed out a scratchy smoker's laugh, more wheeze than chuckle. "That's what I like about you, Jackie-girl: You've got a great butt and you're as sharp as a tack. 'Lafter.' That a word? Doesn't look right.

What the hell, close enough. Eight points. Write it down." He stabbed his finger at the score sheet and ignored her skeptical look. "You're right, I'm plenty diversified. Matter of fact, I just bought myself a shipping line out in California—bunch of old rust buckets, but they've still got enough life in them to haul containers of scrap back and forth to Japan and Korea and Taiwan. I'll be taking the plane out to San Francisco to close the deal tomorrow."

Plane? That had a nice sound to it. We like planes. I sprayed one wall of cabinets with 409 and began rubbing at the gluey fingerprints.

"Why don't you come along? I'll take you to dinner at Fisherman's Wharf."

Madam gave him a blank stare.

"Hello, I'm just kiddin'. We'll go to Postrio."

"What kind of plane? I'm not flying across the country in some little puddle jumper."

"It's not a puddle jumper," he bragged. "It's one of those new Boeing Business Jets. You know, a BBJ?"

"I'll let you know at dinner."

My God. A *Boeing Business Jet?* It's a private 737 for heaven's sake. Well, why shouldn't she have dinner with this profane, racist, walrus, pig? Even if he did have a reputation as a sexual pervert. He wouldn't try anything with her that she didn't want him to, and she needed some fun. So what if he was a diamond in the rough? At least he was a diamond who could back up his business, unlike Ryder, a flawed, dark zircon at best. As dark and bottomless as the hole behind his fake eye.

"I better get going if I'm gonna be able to keep our dinner date tonight. Gotta get my beauty time in." Junior struggled to his feet and I could hear all the champagne, tuna fish sandwiches, potato chips, and DoveBars whooshing their way below his belt, flooding his stomach, putting unimaginable pressure on his bowels, liver, kidneys, and bladder. The possibilities for medical calamity swamped my mind.

At the front door, when I handed him his hat and helped him into his coat, he squinted at me good-naturedly and cocked his pudgy hand as if it were a six-shooter. He clicked his tongue a couple of times, fake bullets from his little gun. "Nigel," he said, evidently by way of thanks.

Then, he swatted Madam's bottom.

"I'll pick you up at eight, baby girl."

———

"I know what you're thinking," Madam said from behind her dressing screen as I drew her bath and she stripped off her exercise clothes. "I think he's more than I can take, too."

"Well . . ." I began.

"Do you think he meant it? When he apologized for the 'nigra' remark?"

"It doesn't make much difference. The fact is, Madam, you need to start somewhere. You need some options."

"And an option with his own Boeing is pretty attractive?" she finished my sentence.

"It's not as though you're going to marry him, and you seemed to be having a good time."

"You're right. He's fun to be with. No strings. No pressure. He's just a great big teddy bear."

"A great big, *rich* teddy bear."

Madam peeked around the screen and gave me a big smile. "No kidding. But I'll tell you one thing, that is some kind of sick family—him and Bianca and Patty, and this Daddy Rex person? Give me a break. Every one of them is standing in line waiting to screw the next person. He blabbed just about everything, except for whatever it was their father used to do to them. I'll bet that'd curl your hair."

"I don't even want to try to imagine."

"He came right out and said he was glad Lynette's dead. His own sister. Can you believe it?"

"Do you think he blew up the boat?" I asked incredulously.

"No, no, Nigel. Nothing like that. I think he just meant he would wait them all out. He might not lift a hand to help, though, if one of them needed it. I wouldn't look to him for a life preserver if I were Patty or Bianca and I were going down for the third time."

"Have they discovered anything more about the *Kiss-Kiss?*" I wanted to get off this subject and went busily to work on her double espresso shake as the tub filled.

"Not yet." She twisted her hair up on top of her head and anchored it with pins. "Junior said they've figured out for sure the explosion was caused by some kind of bomb stuck on the propane tank."

"So there's no chance it was an accident?"

"Nope." Madam dropped her robe, climbed quickly into the tub, and disappeared up to her neck in bubbles. "Creepy, isn't it? I mean, we literally escaped with our lives. What if we'd spent five more minutes saying goodbye?" she wondered out loud.

The question required no response. "Do you think it had to do with the Renoir?"

"I've been wondering about that, too. It's a pretty extreme way to cover up a theft. I mean, it was a good Renoir but not what I'd call a great one. Not worth eighteen lives."

In bed that night, before my sleeping pill kicked in, I wondered why a man with all Junior Hammond's money and power would need to cheat at Scrabble. He knew what he was doing, he knew the word was wrong, but he took the points. He had to win. What *had* his father done to him and his sisters?

Daddy Rex, I thought as I drifted off, now there was a name with some serious psychological implications.

21

"The only thing I'm looking forward to about this evening is seeing Armand," Madam said as our limousine came to a stop in front of the Museum of Modern Art. "You can throw the rest of it right out the window."

"What about Ryder?"

"Don't you think he's gotten the message by now, Nigel? I mean, I haven't talked to him for six weeks." She ground her cigarette out in the tiny door ashtray.

"I wouldn't count on it."

"Maybe someone will push him off a cliff. God, I *hate* these parties."

Bright lights extended their welcome through the institution's soaring glass facade into the frigid evening, illuminating the excited, glittering crowd that proceeded up the escalators to the second floor gallery. How incredible it was that I, Nigel Weatherby-Smythe, convicted felon, butler, and child of post-war England, where the concept of having "enough" of anything was completely foreign—would even dare to cross the line and join these people as an invited guest. But here I was in my proper evening jacket, cummerbund and tie, tucked white shirt, and ribbon-striped pants.

Madam was nervous. Not only because she was an artist, and as we all know, artists are notoriously shy, social foot-draggers, so totally ego-centric, they think they have a monopoly on insecurity. Madam is no exception. But tonight, her bad humor and nerves came from sources other than standard, everyday, humdrum neuroses. She was the de facto star of the show and would be required to speak positively and act graciously about her mother and her mother's works, a challenge under any circumstances. Also, it would be the first time she would be seeing Armand since the incident on the *Kiss-Kiss* and, perhaps most significant of all, it would be the first time she'd have contact with Ryder since we'd left Middleburg six weeks ago.

She might have been nervous. I was fine. The confrontation with Ryder in Paris had been very out of character, not only for our relationship, which was limited to sexual bossing around, but for me. I'd spent my life dodging the hard questions; it was so much easier simply to do as I was told. But over the last forty-eight hours, through three calls from him to Madam, who had instructed me simply to say she was unavailable until the party, and "whatever you do, don't tell him I'm going to California for dinner with Junior," my new resolve had been tested and held. Ryder accepted these rebuffs without comment, wise-crack, or threat, which made me suspicious. Over the phone, he and I respected our assigned roles. I kept a proper demeanor, and he treated me as he would any servant who answered the phone. Each time I heard his voice, my gut tightened and I had trouble getting my breath and, I'll admit, I did have a sip of sherry after we'd hung up. But I never weakened. I wondered if, at this late date in my life, I was actually beginning to build "character."

Several times, I reviewed the section in Lady Atchley's manual about self-control:

No matter how extreme the situation, unless it is life-threatening, never allow your own opinions or feelings to interfere with those of your master. Remember, you are there to serve at his leisure, and strict discipline over yourself must be maintained at all times.

Madam invites me to escort her to galas because I am the perfect companion: I stay nearby, silent and smiling, never participating in the conversation, am never *expected* to participate, I mean, who's kidding whom? I know who and what I am, and if anyone who doesn't strikes up a conversation with me, I set them straight as graciously and expeditiously as possible. No one pays a thousand dollars to come to a party and talk to the help, although occasionally, the help themselves go astray and mistakenly think it's only money that makes the difference between them and their employer. To wit: Mrs. Duke's man, who ended up a bloated laughingstock in smeared makeup and diamond stud earrings, stripped of her goods, his dignity, and finally his life.

Me? I'm the backdrop, the wife of the famous CEO, the husband of the movie star. Or vice-versa. However, I'm sure those individuals mind being completely ignored or worse yet, humored, and rightfully so. But I consider it one of the perks of my job, although as you've probably gathered by now, I wish Madam were more attached to the world of classical arts than the modern. I mean, Andy Warhol is as far as I can go. All the rest, to me, is sheer dementia. I'd much prefer to attend an opening of, say, Cartier jewelry at the Metropolitan Museum than one for Constanza di Fidelio at the Museum of Modern Art. But, as my mum used to say, "When you get a lemon, make lemonade," and that attitude is such an ingrained part of my nature, it's simply not in me to be unhappy for very long. And tonight? On an occasion as brilliant and long-awaited as this, with a crowd so incredibly chic and mainstream, I blended right in. What if she were to get married, or take a permanent, public lover? What would happen to me?

Please don't misunderstand. I want Madam's happiness as much as she does, but what if she were to make a true love match, not a demon like Ryder or a buffoon like Junior? What if a relationship developed with Armand Weil or someone equally winning. I wouldn't try to undermine it, but the possibility scared me to death. What if she let me go? She might as well put a gun to my head and pull the trigger, because if she sent me away, I would be floating down the Nile in a leaky, little reed basket like the baby Moses, my fate left to the gods and the tides.

These were my thoughts as Madam, looking like a goddess in a black Prada sheath and a single rope of pearls, stood in the receiving line with Bianca and Charles Roosevelt. I stayed right behind her, ready to refill her champagne or run quick errands. She greeted Mary Anne and Ryder as smoothly as if she were spreading soft butter on bread, kissed Armand's cheeks cooly, without implication or innuendo, and hugged Junior Hammond as enthusiastically as if he were a long-lost brother.

We were all on our best behavior.

Out of the corner of my eye, I watched Ryder drift from circle to circle making small talk because Mary Anne, who was on the board of Chase Manhattan, was deep in highbrow conversation with David Rockefeller and Henry Kissinger.

As he circled, never too far from his wife, he kept a constant eye on Madam, waiting for an opening, like a shark on a leash. There was a string around his tail tied to the handle of Mary Anne's pocketbook.

After an hour, the line broke up and all three Hammonds—Bianca, Patty, and Junior—who had underwritten the occasion, invited Madam to join them beneath Constanza's whopping *Galileo* for a photograph. From across the room, she looked like a black swan surrounded by ostriches.

"Have you ever seen a bigger bunch of assholes in your life?" Ryder muttered over my shoulder. He was so close I could smell his aftershave.

"Pardon?" I asked. My heart started to pound.

But he didn't repeat the remark because Madam was headed toward us. I could tell he was a little unsure, a little rattled by my brittle attitude, the skeptical, aggressive, just-try-it look on my face, and the white knuckles on my scotch glass. I turned the knife before disappearing behind my mask of servitude.

"Claude told me about the Italian child."

22

$\mathscr{I}$ think I forgot to mention that one of the days in Paris while the workmen buzz-sawed and hammered the shipping crates, Claude La Gallienne and I went around the corner for an aperitif and sandwich. It was a rainy winter afternoon, and inside the café, the white mosaic tile floor was slick and muddy. Condensation streaked the windows, and the overheated air was soupy with smoke, wet wool, and unwashed bodies. We took a table by the window and ordered Pernod and baguettes with country ham and butter. I asked him how well he knew Ryder McCormick. Claude said he'd known him for at least thirty years, and told me that from the first moment he'd laid eyes on Ryder, who was notorious for guzzling Constanza's booze and never replacing it, he'd held him in complete contempt. "I spit on men who live off women," Claude had said, and punctuated the remark by pretending to spit on the mucky floor. "They are *merde* beneath my feet."

"Fair enough," I said.

Into our third Pernod, whose powerful anise-flavored liquor hits you hard and then hits you harder, he leaned toward me over the table and told me a story he swore was true: A number of years ago—maybe twenty-five or thirty—the hostess at a house party Ryder and his then-wife were attending in Sardinia had him arrested for rape and kid-napping her eleven-year-old daughter. But her husband—the girl's step-father—had the charges withdrawn, claiming it had been a misun-derstanding, that the girl was uncontrollable and had run away. The po-lice were paid off and hushed up with Ryder's wife's money. The child was never found. Do you think he murdered her? I'd asked. Of course he did, Claude answered. Probably threw her down a well. Do you think Madam is in danger? Claude responded with a shrug and a disinter-ested, *Qu'es qu'on peut fait?* He had known Madam virtually her entire life and observed the situation with the dispassion of Constanza's most trusted business associate, who knew better than to cross the line and interfere in her personal affairs.

"Why haven't you returned my calls and why aren't you wearing the ring?" Ryder whispered as he kissed Madam's cheek. The skin was tight around his eye and his fingers squeezed her upper arms hard enough to leave pale marks.

"Why are you still married?" She smiled back guilelessly.

"Touché."

"Besides, I was afraid if Mary Anne saw it, she'd want it back."

"You are in high spirits tonight."

"Yes. I'm happy to get this show up and over. These canvases bring back too many memories for me."

Ryder looked up and down the vast gallery and nodded. "Your mother was a lost soul."

"Is that why you loved her so much? Someone a little more lost than you?"

"You know I never loved her the way I love you."

Madam studied him hard. "You are such a fucking jerk . . ." She be-gan but stopped cold when Armand materialized at her side.

"Good evening again, Jacqueline. Good evening, Ryder. Am I inter-rupting anything?"

"Of course not," Madam answered.

"Then permit me to congratulate you on this brilliant show." He kissed her cheeks. "I know how hard you worked to put it together."

"Actually, I can take virtually no credit, Armand. The Hammonds gave all the money and the museum did all the work. I'm just along for the ride."

Ryder, unwilling to show his fury and frustration over Armand's crashing his and Madam's conversation, noticed someone—someone non-existent—across the room frantically trying to get his attention, and excused himself, leaving them alone.

"How have you been?" Armand asked, searching her with his eyes, first her face, then her mouth. The electricity between them was palpable. "I've missed you."

"You have?" Her face flushed.

"Yes." His lips tilted in a half-smile. "Very much. Come walk with me and show me the collection. No one will be brave enough to interrupt us, we could be making a deal." He tucked her arm in his and they strolled slowly down the gallery, pausing before *Pegasus*. I stayed close at hand. "Your mother really was mad, wasn't she? But she's making many people rich, myself included. Before she died, I brokered this painting for eight-hundred-thousand. Last month, I resold it for fourteen million, proving there is no accounting for taste." He paused. "Have you thought about our conversation last December?" His hand stroked hers, then he spread her fingers and fitted his in between them. The intimacy of the gesture made her gasp.

"Constantly."

"What are you going to do about it?"

"I don't know." Madam sipped her drink. "Maybe nothing."

"Will you have dinner with me tomorrow? I can change my plans to be in New York for one more day."

They stopped at a buffet table. The canapés were exquisite little tidbits created in the vibrant colors of Constanza's works, which, frankly, in my opinion, looked much more appetizing as sushis on trays than as paintings on the walls.

"Let me see," Madam said as they moved away with a colorful selection and paused out of range of the crowd, "which one shall we demolish first? How about *Venus Descending?*" She laughed and fed the delicacy to the Frenchman, never taking her eyes off his.

"Let me ask you, are you a skier?"

Madam nodded. "Of course. I'm a terrific skier."

I'll just tell you right now: This was a complete lie. To my knowledge, Madam had not been on skis in her life. And she could certainly not afford a broken arm at this point. It would put her out of business and into the hoosegow.

They stopped in front of *Elixir d'Amor,* a jumbled, fragmented torment of broken cups, broken hearts, and shredded letters.

"Come to Aspen. I'm having a few friends for the first weekend in March. I would like you to come. I'll have my office arrange it. I'll send the plane to fetch you."

There it was, the invitation. The house party in Aspen. The vault. The paintings stolen from the Gardner Museum. The builder's plans for the house. The FBI and the Internal Revenue Service. The serpent raised its head and hovered above them, smiling and swaying slowly, and for a moment I thought she was going to tell him everything, but he didn't give her the opening.

"It would give us a chance to have some time together. You'll know just about everyone there, the Pradzynskis, the Kowalskis, the Burneys from Oklahoma. And I'll take a few days off, I'll dedicate myself to you completely."

"I'll bet you say that to all the girls."

"I don't have a lot of 'girls,'" Armand shrugged slightly. "The emotional toll and bother are too great." He cast his eyes around the hall. "I don't play around. You know how I live, everyday a different country. I live on the edge, I am addicted to the adrenaline of the deal. For me, it is better than sex."

"Let me be sure I understand, I'm supposed to see this as an irresistible invitation?" Madam was laughing. "How will you entice me into bed? With a Sotheby's catalogue?"

"Yes, and I hope you'll understand when I scream 'SOLD!' at the end. For me, that word is the greatest aphrodisiac of all."

"How could I say no? You are too smooth for words."

"Seriously, *chérie,*" he drew her closer, until their lips were almost touching, "you must believe I will do anything to get you. I've been patient these last two months while you've been working, but no more. And if you think I'm interested only in getting you into my bed, well, that would be only partly true." Armand laughed. "I am, after all, a Frenchman."

"And I am, after all, a Frenchwoman, at least at heart." Her eyes smiled directly into his. "I'll look forward to it," she said as another guest approached. "Get some rest. Too much après-ski can wear you out."

"You can't tie her up all evening," the woman scolded good-naturedly.

"I wouldn't dream of it." Armand kissed Madam's hand and blended back into the party.

On the other side of the room, I saw Ryder's face harden and his eye flash like a hollow-point bullet as Junior Hammond—all in white and looking sort of like a very chubby Colonel Sanders—told him what he probably thought was a joke.

23

$\mathcal{T}$he reception whirled along, with Madam and the Hammonds
working the crowd like professional politicians.

"Let's take a break," Bianca whispered to Madam.

They found a less-crowded gallery and sat down on a long marble
bench to catch their breath.

Madam leaned back against the wall, crossed her legs and closed
her eyes. "This was a great idea," she said.

"I couldn't stand up for one more second. My feet are killing me."
Bianca kicked off her shoes, size twelve, dyed-to-match satin pumps.
Her toes were covered with corn pads, and it looked like she had
bunions. She sagged against the wall and planted her wrecked feet flat
on the floor, about eighteen inches apart. She wiggled her toes.

"Congratulations, Bianca, on a huge success," Madam said.

"Can you believe it? But listen, I want to ask you something before I have to go back to work prying money loose from this bunch." Bianca raced ahead like a freight train. "My baby bro', Junior, told me he's been having the most delightful time with you. Did you really go to San Francisco for dinner with him last night, or did he make that up? He's always making up these wild stories about all the famous women he goes out with, when we all know he's only comfortable with chorus girls."

"No," Madam smiled. "I went and we had a ball."

"Well, I hope the little guy behaved himself."

"Complete gentleman."

"I hope he didn't try to take you to Fisherman's Wharf for dinner."

"He did and I said absolutely not."

"Good for you. Most of the girls he takes on these trips are so excited to fly in that silly plane of his that they put up with being taken to some cheap tourist trap. He usually leaves them there, buys them a first class ticket home or wherever they want to go."

Madam smiled. "He's definitely got a style all his own."

"I guess we all do. I'm glad he and Patty are both here tonight. We were never real big on family togetherness, but since Lynette got killed, we've been sticking a little closer. Patty came in all the way from Kathmandu, or Timbuktu, or one of those. I think Junior came just to see you. Just look at him talking to Armand. They always have some kind of deal going on. I swear, those two are like brothers. Oh, hi, Nigel. I'm sorry, I didn't see you there. How are you doin'?"

"Wonderfully, thank you, Madam."

"Did you hear the news about Lynette's boat?" she asked. Her voice was relentlessly loud, and she seemed addicted to the sound of it.

Of course we'd heard about Lynette's stupid, bloody, frigging boat, I wanted to scream. We were *on* it, you idiot. I was starting to get tired and grumpy. She thinks *her* feet hurt. I wiggled my own toes inside of my patent leather dance pumps, which used to fit perfectly until I started wearing running shoes instead of well-constructed brogans to speed walk around the city. For what usually could be counted on as a maximum two-hour reception, the evening had already gone at full pitch for an hour and a half and it didn't look like anyone was about to leave. I know I made a big deal about saying how much I enjoyed these parties, but there are limits.

I studied Bianca more closely. Her hair might as well have been a platinum football helmet for all the movement it had. And anyone with a neck like that should not wear dangling earrings, I don't care how much they cost. I was getting to hate her more every second.

"They know now for sure that someone blew it up. I'll tell you, I'm not totally surprised she got murdered. She made lots and lots of enemies. We all have. It's hard having so much money sometimes, a big responsibility. People are almost always mad at you because they think they know how you should spend your money—usually on them—and when you don't, they turn on you like greased lightning. It's no wonder rich people never have any friends; we're always getting screwed. Daddy Rex kept telling Lynette to hire a secretary, a publicist, and a bodyguard. I did, years ago. But why am I telling you this?" Bianca giggled. "You're the one who spent three weeks with her on that silly ship, you know what she was like: mean as hell."

"I've got to tell you," Madam held her glass in my direction for a refill, her eyes casting about for a rescue, "I never had any problem with her. As a matter of fact, I really liked her. I had a great time. The boat was beautiful and comfortable to work on; I was sorry to leave."

"Humph," Bianca snorted and looked at Madam as though she'd lost her mind. "I don't know how you took it." She rummaged around in the deep folds of her voluminous gown and extracted a jeweled cigarette case and lighter from a hidden pocket, lit a cigarette and waved the smoke away from her face.

"I don't think you're supposed to smoke in here, Bianca."

"Tell me another. Who're they gonna call? The cigarette police? I don't exactly see that many multi-million dollar donors falling out of the trees, do you? Now, what was I talking about? Oh, yes, Lynette. What that girl needed was a few hormone pills. I started taking them and they settled me right down."

"You are too much, Bianca." Madam sounded exhausted. "Will you excuse me? I think I'll zip into the ladies room before I get back to work. There are still people I haven't talked to."

"I hear ya." Bianca dug into another pocket, withdrew a tiny mirror and tube of lipstick, and made the necessary repairs. "I hope you're enjoying yourself, Jackie. You sure deserve it after what that maniac of a mother put you through."

"Did you know her very well?"

"Who? Your mother? Never met her, but all you need to do is look at her work—the sheer drama of it couldn't come from a kind-hearted person. She was obviously insane. Okay, that's it. Back to business. I've still got a lot of money to raise. Don't want to leave anything on the table." She crammed her feet back into the pumps, put her hands on her knees, levered herself to her feet and then *dropped her burning cigarette into my full glass of champagne.* "Thanks, Nigel," she said. "You're always around when someone needs you."

Madam looked at me wide-eyed as Bianca's big butt trundled off. "This can't possibly go much longer," she said and headed for the powder room.

Lord, deliver me.

I was taking advantage of the break to catch up with a couple of friends, men such as myself who were escorting their ladies, when I heard shouts and ran into the main gallery.

Bianca's hand clutched the arm of the woman she'd been talking to. Her mouth hung wide open and her expression was as stunned as that of a cow in an abattoir. The color drained from her face as if a window shade had been drawn.

"Bianca, are you all right?" the woman screamed at her again.

"You know, I, I . . . Oh . . . Ow . . ." Her eyes got wider and a wad of spittle appeared at the corner of her mouth. "Ow," she gasped again as a look of sheer panic took over her face.

"Bianca?" said someone else. "What's wrong? Are you all right? Are you having a heart attack? Are you choking? Oh, my God. Does anyone here know the Heimlich?" Voices screamed as Bianca began to wobble. "Bianca's choking! Bianca's having a heart attack! Somebody do something!"

I handed my drink to a member of this useless mob of ineffectual boobs, spun Bianca around, and performed a picture-perfect Heimlich maneuver on her, but nothing came out. I tried again. And again. Nothing. Instead, she collapsed over my arm like a rag doll, pulling me to the floor with her weight, a champagne flute clenched in her hand like a rattle.

Pandemonium ensued. People screamed for 911. A man, presumably a doctor, helped me move from where I'd landed on top of Bianca, my arm trapped by the sheer bulk of her, and we rolled her onto her back. He began to perform CPR and kept it up until the paramedics arrived. They laid an oxygen mask over her contorted red face and raced her off to the ambulance.

I know this is a terrible thing to say, but it was a very effective way to end the party.

24

"It wasn't your fault, Nigel," Madam insisted for the hundredth time as we rode home from Columbia-Presbyterian. "Really . . ."

We'd waited for two hours in the steamy, anonymous, emergency room with Bianca's husband, her brother and sister, the museum's horrified president, and its director of public relations.

Scattered around the room awaiting word on their own personal traumas and tragedies were various hollow-eyed, frightened, people, all of us caught off-guard and thrust together by one of life's unexpected curve balls. We were sharing unspeakably intimate moments with total strangers—instances that literally meant life or death. How incredible it is that we spend years and years of our lives building our own personal worlds, controlling our environment and surroundings, carefully choosing our friends, our jobs, our lovers; we dedicate ourselves to making our own world as perfect as it can be, we talk endlessly about how we would like to live and die, but in the end, all is grace and favor.

Finally, Bianca's doctor had come out and asked Charles to accompany him into a consultation room. At that point we knew it was over. "I'm sorry," I'd heard him say as he closed the door, "there was nothing we could do."

I rolled down the window in the limo and let the icy fresh air blow across my face.

". . . Not any more than it was mine or anybody else's," Madam continued. "She died of a massive heart-attack. You couldn't have done anything. The doctor said she was dead before she hit the floor."

Her words didn't console me, I thought as I went back to my musing. I'd prepared for years, taking classes, using ridiculous blow-up dolls, for just such an emergency. I'd received Red Cross merit badges for my Heimlich and CPR expertise, yet when my turn came to act, the person had died. I was devastated. I, Mister Perfect, Mister Know-it-All, *couldn't tell the difference between choking and a heart attack.*

"I'm going to take the dogs," I told her when we got home. I strapped on their little winter Burberrys and put two precautionary Fishermen's Friends beneath my tongue.

"I'm coming with you."

"It's too cold."

"I can take it."

I tucked my muffler tight around my neck, clamped on my earmuffs, and we set out for a walk along the dark, frozen streets. There was no traffic to speak of, beyond the occasional taxi speeding past and sending up sheets of slushy black water.

"Come on, Nigel," Madam said after a couple of silent blocks. "I'm sorry she's dead, but it's not as if we'd lost our best friend. I mean, we didn't even know her very well."

"It's not so much her I'm upset about," I admitted, "it's *me.* I thought she was choking."

"Frankly," Madam said, "I'm surprised Bianca lived as long as she did." She was huddled deep in her fur, with the collar pulled tightly around her ears. The gardenias were long gone. "She was at least sixty-five, and I'll bet she weighed at least two hundred and fifty pounds. She could have died of a dozen different things. Don't you agree?" She was knocking herself out to humor me.

"Please, Madam, don't try to jolly me up. I am flawed and incompetent."

"For heaven's sake, Nigel, let me get my violin. I think you should try to look at this scientifically, considering you're such a big medical expert. She was obese, what else could she have died of?"

"Well," I said, unwilling to release my guilt but succumbing to her niggling appeal to my diagnostic skills. "Her weight would make her susceptible to an array of ailments."

"Like what?" Madam pushed. "Tell me all of them, A-to-Z, we have the time."

We were moving fast, but no matter how quickly we walked, the dogs were ahead of us. Pulling.

"A-to-Z? Hmmm. Let me see. I would start with the obvious, the full spectrum of acute arterial conditions. But there is also a wide range of abnormalities, from glandular and intestinal to diabetes and stroke, kidney, gallbladder disorders to, well, I can't think at the moment exactly what starts with Z but obesity affects everything, so I know there's a Z in there somewhere."

"Zinc something, probably," Madam offered. "She smoked, of course, which we all know, like it or not, is a death sentence."

That particular reality took the chatter out of us for a number of steps. I *love* to smoke, but every now and then I run across the statistics about how smoking kills more people in America every year than AIDS, suicide, homicide, car accidents, and so forth.

"I think it was high blood pressure, fat, smoking, and booze," Madam pronounced as we entered Battery Park, putting an end to the subject. "The whole family looks bad. Except for Patty. I thought she looked to be in pretty good shape, didn't you?"

Patty Hammond, the youngest, and now only surviving sister, was an outdoors woman. She owned and operated Hammond Adventures, a company that arranged treks to Nepal and Bhutan. She was often featured on the Discovery Channel and in magazines because, for an outrageous amount of money, her company took groups of semi-in-shape rich folks into the farthest reaches of the Himalayas on what could only be called Outward Bound, character-building experiences. She had the wind-burned skin and rugged manner of an independent individualist. "I'm more at home with a mountain bike or a mountain goat than a bunch of dressed up drunks," she'd declared in a *Town & Country* profile of the family. But Patty Hammond's tough love was obviously what the dressed up drunks wanted, because her expeditions were booked years in advance.

"I quite liked her, comparatively," I said half-heartedly. "She seemed like a real no-nonsense kind of person." We walked a few steps further in companionable silence. "Not to disregard or diminish what happened to Mrs. Roosevelt tonight," I said presently, "but I was interested to hear that you are such an expert skier."

Madam's laugh sailed into the darkness, bright and filled with delight at her own brashness. "What else could I say? It just popped into my mind. I don't want those IRS people to keep coming back into my life. They scare me to death. They're already taking all my money, and helping them is my only chance to get out of this hole. The thought of having the farmhouse taken away is so terrifying I'd do anything to stop it. I was afraid if I told Armand I didn't know how to ski, he'd uninvite me. What a mess."

"Where are you going to get the clothes?" I asked. "You'll need parkas, gloves, ski suits, hats, goggles, mukluks."

"Mukluks?"

"Plus there's lots of equipment." I smiled over at her. "Like skis and so forth."

She laughed again, shaking her head. "I don't know why you stay with me, Nigel. I know it's like living in a madhouse."

"I'm very happy working for you, Madam. When my colleagues describe their situations—you can't imagine how lucky I feel."

"How much do skis cost?"

"A great deal, I think."

"Crap."

"What kind should I get?"

"I haven't the vaguest idea, but I'd be happy to research it for you."

"That'd be wonderful. The whole thing makes me hyperventilate."

"Are you happy with how the rest of the evening went?" We were going along at a fast clip now, on our way home. I scooped up the now weary dogs and handed one to Madam.

"You mean Armand?"

I nodded.

"Or Ryder?"

"Both actually."

"Or Junior?"

"All right, then. All three."

"Well, let me put it this way: If Bianca hadn't died and Armand had asked me to run away with him tonight, I would have. I'd be in some amazing suite at the Four Seasons right now. I looked at him and Ryder together and thought, what on earth have I been doing? I was pretty sure that when I saw Ryder tonight, I'd feel *something*—happy, excited, mad, whatever—but I didn't. It was a big zero. It's over. I wish he'd just go away and I'd never have to see him again."

"I'm afraid it's not going to be that easy," I said as we rounded the corner and watched Ryder disappear into our building.

"Shit," Madam said.

25

I could not have said it better. I knew too much. Whereas before I'd seen a man who, for better or for worse, was a fact of our life, now I saw a real danger. He had all the potential to become the sort of fringe desperado we read about in the papers, who kills everyone he loves just so no one else can have them. As far as he was concerned, Madam was his personal property and she was slipping from his grasp. I knew enough psychology and physics, enough about equal and opposite reactions, to know that, as much as he liked to receive pain, he could be equally capable of inflicting it.

As if to emphasize the theory of equal and opposite, when we got indoors, as full of fun as the atmosphere in the living room had been two days ago when Junior sat on the floor playing Scrabble, it was now charged and tense. No candles tonight. Instead, Ryder had switched on all the track lights, bleaching the living room with a stark halogen glow.

"You can say good night now, Nigel," he said thickly as he held a match to the newspaper beneath the Georgia fatwood kindling. My well-laid fire flared up furiously. He was drunk. His hair was messed up and he had removed his glass eye and covered the hole with a black patch. "We won't be needing you any further this evening."

I looked to Madam, who shook her head indicating that I should stay close by. She stood stiffly near the hearth, trying to remain cool, but I knew she was both annoyed and afraid. Ryder was angrier than she'd ever seen him.

"I'll be in the kitchen if you need me," I told her.

This was a high-stakes situation. How much, I wondered, as Ryder and I stared at each other across the room, was either of us willing to risk? Would I risk my job to save her life? Would he risk his life to keep his prize possession? I left the kitchen door ajar.

"What the hell kind of game do you think you're playing?" His voice was threatening, meant to intimidate.

"What do you mean?"

"Don't pull any of that 'what-do-you-mean?' bullshit, Jacqueline di Fidelio. You can't lay that wide-eyed little girl crap on me, I *know* you. Remember? This is me, Ryder. I *own* you. I've spent my life grooming you."

"Ryder . . ." she began.

"Don't interrupt. You know you're mine and you've known it from the day you first laid eyes on me. I saved your life. My own perfect little three year-old." His voice became melancholy. The cork in the brandy bottle popped like a muffled gunshot and he slopped the liquor into two snifters. He offered one to her but she turned away and he slammed the glass onto the mantel. "You've always been mine. If you think for one second I'm going to let you throw it all away now on some faggy little French Jew or that slimy Texas shitkicker, you don't know me as well as I thought you did." He drained his snifter and refilled it.

"I'm not your little girl anymore, Ryder." Madam made every effort to keep her voice steady and reasonable, but no one could provoke her faster, and one of her most prominent characteristics was that she liked to fight. She never backed down, especially against Ryder. It was like a competition, some kind of sick addiction, to see who could inflict the most damage. "The time away from you has helped me see what you've done to my life. And for what?"

"What do you mean, 'for what?' You know as well as I do we were meant to be together."

"You can't see it, can you?"

"See what?"

"How wrong this is. I'm the first one to admit that when you and Mother were lovers, I wanted you because I thought I was in love with you. Now I see it was because I wanted to hurt her, to get her back for all the pain she caused me. When she died, I was ecstatic. I could have you all to myself. But don't you see, Ryder? It's not working. It's not right. It's sick."

"Thank you, Dr. Freud."

"It doesn't take a psychiatrist to see how warped our relationship is."

"What's gotten into you? This is not my Jackie talking." He lurched toward her. The brandy had pushed him from drunk to unsteady. He reached out to her and she side-stepped him, forcing him to catch his balance on the mantelpiece, and knocking her glass to the floor, where it shattered. They both ignored it.

"It's beyond sick, Ryder. Come on, you know it as well as I do. Let's just call it quits. Why don't you just go home?"

I could tell she was beginning to lose her patience. Her tolerance was severely limited at best, and I sensed she had given him all the reasonable understanding she intended.

"Don't think for one second you can get rid of me as easily as that."

"Really? I can get rid of you any time I want. You want to know another thing? After all those years of wanting you, I now know you aren't what you seemed." It was clear, from my listening post in the kitchen, that time was up. The bell had rung, the gloves on. "You aren't some knight in shining armor riding a white horse—you're a brainless, gutless wonder. And I'm not doing it anymore. Face it." She pointed at the door. "It's over. Go home. Amscray."

Here's what we all stupidly or naively or wishfully think when we utter those words to end an affair: The End. Just get your gear and get out and never contact me again. We can't wait for that other person to be gone, and we can't understand why he doesn't just do what we tell him.

But it never works that way. The other guy has his script. So inevitably, whether it's from respect, exhaustion, or not wanting to come off as a totally heartless bastard because we have, after all, shared intimate moments with this person, we are somehow required to stand by and let him have his say. It's tedious and dreary and we want to say, Why don't you just shut up and hit the road? Go tell someone who cares. But we can't. We have to take it, and it makes us dislike the other person all the more.

Ryder stared into the fire. His jaw was set and he did not speak. The silence was interminable.

"You've had too much to drink." Madam crossed her arms over her chest. "And I am asking you, very politely, to leave."

Stick to your guns, Madam, I prayed.

"Oh, Jackie, honey." His voice was soft and the tone contrite. He turned, grabbed her shoulders, and pulled her to him. When he spoke, his face was very close to hers. "How can you say what we have is sick? Can you even begin to imagine how much I love you? How much I need you, even to breathe?"

Madam didn't answer.

"All I want is for you to keep away from other men. Armand Weil, particularly. You know how jealous I get." He tightened his grip, and although he tried to keep his tone gentle and rational—so *rational,* only an *irrational* person wouldn't want him—we all know that manipulative trick—it didn't work. The threat was obvious.

Madam stepped back and drew herself up and straightened her spine. Her folded arms formed a hard barrier between them. "I'm not your property, Ryder. Let go of me."

"You stay away from Armand Weil," he lashed back furiously. "Do you hear me? You're turning into a goddamned whore."

A heartbeat of silence.

"Do you hear me, goddamn you?" he roared. "Stay away from him."

"Fuck you," she said.

A ringing slap. I flew through the door.

"And I want you to keep away from Junior Hammond. Do you understand?"

"Let go of her!" I yelled.

"Get the hell out of here," Ryder warned but I kept moving, darting around the chairs. I felt a sharp chrome edge slice through my pants and into my thigh.

She was standing firm and solid as an oak but had squeezed her eyes shut, expecting another blow. Instead, he grabbed her jaw, forcing her lips into a pouty grimace, and shook her head savagely back and forth. "Look at me, goddamn you. Do you understand?"

"Let go of her," I yelled again.

I had reached them and Ryder turned to look at me. He appeared to have lost his mind. "Get out of here, you filthy little fairy," he snarled.

I clenched my fist into a tight ball, cocked my right arm back, and then *BANG!* smashed him in the nose as hard as I could. Ryder dropped his grip and staggered back, blood running over his mouth and pouring down the front of his white shirt.

We were all absolutely stunned.

"Get out of here, Mr. McCormick," I said evenly. "Now. Or I'll kill you."

26

We watched him walk out the door, trying to gather some dignity around himself, but it didn't work any better than the way he tried to drape his overcoat around his shoulders, as if he were leaving for the opera. It hung cockeyed, and one sleeve was inside-out. The fringe of his white silk scarf dragged on the floor. His walk was a semi-staggering, movie monster shuffle, one deliberate step at a time. As he thumped down the circular wrought-iron staircase, he muttered unintelligible epithets, but the tone of his message was clear: We would be sorry. Neither of us moved until we heard the door slam behind him, and only then did I race across the living room and down the stairs to slam the dead bolt home. I had never been so afraid in my life.

Madam was picking up the shards of the shattered brandy snifter slowly, as though she were in a dream. Her cheeks were bright, angry red from where he had slapped her.

"Here, Madam, please. Let me." I held out my cupped hand and she dropped the bits of glass into it. "You go to bed."

"You saved my life, Nigel."

"Possibly." I had no energy in me to deny it.

"What do you think he'll do?" She lit a cigarette, her hand shaking so hard it almost extinguished the match. She struck another and held it to the candles along the sideboard behind the sofa, then walked over to the light panel and switched off every single one of the lights. With the quiet, familiar incandescence of the fire and candles, a huge calm descended over the room. All of a sudden we were warm and safe in our house. Control and sanity restored.

"Nothing, if he's smart."

"Thank you, Nigel," she said. Her voice was breathless, almost inaudible. "Thank you for everything."

"All in a day's work," I replied, hoping to bring a little levity to the situation. A silly, self-conscious, futile gesture.

"No, I mean it. I don't know what I would do without you. Where did you learn to punch like that?"

"Good night, Madam."

I left her sitting in front of the fire, staring into it. I couldn't tell her I'd learned to fight in prison out of self-defense, ending up the institution's bantam-weight champion instead of its sweetheart. I double- and triple-checked the locks on the front door and retired to my room, where I poured myself a hefty tot of Armagnac and collapsed, completely drained, on the chaise in front of my own small hearth. As it turned out, the sharp edge of the chair had sliced neither my pants nor my leg, but a deep bruise had begun to emerge. It was late, and I was too tired to do anything about it. My last thought before I drifted off was that maybe Ryder would do the gentlemanly thing, do us all a favor and jump off a bridge. I could picture him floating face-down in the Hudson, his dance pumps left sitting side-by-side on the bridge with his watch and ring and a note with Madam's phone number tucked in the toe of one, his reading glasses in the other, his cashmere coat flying behind him like Superman's cape as he fell. Did he scream? Probably like a baby.

I was still lying there, fully clothed—sleeping so deeply I might as well have been drugged—when, I don't know how many hours later, the phone rang. The clock said seven. Outside, the morning was dark with dense fog. I struggled slowly to consciousness.

"Miss di Fidelio's residence," I answered.

"Turn your television set on. Channel Four." It was a colleague, one of the fellows I'd chatted with last night. "You won't believe it. Mrs. Roosevelt was poisoned." Then he rang off. The phone rang again, and it was someone else telling me the same thing.

I knew it! Food poisoning. Never fails at these big affairs. What would it be this time? Salmonella? Botulism? Amoebic dysentery? It would be the kitchen help, of course. Cheap labor, people without papers who knew enough to peel a potato but not enough to scrub up before touching it. Typhoid? Cholera? Cholera is bad. Your insides simply run out in a constant stream until they're gone and you're dead. Do you know, in developing countries—like Africa, of course—there are special beds called "cholera beds," just a canvas sheet stretched on a rack with a hole in the middle and a bucket underneath. Do I need to say more?

Fifteen seconds into the story, I thundered down the hallway, my hard-soled shoes sounding like a herd of escaped wild horses on the wooden floors, and into Madam's pitch-black bedroom. "I'm sorry to disturb you, Madam," I spoke firmly, in spite of being out of breath. "But you must wake up."

"What is it, Nigel?" she said groggily and raised one corner of her sleeping mask. "Tell Ryder to leave me alone."

"No." I pulled open the tall shutters and gray light timidly crept in. "It's not Mr. McCormick. You have to watch. It's about Bianca Roosevelt. She died of food poisoning, but the police don't think it was accidental—they think she was *murdered*."

"What?" She bolted up and ripped the mask off.

"Murdered, Madam. They say Mrs. Roosevelt was *murdered*. Come into the kitchen."

I dashed back through the apartment like a madman, turning on everything—the television, the coffee, the oven, all the lights. The coffee had scarcely begun to brew when she stumbled in, tying her kimono around her and looking much older than her forty or so years. The scene with Ryder had etched itself into her face like a fingerprint in wet cement.

The story was so big, reporters just kept repeating it over and over: Bianca Roosevelt hadn't died of a heart attack. She had been poisoned. But it wasn't *accidental* food poisoning. She had been murdered!

We stood at the counter and devoured two plates full of orange rolls and an entire pot of coffee, to which Madam added cream and three heaping tablespoons of sugar, while the television screen showed a file tape of a wiggling, prickly fish being eviscerated by a Japanese master chef as the reporter explained how this particular delicacy—Fugu, a Japanese blow-fish—had to be prepared just right, otherwise it would become deadly.

"That fish is so disgusting, I can't believe it," Madam said, licking sticky orange glaze off her fingertips.

Then they interviewed the caterer who, understandably, was in a desperate state of shock, watching his business evaporate right before his eyes. Like us, he had been rousted from bed and caught unprepared by television cameras at his front door. "We would never, ever, consider serving Fugu. It is far too dangerous. That sushi did *not* come from *my* kitchens."

Madam looked at me.

We said, "Junior," at the same time.

The police had no comment except that they were launching a full investigation, nothing had been ruled out. A reporter asked if the NYPD was aware that Mrs. Roosevelt's sister's yacht had been blown up in Florida a couple of months ago, and the chief replied in the affirmative and said they'd already been in contact with the Palm Beach Police. That was the end of the news conference.

Madam switched to A&E and then muted it. "I don't think it really could have been Junior, do you?" She had tucked her hair behind her ears, which made them stick out unbecomingly.

"No." I gathered up the plates. "I think it was a complete fluke. Random. Wrong place, wrong time. They'll find out it was some sick waiter with a big ax to grind with his boss or his wife or lover or dog, or the city or the police or the immigration service and he decided to get even by working the room with a couple of deadly sushis on his tray."

"You sound like an authority, Nigel. Maybe it was you," she teased.

"We read about these things all the time, Madam."

"Poor Bianca. Talk about bad luck."

Or good. I kept my mouth shut. My opinion of the Hammonds is pretty well documented by now. Lynette had been a whining cow, and Bianca was a dirtbag. My most vivid memory of her would always be her dropping her burning cigarette into my glass of Veuve Cliquot. It was a perfectly succinct and lasting definition of her character. And Junior? A racist pig. I've said it before and I'll say it again: They were not our kind of people. The poisoning completely absolved me of any residual guilt I might have had from not saving Bianca the night before—everyone knows there's no coming back from Fugu.

My own feelings were perfectly reflected by Madam's actions.

She yawned and stretched. "The world has gone mad. I'm going back to bed. One Hammond more or less doesn't make one hell of a lot of difference in my life one way or the other."

Hear! Hear!

I turned up the heat in the apartment. It was freezing and pellets of snow started hitting the windows like BBs. I'd had enough of New York. I wanted to go home to Virginia. The phone rang. "Miss di Fidelio's residence." It was just minutes after eight.

"Armand Weil calling," a professional female voice informed me. "Is Miss di Fidelio available?"

"One moment, please."

I'm embarrassed to say that's really all it took for either one of us to completely forget about Bianca Roosevelt. We didn't even go to her funeral, although we stayed in New York for another week.

Armand, who claimed he never remained in any one place for longer than twenty-four hours, changed his schedule and for seven days— sandwiched between meetings, international auctions, and conference calls that seemed to go on twenty-four hours a day—he and Madam had lunch, dinner, and long, long hours into the night, every day and every night. If he was the world's most accomplished art thief, he hid it well.

Joy descended upon us. Light had come to replace Ryder's dark. I cannot remember a time of greater happiness in our household. If Ryder had brought out the worst in Madam, Armand brought out the best. She smiled constantly and called Armand by all sorts of silly pet names: Pookie, Chou-Chou, and so forth. They sent each other flowers and telephoned often, just to say how much they loved each other. Their infatuation was so complete that, on one hand it made me feel as elated as they were, and on the other I could not help being envious. I ached for someone to love as well, someone who would be as nice to me as I was to her, or him.

Madam put it succinctly, "Every other time I've thought I was in love, I've been the one doing the giving. It's never been completely reciprocal. I've never experienced anything like this before, where everything I give comes back bigger. Where did this man come from? It's like he dropped out of the sky."

That's what we all want, isn't it? A deus ex machina.

By the time we returned to Middleburg—where she put the finishing touches on a portrait of the eight-year-old daughter of a local divorcée and collected a nice check—they were completely pledged to each other, and he promised to try to work less. Who knows if he was telling the truth.

I supposed that telling him about her assignment to spy on him to save her own skin was always at the tip of Madam's tongue, although she and I never discussed if she'd told him or not. Still, I know if she had, she would have told me. Personally, I don't think I could have taken the pressure of not telling him. But I've never had a long-lasting, honest, relationship, so what do I know?

I spent my time getting the gear together for our trip to Aspen, and what a lot of gear it was. Unfortunately, because it had to look like she knew what she was doing, the stuff couldn't be purchased in New York. It had to come from a top shop in an exclusive resort. We'd received catalogues over the years from a boutique named Gorsuch, and I called them to ask for their guidance.

"You're in luck!" the manager said. "We've just marked everything down by ten percent!"

But at those prices it didn't make much of a difference. With seven thousand dollars in merchandise and a thousand in overnight freight, Madam was, as they say in the Marine Corps, "good to go."

Here's what she had:

1	*Prada parka—retro, severe, fitted, in European*	
	slate gray	$ 1,200
1	*pr. Prada stretch pants—blue-based red*	350

1	pr. Prada straight-leg ski pants—slate gray	500
1	Sonja Bogner one-piece bad weather ski suit, feminine, chic, sleek but heavy coated twill microfiber-black	1,500
6	Postcard micro-fleece turtlenecks—assorted colors	900
1	Prada beanie	110
1	hand-knit, bad weather hat from England	168
1	pr. Technika gloves	200
1	pr. Briko goggles	100
1	pr. Prada after-ski boots	350
1	pr. fur-trimmed Technika after-ski boots	300
1	pr. Technika ski boots	600
1	pr. Atomic skis w/Marker step-in bindings	1,200
1	pr. Goode ski poles	350

	7,770
less 10%	770
	$7,000

When we left for Colorado ten days later, the New York police still had no leads on who had planted the deadly sushi, and I didn't think they'd come up with any. I thought that whoever had done it was long-gone, back to whatever third-world country he'd come from.

More significantly though, there had been no communication from Ryder, which made me feel like we were living with a time bomb in our midst. Madam had taken his ring to Harry Winston and sold it for twenty thousand dollars, which only reinforced the likelihood that Ryder had stolen it out of his wife's jewelry box. He would never have had the money to buy such a piece himself.

27

ASPEN

"What do you mean, 'there's no first class'?" Madam said to the agent at the United Express gate in Denver when we checked in for our flight to Aspen. She had on a couple of other new items she had gone out and bought herself: a full-length coyote coat, cowboy boots, and a cowboy hat.

"If I may, Madam," I'd said when she came home with her purchases, "to me, wearing mink or chinchilla is fine. It's like eating beef or wearing leather shoes because they're raised to become the product. But coyote is a little too close to the edge of humane. You know, coyotes are actually wild dogs. Can you imagine someone making a coat out of your *dogs?*"

The yorkies had looked at us, their little black eyes glittering with fear. They knew what we were talking about.

"Come on, Nigel."

"Truly, Madam. They're shot or trapped in the wild only for their fur. That's all they're good for—you can't eat them. How many people have you heard of eating coyote stew? Not many, I'm sure."

"Nigel, calm down. It's *fake.*"

The cowboy boots were Luchese.

"What about these?" she had challenged good-naturedly, pointing to her size ten feet hidden inside three thousand dollars worth of reptile skin. "These are real. Think of all the snakes and Gila monsters who died to make my boots."

"You've got me there, Madam." I took the new coat, it was light as a feather, and hung it in the closet. "Your boots remind me of what you said when Bianca was murdered: One Hammond more or less doesn't make a whole hell of a lot of difference in my life. That also sums up how I feel about reptiles."

"Me, too."

The hat was just a hat, fawn beaver with a woven leather band, nothing fancy. It did provide several inches more height, which made Madam a good foot taller than anyone around her, and a foot-and-a-half taller than the agent at the check-in counter. He was not even slightly fazed.

She hadn't said anything to me, but I knew she was peeved that Armand, who had originally offered his private jet to fly us in, had withdrawn the offer at the last minute because he had to deliver a painting to Saudi Arabia. But he *had* sent a limo to pick us up at home and he had bought us first class seats on a United 777 from Washington to Denver, which wasn't exactly a Gulfstream Four but was very nice for a domestic carrier.

"It's all one-class seating," the agent answered.

"You've got to be kidding."

"I'm not."

"Is it at least a jet?"

"Yes. Four engines." He busily tapped in our names. "And if it makes you feel any better, Jackie, everyone on these flights is always in as much shock as you are at this moment. Nobody who goes to Aspen has ever flown coach before in their lives."

"Well, that doesn't make me feel any better," she said and snatched the boarding passes out of his hand. "And it's Miss di Fidelio."

I'd never been to Aspen but, in spite of my ignorance, I was a member of its long list of critics:

The town is from a different planet.

There are only rich people there.

The help has to commute a minimum of an hour (for some it is as much as three hours!) to work each way every day because their employers provide no housing for them. In California's Coachella Valley, home of Palm Springs, Palm Desert, Indian Wells, and Rancho Mirage, where there is so much money it makes Aspen look like Hooterville, the state law mandates that each town must have enough low-to-middle income housing for the people who work in it. Not only does this result in a somewhat more well-rounded community, it also provides for a much more stable workforce. In the Colorado ski areas, on the other hand, there are two kinds of workers: rich kids who will do anything for a winter in the Rockies and a free ski pass, who can afford to rent run-down, tear-down, condos for ten-thousand a month but, when it comes to hard work, are totally undependable; and illegal migrants from Mexico and Central America who are so desperate they will do anything. They have flocked from mind-numbing tropical poverty to spend their lives on busses that rumble through blizzards ten thousand feet above sea-level; over Vail Pass, through Glenwood Canyon, down the Roaring Fork Valley, past trendy Carbondale and magnificent Mt. Sopris, past Basalt with its vast trailer parks and million-dollar chalets, and into Aspen during the blackness of night. They never even see the beauty they're traversing. It's an outrage, because no matter how much they're paid, for all intents and purposes, they are slaves. These are invisible members of the human race, treated with no respect or humanity, expected to take it or leave it. Unfortunately, if or when they can't take it any more, there are fifty people waiting in line behind them. I cannot even imagine how hard the conditions must be where they came from, if this is better.

None of which has any real or discernible effect on Aspen or the people who live there and go there to play. And it shouldn't. They're paying an absolute fortune, an insane amount of money to ski, party, and go about the town unmolested by reality. They're on vacation, not in an anthropological seminar.

I flew to Aspen—made brave by the four oversized jet engines on the intrepid little craft—armed with all these opinions and pre-judgments, many of which would turn out to be correct, but I was unprepared for the overpowering natural beauty of the place or the massiveness and majesty of the Rockies as we flew high above them. We were seated in the first row, and Madam made me sit by the window while she took the aisle. "If we crash I want to be the first one out of here," she said. A well-dressed gentleman from Minneapolis, stuck in the tiny seat between us, studied a stack of Smith Barney newsletters the whole way, unperturbed by the fact that the captain came on the public address system a minute or two before take-off and announced, "We expect some turbulence on our quick hop over to Aspen today, so I've asked the flight crew to remain seated throughout the flight." And then we bolted off the ground and headed up, up, up, the four engines straining under the dead weight of skis and boots and rich people fearing for their lives.

Within two or three minutes we were in the mountains, and they seemed so close I could have reached out and touched their snow-blown peaks. It made my heart skip. In the high meadows and valleys I could pick out frozen lakes in shining chains like silver disks on the necklaces of the gods, and an occasional cabin, silent and snowbound. When our plane hit an air pocket and we dropped what seemed like ten miles, plummeting flat-bottomed toward the jagged rocks, then bounced as though we'd landed on an invisible cushion, everyone in the plane clapped and laughed. I think it was the most fiendishly dangerous and thrilling ride I've ever had.

Suddenly, although there was no sense of descending, the sound of the engines changed and the mountains began to grow closer and take on the appearance of half-melted marshmallows, softly undulating mounds of snow edged with rocky cliffs and buttes. We sailed over large ranches and along a frozen riverbed, and just as we headed straight toward a mountain and I was sure we were going to fly smack into it, the land fell away, simply disappeared, and we touched down gently on the runway, rolling past a parking lot full of at least fifty private jets.

By the time we landed at Sardi Field at twelve-fifteen, the migrants had been at their jobs for hours, their train of double-length busses replaced by a steady parade of gleaming Cadillac Escalades, Suburbans,

Expeditions, Range Rovers, Discoveries, and Explorers. We taxied past the private fleet of Learjets, Gulfstreams, Citations, Falcons, and Jet-stars—the people working around them waved at our plane as if they were actually glad we'd arrived—and came to a stop at the terminal. The roof had a jagged design to complement the ruggedness of the surrounding peaks. A huge, friendly greeting sign hung over the entrance: WELCOME.

"Look," said Madam, as a wide stairway was rolled to the door of the plane. "They still use stairs here. Isn't it charming? You go first, Nigel. Make sure Armand's here."

28

When I emerged from the plane, the first thing that happened was that the sun completely blinded me. I've never seen such glare. Tears poured from my eyes in spite of my dark glasses. And then, as I walked toward the terminal and a cloud passed overhead, I realized that in the sun it was warm; in the shade, it was cold as hell. The air was exhilarating, sharp, and clean. Without question, the healthiest air I'd ever breathed.

Armand met us, as I knew he would. I believed his intentions toward Madam were entirely honorable—he was an honorable man. I've known criminals, intimately, and he exhibited none of their characteristics. He wasn't furtive or paranoid. He conducted his business openly, in front of Madam, sometimes even in bed. He didn't excuse himself, retreat to another room, speak in whispers, or babble in truncated codes. Much of what he did was confidential, to be sure, but he trusted her.

Oh, God, what am I saying? He trusted her, and she was spying on him for the government. Brutal.

His ski clothes had been selected with the same sort of careful eye to understated power he gave his business suits. The man was a rock of style and substance. He had on a black baseball cap with no logo, a bright red Armani parka, black stretch pants, and dark glasses. His face was more tanned than usual, which made his teeth, beneath his black mustache, as white as the snow.

"Jacqueline." He rushed halfway across the tarmac to greet her, wrapping her in his arms and kissing her on both cheeks. "I am so glad you're here. Look at you in your hat and boots. You look like a native. Hello, Nigel." He shook my hand with a good, strong, genuine grasp. "Welcome to Aspen. How was your flight? Everything okay?" He took Madam's hand luggage. "I'm sorry I couldn't send my plane, but, you know," he gave a Gallic shrug, "business."

So what else is new? We never will have a plane. Even if she married him, he'd probably never let her use it. We needed someone who was so rich his plane was for *fun*. Whose company, or better yet, *companies,* had their own planes to use for business. That was the one problem with Armand, as far as I was concerned—business, business, business. Unfortunately, the ones whose planes were for fun were the ones like Junior. Nobody gets to have everything.

"It was perfect," she answered, her words coming out in puffs from the cold. She was so happy to see him, she would have said anything on earth, even the most horrible natural disaster, was perfect. "We were totally comfortable thanks to all your special arrangements."

"Good. Good."

"Is everyone here already?"

"Yes, they all came in last night. You're the last to arrive. Everyone's on the mountain."

"All I want to do is kiss you," she laughed. She had her arm locked into his as though it were a life-preserver. "Did you go skiing this morning?"

"Of course. The snow is spectacular. There's still time for us to get in a couple of runs this afternoon if we hurry. We'll grab a light lunch at the club. Have you been there yet?"

"Where?"

"The Aspen Mountain Club."

"No," Madam answered enthusiastically. "I can't wait. I've heard so much about it." She had absolutely no idea what he was talking about.

I knew all about it, but the chances of my ever seeing the Aspen Mountain Club—a private affair situated halfway up Ajax Mountain—were virtually nil. The founders' initiation fee had been one-hundred-thousand and they'd sold out in a week. The standard initiation was then reduced to fifty thousand. The members weren't really my crowd anyway, or rather, the crowd I would choose if I had a choice. They weren't Madam's either, but I knew they were about to be, if they were Armand's.

"One change," Armand was saying. "The Burneys canceled at the last minute and I invited Junior in their place. He's been through so much, I felt sorry for him. That family seems to attract disaster. Also, I'm on to a couple of pieces he'll be interested in."

"Terrific." She huddled closer. "I love Junior. I think he's one of the funniest people I've ever known in my life."

"I wouldn't go so far as that, but at least his heart's in the right place."

Huh? I'm so ambivalent sometimes, I can't stand myself. The truth is, according to Madam, Junior is fun, a big spoiled rich kid with a heart of gold, but I swear to God, if he called me a nigra again, I'd—well, I'm not sure what I'd do. Kill him, maybe.

All this while, Armand had been leading us through the terminal and out to the parking lot, where we stopped at a twinkling navy blue Ford Excursion so big it looked like a locomotive. I'd read about these cars: They had forty gallon tanks and got eight miles to the gallon, which seems cockeyed and hypocritical in a town that prides itself on its environmental awareness.

"Nigel, do you need help with the luggage?" Armand asked.

"No sir," I answered, stowing my carry-on on the floor behind the driver's seat. "I'll be right back."

"Take your time," he said. "We're on vacation—no rushing." He turned to kiss Madam, pinning her against the voluptuous hood of the car like a teenager.

I studied my surroundings as I waited for the luggage. The baggage claim area was jam-packed, wall-to-wall, with attractive people. Even the luggage handlers looked like tanned movie stars in their jeans and Sorel boots, Bogner parkas, and cowboy hats. I flagged down one with a large cart and we made small talk as we waited for the bags to start flowing in on the conveyor. By the time he'd lifted the four Eddie Bauer duffles, packed with clothes Madam could not afford and would never wear again, onto the cart, found her boot bag, which looked like everyone else's, except for the thin scrap of brown Hermès ribbon I'd tied on the handle to make it easier to identify, and transferred her ski carrier, he'd asked me if I'd like to join him and some of his friends for a beer after work.

"Just give me a call. Here's my number." He handed me a card. Jeremy, it said. "Everybody's pretty laid back."

"Thanks," I said. I wasn't going to give Jeremy a call. I didn't make my friends among anonymous baggage handlers, no matter how handsome, but the invitation reminded me of how alone I was, how lonely my profession is. If I wasn't serving time in jail at the grace of Her Majesty, then it was at Madam's. Always someone else's grace, never my own. It was the trade I'd made not to accept responsibility for myself. Fernando's face flashed through my mind—his slightly obvious toupee and snappy, pencil mustache, the gusto of his belly laugh and his wry sense of humor. I hadn't met anyone even vaguely like him who was worth a nickel of my time. It had only been a couple of months ago—although it seemed like years—that Lynette Payne's yacht had vanished into a ball of flame. I'd been in New York almost the whole time since then, while most of my buddies were with their bosses in Florida or the islands for the winter. But, of course, most of them were working for geezers.

And now I was in the baggage claim area of the Aspen airport getting hustled by a twenty-five-year-old. What on earth has become of discretion? This boy was a child, a fool, and playing a dangerous game. He was the epitome of how people these days approached every aspect of life: Let's just do everything in public. Let's just do what the Beatles said: Let's do it in the road. Just the opposite of what's proper. David Breashears, the man who's climbed Everest five times (and made the IMAX movie during that deadly climb in May of 1996 when twelve people perished attempting to descend from the summit) was a real first class fellow. When he and his team completed their ascent, they came across the bodies of the two dead expedition leaders, but he kept the lens covers on his cameras out of respect for them. "Just because it happened, doesn't mean it's public," he said. Bravo, Mr. Breashears. Let us follow his example. Let's *not* do it in the road.

I gave Jeremy a twenty once the bags were loaded into the car, avoiding his attempt to brush my hand, and once I was buckled in, Armand pulled onto the plowed highway and proceeded toward town at a maddeningly slow pace. He was on the phone before we were out of the parking lot.

"Just one more call and I'm done, darling," he said. Six times. We crawled along in the right-turn-only, busses-only lane, sticking behind a local school-style bus as though it were towing us. It had racks packed with skis running along its sides. When it stopped, we stopped. Skiers piled on and off. Traffic flew past. Bus fumes filled our car.

Every now and then, as if to demonstrate how happy he was that Madam was with him and how sorry he was that his business was interrupting their good time, he'd point out the window and mouth words like "Buttermilk," or "all golf course around here," or "Aspen Highlands," or "Music Festival tent over that way." Madam looked wherever he directed and did her best to look interested rather than disappointed. Or miffed. We crept across a rickety, pot-holed suspension bridge, and the gorge it traversed was so deep, the bottom—where, a sign claimed, Maroon Creek ran—wasn't visible. Mansions clung to its shadowy cliffs.

We passed a sign at the city limits: Aspen, Colorado. Elev: 7908 feet. My head began to throb. I was probably suffering from a little altitude sickness, oxygen deprivation, and so forth. Like exhaust fumes.

I reminded myself of two things: I was here to do my job, which was to make Madam's life comfortable; and she was here to see if Armand Weil had stolen the Gardner Museum pieces and hidden them in a large vault deep in the mountainside beneath his house. That done, the government people would leave us alone and stop trying to wreck our life. This was a business trip for both of us and it was important to keep that in mind. I reached inside my jacket pocket and fingered the envelope that held the floor plans provided by the FBI.

Once past the snow-covered fields, we made two sharp turns, one right, one left, passed the bus, and emerged onto a snow-banked boulevard with old-fashioned street lights, trees still twinkling with Christmas lights, and brightly painted, restored little Victorian houses, interspersed with 1960s motels done up as chalets and given Old Country names such as Ullr Lodge, Tyrolean Lodge, Innsbuck Inn, Christiana, L'Auberge d'Aspen. Nothing local until, finally, the Molly Gibson.

Armand took a right onto Mill Street—I saw the famous old Hotel Jerome there on the corner—and showed us the town, wending his way along snow-packed streets lined with two-story, red-brick Victorian buildings filled with restaurants and so many chic boutiques we could have been on Madison Avenue. The sidewalks were bustling with unbelievably good-looking people, most of them in tight-fitting ski clothes, some in full-length fur coats—coyotes included—and, I was glad to see, Prada after-ski boots just like Madam's. "One of the must-haves," the Gorsuch manager had insisted. We passed the skating rink; the plaza with its steps leading to the Silver Queen Gondola and its milling crowd of skiers waiting to board; Gorsuch itself, in the Little Nell Hotel, and the tiny Aspen Book Store. "There it is, Aspen," Armand announced, "now we'll go home."

Moments later we approached the Hotel Jerome again from the opposite direction, turned down a steep hill, and started up the opposite side of the valley. All around us, packed like sardines, were private houses as large as the American Embassy in Paris. There was no air between them, and with all their different styles of architecture, tucked into each other as they were, they looked like super-impositions in an architect's sales brochure.

We crossed a beautiful, hand-laid stone bridge over a frozen creek and started to climb what Armand, who had finally hung up the phone because the terrain required both hands on the wheel, explained was Red Mountain, so named because it was made of a heavy clay that turned red in the rain. Little snow stuck to the side of Red Mountain since it had a southwestern exposure, and there were almost no trees except those planted to screen the gargantuan residences. Half way up, he turned off the road, crossed onto a snowy plateau, and passed through an electronically operated security gate set in a split-rail fence.

"Welcome, my darling, to my little hideaway." He took Madam's hand and kissed it.

One more turn, and the property—concealed behind a thick screen of towering Colorado Blue Spruce and groves of bare aspen trees—opened to reveal a sandstone and glass house, its flat roof studded with chimneys. Unlike the houses we'd been passing, Armand's, in the school of Frank Lloyd Wright, fit unobtrusively into its pristine setting. The driveway was heated. Before we pulled into the garage, I looked out at the view of the entire Aspen Valley, the town itself, and the main ski area beyond. We had entered a postcard.

"I'll be ready in ten minutes," Madam told Armand, giving him one last smooch before we headed down a gallery-like hallway hung with paintings most museums would sell their souls for.

29

"What do you want to wear skiing?" I asked once I'd gotten all her gear—except the skis and boots, which stayed in the special ski room next to the garage—into her bedroom.

It was a sleek suite with butter-soft, fawn-colored carpeting. Three of the walls were paneled in pale wood to match the furniture, which had simple, clean lines. The fourth wall was glass with floor-to-ceiling sliding doors that opened into a private garden, now buried under three feet of snow, and looked over the town and the mountains. Everything that could be built-in, was: drawers, cabinets, bookshelves, bedstead, and bed tables. The lighting was recessed. It was a house built to display art, and in Madam's room, an eight-by-ten-foot Helen Frankenthaler over the king-sized bed provided the only color but for the sky. To the right of the bed was a fireplace. A bottle of champagne sat chilling in an ice bucket on a glass coffee table.

"Pull out that negligée, Nigel. Quick." She was busy yanking off her earrings and her turtleneck travel sweater, tossing them on the bed as she rushed into the bathroom and turned on the shower. Her makeup and beauty products clattered as she dumped them onto the sandstone counter.

"Sounds just right."

The negligée was French, champagne silk-satin trimmed with marabou, and had cost twice as much as the skis.

"Open the champagne. Light the fire." The shower door banged shut.

"Done. And done."

Moments later, she was out of the shower, toweling off, fluffing her hair. I continued to unpack her gear. The foul-weather ski suit was so warm I think an astronaut could wear it on the moon.

There was a knock at the door.

"Jacqueline?" Armand said. "Are you ready?"

She smiled at me, crossed her fingers, and whispered, "If I have to go skiing, I'm a dead duck." Then she called out, "Almost, darling. Come on in."

I opened the door. "Please," I said and stood aside as he entered.

Madam emerged from the dressing room. She was brushing her hair and the sheer peignoir was in the process of working its way open. "I'll be ready in just a couple of seconds. Why don't you pour yourself a glass of champagne and by the time you're done, I'll be all set. I think that's it for now, Nigel, thanks."

"Very good, Madam." I closed the ten-foot-tall door behind me.

There would be no skiing today.

On the flight from Dulles to Denver, Madam and I had discussed at great length how we would determine if the house was laid-out as billed on the FBI's pilfered floor plans. By the little I'd seen so far, it was.

"I think that while everybody's skiing, or working out, or whatever it is we're going to be doing," Madam had explained, "you should check the place out."

"Me?"

"Well, of course. I can't do it. I'm out here to be with Armand. You're the one with the free time."

"Madam," I'd said, "I'm very uncomfortable doing such a thing. Snooping like that."

She had then given me a look with her blue/black eyes that delivered equal doses of compassion and steel, a look that said she would brook no nonsense. "Nigel, do you think I don't know anything about you?"

"What do you mean?" I'd squeaked, as my forehead began to dampen.

She'd covered my hand with hers. "I know you were in prison for safe-cracking. I know you were the bantam-weight boxing champion at Kingswood Prison. I know you've been reading up on museum security procedures and alarms on the Internet. I know you might possibly have even more neuroses than I do. And," she'd concluded gently, "I know you're the one who needs to scout out the place while I distract Armand."

The devil, you say. She and I had stared deep into each other's eyes for a full minute and then we both began to laugh. Even though I'd been out of prison for more than a dozen years, I felt free for the first time. We'd laughed so hard, I didn't think I could stop even if I'd wanted to. I was free, free, free! My darkest secrets known. Except for my clandestine relationship with Ryder, the thought of which finally enabled me to gain some control.

"Besides," she'd added, "I wouldn't call it snooping. I'd call it reconnaissance."

"I love you, Madam," I'd said.

"I love you, too, Nigel."

30

So now, here we were. Madam and Armand had gone to bed for the rest of the afternoon, and I would scout the house and grounds as unobtrusively as I could, making sure the subterranean vault was where it should be.

I took my time getting to the kitchen, visiting as many rooms as possible. The layout of the main areas was elegantly simple. The living room, dining room, and study, or great room as they're now called, were centrally located, with two guest wings, each with three bedrooms off on either side. A stairway, eight-feet-wide according to the plans, led up to the master suite. The same subtle, muted colors had been used throughout: polished sandstone floors, pale taupe carpeting, pale wood-paneled walls, down cushions covered with soft chenille on sleek, modern furniture. Everything was about light, about bringing the outside in, and . . . the art. The placement and lighting of each piece was meticulous. The range of Armand's collection was comprehensive, from Old Masters to Impressionists, to the great contemporary painters of the twentieth century—Motherwell, Kline, Pollock, and relative newcomers like Pradzynski and Smith. It was the finest possible private museum.

A quick scan of the security system indicated that it was as the FBI had described—state-of-the-art when the house was constructed ten years ago, but totally inadequate for today's thieves. There were heat and motion detectors but no miniature pin-hole cameras or sound sensors. It was a sign that Armand had become lax and over-confident about the safety of his collection. I wondered how much, if any, insurance he had.

I also wondered, as I stopped to appreciate a Thomas Hart Benton—a beautiful piece depicting a man toiling behind a plow, he and his horse straining their bulging muscles to the maximum, his sun-bonneted wife waiting patiently beneath a gnarled, leafy tree with a gingham-covered lunch basket—just how many were stolen and how many were acquired honestly; how many, if any, of the paintings were the real McCoy, and how many were copies? Unfortunately, I wasn't nearly expert enough to tell the difference.

Shortly, I heard sounds coming from what I knew to be the kitchen and headed in that direction. On my way, I passed the stairway to the basement, just where it was supposed to be. I tried not to hear the paintings down there calling my name, but my heart began to race a bit. I was desperately trying not to look forward to any sort of dangerous adventure, but I was still giddy from the liberation of my recent conversation with Madam. The *Mission Impossible* theme kept playing in the back of my head, and I could feel that same adrenaline rush that had gotten me in trouble in the first place, beckoning like an illicit lover.

The household crew, Suzie and Matt—a buxom, friendly couple from Idaho—were in the kitchen. I introduced myself.

"Matt'll help you out to the bunkhouse with your gear," Suzie said over her shoulder from the sink, where she was stripping asparagus with a small paring knife. "Then come back in and I'll give you some lunch."

"Right-o," I answered with a cheerfulness I didn't feel. Bunkhouse? I didn't like the sound of that. I followed Matt, who was bearded and as big as a lumberjack, through the back door and down a shoveled path into the trees. We walked in silence for probably a full minute, arriving at a smaller version of the main house. Matt unlocked the front door and held it open for me to pass. The living room was comfortably furnished and there was a well-equipped kitchen.

"This is lovely," I observed, trying to make conversation with this silent stranger. "Hardly what I would call a bunkhouse."

He shrugged. "VCR's busted. You're down here."

I followed him to the end of a fairly long hallway. We passed four closed doors on either side, each with a shiny brass deadbolt.

"Got you in the bridal suite," he said without humor as he unclipped a key from his ring and opened the door. "You'll be plenty comfortable. Good idea to keep your door locked at all times. We get druggies around here. Steal anything isn't nailed down." He handed me the key. "That works in the front door, too. Come on back when you're ready."

The basic style was the same as Madam's room, except the carpet wasn't quite the same quality, the view was only of the trees, there was no fireplace, and the paintings above my bed were a fire-and-water-damaged set of Grandma Moses primitives. For staff quarters in a Frenchman's house, it was pretty good. On a scale of one-to-ten, I gave it a four.

After I unpacked, hanging my three dark suits and six white shirts in the narrow closet, arranged my toiletries, and freshened up in the clean, compact bathroom—Armand had skimped again, using small-scale stainless steel fixtures intended for ships or motor homes—I hurried back down the snowy, tree-lined path, my breath visible in bursting clouds. Tucked in the woods sat another building that I knew was Armand's suite of offices. A navy blue Ford Explorer was parked at the door. Smoke curled invitingly from the chimney.

I was tempted to stick my head in the door and introduce myself to whoever was there, but it was too damned cold, it must have been ten below, and I finally ended up running as fast as I could, slipping and sliding in my hard-soled city shoes, back to the main house and into the now-empty kitchen, which was as clean as an operating room and smelled of fresh ginger and roasted garlic. The stone counters and freshly scrubbed floor gleamed. A dozen bundles of pencil-thin spring asparagus tied with strips of lemon peel soaked upright in a pan of water, and next to them was a square pan of what looked like elk steaks marinating in soy sauce and smeared with a soft garlic and pungent ginger paste.

Two places, with red-checked napkins and reed placemats, were set for lunch on the counter, and while I waited for Suzie and Matt to reappear, I helped myself to a handful of cashews and studied the seating chart taped next to the swinging door in the pantry.

Jacqueline di Fidelio

Junior Hammond and guest

Victor and Babette Meredith. (I didn't recognize the name.)

Thomas and Maria Weicker. (Thomas was a Pole or a Czech who lived in Toronto. His realistic street scenes were big in Japan.)

Count and Countess Hubert de Varon

Mr. Weil

What a perfect ten. For an Agatha Christie book.

I was itching to get to the basement—the urge was spreading on me like poison ivy. Da-da-da-daaah. Da-da-duh-duuuh. I pushed an unruly hank of hair off my brow and wished I had a buzz-cut like Tom Cruise.

Suzie bumped through the door, dust rag in hand. "Ready for lunch?" she asked. She was slightly overweight—nothing like Bianca Roosevelt, but as plump as you'd like your cook to be. Someone who obviously enjoyed food and partook regularly. Her blonde hair was pulled into a twist and her yellow and red chef's apron said "Picasso Rules." She had on jeans and hiking boots, and her denim shirtsleeves were rolled up, showing well-muscled forearms. Her hands were wide and clean.

"Yes," I said eagerly. "I'm hungry."

"Well, just plant your butt right there," she indicated a stool, "and I'll be with you in a jiffy. Do you know all the guests?"

"I think I do, except for the Merediths."

"He's the guy who owns that big leasing company—planes, trains, boats, and automobiles. You know, super-tankers. Seven-forty-sevens. Oil field equipment. Mega-collector of early twentieth-century industrial realism; you know, that Russian revolutionary stuff. His wife's been his wife for about thirty years. Nice couple, not like some of the art groupies he invites up here." She turned on the flame beneath a covered pan, lifted the lid, stirred, whapped the spoon a couple of times on the edge of the pan, and replaced the top. "The de Varons are just friends of Armand's, not especially rich, no important collection, just friends. Normal people. Hubie and Veronika."

"Right. I've met them a number of times."

"And Armand's high on Weicker these days. Coors or Diet Coke?"

"A beer sounds fine, thanks."

"Be careful at this altitude. A little liquor goes a long way."

"I'll keep that in mind." I poured the golden, foamy liquid into a pilsner glass. "The bunkhouse is nice."

"We like it. Monte Cristo sound okay?"

"Yes. Wonderful. Are those elk steaks?"

"Sure are."

"I never serve elk because it always turns out tough and harsh."

"This marinade makes it melt in your mouth. I'll give you the recipe. Soup?"

"No thanks. How many of us are in the bunkhouse?"

"This weekend? Just you, William, Matt, and me."

"William?"

"Armand's assistant."

The back door crashed open, aided by a strong kick from a heavy boot, and Matt, trailed by two identical Alaskan malamutes, tromped in loaded with firewood, which he dumped noisily into a bin by the back door. The dogs went immediately to their rugs and never took their eyes off Matt.

"You want a Monte Cristo, honey?" Suzie asked. "Or Cantonese saffron chicken noodle?"

"Both."

"Plant it."

He put his butt on the stool next to mine without being told twice and sat like a five-year-old, eagerly waiting for his lunch. Spoke not one word. Typical westerner: close-mouthed, suspicious, contentious, and invariably easy to trick. I knew I'd be able to talk my way into the basement in nothing flat.

"What are your dogs' names?" I asked.

"Sugar," he grumbled. They perked up their ears.

"What about the other?"

"They're identical twin litter mates so I call them both Sugar. They don't know they're two different dogs."

Interesting.

"Do you stay here all year?" I asked. Suzie placed a steaming bowl of soup before Matt.

"Yeah."

"Now, honey," she teased. "You know that's not completely true. We're not here *all* year," she said to me. "We go to the Club Med in Cancún for a couple of weeks in the winter and then up to Lake Arrowhead with our folks in the summer."

"Sounds nice."

"Ummm." Matt shrugged and sucked in a mouthful of Cantonese saffron noodles that whipped around his beard like yellow worms before disappearing between his lips.

"Is Mr. Weil here very often?"

"Couple of weeks in the winter, couple in the summer."

"This is a big ship to keep afloat for a month a year."

"Lots of places up here a lot bigger than this and some years no one comes to 'em at all." Matt ended the exchange.

On the other side of the counter, Suzie flipped the batter-soaked sandwiches, and as their toasty fragrance began to fill the air, my mouth began to water. I didn't know how many years it had been since I'd had a Monte Cristo. I avoid them because they're nothing more than pure fat—ham and cheese grilled in butter between egg-and-milk-dipped white bread—but when she opened that jar of Fortnum and Mason currant jelly and spooned it onto the plates, I decided I wanted two.

"Everything's probably self-contained," I observed between bites—it was like eating delicious feathers, little mouthfuls of butter-jelly air. "Generators and all. Pretty complicated, I imagine."

"Yeah. Our heating, ventilation, and electrical systems are as fancy as a nuclear sub's," he bragged.

"And probably just as hard to run."

"Nah. Pretty easy if you know what you're doing. I was in the Navy, worked in the engine room of the *Daniel Boone*."

"So you really know what you're doing."

He gave me a contemptuous snort.

"I'd love a tour."

"You would?" He looked at me skeptically. "Really?"

"Really," I said firmly.

"Okay," he shrugged and sucked in a big slurp of espresso.

Candy from a baby.

The basement had a wine cellar with more rows of racks than many liquor stores and a central table for twelve; a fully-equipped gym with a treadmill, StairMaster, weight equipment, a sauna, steam room, and racketball court; a mechanical systems room with generators, furnaces, hundred-gallon hot water tanks, air conditioning and electronic communications networks big enough to serve a good-sized hotel; and a brightly-lit gallery hung with a dozen Peter Max bouquets in a dozen different colors. There were closed double doors at the end.

"What's down there?" I asked.

"Store room. I've never been in there but William says it's full of paintings. He and Armand keep it locked. Well, that's it." Matt shut off the lights and I followed him back up the stairs. "You've seen the works."

"Impressive. Especially that compressor."

"She's a beauty."

"Jackie's looking for you," Suzie said when we got back to the kitchen. It was after four o'clock.

"Jackie?" I asked.

"You know," she gave me a funny look. "The lady you work for."

Armand. Jackie. What happened to sir and madam? No manners in the Rockies. Why don't we do it in the road?

31

"Armand says there's a gym downstairs." Madam was pulling on her leggings. I'd passed Armand on the way up to his room. He had on a white terry cloth robe and I'd heard his phone ringing in a pocket.

"Yes, a wonderful one. Do you want me to show you where it is?"

This was silly. We were speaking in code, as if her suite were bugged.

I led her back to the pantry and down the stairs to the basement, past the wine cellar, to the glass door of the mirror-walled gym. She indicated with her head down the hall toward the locked doors at the far end. "Is that it?"

"I think so. It should be."

The gym was empty and the house was quiet. The other guests, too tired for more exercise after their day on the mountain, had all returned and gone to their rooms for naps or for a deep soak in their individual Jacuzzis. I could hear the four one-hundred-gallon hot water tanks humming in Matt's engine room.

"I'm going to keep an eye out here," Madam said. "You go see what's what."

My hair stood on end. "Me?" I whined. "I really don't want to, Madam. What if someone comes?" Now that the time to stand and deliver had materialized, I didn't like this nearly as much as I thought I would. Not at all. This wasn't daring or romantic, it was foolhardy. Memories of prison flooded my mind and I could feel my bowels begin to threaten.

"Just pretend you're admiring the art. Go on, Nigel. Nobody's going to come down here, they're all asleep."

"What if someone does?" I hated the sound of my voice, it had gone all high and nasal on me. "How will you alert me?"

"You mean like a signal?"

"Yes, a signal."

"I'll have a coughing fit."

Talk about a rinky-dink operation. "You're never going to make it in the big leagues, Madam."

"Go on." She was growing impatient.

"All right," I said, petulantly. "I will." I cleared my throat and squared my shoulders, pretending I was brave and that this was not reality, that I was in a movie. I approached the door like a true professional actor: cautiously, respectfully, and confidently. I would take no back-talk from this goddamned door. I think I was also experiencing some arterial fibrillation because a non-stop flutter winged my chest and my breath came in shallow little puffs. I didn't bother to mention this to Madam because she would have been completely unsympathetic—our whole future depended on me at this moment, on my prowess. Oh, how I hate to be counted on. I lost my nerve. I stopped and turned to Madam.

"All I want to be is a cheerleader."

"For God's sake, Nigel, will you just *do* it? You're there. Just check out the doors."

They had a standard deadbolt, nothing fancy. I jimmied the lock easily with my Visa card, and peeked inside. There was a stairway, as wide as the doors, and in the darkness, I could make out the landing at the bottom. Across the landing were what looked like sliding steel gates, the kind used at banks or department stores, with a big lock in the middle where they joined. Talk about rinky-dink. I glanced back at Madam. She motioned me to go further, and just as I stepped through the door, she sneezed violently and began to cough. I looked back, and saw a man's foot appear around the corner. Madam coughed more; she could have passed for a tubercular. I was in no-man's-land. Jesus Lord, if I get caught down here, I'll be in jail forever. I slipped inside, pulled the door closed behind me, turned the lock as quietly as I could—hopefully the sound was covered by the racket of the coughs—and started to pray.

Then I noticed a peephole in the door and put my eye to it. A man in a sport coat and slacks, presumably William, Armand's assistant, had his arm around Madam's shoulders and was helping her toward the stairs. She was doubled over with her fit and limped along beside him. The second they rounded the corner, I let myself out and raced back down the hall, through the gym, and into the steam room, where I stripped off all my clothes and lay on the slippery white tile bench praying I would die.

32

*M*att had dusted himself up pretty well for dinner, putting on clean Levis, a pressed white shirt, a plaid wool tie, and a white apron. He was in charge of the dining room, and I was acting as his assistant. Most of his direction was given with a jerk of his bearded chin or an off-hand wave of his meaty arm; it was a little like mind-reading to determine exactly what he wanted, but this wasn't exactly rocket science, and certain specific actions had to occur before the next could follow. For instance, the first course—vegetable broth with cheese croutons—had to be cleared before the next—the elk steaks, asparagus, and grilled slices of roasted-red-pepper polenta—could be served. We seemed to get along just fine.

"You stole her right out from under my nose," Junior Hammond proclaimed from where he sat between his companion for the weekend,

Kiffany, a late-youngish/early-oldish woman who looked as tough as a bear, and Madam, the unofficial houseparty hostess.

Madam had on red shantung pants and a black cashmere tunic that kept threatening to slide off one of her shoulders. The gardenias in her hair were fresh and fragrant. She was the only one who was not sunburned, but her cheeks bloomed with happiness and she smiled down the table at Armand through the candlelight.

As impossible as it may sound, Junior appeared to have gained weight since New York. He looked hot and uncomfortable in a tight Tyrolean jacket. The heavy boiled wool had begun to shred down the back seam and the braid-trimmed sleeves crept up his arms. Junior's omnivorous instincts were more fully developed than any man's I'd ever seen. He fed himself like a bull elephant frantically ripping off tree tops and cramming them into his mouth with his trunk. He ate insatiably, with his arms bowed protectively around his plate. He'd chew only once or twice, add a quaff of the '78 Chateau Petrus, mush it all together and swallow. Never touched the asparagus.

"What are you talking about?" Armand laughed.

"Jackie girl, here." Junior used his knife to point to Madam. "Things were going just fine, I was even getting to first base—although she may deny it, I know I was—and then, whammo, you *steal* her."

"Junior, will you stop," Madam was laughing, too. "Besides, you weren't even close to first base."

"I'll tell you what. I'll make you a bet. This Armand character, I know him, he's my best friend, and if you can crack through and get him to spend one day—I'm talking twenty-four hours—without doing business, I'll give a million dollars to your favorite charity."

"What if I can't?" She went along.

"You have to give me another run at you."

"Give you another *run* at me? You mean like I'm a target and you're a bull?"

Junior roared with delight.

"Deal," said Madam.

Oh, Lord, I thought.

"Hot damn." Junior raised his tightly-wrapped arms into the air, shredding the jacket even further, and curled his hands into balls, keeping his index fingers out straight like the six-shooters he liked to wield, cocked his thumbs, and fired. "I get another shot."

"Not so fast," Armand said good-naturedly. "You have to give me a chance."

"Okay," Junior said affably. "I'll even let you pick the twenty-four hours."

Madam turned to Armand. "Well?" She smiled.

Everyone at the table knew Armand well enough to realize what a completely impossible challenge this would be for him despite his best intentions. He rolled the deep-ruby wine in his glass and took a thoughtful sip. "All right. The middle of May. Come to Nepal with me. I'm meeting some friends to take one of Patty's treks. I promise you, I will not talk on the phone for a week."

Everyone laughed and clapped. Madam grinned at Armand. A tight little grin, more a pursing of the lips, a locking of the jaw actually, if you knew her well, which I did.

I almost screamed. I've never been to Nepal, but I've heard enough stories about the conditions there to curl my hair. This would be one trip she would have to take on her own. Even if she invited me, I would have to decline. I wouldn't be caught dead over there. They don't even have plumbing.

"No way," Junior complained. "How will I know you're not lying? I'm not going on one of Patty's stupid, goddamn hikes. She hates me. She'd push me off a cliff." He turned to Madam and took her hand. "You would *hate* it. My sister treats her customers like *dogs*. She only lets you take what you can carry. Her trips are barbaric."

"That is singularly untrue," Armand said. "They cost ten times more than anyone else's partly because they are so comfortable."

Madam's eyes swept back and forth between the two men before settling on Armand. She rearranged the tunic on her shoulder, then touched her napkin to the corner of her lips, never taking her eyes off his as she contemplated her reply.

"Armand, my dearest darling," she finally spoke. There was lightness and humor to her voice, but only a thin veneer's worth. "I thought you knew me better than that. There is nothing on this earth, not you, or even Junior's million dollars for my favorite charity, that could get me to go to Nepal, or Bhutan, or for that matter, anywhere there's not a Four

Seasons Hotel. For any reason. I'd be totally miserable. And what's worse, I'd make sure you and everybody in a hundred mile radius was as miserable as I was. You'd end up pushing *me* off a cliff just to shut me up. It would be horrible."

"It will be divine. We'll share a sleeping bag."

"Are you *insane?* A sleeping bag? I'd rather be shot than camp out."

"I'm with you, Jacqueline," Countess Veronika chimed in.

"Me, too," said Babette Meredith.

"See?" Madam held her hands out. "I have a rule: Unless it's business, I never stay anywhere that isn't nicer than my home. I'm afraid you'll have to come up with some other suggestion. Nepal is definitely out."

Right on, Madam.

"I'll make sure we have lots of help," Armand said. "Lots of porters." And then, I could have sworn, he looked directly at me.

Not on your life, mister.

"Not enough nig . . ." Junior began but stopped mid-word at a piercing glance from Madam. ". . . *Sherpas* on the planet to get me on one of those things." Nobody had to point out that for Junior to make a trek, he'd have to lose at least two-hundred pounds, and once he finally got out on the trail, if his sister didn't push him off a cliff, the nigras most assuredly would. I'd be leading the charge.

"I'm sorry to say, Armand, I'm totally with Junior and Veronika and Babette on this," Madam said. I wondered if anyone else noticed how much tighter her voice got each time she spoke. "There are not enough Sherpas on the planet. My makeup alone takes up one whole suitcase. How about Bali? Let's go there for a week instead."

"Bali's lovely," Mrs. Meredith said. "We were there last month at the Four Seasons. Absolutely magnificent."

"I'm already pledged to the Nepalese trip," Armand said cautiously. "Let's see what we can work out." For the first time, I sensed competition between them.

The rest of the table ignored the tension and headed into new territory as Matt and I cleared. The conversation revolved around various trips where the guests had been forced to "rough-it," such as a trip to Antarctica and the Galapagos Islands where all the food on the ship had spoiled and everyone got food poisoning and they only had potato chips and beer for ten days. Or when Mr. Meredith and some of his pals had gone fishing in Alaska and the pilot who was supposed to pick them up crashed in a ball of flame and no one knew they were out there until his wife called the National Park Service. Or, when Madam and I got stuck at the end of the runway in Dakar for twelve hours in a full 747, in July. You want to talk about *miserable,* I wanted to say.

Across the table, Matt's eyes searched out mine and he held up an empty bottle of wine and three fingers. At the same time, Junior struggled to his feet. "Where's the little boy's room?" His body radiated heat like a furnace, and his turtleneck looked as if it were strangling him to death, pushing all his blood into his face.

"Allow me to show you, sir," I said. "I'm on my way for more wine." As he followed me out of the dining room, his breathing was labored, each breath almost a gasp.

"Are you feeling all right, Mr. Hammond?" I asked.

"Altitude's about to kill me."

He sounded as if it were true.

We had reached the guest bath and I flipped on the light. "Is there anything else I can do for you?" I asked.

"Not unless you want to come in and hold my dick." He let out a rattling blast of gas and closed the door.

I hated his guts.

The basement was quiet as a tomb, not the slightest indication there was a raucous party going on overhead. As long as I'm down here anyway for the wine, I thought, I'll take this opportunity for another quick peek into the vault. I tiptoed, even though my footsteps were silenced by the thick wall-to-wall carpeting. Tom Cruise would have been impressed. Da-da-dah-dah. Da-da-duh-duh. When I reached the doors to the vault, I saw just the thinnest band of light along the bottom. Was someone in there? And then I heard footsteps on the cement steps behind them. Coming up.

Oh, my God. I turned and ran as fast as I could to the wine cellar, rushing into its farthest depth, darting beyond the racks of burgundies, beyond the bordeaux, all the way to the sauternes, where I crouched like the coward I was. My heart was pounding like a jackhammer.

"Is anyone in here?" a voice called.

I didn't answer. I don't know why. I wasn't doing anything wrong, I had come for more wine, that was my job. But I was completely paralyzed with fear, my breath locked in place around my racing heart. I had an overwhelming urge to urinate.

"Huh," the voice said again. "I could have sworn I heard someone." He turned off the wine room lights, closed and locked the grilled door, and left. It was quiet, with only the sound of his padded steps going away, ascending the stairs. I was in pitch blackness—not a hint of light anywhere, sealed in, just like the man in *A Cask of Amantillado*. I heard the door at the top of the stairs close. All I could think about was how badly I needed to go to the bathroom. I couldn't stand it any longer. I got stiffly to my feet and, feeling my way to the far end of the row, unzipped my trousers and there, among the collection of thousand-dollar-a-bottle dessert wines, went on the floor in what I prayed was a corner.

I couldn't believe it. I was locked in. What a fool. I tried to feel my way back, going slowly along the racks, but they had become a maze. Just when I was sure I was near the door, I'd dead-end into another wall of bottles. I wasn't afraid. I knew, sooner or later, Matt would wonder what had happened and come fetch the wine himself. But, in the meantime, I'd never felt so stupid in my life. Fortunately, within a matter of minutes the lights came back on and Matt came to my rescue.

"What happened?" His smile was big from inside his beard.

"I was back pulling the bottles, and all of a sudden it went dark and the door was locked."

"Must have been William. He gets all paranoid when I leave the wine unlocked." He handed me four bottles of the Petrus and jerked his chin toward the back of the cellar. "Might as well grab four of those Yquems while we're here, save us a trip."

"Oh, let me. I'd already selected them." I dashed back to the dessert wine section. If he discovered what I'd done, that I'd left a puddle in the corner, I'd have to kill myself. Or blame it on the dogs.

33

*W*omen, I mused, as I refilled the wine glasses, if they want—or in our case *need*—to have a lot of money and aren't able to earn it themselves, they have three choices among the kinds of men they can marry to get it.

There are men like Armand, dashing, driven, and self-made. These are men who can generate huge sums and are typically charming only in short bursts, like sound bites, between meetings. Madam could have (although she hadn't) complained that Armand worked too much; but on the other hand, it kept him surrounded by interesting people—those who could afford to do business with him, who shared his interests in the collection of world-class art or wanted to learn from him. He was like a steam engine, a self-perpetuating machine, an energy field all his own who was able to serve what looked like an unlimited quantity of exquisite wine, to fly unpasteurized cheeses directly from France on his own jet, be beguiling when the situation required it, and vicious as a barracuda all the rest of the time.

Or there are men like Junior, who had inherited their wealth and worked just enough to perpetuate it, but who, by and large, took luxuries for granted and let others on their payroll make the deals. These men were engaged to an extent *in* the club because they owned the companies, but they were not *of* the club, that wolf-pack of super alpha males who made things happen.

Or, finally, there are the men who had inherited their money and did nothing but hang around the clubs, bums like Ryder. Now, which would *I* prefer for Madam? Armand, *bien sur,* but with Junior's schedule and money. But then, he wouldn't be Armand.

It had begun to snow, a peaceful falling of flakes as large as rose petals.

"This is our special springtime snow," Armand explained. "It's called corn snow, light and fluffy. It's so forgiving, it makes everyone ski like a champion."

"Good," said Madam. "I'll need all the help I can get."

"What time are we going to head out in the morning?" one of the guests asked.

"Whenever you like," Armand replied. "Matt will drive you to the lift. But I think ten o'clock is usually best. By then the crowd at the bottom has thinned slightly and you don't have to wait quite so long. Or you can stay in bed and simply come to the club for lunch at twelve-thirty."

I placed the cheese platter on the table between him and Countess Veronika.

"I want everyone to try the Louveran," Armand said. "Suzie left it on the counter for two days. Wait till you taste it with the Petrus . . ." He kissed his fingertips. "I bought this particular vintage at auction. It's a 1978 Colombard Vineyard. Almost as magnificent as you, Jacqueline." Madam blew him a kiss and raised her glass.

The dining room was laden with candles. On the table were six tapers in wrought-iron candlesticks with hammered iron cut-outs of elk soldered to their bases, and two dozen votives in little iron cubes with cut-outs of stars on their sides, and there were more on the sideboards. The flickering light made the cheeses look like creamy clumps of molten gold and turned the wine dark purple, almost black.

"Junior," Madam asked, "how is your father doing? Is he beginning to recover from Bianca's death? And Lynette's? What horrible blows for him."

Junior's jowls expanded and contracted like bellows as he nodded his head. "It's sad. His girls were his little darlings. It's really knocked him down. Ever since Mama died, the girls have looked after him, taken turns going down to the ranch every couple of weeks, making sure the Mexicans were doing right by him."

He just couldn't resist, could he?

"I go down every now and then, but the girls were his babies. Daddy Rex and his babies—he always had Mama dress them up like twins, even though they weren't, all in ruffles and ribbons—and then he'd drive them all over the county in his Cadillac convertible and they'd sit up on the back like little beauty queens."

"Don't you have another sister?" Victor Meredith asked, looking curiously from Armand to Junior. "Weren't we just talking about her?"

"Patty," Junior answered, slathering hunks of butter and Camembert onto a cracker. "She's my baby sister. She and Daddy Rex have never been close. She's pretty damn independent. Kinda masculine. Bianca and Lynette were girly-girls, and that's how Daddy Rex likes 'em."

Girly-girls who looked like football players in drag. I filled Junior's glass for the fiftieth time. It was opaque and gooey with fingerprints.

"Like Kiffany, here." He squeezed his consort's thigh. She let out a little squeal. "She's as girly as they get."

At that moment, Madam's eyes met Junior's and with that one look, she stripped away all his buffonish pretense. She could see into people. That was her profession—to look deep, watch carefully, and listen patiently for the subtext. While no one else at the table probably noticed, a look of intense longing came across his face—an expression that revealed all the pain of his sisters' being their daddy's favorite, of him being their daddy's disappointment, of his loneliness for the love and understanding of someone as solid as my Madam. It even made me a little sorry for him. At that moment, he reminded me of a very, very sad pig.

"So!" Armand clapped his hands and rubbed them together. "Eleven o'clock. What shall we do? We can stay here and have a little chocolate soufflé and Chateau d'Yquem and watch it snow, or, I propose we go to town, listen to Bobby Halladay at the Caribou Club, and have a coffee or a brandy."

The table murmured a round of assent and got to their feet.

"Armand," Madam said, "do you mind if I don't come along? If I just go to bed? I'm completely exhausted—it's after one o'clock at home and you know me, I'm asleep by ten."

He ran his hand across her shoulders and pulled her close, then kissed the side of her head. "Do you mind if I go?"

"Of course not. They're your guests. Just don't be gone too long."

"Should I waken you when I get back?"

"I can't wait." She turned her body to his, and I felt as if I were standing next to an atomic bomb.

Madam's nightie, a caramel-colored cotton jersey trimmed with white binding, was laid out on her bed, a fresh carafe of water was on the bed table, the fire crackled cheerfully, the lights were dimmed, and I was just on my way out of her suite and over to my own, when she opened the door. "Is there anything else, Madam?" I asked.

"Where do you think you're going?"

"I . . . I . . . I thought I'd retire," I stuttered.

"Are you kidding?"

"Pardon?" A creeping feeling of doom began to spread.

"We have to get to work, Nigel. Down to the basement."

"Oh, Madam. Oh, Madam. I have a very bad feeling about the basement. We have to find another solution. I got locked in the wine cellar tonight. I don't want to go down there again. Please."

"Don't be ridiculous." She was busily unzipping her travel bag, from which she withdrew two matte black, rubber-encased flashlights, the sort security guards carry—each one must have had five batteries stacked end-to-end. Then came two disposable flash cameras, each with thirty-six exposures. "You didn't think I really wanted to go to bed, did you? I'm *dying* to go to the Caribou Club—it's the most talked-about club in the country. You know me better than that, Nigel."

Yes. Unfortunately I did. Deep down I'd known nothing about this holiday weekend was going to be pleasant or easy.

"I just want to get this part of the trip over with so I can relax and have a little fun. I know he doesn't have any stolen paintings down there." She was looking out the window, watching for the headlights of the Ford Excursion to depart. She turned to face me. "I *hate* this. I want to tell him, but I keep thinking if I can just get into that vault, snap a bunch of pictures to prove the paintings aren't there, I won't ever have to think about it again. He'll never have to know." The headlights arced through the snow like beams from a lighthouse, pointed out the gate, and disappeared down the mountain. "Come on. Let's go."

I trailed behind her along the dim gallery, illuminated only by the gentle spotlights on the paintings, down the stairs to the dark basement, where we clicked on our flashlights and followed their white circles to the tall doors. She took my torch and held both beams on the lock while I jimmied it open for the second time that day. We crept inside, closed the door behind us, and descended the wide cement steps to the landing and the locked accordion gates. Instead of beckoning me, as it had earlier in the day when it was only a fantasy, the vault felt like a giant, hostile, silent cave, full of sticky cobwebs and dangerous monsters. It smelled of cold cement, oil paint, and old canvas.

"What do you think?" She turned the flashlights on the gate locks.

"Basic," I said and went to work. There was a central key lock and a padlock attached to a chain that ran through the open grillwork on either side.

"Oh, my God," Madam suddenly said. She had moved the beams from where I was working, leaving the locks in the dark, and shone them into the vault. "Will you look at that."

Hundreds and hundreds of paintings hung on metal frames that reached twenty feet high. "Madam," I whispered. "The light."

"Oh, I'm sorry."

My hands were shaking but I finally got both locks undone and we slid the gates far enough apart to squeeze through. The vault was packed with paintings of every size, style, and medium—oils, pastels, watercolors, and acrylics. Directly in front of us, at the bottom of the stairs, in the center of a wide aisle that ran between the racks like an alley, sat an Ormolu desk as large and imposing as a dining table. A red and gold Napoleonic crest, large as a Roman shield and intricate as a wedding cake, was attached to the front by gilt wings that curved back up to the table top. This must have been the emperor's personal desk, I thought, not only because of the crest, but also because gold trim flared out from its corners like large epaulets. Two double candlestick lamps, a telephone, a fax-machine, and a good-sized humidor sat on its glowing surface. An armchair with a Napoleonic coat-of-arms was on the far side, with two visitors chairs in front.

"You start over there," Madam indicated the section to the left. "I'll start here and we'll work toward the center. You do know what the Vermeer looks like, don't you?"

"Girl with a violin?" I asked.

"Yes, and just in case, the other three major missing Gardner works are Rembrandt's *Lady and Gentleman in Black,* she's in a chair to the right in front of a red curtain, and he's more central, full-body."

"Righto."

"*Storm on the Sea of Galilee,* another Rembrandt."

"Madam, we should get started."

"One more, the Manet, *Chez Tortoni,* waist up, man in a black top hat."

"Thank you."

Each panel held as few as two, and as many as eight paintings, depending on their size. I knew the Vermeer was tiny, so I flipped through the bigger paintings as fast as I could, but I couldn't help noticing that most of them looked very, very familiar. And then, there it was, right before my eyes: the Renoir. Lynette Payne's Renoir of the flower market. *Matin de Juin.* I had just opened my mouth to call to Madam when all the lights came on.

34

"What do you think you're doing in here?" a man's voice demanded. I peeked around the edge of a panel and saw him addressing Madam, who returned his glare with her own. I don't think he knew I was there. Oh, Lord, what to do. I was getting to hate my job. I wasn't Madam's mother. I didn't need to risk bodily harm to protect her. She was twice my size, and in fact, she was a lot bigger than this man who confronted her. So why did I find myself tiptoeing up behind him, my flashlight held like a cudgel in my hand?

"Hello, William," she said calmly.

"I repeat, Miss di Fidelio, what are you doing in here?" He had a slight accent, possibly Welsh.

He was about my size. Bald.

"I can't tell you," Madam answered.

I edged closer and closer, until I could see the wrinkles in the seat of his pants, and a light sheen of oil on his smooth pate. He smelled of almond soap.

"I'll have to notify Mr. Weil." William pulled a phone from his jacket pocket and flipped it open with one hand. I heard the beep as he pushed the send button.

My arm was raised to strike. I held my breath. And then, at the last second, just when I was about to squeeze my eyes shut and do it, he turned around. He had a *gun*. Pointed right at my mid-section. Oh, my God. I didn't know he had a gun.

"Don't shoot!" I screamed, dropped my bludgeon, and stuck my arms straight into the air.

William took a couple of steps back and spoke into the phone. "Sorry to disturb you, sir. But I got an alarm in the vault and discovered Miss di Fidelio and Mr. Weatherby-Smythe snooping around with flashlights."

"We were not *snooping*," Madam snapped at him. "We were reconnoitering."

"Yes, sir." William said and closed the phone. He indicated the desk. "Will you please sit down," he said politely, removing Madam's torch as she passed him, "until Mr. Weil arrives."

There was something very familiar about William, and as I sat in my assigned seat and studied him, it hit me. "Fernando?" I said tentatively. "Is that you?"

He gave me an affectionate smile, his small teeth an even string of pearls beneath his now-full mustache. "Yes, Nigel, it's me."

My heart soared. "You're alive?"

"You two know each other?" Madam said.

We ignored her.

"But how?" I said.

"It's a long story, too long for now. But my name's William, not Fernando."

I was too stunned to speak. I just gaped, my mouth hanging wide open, like a big fool.

"What's going on here?" Madam drummed her fingers on the table impatiently.

"I think we should be quiet until Mr. Weil arrives," William said.

"You aren't really going to hold us prisoner, are you?"

"I'm sorry, but those were my instructions from Mr. Weil."

"At gun-point?" She was remarkably cool.

"No, probably not." William loosened his grip on the firearm, but it remained alongside his hand on the gilt-edged leather desk top.

I studied him. He was as wonderful to look at as I remembered. More wonderful actually, without the toupee. Not handsome at all, just full of life. His dark eyes flashed over at me and I saw in them the ironic humor I had loved so much. I wanted to jump across the table and hug him, I was so happy. He was literally back from the dead. I wanted to jump for joy.

"Wait a minute," Madam said. "I know who you are. You were Lynette Payne's butler. Right?"

"Yes, Madam, that is correct," William said politely.

"I thought you were dead."

"As you can see, I am not."

"But . . ."

William jumped to his feet as footsteps quickly approached down the hall, and then Armand appeared at the open doors and marched down the steps like a Gestapo officer to where we lingered like prisoners of war awaiting orders for our execution.

He was furious. "What's going on?" His voice was controlled but his eyes were on fire. And Madam, who by then had worked up a pretty good umbrage of her own, began to get to her feet. "You sit down!" Armand roared.

"I discovered them in the dark, using these industrial flashlights to sort through the racks, Mr. Weil," William offered. The torches incriminated by their sheer size—these were not typical traveler's aids to find the bathroom in the dark, or even what a cat burglar would use to crack a safe.

"Jacqueline?" His eyes searched hers, nonplused. "Please convince me you had a good reason to do this."

We waited. Her normal reaction would be to attack, head for his eyes with her nails and scratch them out, not literally, but she was an accomplished offensive player, a stare-down artist. I counted to ten while they glared at each other, anticipating the launch, and then a remarkable, once-in-a-lifetime occurrence: She started to cry. I was astonished. I guess the months of pressure had finally gotten to her and she could not control her feelings any longer. She broke down. Not the movie star weep women occasionally use when all else fails, but real sobbing, as though her heart had cracked in two. William pulled open the desk drawer and handed her a tissue, but Armand watched coldly, unmoved. Finally, I couldn't stand it anymore, and moved to comfort her.

"Leave her alone," he ordered. "Let her get a hold of herself. I want to hear her story."

The bastard.

"I do have a reason," Madam finally said. "But I don't think you're going to think it's a very good one."

"I'm all ears. Take as long as you like."

He remained standing, his arms crossed unsympathetically across his chest, zero expression on his face, his sapphire eyes now black and hard as coal. She told him the whole story; about how the IRS and the FBI had come to the farm in November and offered her a deal she had to accept. She described in detail how the agents had provided Armand's schedule and a map of his house, and suggested how she could get close to him, starting with painting Lynette Payne's portrait. They knew the Hammonds were among his biggest clients and that he would be unable to decline an invitation from any one of them. She told him everything, and the more she talked the angrier he became.

"You mean all this has been phony?" He was incredulous. "All this love is fake? You have been manipulating me right from the start?"

"No." She started to cry again. "I love you so much I can hardly stand it. You can't imagine how this has been making me feel, Armand. I'm glad you know, glad it's out. The lie was killing me. I was going to tell you anyway."

"When?"

"This weekend."

"And you honestly thought I had the stolen paintings? You think I *steal* to make my living?" I kept my mouth shut, but judging by the trillions of dollars worth of famous works hanging in this cave, it was a reasonable assumption. She shook her head and drew in her breath, struggling for composure.

"Do you think I'm a thief?"

"No." Madam blew her nose noisily, mopped the tears off her cheeks, and pushed a few undone strands of hair off her face. "No, of course I don't think you're a thief, but—" There was the glimmer of a twinkle in her eye, which I prayed Armand would not see. This was no time for mischief or an attack of hysterical laughter, "—I must say, I am more than a little curious about what you are doing with some of this stuff."

"You think I stole all these paintings?" His eyes cast down the racks. "Some of the most famous, valuable paintings in the world are in this vault. If they've all been stolen, don't you think someone would notice?"

"You have to understand," she pleaded. "It doesn't matter what I think. Their threats were absolutely devastating. They were going to take everything. Everything. My farm, all my possessions. You're a rich man, Armand. Powerful. You have yourself protected. I don't. I barely hold it all together. Ask Nigel—his paycheck bounces half the time. I didn't have any choice but to cooperate. I don't blame you if you don't ever speak to me again, but I want you to know, I love you more than you can imagine. It's true, I manipulated you and tricked you. I wish it weren't so. I'd do anything to change it."

"You are a pathetic bitch," he said and turned his back on her.

We all sat, afraid to breathe.

Eventually, Armand sat down on the steps, put his elbows on his knees, and ran his hands tiredly across his face. He and William stared at each other. My elation at seeing Fernando, now William, was tempered by the fact that Madam and I had obviously stumbled onto some sort of an art fraud operation of monumental, international proportions. As the men continued their silent communion, I sensed we were in great danger. It would be easy for them to make us disappear.

35

*G*et a bottle of brandy, William," Armand said. "The four of us need to talk."

No one moved or spoke while William was out of the room, we kept our eyes and thoughts to ourselves. I studied the floor and walls and ceiling. They were the most perfectly poured concrete I'd ever seen, not a flaw or air bubble disturbed any surface. We were deep in the mountain and we could scream as loudly as we wanted, no one would ever hear us. No one would ever find us. We were entombed as surely as if we were truly buried.

William returned with a bottle of Armagnac and four snifters and, as he poured, Madam examined him carefully. The longer she studied him, the deeper her frown became. I suppose it was registering with her that William was supposedly killed when the *Kiss-Kiss* exploded, but here he was. Furthermore, whoever had blown up the ship had not been apprehended, and it was possible he had been the bomber. He felt her eyes on him and returned her gaze calmly, a tiny flicker of something resembling a smile at the corners of his mouth. Was it a smile? Or the cruel little twist of a madman?

Oh, shut up, Nigel, I thought. Don't get any more carried away than you already are, or than the situation demands. But it wasn't impossible, was it? I mean, look at the circumstances.

I think it was just beginning to dawn on both of us, as we sat surrounded by hundreds of possibly stolen paintings, being served brandy by a potential mass murderer under the watchful eye of his mastermind, what gigantic peril we were in. And Madam didn't yet know the most condemning fact of all, that Lynette's rare and priceless Renoir was hanging right here, in this solid-cement, escape-proof basement, thousands of miles from the ship, ten thousand feet above sea level, in Aspen, Colorado. That, to me, more than anything, sealed the indictment against him.

"I'll do whatever you want," she said to Armand, breaking our heavy silence. "I'll do anything if you won't kill us."

"*Kill* you. My God, is that what you think I'm going to do?" Armand and William both began to laugh. "No wonder I fell in love with you, Jacqueline. You have the most wonderful imagination. Kill you? That's a good one." The words were jocular and kind, except they were spoken with no conviction or emotion. They emerged flat and dangerous as a serpent's warning hiss.

I struggled to keep my hand from shaking as I raised the snifter to my lips, which were threatening to quiver. It was not a good sign that Armand had laughed, because it introduced a new, particularly heartless element into his repertoire—the looming possibility of disengaged brutality. We were far from being out of danger. William sat back in his desk chair—Napoleon's chair, speaking of brilliant, heartless nuts—and was spinning the chamber on his revolver.

"Let's recap," Armand said tightly. "You're here to find out if I have stolen the paintings from the Gardner Museum, which I guarantee you I have not."

"Fine," Madam said, and prepared to get up. The back of her hair was starting to come unpinned, and the gardenias fell to the floor.

Armand came over, picked them up, smelled them, and laid them absently on the desk. "That's all I needed to know. I'll tell them."

"Sit down, Jacqueline. It will not be so easy." He slipped his cigarette case from his jacket pocket and offered it around. Madam accepted one of the thin cigarettes that Dunhill custom-blended for him. I declined. "Perhaps you would prefer a Havana," he said to me. "As I recall, William told me you prefer fine cigars."

I swallowed but did not answer as William opened the humidor and rotated it in my direction. "Please," he said. The selection was irresistible—the full range of Cohibas. I was careful not to meet his gaze as I helped myself to the largest, a seven-inch-long Esplendido. If this was going to be my last, I wanted to make sure it was a good one—a cigar worth dying for.

"As you can see," Armand had returned to his seat on the steps—carefully shaking out and straightening the creases in his gabardines before bending his legs—and waved his arm over the vault as if in a benediction. "You and your—what exactly are you Nigel? Aide de camp?—have stupidly bumbled your way into a major aspect of my business. Now I need to determine just how compromised I have been."

"Whatever this is," Madam said. She was calmed by the cigarette, more assured. "Whatever you're doing, I don't care."

Armand laughed. "You are such an innocent. Put down the gun, William. You're making us all nervous. Put it away. Out of sight." He waited while William pulled open the desk drawer and laid the gun inside, pushed the drawer closed, locked it, and pocketed the key. "Thank you." Armand put his elbows on his knees and clasped his hands together—I noticed for the first time how incredibly long and thin his fingers were—and looked directly at Madam. Looked at her hard, as if he were trying to see all the way to the deepest depths of her soul. "I think it is very important for you to understand what I am doing, Jacqueline, because it's not nearly as ominous as it may seem. As you have no doubt noticed, this room is divided into two parts. All the paintings on the right are real, all the ones on the left are fakes. Most of them belong to clients, a few are in my own collection. The clients own the real ones *and* the copies. It all has to do with insurance. You know as well as I do, the cost of insuring works of art is prohibitive and many collectors choose not to insure them, but instead have copies made to hang in their homes. I'm certain you've come across this before, *n'est pas?*"

She nodded her head. "Often."

"Well, this is where many of the originals are. The owners give them to me for safekeeping. But, as you know, not all owners are honorable." Armand placed his hands together and seemed to examine them for a moment, as if he were praying. "There are certain collectors who *do* insure their works, arrange to have the copies stolen, claim the insurance, and then, after a reasonable period of time has passed, I assist them with making arrangements to have the original painting emerge quietly and sell privately. It's a very simple explanation and while it is not entirely legal, it is a common practice." He turned his eyes back to her. "Do you understand?"

She gave him a tentative, almost conspirational smile. "Perfectly. Everybody knows it goes on."

"That's what you're looking at—this is where all those missing pieces end up. If I were to take you through the racks, you wouldn't believe what we have down here—works much more valuable than the Gardner pieces. Now granted, outsiders might look at our operation and consider it grand theft, but William and I are in what we—and our clients—consider a service business. We never operate without the consent of our clients. We are *not* in the business of murder or intimidation, as I'm afraid you've come to believe over the last few minutes. But when the alarm went off, I'm sure you understand, we had to respond as if the worst had happened. As if we had a thief in the vault."

Madam gave me a dark look that said she would have words with me later. "Where exactly is the alarm?" she asked Armand.

"The landing is weight sensitive. If even a feather lands on it, it goes off."

Well, that was a new one on me. An entire cement slab, about ten feet square. It was just a giant scale.

The brandy had given me courage. "May I ask a question, sir?"

"Of course."

I faced William. "What about Mrs. Payne's Renoir? How did it get here?"

"What?" Madam said. "What are you talking about?"

"It's here, Madam," I answered, not taking my eyes off William's.

"Over there on the racks of fakes. And probably over there on the racks of originals."

"You're kidding." She looked at Armand incredulously. "Please tell me you didn't blow up that boat."

He held up his hands. "No. No. No. My God, Jackie, what kind of person do you think I am? You think I'd steal artwork from museums and blow up eighteen people to get my hands on a fake painting?"

She shook her head. "I certainly hope not."

"Never. But that explosion has complicated life tremendously."

We all turned to William.

"Don't look at me," he said. "I didn't blow up the boat."

"Well, then, what happened?" I pressed. The enormity of it all was settling in, making me dizzy, and deep down in my stomach I could feel the blue pilot light of my anger smoldering, threatening to ignite. I tried hard not to sound accusatory, which was, in fact, what I felt. "When I walked through the main salon, the Renoir was gone. Eighteen people ended up dead, and you and the painting show up here."

"Go ahead and tell them, William," Armand said. "We must tell all here, the stakes are high."

"I promise you, on Saint George's grave," William said, trying ineffectually to make us—me—smile. "I had nothing to do with the explosion. My assignment was to remove the painting at the end of the evening and take it off the boat. So once the guests were gone, just you and Miss di Fidelio were left and she was down on the platform with Mrs. Payne—it never crossed my mind you'd go upstairs again—I quickly removed it from the frame, rolled it up, slid it into a Fedex tube, tucked it into my jacket, and went below. I'd tied up a jet ski on the opposite side of the ship and I left just before you did. I was going over to the Federal Express drop-off and coming right back."

"You mean you planned it so the theft would be blamed on one of the guests at the party?" Madam asked.

Armand's expression indicated anything was possible, and in any case, it would have nothing to do with him. He exhaled a cloud of smoke. "Whoever. These things get tied up for years and years."

"When the boat exploded, I couldn't believe it," William continued. "I was horrified, as we all were, and when I called Armand, he arranged to fly me to Aspen that night because if anyone found out I was alive, I would be the prime suspect. So I've been keeping a low profile up here ever since."

My fury was mushrooming at an alarming rate, blossoming like a nuclear cloud. That son-of-a-bitch. Everyone in this stupid vault was a consummate liar. We had all said we loved each other at one time or another, and I think that those were the only truthful things we'd said to each other. But the fact was: many of the characteristics we loved about the others were put-ons. William wasn't a lonely butler, Madam hadn't set out to capture Armand's heart out of true affection, and Armand was as phony as a three-dollar bill. And I? Well, we all know enough about me. Who was who? And what was real?

"So you've *never* been a butler?" I asked. "Elena wasn't your wife?"

"Elena was my little sister. We were orphaned in the war and have worked together since we were children, starting off as pickpockets."

"Sort of like *Oliver?*" I asked sarcastically.

William's expression suggested he would like to receive a little sympathy. "It's not a joke, Nigel. I was devastated to lose her."

"Good," I said. "So maybe you, too, have suffered a little from this terrible tragedy, you crooked bastard."

"You aren't exactly what I'd call as pure as the driven snow," William shot back. "Being a jailbird and all."

"That was a *secret,*" I screamed and lunged across the desk. "I *trusted* you."

"Gentlemen, please." Armand leapt up and grabbed my shoulder in a vise-like grip. "Calm down, Nigel. This is getting unnecessarily hostile." I was consumed with anger. Madam raised a hand in my direction and patted the air for me to back off, but I was focused on William on the other side of the Napoleonic slab. What a liar and a turncoat he was. Whom could I ever trust? Whom could I ever love, if this was what happened? It wasn't fair. I had told him everything. We were *friends*.

"William and I have been partners for twenty-three years," Armand said. "He and Elena have posed as a variety of couples. Butler and maid, doctor and nurse, tycoon and secretary. Whatever it took to get them close enough to the works to have them vanish or be replaced."

"That's why I made such a big deal about saying I was leaving Mrs. Payne to go work in Connecticut," William explained.

I wanted to cry. I felt like such a stupid dupe, so totally betrayed, I couldn't stop the tears from running down my face. I turned away.

"But now, we have a complication," Armand continued matter-of-factly. His voice had gotten cold and analytical again. "Our business has been discovered. What to do with you." He studied Madam carefully.

"Well," she said, "I have an idea."

"Yes? I'm open to suggestions."

"Why don't you make me a partner?"

"A partner?"

"Wouldn't you like to have some of my clients as yours, too? I have access to a lot of people with important collections." She sat up straight in her chair and leaned toward him. Her red shantung pants glowed, as though she were already bleeding to death. She sounded pathetic. Wheedling was unbecoming and she knew it. "Oh, Christ, Armand. Forget it. What am I talking about? They're probably all your clients already, anyway. Why don't you just go ahead and shoot me? Get it over with. I don't think there's any solution. You won't believe how sorry I am, or how much I love you. I don't care what you do to make your living. I wouldn't care if you painted all these stupid things yourself to sell on the beach in Acapulco. You might just as well get that gun out of the desk and pull the trigger. This has been the biggest screwed-up mess of my life. The one time I really fall in love and the whole thing gets wrecked."

"Ditto," I added miserably. I agreed with every word. They might as well just kill us and shove us in the corner of this giant catacomb, get the whole mess over and done with.

"Come here." Armand took her in his arms. "Nobody's going to shoot anybody. No more talk about shooting." He stroked her hair and stared into the vault as if he were standing on a cliff above the sea watching for a ship. "Do you know you have captured my life, Jacqueline di Fidelio?"

William and I waited silently to see what that meant, what would come next. Our futures were in his hands. "Here's what we're going to do," Armand finally said. "I'll pay your tax bill and you'll help clear my name with Interpol and the FBI. I had no idea they might be on to me, the United States government never gets involved in these issues. It could doom my entire enterprise. I'm sorry you were trapped into this. I understand how hard these things can be and that you didn't have any choice."

We were all sorry, sorry for how everything had been handled, sorry for the dead, sorry for causing this anguish, but it was only I who would end up alone. I looked at William and I wanted to kill him. How dare he cause me such pain.

Later that night, just as I was ready to turn off my reading light, there was a knock at my door. All was forgiven.

36

*W*ouldn't that be a perfect ending? It's not the way it happened, but it made me feel so good to say it: All is forgiven.

I don't know where I got my lack of mercy, my suspicious nature, my inability to forgive, even when I say I have. My mother wasn't especially angry or suspicious, so it must have been my father, whom, as you know, I met as a wee child, but about whom I have no recollection except for my mother's descriptions of his heroism in battle and his sacrificial death. The white cross on his grave in Bayeux: John Smythe (I added the Weatherby to give myself a little more panache) 1918–1945. I don't know why I let things fester in my soul, but I do.

I ate my oatmeal and banana and sipped my tea and watched it snow from the cozy warmth of the bunkhouse kitchen. Matt and Suzie were already over in the main house, stoking fires and preparing breakfast for the houseguests, who'd spent a lively evening at the Caribou Club and slept soundly, oblivious to the first act of a dashing little real-life drama being played out in the basement. William had been up and gone to work before I emerged from my room, where I'd spent a restless, tortured night. It would take me ages to recover from his duplicity. I didn't care if he was a crook, I used to be one myself. But he was a liar. Oh, hell, what am I saying? I'm a liar, too. I bit into a slice of dry toast.

At eight o'clock, I balanced a breakfast tray on one hand and knocked softly on Madam's bedroom door.

"Come in," she called.

Snow-flattened morning light made the room feel cold in spite of the fact that all the lights were on and the fire had already been stoked to a roaring blaze. She and Armand were sitting in bed, covers to their waists, with CNN on the television. Armand's chest was well muscled, tan, and hairless. He was wearing his glasses and reading the *Wall Street Journal,* which William had dropped at the door earlier. Madam had on the lace-trimmed nightgown that matched the peignoir.

"Good morning, Madam," I said with a jauntiness I did not feel. "Sir. Good night's sleep?"

"You aren't going to believe this, Nigel, but guess what I'm doing to-day?" she asked.

"I could not begin to guess, Madam."

"Going skiing."

"Wonderful," I answered. "Seems a perfect day for it. It's only twenty or thirty below and snowing." I poured her coffee into a plain white breakfast cup.

The dynamics among us had changed, as they obviously had to. We now knew so much about each other, it was as if we'd been transformed or melded into an accidental family, or a gang of thieves, of highwaymen, desperadoes on the lam, hunted, fearful, and suspicious of everything and everyone, including and perhaps especially, each other. I tried to pretend it hadn't happened, tried to act as though everything was the way it had been before our wrenching discoveries, but I was still weepy and slightly afraid of what Armand would do. Apparently my phony good spirits were obvious because Armand read them perfectly and very kindly sought to reassure me.

"Nigel, we opened up a lot of doors last night, and there's no going back. We know more about each other than many friends do after years and years. We can either accept what we've learned and choose to hold together, work together, enjoy each other, and grow closer, as we were beginning to do before our revelations, or we can choose anxiety and mistrust, and destroy all our lives." He reached over and took Madam's hand. "Your Madam and I talked all night, and we realized that in spite of our counterfeit beginnings, what we feel for each other is genuine."

It could be argued that Armand was overheated, still at that stage of infatuation where he would say whatever it took to get what he wanted, to get between Madam's legs. But on the other hand, Armand wasn't a child, nor was he inexperienced. In spite of his kind, generous words, he had been manipulated, duped, and one of these days when things cooled to mere boiling, he was going to figure that out and then we'd see where we were. Like Koebler-Ross's five stages of grieving, he was still in denial, but anger and then revenge were just around the corner.

"I'm delighted, sir. Very relieved."

"Armand's going to teach me to ski." Always the chameleon, I thought. Love me, love me, love me. What can I do to get you to love me? I'll do anything.

"You're a brave man, sir." I handed him a cup of coffee and smiled.

The guests were suited up and gone at ten, just as Armand had recommended the night before. And since I had no household duties and my one assignment—finding out whether the stolen paintings were there, a question to which I still didn't have what I considered to be a satisfactory answer—had been suspended by mutual agreement, I decided to explore the town.

"Will you let me buy you lunch?" William asked as I pulled on my brand new Sorel boots and prepared to walk down the hill.

"No thanks," I said.

"Are you ever going to forgive me?"

"Not likely."

"I'm sorry."

"You should be."

"I hope you'll change your mind. I really would like to explain. Every word I told you on the boat was true."

"Tell it to someone who cares."

As I trudged to town, the sun came out and I felt I'd been delivered—not a deliverance from reality, nothing could change the facts, but at least from the darknesses of the night. I decided to begin my day again. I walked across the meadow and started down Red Mountain, crossing the lovely stone bridge that arced over the tiny frozen creekbed. I passed a dog grooming shop called Barking Beauties, and it made me miss the dogs. There were dogs everywhere, mostly huskies and malamutes. Our dogs would love it here.

I turned down Hopkins Avenue, spotted Caribou Alley across the street, and decided to go in—not into the club itself, but into the entryway. I just wanted to see what it looked like, what all the hullabaloo was about. What could they do, throw me out? After last night, it would take something much stronger than threat of expulsion from a private alleyway to raise my pulse. The passageway was ablaze with masses of tiny white lights that circled the edges of the ceiling. There was a jewelry shop on one side and a beauty salon on the other, and at the far end were mahogany doors with "C" shaped golden handles. Above was a half-moon of etched glass with interlocking "Cs." This was it. Mecca. The Caribou Club. The place Madam had been dying to see, and probably now would go to regularly. No sign, only a brass plaque on the door: "PRIVATE." Two couples, beautiful people and no doubt recognizable if I'd been more up on my movie stars, pushed past me and went in. "Harley, darling," the woman in the real coyote coat said. "Aren't you looking smart in that vest." The doors closed behind them with the hush of a secret handshake.

Across the street I spotted a small café, Zélé. Bustling with smartly dressed nonskiers like myself, it looked like just the place for a coffee. I took a tiny table out in the sun and studied the menu. It left my beloved Starbucks in the dust, with Raspberry Mocha, Orgeat Latte (Espresso, steamed milk, and almond), Espresso Cioccolato, Frappes, and fruit smoothies, like a Rocky Mountain High, with blueberries, strawberries, raspberries, and yogurt. There were a dozen different fruit and vegetable juice concoctions: Aspen Cooler, Tropical Snowdance, Rocky Mountain Sunrise, Key Western, or Caesar's Choice, which was made with carrot, tomato, and celery. I ordered a double cappuccino and a carrot muffin and sorted through a copy of the *Aspen Times*. The real estate was expensive, but nothing compared to Palm Desert or Indian Wells. The muffin was loaded with dates, raisins, and shredded coconut. It was so good, I ordered another.

Then I set out to explore the town. I looked in everyone's windows, Louis Vuitton, the Baldwin Gallery, Celine, Chanel. The Hard Rock Café and Planet Hollywood were small and empty. There was a Federal Express drop-off box and an ATM on every corner. I ambled along, visited with a relaxed husky lying atop a brick wall in the sun, and got some cash from a ski-up machine. I smiled at everyone and they smiled back. When I rounded a corner onto Hunter Street, I saw a shop with a bright blue and red sign: Himalaya Mon Amour. William's Explorer was parked in front. I then remembered Armand's invitation of the night before: a Nepalese trek. I guess he was serious.

A tiered cone of golden bells jangled merrily when I pushed open the door, followed by a total immersion of my sinuses and senses into a loony bin of incense and music that clanged in a random combination of bells, cymbals, and flutes. The shop, which looked deceptively small, turned out to be three rooms deep, each more cluttered than the other with brass trinkets, carved Buddhas, brightly embroidered shirts and blouses (mostly red). There were shelves and shelves of books, portraits of the bespectacled Dali Lama—always smiling, always peaceful—in every possible size and medium, and heaps of tapestries. Strings of prayer flags—some as large as pillowcases, others as small as handbooks—fluttered from the ceiling.

William's back was just visible in the very last room. He seemed to be poring over a map with a small, caramel-skinned man. I approached tentatively. "Nigel," William stood and greeted me warmly, his reading glasses perched on the end of his nose. "So glad you're here. Allow me to introduce you to Mr. Sinuwa. He is helping me finalize arrangements for the trek."

"I thought Patty Hammond was arranging everything."

"Well, she is leading it, certainly, but she isn't particularly helpful about getting us outfitted or telling us what to expect. Mr. Sinuwa is Tibetan and knows everything."

"Please don't let me interrupt."

A large map under a sheet of Plexiglas covered the table, and Mr. Sinuwa had marked it with a red grease pencil, tracing the route of our trip.

"Dolpo," Mr. Sinuwa said, tapping the map.

"Dolpo?" I asked.

"Very beautiful. Very beautiful flowers, very beautiful rivers," Mr. Sinuwa sang. "Very holy."

37

*H*ere's what I think: People who say coach is just as comfortable as first class probably haven't flown first class. And people who say first class is just as comfortable as having your own jet are just plain fools.

I'd never flown in a private jet before, so when Madam, Armand, William, and I packed up three days later to go home, here's what we did: Matt drove us to the airport, but not to the main terminal, which teemed with Aspen's perfumed masses. We went to the *private* terminal, and we didn't even stop to go inside. We drove straight to Armand's big, shiny, white Gulfstream Four! Right to the steps! The pilots, wearing black uniform suits with gold-braid trim, were standing there to greet us. A couple of ramp men in red Bogner parkas, pressed Levis, Sorel boots, and red baseball caps with the Sardi Aviation logo, loaded the bags. I didn't have to do anything! Except stand around with William while

Madam and Armand got on board. By the time we got on, they were already seated in the main cabin—a luxurious little boudoir-sized love nest with four kidskin upholstered swiveling armchairs and a sofa that opened into a double bed. William and I would sit in the two-seat business cabin up front. I still didn't have to do anything because there was a flight attendant!

Wow.

William just looked at me and laughed.

The captain, a trim fellow of forty or forty-five, went back and consulted with Armand and then returned to the cockpit, hung his jacket in the closet, tucked his hat onto a little shelf, and took his seat next to his co-pilot. When they started the engines, he didn't even close the cockpit door, so I could watch everything. They put on their headsets and talked on their radios and flipped switches and checked gauges and looked at their watches and consulted clipboards. Finally, the captain adjusted his headset, put his big square hands on the control handles in the center console, and pushed them forward. The engines slowly came to life and powered us to the end of the long, long, runway. Past all the poor schleppers who'd just spent a minimum thousand-a-day per person for a skiing vacation and now clumped up the stairs onto a cramped United Express jet that didn't even have first class. I think that stinks. There should be first class; these people don't care how much it costs, they just want to be comfortable.

Our captain maneuvered the plane into position and brought it to a dead stop, and I watched as he and the co-pilot pushed their feet down hard on the brake pedals and at the same time moved the power lever forward until it was at full throttle. The engines roared and roared and roared, louder, louder, and still louder. It seemed we were going to sit there forever until the engines either flew to pieces or blew the tail-section off the plane, but suddenly, the pilots took their feet off the brakes and we shot forward with all the furious force those two giant jet turbines could work up. They pushed us down the runway like a runaway freight train and launched us off the ground like a shuttle mission. Practically straight up. Oh, God. It was fabulous. It was the most fabulous, exciting thing I've ever experienced in my life. The powerful thrust and howling scream of the engines, the steep climb, the closeness of the mountainside—it was literally right next to our wing—the sudden soaring into the wild blue. I collapsed back into my seat and let out my breath. Exhausted.

All I wanted to do was do it again.

After the thrill of the take-off, the rest of the trip was totally uneventful, a nice light lunch of a chicken Caesar salad and a fine Puligny Montrachet. What waited for us at home? Ryder. I hadn't thought of him in days. He'd probably planted land mines all over our property.

William and I had reached a truce of sorts. Things could never be the way they'd been before, but if developments continued between Madam and Armand in the direction they seemed to be going, I would have to manage to have a cordial relationship with him. He had apologized to me countless times; I told him I accepted and made every effort to bury my feelings and share an after-dinner glass of whiskey and a cigar in the spirit of good-fellowship. I did these things, concealing my feelings, because I was genuinely happy for Madam. Armand was everything she, and in turn I, had hoped for, and she seemed to provide him the same joy.

Much to everyone's surprise, and to Junior's sad-eyed disappointment, Armand had gone for twenty-four hours without talking on the phone, even earlier than he'd promised. He and Madam were glued together like Siamese twins the whole time in Aspen. Maybe the added element of complicit larceny had increased their mutual attraction—they'd talked and laughed about it constantly when the other guests weren't around. He'd bought her so many beautiful gifts, she had to buy another duffel bag to get them home, and she did a lovely pencil sketch of him on the sundeck. I think it was the best portrait she'd ever done, which only reinforced what seemed to be a deep connection between them. He would pay the taxes. He would save us from a life of poverty. Overall, Aspen had been a delightful and enlightening experience. Madam found Armand, and I was learning to compromise. Also, I'd seen the magnitude of Armand's and William's expertise. Every famous missing work—except those from the Gardner Museum—was in their vault.

I leaned back in my seat and closed my eyes. William reached over and patted my arm. "Everything's going to be fine, Nigel," he said. What did he think, I was a child in need of reassurance? Would everyone always underestimate me because I was a bit frail? Couldn't they see that inside I was a giant?

All good things must come to an end, including our ride on the Gulfstream IV. We descended almost as steeply as we had ascended and landed smoothly at Manassas, a small municipal strip just fifteen minutes from the farm. A Lincoln Town Car was there to meet us, and while Madam and Armand said goodbye, the driver and I transferred the luggage, only half of which would fit, meaning I would have to come back and retrieve the rest. I didn't mind. I was just glad to be home. William stayed on board. I had no idea when I'd see him again.

As we drove past the end of the runway, the jet screamed over our heads and disappeared almost immediately into the deep twilight. They would be in Paris well before breakfast.

38

SPRINGTIME

*I*f that's what you want to do, Madam. But if I were you, I'd want to be on record as having registered the strongest possible protest."

It was a glorious Virginia spring day, the sort Southern legends are made of. The dogwoods were in bloom and their blossoms floated above our heads like planes of delicate white handkerchiefs, or flights of silver dollar-sized white butterflies. Gigantic banks of pink and fuschia and white azaleas pushed themselves over the edges of the path to Madam's studio like a floral obstacle course. The air was luscious and warm and it was too early for the onslaught of summer bugs, although I now kept the dogs on their heartworm medication year round. We had three new fawns added to our little herd, their spotted coats irresistible, their eyes the most trusting I'd ever seen.

I was setting up lunch on the porch of the studio. We'd been home from our ski trip for two weeks, and she'd just started a commission in Washington painting the first lady, which meant that even though she was in the city and spent three nights a week in a small suite at the Four Seasons while I remained on the farm, we would basically be home all month. It is best to stay home in April. T. S. Eliot was right when he said, "April is the cruelest month." It's the month when California has the most earthquakes. The month when two home-grown terrorists blew up the federal building in Oklahoma City, killing sixty-five people and wounding hundreds. The month when two boys murdered thirteen of their classmates and wounded countless others in Colorado. Given time, I could name dozens and dozens of examples, but I don't like to dwell on tragedy. I will conclude by pointing out that April is the month of Hitler's birth. To me, Hitler was the devil incarnate, and April is the month when we all should just mind our knitting and be extra kind to one another. I suppose it's because it was April that Madam felt compelled to torture me.

"He says it will be fabulous," she countered. A bee buzzed around her shocking pink leggings.

"You don't think he would tell you if it were going to be anything but fabulous, do you?" I didn't like the snippy tone in my voice. "What I mean to say is, Mr. Weil loves you, Madam. He'd say anything to get you to go with him."

"Nigel. I *am* going with him. It's *you* I'm talking about."

"*Me?*"

You have no doubt figured out by now what we were quibbling about: Nepal.

"Absolutely not. I would be of virtually no use on a Nepalese trek. I am not strong-backed, my general constitution is weak, and I am petrified of heights. William and Mr. Weil will take beautiful care of you."

"I won't go if you don't."

"That is a low approach, Madam."

"I'm serious."

"Well, what precisely is it that we would do in Nepal? How do we get there? What is the time difference? Where would we get water to drink? What should be done with the dogs? Shall I continue?"

"Nigel, I promise you, it's going to be fun—the trip of a lifetime. Armand's working out all the details. We leave on the fourteenth."

"That's only two weeks. What will we take?"

She looked at me with eyes full of laughter. "Calm down, Nigel. The fourteenth of *May*. We have six weeks to get in shape. Don't worry, I'll take care of you. Oh my gosh. Look what time it is. I've got to clean up and get my nails done. He did say six, didn't he?"

Only the hundredth time she'd asked.

She jumped up without touching her lunch and ran back to the house, so I took her seat at the little outdoor table with its Constanza di Fidelio hand-painted ceramic tile top—more zodiac images that looked like Lilly Pulitzer on drugs. I estimated we could probably sell it for a few hundred thousand, not enough to make a dent—and ate the meal myself. Cold sliced Westphalian ham, Jarlsberg cheese, powerful Dijon mustard, a large pile of cornichons, and iced tea. The whole time I ate, I thought up ways to get out of going to Nepal, but every excuse ended up with having to quit my job. I tossed a piece of lettuce onto the grass, lit a cigarette, and sat back. Shortly a rabbit ventured out from beneath an azalea bush and munched it up. Although he kept one eye on me, one soft ear forward and one back, he was completely unafraid. Stupid little rabbit.

I knew I should be getting back, I had a million last-minute things to do to complete preparations for the weekend, but I decided it might be wise to check first on our neighbors. You know who I mean. Madam kept a pair of Nikon zoom-lense binoculars for "bird-watching" in the studio. They hung from a nylon mesh strap on a hook just inside the door. She said they were for bird-watching but I know as well as you do they were for just the purpose I was about to put them to: spying on the Mc-Cormicks. I went in and retrieved them—dodging Constanza's painted gaze, which had been looking a little derisive lately—and crossed the lawn to the split-rail fence and hedgerow, where I took up my customary spying position. The McCormicks' red brick manor house was completely visible with the binoculars. I searched the estate carefully, and it looked as though they were still away. The curtains were drawn upstairs and down, and there didn't seem to be any activity around the parterre where the first bloom of roses was about to burst open in Mary Anne's garden. It had been designed by Ellie Comfort, one of England's top landscape architects, and was paved with ridged stone walks so that Mary Anne could tend her rose bushes from her wheelchair. The pond where her swans floated on untroubled waters, and the greenhouse where she visited occasionally to check on dormant orchids, hydrangeas, and cyclamen, seemed similarly vacant. When the McCormicks were home, a white canvas deck umbrella remained unfurled at the end of the dock, Mary Anne's favorite refuge. She would sit there for hours on end, watching the fish jump, feeding the swans, reading business papers and gardening books, and talking on the phone. Today the umbrella was tied down and the weather-beaten table was bare. The stable man's car was in its usual spot, but all the horses, including Ryder's large chestnut, were grazing in the pasture, soaking up the warm spring sun. It was so silent only the air itself hummed.

When I got back from my scouting mission, I went up to her dressing room. She'd slipped into a cotton blouse and slacks and had just finished sinking a large comb with two fresh gardenias attached to it into her chignon. One of my first jobs every morning was to wire the gardenias to the combs. She bought a dozen a week. They were unbelievably expensive, but I was only occasionally able to convince her that she could tuck in a hibiscus or rhododendron or, especially now that it was spring, a cherry or apple or dogwood blossom. "Where do you think the McCormicks have gone?"

"No idea, but let's not kick a sleeping dog."

"I agree he's a dog, but you don't really think he's sleeping, do you?"

She looked at me in the mirror. "I don't want to think about what he's doing, Nigel. I don't want to think about how I behaved with him or how he almost made me lose my faith. He was like a black hole, sucking me in, dragging my light out. Being with Armand is like being around the sun. I can see the difference in my work. This portrait of the first lady is coming out with the most wonderful lightness. Maybe lightheartedness. I don't know how to describe it, it's different."

"Umm," I answered. It was impossible for me to kick Ryder into the background that easily, and the longer we went without hearing from him, the more uncomfortable I became. It wouldn't do me any good to mention him again, but he was always back there, swirling on the ground like killer fog. "Have you given much thought to what you would take to Nepal?"

"None. I was hoping you would do that for me." She lined her lips with a dark pencil and filled them in with burgundy lipstick. "I've been to the Nepalese Center in Washington a few times, and I got you this book. They said it would tell us everything we need to know." She handed me a thick volume: *Nepal for Beginners*. "Also, Armand has arranged to have a Buddhist monk come over a couple of times a week before we leave to teach us a few words of Tibetan, and to tell us about Buddhism and local customs and so forth so we don't insult anybody. Apparently where we're going is more Buddhist than Hindu, or the other way around, I'm not really sure. The Nepalese are the most spiritual people on the planet. They're very sensitive. I've started meditating, and it's bringing me a lot of peace."

She hung an unusual necklace around her neck. It looked alive. "What on earth is that?"

"Isn't it amazing?" She fingered the long, sharp objects. "They're amulets—Buddhists consider these very good luck. Very good karma. It was delivered to the hotel yesterday. From Armand. It's musk deer teeth."

I felt like I was having an out of body experience.

"You aren't thinking of becoming a hippie are you, Madam?" We had been through phases before.

"Don't be silly. Oh, no," Madam gasped. "What is *she* doing here?"

A flash of light off a windshield had glinted on the ceiling, and we watched out the window as the Internal Revenue lady got out of her tired little Toyota. We still hadn't gotten the money promised by Armand, and Madam was reluctant to bring it up. If she didn't mention it this weekend, I would.

"I told Agent Romero the paintings weren't there. Armand doesn't have them and he doesn't know who does. What more can I do?"

They stood in the entry hall. The days of coffee, orange rolls, and basic hospitality were long gone. Now it was straightforward thrust-and-parry, with the IRS doing the thrusting and Madam parrying with all the skill of an elephant. The subtleties of political manipulation were so foreign to her, she may as well have held the meeting in Chinese.

"As you know, our arrangement was that if you located the paintings, your tax, including the interest and penalties, would be forgiven. That was the offer, as I'm sure you will recall. Since you've been unable to locate the goods, the taxes are still due, and since no payment has been made since we first contacted you last November, the interest and penalties have continued to accrue. The balance, as of this morning, is nine hundred and twenty-three thousand dollars. The director has agreed to another extension, and if the government receives the funds by the end of this quarter, June thirtieth, that is the amount you owe. If the government does not receive the funds by that date, foreclosure proceedings will commence forthwith."

"Nine hundred and twenty-three thousand?" Madam studied her with outright contempt. "You just have no soul, do you? No good karma. I'll bet you enjoy this part of your job, ruining people's lives. I'm sorry for you. Unfortunately I have a feeling that with each subsequent incarnation, you are moving down, not up, on the food chain."

Madam was beginning to talk the talk, but she wasn't exactly walking the walk. I think she needed more direction in her meditation efforts, which—given the little I know about Buddhism and related subjects—I have always understood to be useful in calming one's temper, not inflaming it. I also don't think that the subject of reincarnation is supposed to be used as a threat.

But the IRS lady didn't understand, or *care* about, the finer points of Eastern philosophies any more than Madam did. Bottom-line: This conversation was nothing more than a verbal slug-fest between two bitches who hated each other's guts.

"Miss di Fidelio, may I remind you, most of the people in this country are law-abiding citizens. They pay their taxes on time. You are one of the exceptions. You failed to plan for yourself. You have simply taken one hundred percent of your income, which is substantial, and spent it. Do I enjoy informing you that your home and possessions are subject to forfeiture? Not particularly. But I'm not the one who caused your problem, you are." She slipped a card out of a little plastic wallet. "Here's my number. Call me when you're ready to settle your account."

Ms. Collier returned to her car, but before she got in, she scolded, "I'm sure you're aware that April fifteenth is just around the corner. Don't forget to file your taxes."

See what I mean about April?

Thank God for Armand. He arrived from Paris like Louis Quattorze, loaded with wine, champagne, cheeses, a solid gold dual-time-zone

Rolex, a black Armani pantsuit with wide turquoise piping, and—we hoped—$923,000.

"How long will you be with us, sir?" I asked as I took his Hermès valise from the driver.

"Just tonight. Unfortunately, I have to go to Mexico City in the morning."

"Oh, no, Armand," Madam said. "I thought you were spending the weekend. I've planned all kinds of things."

"*Non, cherie.* Tonight only."

"But we haven't seen each other for two weeks. You *have* to stay." The color was high in Madam's face. She was preparing to dig in, engage in a little trench warfare, a little hand-to-hand right out there in the driveway. The driver looked to Armand for instructions. "Eight o'clock, please, John," he told him, and the man climbed quickly into his car and left without comment. "Next weekend, perhaps, I'll be able to stay longer. But tonight is all I can do. Come, my magnificent Jacqueline," he slipped his arm around her waist, "I'm as disappointed as you are but let's not spend our evening fussing, you know my time is not my own— like you, I live at my clients' whims. Show me your farm, show me that famous studio of yours." He had the touch. He'd disarmed her without a drop of blood being shed. His tone of voice made it clear he would not budge from his schedule, it was fixed, primary. She was secondary, she could either choose to fit in or not. The subject was closed.

I admire men like Armand. They're their own breed of cat. They're different. For them, the competition of business is everything. When they decide to take time off or buy gifts or fall in love, their involvement is as intense and genuine and temporary as their attention to a deal until it's done. Usually, of course, they exercise the niceties only to prove to themselves and their colleagues how much they can afford, to show just how far they've come. Usually they're also socially inept, insecure, and immature, which Armand, of course, was not. He was the most socially accomplished man I'd ever known—a satin toga draped over a marble statue. He understood artists well, knew their temperament, knew a strong, loving hand was what it took, knew they would trade everything they owned for a little love and kindness and admiration of their art.

They went to the studio and closed the door. Armand, the alpha male, eradicated every last scent of his vanquished foe from the cave.

The driver fetched him at eight o'clock sharp.

"Did you get it?" I asked as soon as he was gone.

"Get what?"

"The *money*."

"You mean did he have nine-hundred-thousand dollars in cash with him? No. But his Paris bank is going to wire it to my bank on Monday. Don't worry, Nigel." She looked incredibly sad.

"I'm sorry he had to leave," I said.

"Just once in my life I want to be what comes first. I want my lover to say, forget the business. Forget everything and everybody. I'm just going to be with you and do what you want, for as long as you want, and you'll never have to worry about anything again for the rest of your life."

"That's not going to happen with Armand."

"I know," she said with resignation. "Nobody gets everything. But I don't think I'm asking for so much."

Health. Love and Happiness. Intelligence. Money. We each get three out of four. People are always thinking: money, money, money. Not realizing that by the time one of the other pieces falls away, it will be too late to get it back.

Maybe I'm becoming a hippie.

The weekend now loomed ahead. Just Madam, me, and the Dali Lama. Or so I thought.

39

*I*t was a little after three o'clock on Saturday afternoon when the doorbell began to ring incessantly. I put down the silver candlestick I'd been polishing unnecessarily, wiped my hands, removed my apron, and went to see who it could possibly be.

Junior Hammond. Carrying a case of Dom Perignon 1985, five board games still in their shrink wrap: Parcheesi (Deluxe Edition), Sorry, Trivial Pursuit (Baby Boomers Edition), Checkers, and Chess. A suitcase of clothes. "Where are they?" he demanded. He had on a Hawaiian shirt, tent-sized trousers, and sandals with white socks.

" 'They' who, sir?"

"Jackie and Armand. They didn't think I was going to let them have an entire weekend alone, did they?" He pushed his way past me into the house.

"Mr. Weil left for Mexico City early this morning and Madam is in her studio. I'll get her for you." Junior drew in a deep breath and shook his big, jowly head.

"That stupid jerk."

"Sir?"

"Armand. He has his priorities all screwed up. He's going to lose her over some stupid painting."

Unfortunately, I could not disagree. "I'll tell her you're here."

Madam and Junior spent the rest of the weekend—Saturday afternoon through Sunday evening—laughing their heads off, sitting on the terrace during the daytime and on the floor of the library after dinner Saturday night playing the games and drinking the champagne. By the time he left after a late Sunday lunch, most of the champagne was gone and so was Madam's anger at Armand. Junior had convinced her to forgive him.

On his way out the door, he handed me a twenty. His lack of class seemed unlimited.

40

NEPAL

*A*RMAND. ARMAND. CAN YOU HEAR ME?" Madam shouted into the compact Global Star satellite phone, which was significantly heavier and more expensive, but not much larger, than a regular cell phone.

Outside the glass-less windows of our hotel room, the teeming streets of Kathmandu churned up billows of dust and the stinging fumes of rancid yak butter burning over charcoal fires. The din of street vendors' cries, silver symbols attached to human fingers, and bells attached to cow-ankles was a constant annoyance. The sun was hot and the humid air that rolled in was fetid with the stench of waste and cooking smoke and exhaust from the falling-apart, bulging busses and third-world lead-burning sedans that rumbled past endlessly beneath our window.

"Of course I can hear you, darling, you don't need to shout," he shouted back loud enough to hear from across the room. "The connection is perfectly clear. You sound like you're next door. The new technology on those phones is remarkable."

"Fuck the technology. Where in the hell are you?" Her hair was in complete disarray, falling in long hanks from its straggling chignon. Perspiration slicked her face and arms. Her thin cotton skirt was glued to her legs.

"Didn't William tell you? Isn't he there with you?"

William and I stood motionless by the door next to the mountain of luggage, keeping our distance from the quarrel. The room was small and threadbare, layers of dirt rounding the corners where the walls met the floor. The thin, worn, blue chenille bedspread was dark with the stains of those who had sweated side-by-side there before us and if you looked at it closely, you could see it move—alive with bugs. That was the icing on the cake.

"Yes, William's here. William's always here. It's *you* I'm interested in. I want to hear it from *you.*"

"Didn't he explain about the Caravaggios that were put up at the last minute for auction tonight at Sotheby's?"

"Did I explain that I don't give a shit about the Caravaggios?" Madam yelled in response.

True to form, Armand ignored the outburst. "You and William and Nigel should just go ahead and take the flight to Juphal tomorrow morning. We're already a day behind the others. Patty said she'd fetch us there."

"Look, Armand, this is not going the way it's supposed to. First you tell me how beautiful and romantic this trip is going to be, how we'll fly together from Paris to Kathmandu on your plane, except oops, something comes up, so Nigel and I should fly from LA and you'll be here to meet us in Kathmandu. Okay, we did that, and who's here to greet us but William? I like William and all, but he's not you. And now you're saying you can't make it to Kathmandu but will meet us in Juphal, wherever the hell that is, so now we're stuck overnight in a mud hut with nothing but a hole in the floor for plumbing. I don't know what the hell Patty Hammond told you about our reservations, but we've ended up in a hotel I wouldn't ask my dogs to stay in."

"She said it was supposed to be the best."

"Oh, you must mean the Yellow Flame? Well, the Yellow Flame never heard of us, had no record of our reservation, so they sent us across town to the Rin-Dak . . . a . . . a . . . I don't even know what to call it. Did I mention there's no plumbing to speak of and the electricity's been out in this part of town for several days? No glass in the window, that's 'window' singular, and bugs up the kazoo? And only one room for the three of us? Four of us, if you had deigned to make the trip."

"Now listen, Jacqueline . . ."

"No, you listen. You get your tight little French butt over here now or I'm on the next plane out."

"I promise you, darling," his voice cooed through the ether from the comfort of his leather desk chair in his Paris office, which looked out over the Tour Eiffel and the Jardins des Invalides. "I'm leaving here tonight the second the auction is over, flying directly to Juphal. I'll meet you there tomorrow and we'll hook up with Patty and the rest of the trekkers. Believe me, it *is* going to be a beautiful trip. I'm so sorry this happened, darling. I thought I was doing the right thing having you go on ahead of me; I thought it would be easier on you than coming all the way to meet me in Paris, but I see now it was a mistake."

"Mistake doesn't even begin to describe it." Madam punched the hang up button on the five-thousand-dollar phone and slammed it onto the bed, making the bugs jump. "Fatal error is more what I would call it," she said to no one in particular. "You son of a bitch." She turned away from us. It was so humid, her bra was visible through the back of her short-sleeved white cotton blouse. All our clothes were glued to our bodies as though we'd showered in them. "Don't you ever get tired of doing his dirty work?" She addressed William over her shoulder.

"Fortunately, things like this don't happen very often."

She snorted. "I'm not stupid, William. I see what's happening. This is his payback."

The din outside grew suddenly louder as a group of smiling orange-robed monks in towering yellow hats passed by tooting their recorders, banging their drums, clanging their finger symbols and chanting their chant, the same one they'd been chanting since time began in this ancient civilization. Madam leaned out the window, taking up almost the whole space of it, and sniffed the air like a giant panther. She stayed that way for several minutes, forcing herself to breathe slowly and deeply, trying to regain the transcendental calm she'd been nurturing over the past few weeks with the help of our visiting monk.

"I've never seen anything like this in my life," she finally said. She pulled a handkerchief from her pocket, wiped it over her damp face and around the back of her neck. William and I continued to hang back, trying to decide if this was going to be lemon or lemonade. See where the dust would eventually settle. If good Karma or bad would prevail.

"Incredible. This place is incredible." She shook her head again and turned around, the light framing her figure and making her expression hard to read. She put on her straw hat and dark glasses and picked up her shoulder bag and camera. "I'll be back. Don't take your eyes off that gear." We watched her go and looked again around the shabby little room.

"Welcome to Nepal," I said.

"This is getting off to a very bad start," William observed.

41

The trip over had been endless, with a two or three hour stopover between each long flight leg. Five hours on United from Washington to LA. Sixteen hours on Thai Airlines from LA to Tokyo to Bangkok. Three more on Royal Nepal Air from Bangkok to Kathmandu, a flight that should at least have provided us with some spectacular scenery if we'd been sitting on the right side of the plane. But we weren't, we were on the left. Besides, with the exception of a few of the tallest peaks, the mountains were socked in—nothing but a cloudy sea below us. Madam and I were gray with fatigue.

William wasn't any better. When Armand decided at the last minute to delay his departure until after the Caravaggio auction, he'd sent William ahead on Air France as his advance man, to make his apologies and, as Madam had so succinctly put it, to do his dirty work. He'd flown directly from Paris, via New Delhi, arriving at the Nepali capital's modern Tribhuvan International Airport an hour before we did. Our systems were scrambled.

Thanks to the recent influx of Russian-made, lead-burning vehicles and constant construction, the smog was the worst I'd ever experienced. It made Mexico City's mud-colored, acrid air look and smell as pure as that of the wind-swept plains of Wyoming. The first car in Nepal belonged to a Rana prime minister in 1948. Porters carried the unassembled parts over the mountains to Kathmandu, which had only one road a half mile long. Today, six major roads run through Nepal, most of them little more than rutted tracks outside the cities, and I was quite sure we'd that original car as our taxi from the airport. It and the other taxi—an odd three-wheeled affair we'd hired as supplemental cargo van—were so buried under our gear, their tires were squashed almost flat.

When the taxi shuddered to a stop with a final belch of fumes beneath the ornate portico of the Yellow Flame Hotel, our relief at the way we were received by the efficient, English-speaking doorman, and the wave of air-conditioned air that poured from the door, had verged on giddy, gushy, near-hysteria. The brand new four-star lodging, built in the traditional Nepalese style with whitewashed walls and a dark brown tile roof, its deep eaves supported by intricately carved wooden beams and cornered with upturned dragon tails was, to us, finer, more welcoming, than the Paris Ritz. The image of a shower mesmerized and tantalized us, dancing before our eyes like an oasis in the Sahara: cool, refreshing water splashing over our stiff, aching, sweltering bodies, followed by a massage and a good deep sleep on fresh, cool sheets to rest and renew us before our grand adventure to the enchanted valley.

The man at the reception desk had been so distressed that he had no record of our reservation, he was close to tears. "I regret the phones are out at this time, so I cannot call to find you other accommodations."

"Here," Madam said. "Use my satellite phone." She pulled it out of her leather-bound canvas Hermès tote bag, another gift from Armand, to match the accompanying set of sturdy jumbo-sized duffel bags that were taking up four of the doorman's rolling brass carts.

"I regret Madam, it is of no use. Their phones are as dead as ours." His eyes searched the three of ours before he realized our problem was now his. He intuitively knew we would keep standing there at the desk, staring at him like stupid, weepy baboons, as incendiary as time bombs, until he fixed it. We'd had no idea what to do, no idea where to go, certainly no fall-back plan. We were as lost as Winken, Blinken and Nod on the dark side of the moon. We were on the verge of hysteria, and the man also probably knew from dealing with tourists that the public, especially the rich, spoiled public, can be sweet one moment but turn nasty and litigious in the blink of an eye.

"Let me see what I can do. Please." He'd indicated with his outstretched arm. "Come, make yourselves comfortable." Even though he led us into the lounge and served us strong sweet tea and cakes, we jealously eyed the guests who got to stay. But we didn't belong to this club. We had no reservations, so we were nothing more than dirty, hot, exhausted interlopers camping out in their breezy, cool, grand hotel lobby pretending we belonged, and they, no doubt, were wishing we would leave and stop cluttering up the place.

"I feel like I'm looking through the window, watching the party, when I should be giving it," Madam had groused, looking around sullenly for someone to bring more tea. She had deep circles under her eyes and her face sagged unbecomingly.

"You've read my mind," I'd answered.

"I'm sorry I got you into this, Nigel. I should have listened to you." Her eyes had turned into liquid pools of tears that she struggled to keep from spilling over, but in spite of her efforts, they began to stream down her face. She wiped them away with the back of her hand. "It never occurred to me we'd be stranded like this, that Armand would let such a thing happen to me."

"I can't apologize enough, Madam," William had said. "He never meant for it to go this way, and by tomorrow, I promise you, everything will be one-hundred percent back on track. Believe me."

She smiled sadly at him. "I'm sure you're right. I just need a good night's sleep." She leaned back in the chair, placed her fingertips together, and closed her eyes. "Karma, karma, karma, karma," she chanted and took a deep breath, which she let out with a long hum. "Don't worry about it. *Che serà, serà.* Whatever. Stay cool. I'm okay, you're okay. Way out. Far out. What in hell is it, Nigel, the hippies used to say?"

"Be cool, man?" I offered.

"That was the beatniks. And stop saying 'cool' every five seconds. It's getting on my nerves."

"Cool" had become my mantra. I had become obsessed with cooling off. The fact is, it might not have actually been hot or humid by Virginia standards, but this humidity was different, the most extreme I'd ever experienced. It was tropical, drenching, and paralytic, and the fact we'd not had a change of clothes in almost thirty-six hours and had passed through the sub-tropics of Thailand and India, made me feel caked with dirt, smothered, and molding like yeasty, sodden bread. While we were waiting in the lobby for who knew what to happen—William had been able to contact Patty Hammond on the satellite phone and she'd had a heart-to-heart with the hotel manager, to no avail—we'd each ducked into the modern restrooms and taken a refreshing French bath in carved stone sinks with water that gushed from brass-plated dragon's head spigots, while a pair of smiling attendants stood by with unlimited supplies of fresh towels, good soap, and cologne. I'd scrubbed my teeth furiously and had a change of underclothes. The simple ablutions had sent our spirits soaring. Everything would all be all right. We had more tea and cookies.

An hour later, an assistant manager, who had been sent forth in a motorized rickshaw into Kathmandu, a city that stays as packed with foreign tourists as New York or San Francisco, finally returned, triumphant. And here we were at the Rin Dak Guest House in the Old City. The last room in town. If I made my living writing travel brochures, I would give the Rin Dak a break. I would be generous and gracious in my description of it as "a unique opportunity to experience a step back in time to the twelfth century. No restaurant on premises."

I removed the spread and grimy sheets from the double bed, held them out the window, and shook them, watching the bugs tumble down to the street one floor below, as Madam rounded a corner and disappeared from sight. This was the farthest I'd ever been from anywhere.

"You up for a hand of gin?" asked William.

"You're on."

"I'll go find us a couple of beers."

I dragged the rough square table and two chairs across the wooden floor to the window, and it was only then that I finally really noticed the mountains, those magnificent peaks glimpsed in the distance between buildings. I'd been so preoccupied with all our troubles, I hadn't even taken the time to see where I was, and when I finally did notice, I felt afraid, as though a cool hand had passed over my heart. "What do you think's going to happen?" I had two jacks—diamonds and spades, the king of clubs, ten of clubs, nine of diamonds, six and seven of spades, seven of hearts, two of hearts, three of clubs, four of hearts. I discarded the king.

"You mean between Jackie and Armand?" He picked it up and discarded the jack of clubs. I nodded and picked up the card as casually as I could and put down the four of hearts. The beer, in a bottle with no label, was tart and strong.

William shrugged his shoulders, drew a card, and examined it quickly before discarding the eight of diamonds. "I don't know. I know he loves her more than he's ever loved anyone, but unfortunately, with him, prior experience would indicate that love has never been enough."

"Is he always so thoughtless? So selfish?" I drew the five of spades and discarded the nine of diamonds. William didn't answer, but he didn't need to. His expression did the talking, it was acknowledgment enough. I could see the future clearly. "Do you think he'll show up at all?"

"Of course he'll show up," William said with too much conviction. "He's committed to Jackie and he's committed to this trip. He'll be there tomorrow."

"Oh, God. Poor Madam." I put my head in my hands. "He's not coming, is he?"

We'd been fooling ourselves. He was having his revenge for Madam's deceit.

"Nigel, get a hold of yourself. I've never known anyone who could get himself worked up faster than you. Of course he'll show up. But for how long?" William shrugged again. "That's another story. Hard to say. He goes all out for pleasure, but only in short bursts." He picked up the nine of diamonds and dragged it across the top of his cards before slotting it in. "To tell you the truth, I wouldn't be surprised if it ended up with the two of us looking after your Madam for most of the trip; Armand might just drop in for a few days, but, of course, they'll be the most interesting few days. Those at Phoksumdo Tal—he'll probably just helicopter in and out."

"Do you think I should tell her?"

"I'll leave that up to you. But if it were me, I wouldn't. I could be wrong. He might come for the whole time."

The beer soured in my stomach. "I'm glad you're here, William. I don't think I could have navigated any of this on my own."

"Don't be ridiculous. Gin," William slapped down his cards.

42

*A*n hour later, just as I was beginning to get the upper hand in the card game, Madam returned. She had a young boy with her. He had on a brightly colored tunic and short pants. His intelligent brown eyes were the color of warm tree bark and his lashes were as long as Bambi's. "Come on," she said to William and me. "We're moving."

"What about the gear and supplies?" I asked.

The assembly was enormous. We not only had every possible piece of clothing for every possible kind of weather we might encounter on our adventure into Dolpo, Nepal's "Hidden Land"; I had also brought enough medicines and medical supplies to stock a small hospital, and enough pre-packaged dehydrated food to feed the four of us for a month, in case we got lost or separated from the group. Dolpo—located in Northwestern Nepal, the least visited region of the country, and its lake of other-worldly beauty, Phoksumdo Tal, is home to many rare plant and animal species and sacred shrines. Patty Hammond had gotten special permits for us to travel beyond the lake into the private preserve at the foot of Dolpo's highest mountain, Kanji Roba, an almost-unheard-of privilege.

To say we would be isolated is a ridiculous understatement. Nepal is not for the faint of heart, literally or figuratively. Outside of Kathmandu, the basic elements of western civilization that we take for granted simply do not exist: emergency medical care, emergency rescue, fresh water, sewage treatment, toilets, cooking fuel, basic sanitation. 911. CNN. And to cap it all off, most of this discomfort occurs at dizzying altitudes of twelve thousand feet and up, unless you go to southern Nepal, where the altitude is practically sea-level and you experience the discomforts in a dense, sub-tropical jungle, adding hungry tigers and deadly vipers to the list of hazards. Every tool for survival has to be carried in, and every bit of trash has to be carried back out, all the outfitter's responsibility, to be sure. But . . . better safe than sorry. We had duplicates of everything. It was as daunting to coordinate as to contemplate, and in my planning and requisitioning I had, hopefully, left nothing to chance. But the sheer volume of goods was staggering.

"Don't worry about it," Madam answered, laying her arm across the boy's shoulder. "Chandra will look after it."

Mentally, Madam's solitary foray had gotten her beyond the spat with Armand and let her new friend, karma, take control. It had relaxed her neck, straightened her spine, restored her confidence, reinvigorated her, and brought forth her take-charge attitude. Maybe it was more than karma, maybe it was the famous mystical properties of this remote kingdom, which sits literally on top of the world, or maybe it was simply gratitude to be off the plane. Or maybe, it was because—and this was my theory because it was my plan as well: Like a person who intends to commit suicide and finally has selected the date and method and can then relax and focus—she had decided to kill Armand. Whatever, it was a welcome break.

"Are you certain, Madam?" I asked.

"Positive. Come on, you two. Hurry up. Let's go before we lose the light. We'll be there in about an hour," she told the boy. "Or two." Out we went, following Madam into the extraordinary Kathmandu twilight.

I might have given you the impression that William and I would trail after her like a couple of cringing babies, our faces screwed up as if we were about to get booster shots in our arms. It was a well-documented fact that William was on a par with me when it came to an appreciation for comfort and an aversion to pain, physical risk, and outdoor activities that involved more than a stroll around a city park, preferably Central or the Bois. But since that Aspen weekend, we had been forced to communicate daily about trek preparations via e-mail and phone calls, and in spite of our reticence (some may call it cowardice), we found ourselves bursting with excitement about this unique adventure, which we realized would be fraught with more discomfort and possibly more danger than either one of us had ever faced before. The intimacy of our previous relationship was gone, but you know me well enough by now to realize I would be lying if I said I wasn't happy to have a friend.

Initially, I'd done everything in my power, tried every threat, every underhanded tactic, cited every terror-laden danger, including the massive number of tourist deaths each year in Nepal due to falls off cliffs, unknown viruses and bacteria, and altitude sickness (pulmonary edema, cerebral edema, exploding eyeballs, and so forth), as well as the general lack of emergency medical care, to discourage Madam (and ergo me) from making this trip, but she'd been determined.

"I don't understand why you want to do this," I'd said. "Why not just meet him in Portofino for two weeks? Why expose yourself to such risk?"

"It's the extreme nature of it I love," she'd answered. "If we were going to Everest or something, I wouldn't do it—no interest. But we're going to Dolpo—nobody goes there. It's as exotic and unknown as a Burmese jungle."

Oh, joy.

"Get with the program, Nigel."

Finally I'd just said to hell with it and jumped fully onto the bandwagon with both feet. We all have to die sometime. I guessed I'd go, shattered and spattered, to the bottom of an unreachable, forlorn crevasse. What could I do? It was my karma.

So this evening, emerging from our hovel of a hotel into a whirlwind of the unknown, excitement took me over and I got in the swing of things right off. The sounds and sights were delightful. Just outside the door of our lodging, in a little square paved with cut stones, we passed a retinue of royal bearers whose red, gold, and blue livery was as elaborate as any you'd find at Buckingham Palace. Children swarmed around them, never getting too close, just close enough to admire their uniforms and regalia, and the bearers, some only slightly older than the children, were like their English counterparts: arrogant and unapproachable.

"Wait till you see this," Madam said, marching through the narrow streets, drawing astonished looks from the locals, who had never seen a six-foot-tall woman except in religious drawings. She was like a grand ship sailing forth, her skirt flowing in the evening breeze like a sail in the wind, and we bobbed in her wake like two mindless dinghies. Just happy to be along for the ride, ga-ga at our surroundings.

"Look!" she exclaimed when we rounded a corner and found ourselves in Durbar Square in the heart of old Kathmandu. More than fifty monuments framed the square: temples, shrines, and towers, along with countless market stalls, and a palace that looked like Versailles—the old royal palace, home of Nepal's monarchs since the sixteenth and seventeenth-century Malla kings. Today, the palace is home to the foreign ministry; within its walls are elegant courtyards, exquisite wood carvings, and sculptures of gods, goddesses, and demons. One of the greatest sleeping Vishnu statues in the world is in the palace gardens.

"No visitors," Madam informed us as we hurried past the frilly gates toward an intricately carved Hindu monastery, which, according to Madam, was Kumari Bahal, home of Kumari, the living goddess, who could only be a little girl. When the living goddess reaches puberty, a search is conducted throughout the kingdom for the baby who is her reincarnation. When they find her, they take her from her parents and bring her here and she stays cloistered here for eleven or twelve years and then they find another. I've read that every now and then she is caught peeking from the lattice of her second-floor window, but we didn't see her. Madam's pace didn't give us much of a chance.

We passed through a bazaar so tightly packed with people, it was almost impossible to move, and it was just how you'd envision an Asian bazaar in an ancient trading crossroads like Kathmandu—carpets, shawls, jewelry, pottery, musical instruments, fruits and vegetables, poultry, furniture, incense. The scent of rare spices blended with powerful human body odors and the heavy floral perfumes of barefoot women in bright saris. Men dressed in white leggings, black vests, and hats—house servants to the wealthy—navigated through the crowd with long poles on their shoulders balanced with large buckets of goods hanging from either end. Smiling children ran everywhere. The bazaar sucked us in. We were buffeted, jostled, spun, delighted, bewitched, and enchanted—and then spit out in front of a large temple with a yellow base and a square gold tower. Buddha's face—with its third eye a loop-de-loop in the center of his forehead—was painted on all four sides.

"He keeps an eye on the entire kingdom," Madam informed us. We were exhilarated, changed. "Do you feel it?" she asked.

I nodded, too overcome with emotion to speak. It had finally dawned on us: We were actually in Nepal!

"You know," Madam said to William, as we resumed our march. "In spite of all the hardships of our arrival, our exhaustion, and the fact that Armand has stood us up, I feel totally free and happy. So what if we don't have a good hotel? I feel like I could sleep in the streets." She looked at my doubtful expression and burst out laughing. "I'm kidding. But I do feel somehow transformed. Come on, let's get a move on."

She stopped in front of a medium-sized temple. Its entrance was up a steep staircase banked with matching sets of oversized red stone figures. "This is very special," she informed us. "Look at these statues. On the bottom, there are giants. Next are elephants, then lions, then griffins—half lion, half eagle. Then goddesses. Each one of these is ten times stronger than the one before, and the giants at the bottom are ten times stronger than humans. Don't you love the idea that the goddesses are at the top? Don't you love what that says about how the Nepalese regard women?"

I did not point out that this may have been how they regarded goddesses, but judging by the women I'd seen so far, and by all the reading I'd done, the status of the actual flesh-and-blood woman in Nepal was not quite so esteemed. In fact, they ranked along with, and sometimes even slightly below yaks in the pecking order.

We eventually found ourselves on the same wide boulevard we'd traveled from the Yellow Flame Hotel down into the old city. It was like walking on the yellow brick road or riding a magic carpet, a time machine suddenly transporting us across centuries into a modern area with banks, airline offices, embassies, hotels, and travel agencies.

"Where *are* we going, Madam?" I finally asked. In spite of my euphoria, jet lag and Kathmandu's bad air had begun to weaken my legs, which I'd strengthened so conscientiously in preparation for this journey.

"I could use another beer," William added.

"Almost there," she answered mysteriously. "Isn't this beautiful?"

We had reached a plaza dominated by a great pool, in the center of which sat a white domed shrine.

"Rani Pokhara," she announced as if she visited it every day. "King Pratap Malla built it for his wife in 1670 when their son died. Isn't it magnificent? And check this out," she said, pointing toward the end of the boulevard, "the Royal Palace."

Two or three blocks distant, at the end of a huge plaza paved with flat stones, was a remarkable building that gleamed in the setting sun. Its lines were as clean and precise as those of a Frank Lloyd Wright structure, not a millimeter was superfluous. Two identical, three-story-tall wings of red-gold limestone, with flat roofs and deep balconies, extended from either side of a five-story central tower capped with typical floating double roofs. Each was cornered with an upturned dragon tail. The windows, set far back on the balconies, were deeply shaded with flat slabs of cut stone instead of awnings. A bell tower that looked as if it were made of giant organ pipes stood to the right and had a round Vishnu at the top. In front, across the length of the palace, ran a ten-foot-tall steel mesh security fence, as decorative as it was strong. Heavily armed guards dressed in slate-blue military uniforms with red and robin's-egg-blue epaulets, and bright red and navy felt pillbox hats with little red golf balls plopped on top, patrolled the gates.

"Madam," William said, "don't you want to pause here a moment to admire this? It's quite amazing." He was drenched with perspiration. "Have pity on your brothers."

"We only have another kilometer or two," Madam said, not slowing her pace. "Then we'll all have a big gin and tonic. I'm taking the long way because when else will you get to see these things? I can guarantee we won't be passing this way again. We leave first thing in the morning. Come on." She pulled a sheet of scribbled directions from her pocket and studied it. "It's just across the park and down the street."

It was an enormous park. And a long, long street. Which went up a steep, steep hill and delivered us into a residential neighborhood, up-scale by any standard, where the rhododendron and jasmine bushes were as tall as the trees. We approached a guard house set in a wall that extended up and down the street as far as we could see. Behind the wall was a two-story house, similar in style to, although significantly smaller than, the royal palace. A guard stepped from the booth. It was a United States marine!

"Jacqueline di Fidelio," Madam announced herself.

"Yes, ma'am. May I see your passports, please?"

We handed them over and the young man studied them, and us, closely. He went into the booth and picked up the phone, spoke a few words and returned to where we stood. William's and my mouths were so far open, birds could have flown in.

"Welcome to the United States embassy residence," he said. "Go up the drive. Ambassador Franklin is waiting to greet you at the front door."

43

$\mathcal{P}$atty Hammond has done more for this country than any foreigner, American or otherwise. She is practically considered a deity," the ambassador, a dour, unfriendly man—untypical of someone in the diplomatic corps—informed Madam at cocktails. She was seated in a white wrought-iron chair sipping a tall gin and tonic while he lounged on a chaise like a pasha. An art deco shaker of Bombay gin martinis, which his attendant kept filled, lay within easy reach on a table next to him alongside a bowl of barbecue-flavored tortilla chips.

We were in the garden, surrounded by more varieties of flowers than I'd ever seen in my life, two of which—with blossoms as big and red as watermelons—Madam had tucked into her now clean and shining hair. She had on a fresh white blouse and a loose, almost transparent, flowered skirt. She looked like Ava Gardner.

"Have you ever met her?"

"Only once," Madam answered. "At the Museum of Modern Art for the opening of my mother's retrospective."

"Which I've heard is spectacular."

Madam nodded. "Unfortunately, the occasion was extremely bad luck for her sister."

"So I also heard. Not to mention Lynette's unhappy ending. The Hammonds have a lot of enemies, myself included. All of them except for Patty are as heartless as the Borgias. West Texas white trash."

"I think that might be a little extreme."

"You obviously haven't been around them much. They leave a lot of destruction in their wake and think they're invincible, which, thank God, they're not. Any leads on who killed them?"

Madam shook her head.

"I personally think it was the brother. Junior. Now there's a name for you. A middle-aged man named Junior."

"No. Junior didn't do it. He wouldn't kill his sisters."

The ambassador's expression remained as flat as a plate. "What boat did you get off? He'd kill his mother, his father, his dog, in a heartbeat if it would get him the edge. That guy screwed me on one deal too many. I can't wait until he gets his, and believe me, one of these days he will. Mark my words. Miserable mother . . ."

"Well, he won't be along on this trek so I guess we're all safe," Madam joked lamely, trying to draw him back from what looked like a very dark ledge. "Tell me more about Patty."

"Interesting woman." He held his glass up and kept it aloft until it had been refilled. "Salt-of-the-earth. Completely self-sufficient. Are you familiar with her foundation? The Hammond Himalayan Children's Fund? I'm sure you are, half the cost of your trek will go into it. You do know her treks cost double anyone else's? Extremely comfortable—well, as comfortable as they can get by western standards, you'll still face some uncomfortable challenges."

"We're completely prepared for whatever comes our way."

The ambassador snorted and wrinkled his forehead in a mocking manner. "Everyone says that. Why in hell would you want to go into Dolpo—Upper or Lower—the most empty, god-forsaken place on earth? It's not even pretty. Boiling hot. Freezing cold. And, of course, there's the religious thing. And the caste thing. You've got mostly Hindus here, and

Buddhists there. They don't socialize, of course. And the Sherpas are better than the porters—they don't even speak to each other. They have to have separate kitchens for god's sake. You'll see some weird damn rivalries. I suppose your doctor provided you with Leech-Be-Gone, the newest thing. Those little bastards' bites can bleed like hell."

Madam shivered involuntarily.

"You got splints, tourniquets? Worm medicine for your porters? And malaria pills?" The man was on his third martini and it was beginning to show. He became more of a killjoy with every sip.

"Of course you brought enough toilet paper. Has to be white. You know that, don't you? Stupid little bastards have gotten to be such environmental crusaders—they get advice and money from every environmental protection cult on the planet—they're starting to request you carry everything back out with you. Ever heard of such a thing? Carrying out your used toilet paper? And tampons. I assume you brought enough? Bring those back out, too."

"Uh, Tom . . ." Madam began.

"Damn country is so backward it's hopeless. Can't wait to get home. You know my predecessor thought the place was so dandy, he went around to every province, made friends with all the Rajas and so forth. Left a big damn map in the office, one of those elevated things, and stuck red pins in all the places he'd visited. Know what I did? Threw the goddamn thing away." His chin sank further into his collarbone.

I had completely forgotten that Madam had done Ambassador Franklin's portrait when he was chairman of Paramount Steel. He'd been a major contributor to the president's campaign and thus was offered an ambassadorship. He was enough of a donor that he could have chosen any number of mid-level postings, but he picked this one because he thought he loved the mountains—after all, he'd climbed Mt. Washington when he went to Dartmouth, forty-five years ago—and thought mountaineering was a sport he'd like to get back into. But he'd gotten spoiled and soft and should have asked for Scotland.

"Who else is on your trek?"

"Evelina and James King," William said.

Tom Franklin nodded. "Another Texas loud mouth. Comes over here all the time and tries to throw his weight around. He's an experienced mountaineer, went to the top of Everest once and thinks he knows everything. His wife's an airhead. Who else?"

"Just Mr. Weil, the three of us, and Patty."

"You met her new boyfriend?"

"No."

"Guy's a trip and a half. They go at it like dogs. You practically have to turn the hose on them."

"Where's Victoria, Tom?" Madam blurted out, anxious for a change of subject.

He focused his wavy eyes on her. "Victoria?" he said. "She gave up and went home months ago. Bored out of her mind. Said if I didn't let her go, she'd file for divorce. Couldn't blame her. I've got another eleven months and then it's hasta la vista, baby. Well." He placed his glass on the table with the studied care of one who is accustomed to having too much to drink and equally accustomed to pretending he hasn't. "If you'll excuse me, I'm sorry I can't join you for dinner, but I have a reception at the Royal Palace. Only high point in my week." He heaved himself to his feet with a groan. "Have a good night's sleep and be sure to let my staff know if there's anything at all you need. What time do you take off in the morning?"

"Six," William replied.

"Yes. You need to get in the air early around here, after ten, flying's impossible—all the crazy weather they have. I probably won't see you off, but I'm glad you contacted me, Jackie. The staff'll see you get to the airport in one piece. Good to see you. Good luck."

"Thanks so much for putting us up. I think you probably saved our lives," she smiled.

"Yes, I probably did. For tonight, at least." He frowned and limped slowly across the garden to the house.

44

When we got up, we dressed for walking—the understanding being that as soon as our plane landed, the trek would begin right there at the airport. Because women are expected to wear skirts in Nepal, even when trekking, Madam had brought a number of mid-calf-length cotton and sheer chiffon skirts with leggings to wear under them, so when she appeared at the front door at five a.m. in a khaki skirt, crisp white blouse, ankle-high walking boots with thick white socks, and white rhododendrons in her hair, she appeared to have stepped out of the pages of *Vogue* magazine.

"You look ready for anything, Madam," William told her as he helped her into the embassy's armor-plated white Suburban. He looked quite snappy himself in pressed khakis, a pale blue and white oxford cloth shirt and a wide-brimmed safari hat.

Her face glowed with excitement. "I *am* ready for anything," she laughed. "Bring on the world."

She was especially ready to see Armand, as we all were, but earlier that morning, as I helped her with her hair, I couldn't keep my anxiety about his dependability from spilling over. "What if he doesn't show up?" I'd asked. "What will we do? Will we stop?"

"You are such a little old lady sometimes, Nigel," she'd said light-heartedly. "Of course we won't stop."

The words stung me and I'd been working not to pout ever since. It wasn't my fault if I was trying to bring a little reality to the situation. Someone needed to. She thought I couldn't hear the false notes behind her bantering words.

We were two hours late taking off, due to the unexpected volume of our luggage, which had necessitated off-loading a cargo of unidentified supplies, but at eight o'clock, our Royal Nepal Airlines Short-Take-Off-Landing (STOL) Twin-Otter charter lifted off the runway like a gently bounced rubber ball. Just alley-oop and we were airborne. I'd read that the Royal Nepal pilots, who train in the United Airlines Flight Training Center in Denver, were the best mountain pilots in the world, and only seconds into our flight I could see why: the Rockies and the Alps were *nothing* compared to the Himalayas. They were mere anthills. Smaller than anthills.

We skirted massive peaks—their ice-bound summits glittered forbiddingly in the morning sun—and crossed the range at Pokhara, going deep into the Tibetan Himalayas. Minutes later we passed close to the north faces of Annapurna and Dhaulagiri, two of the world's tallest mountains. We flew deep into stark, steep-walled valleys, their shale-y cliffs completely unforested, devoid of any vegetation except scrub brush, and dotted with red and ochre-colored monasteries and shrines. Wild, impassable rivers, swollen with the spring run-off, raged out of their banks below our tiny plane. We passed over long caravans of yaks burdened with bags of Tibetan salt headed south to trade for barley, a staple of the Nepalese diet. The sure-footed beasts clung solidly to the barren, almost vertical hillsides, unperturbed by the noise of our engines and unfazed by the sure death of a misstep. We flew lower still, dodging through thickening clouds, across green terraces of rice, buckwheat, and barley, onto the fertile Tichurong Plain, the southernmost border of the Dolpo Province, where we found ourselves suddenly in a completely different climate under a high overcast sky, racing above forests of juniper, blue pine, chestnut, walnut, and oak.

Two hours after we'd taken off from Kathmandu, we floated to earth on a barren plain outside an abandoned-looking village named Juphal, on a dirt landing strip, an incongruous concession to the twenty-first century.

"Do you know the chances of Armand landing his jet on this field?" Madam asked.

William and I did not have to answer.

"Zip," she answered for us.

Out the windows of the plane we could see Patty Hammond waiting to greet us with an army of porters. And right next to her, grinning from behind dark glasses with side panels and a braided native Tibetan neck-strap, was her new boyfriend, Ryder McCormick.

Oh, man. Talk about bad karma.

Madam's face turned white as a sheet. "Dear Jesus," she said. "We've got to get out of here."

The three of us looked at each other, the good night's sleep and anticipation drained from our faces. The captain, unaware of the disaster taking place right in front of his eyes, walked past and opened the door of the plane, letting in the soft, moist air. "Welcome to Dolpo," he said, but there was little he could do to entice us out. We sat frozen in stunned silence.

"Hello?" Patty's voice called in through the door after a couple of minutes. "Anyone there?"

"Give us a minute," Madam answered and tossed her phone to William. "Get your boss on the line. Now."

"How were we to know it was a dirt strip?" Armand fought back. His voice was so loud we could all hear it—these phones seemed to have no volume control.

"Did you try a map? Or the aviation authority? Where exactly are you now?"

"New Delhi. I'm trying to arrange a charter, but they say it's too late in the day to fly up there."

"Try."

"Darling, I can't. They won't take off until tomorrow morning. But the charter service has a big cargo helicopter and says they can drop me off wherever Patty tells them to land."

"Did you know Ryder McCormick was along on this trip?"

"*What?*"

"You heard what I said. He's with Patty. I'm looking at him right now through the window, standing out here in the middle of fucking nowhere. It scares me absolutely to death."

"*Jésu,*" he said anxiously. "Let me think what I can do. See if you can stay . . ."

As the sun climbed in the sky, it had gotten hot in the plane and windy outside. Little dust devils swirled around the high plateau, empty but for a small airport building and a handful of flat-roofed mud houses.

"I'm getting out of here, Armand." Madam cut him off. "I'm going back to Kathmandu and then home. If you want to see me, you come to Middleburg."

"No! No! Wait!" I heard him yelling as she flipped the phone shut.

"Get the pilot back in here," she ordered William. "We're leaving."

"I'm so sorry, Miss," the perplexed young aviator explained. "But it's too late in the day to fly back."

"It's only ten-thirty."

"We would not get in the air before eleven and that's too late to fly in the mountains. The drafts are too great. I won't be able to take off until five-thirty or six tomorrow morning."

She called the travel agent. She called Royal Nepal Airlines. She called United Airlines. She called a charter service in Kathmandu. She called the ambassador and had him awakened. "I told you last night," he was unsympathetic. "You can't fly around here unless you take off well before ten." Madam hung up and laid the phone in her lap.

"We are totally screwed," she said to no one.

"Anybody home in there?" Patty called again. "We need to get a move on, we've got a steady five hours back to camp."

"We'll be right there," Madam called back. "Listen you guys," she spoke to William and me. "I don't think we have a lot of choices. There's not exactly a Holiday Inn for us to spend the night. Patty's got all the camping gear at her camp, and what we've got is a bunch of snake bite medicine, beef jerky, and no water. So here's what we're going to do: Fuck Armand. And fuck Ryder McCormick. We're going to go on this trip, but I swear to God, you have to promise you'll stay with me every second, one of you in front, one behind. Ryder's looking for a way to get even, and I'm sure there'll be plenty of opportunities."

"Of course we promise, Madam," I answered for both of us. William nodded his assent.

"We've all trained for this trip, we're mentally and physically ready. We're excited about it. We're much younger and more nimble than Ryder, and I will not let him intimidate me. We're just going to do it."

"Right," I said.

The phone rang.

"Turn that thing off."

"But it might be Armand," William said.

"*FUCK ARMAND!*" she yelled, pulled a lipstick from her pocket, and applied a fresh coat. Sticking the tube back in her pocket, she pressed her lips together and stood up as far as she could in the small cabin. "It's too late for him. He'll just have to figure it out for himself. Let's do it. Nigel, you go first."

"Right."

So, umbrellas in hand, we paraded into the muggy day, into our destiny: Dolpo, Nepal's enchanted, sacred world, into a place as remote as any on the planet, and greeted our executioners as warmly as Mary Queen of Scots did hers when she handed the masked swordsman a gold sovereign and forgave him for what he was about to do, as long as he was swift and merciful.

45

_S_ herpas serve as guides and cooks; they are the elite staff members of all trek expeditions. Patty had brought her head Sherpa, a small, smiling man as gnarled and solid as a tree trunk, and he decided, with remarkable efficiency, how to distribute the load most equitably, who would carry what. Shortly, the porters, who carried their own body weight in packs and duffels suspended down their backs from a single leather strap around their foreheads, headed out in front of us at such a steady clip they were soon gone from sight.

We'd been walking for a couple of hours or so. First we'd descended into a scorched valley where we forged a river via a sturdy cable bridge, and now we were slowly ascending into a completely different topography. Mountains, appearing out of nowhere! It started to mist, making the many shades of green on the mountains sharper. This was not what I'd expected. I thought there'd be chains of gently rolling hills at first, getting progressively steeper as they led to the peaks, but these were more like the loaf-shaped mountains around Machu-Pichu, completely individual entities, thickly carpeted with foliage. Nor was our path what I'd envisioned. I thought it would be a dusty trail, but instead it was an ancient footpath paved with smooth stones that became slick as we climbed into the dense pine and birch forest.

Our order had not changed since we stepped off the plane: Patty's assistant guide—a young Scotsman, named what else but Scottie—led the way. I walked in front of Madam, William behind, his giant Hasselblad camera and tripod bulging from his pack. (Who do you think you are? I'd asked him when I first saw the old-fashioned equipage at the airport. Ansel Adams? He'd just given me a dirty look.) Ryder, who'd greeted us with what seemed to be genuine enthusiasm and friendliness, flavored—I was satisfied to note—with a little tinge of nervous and respectful reticence, brought up the rear with Patty.

I know this sounds crazy, but I think we, Madam and I, were maybe secretly a bit relieved to see Ryder. He was a well-known face, a familiar quantity, and he was on his best behavior. Before Madam could make any cracks about what his wife might be up to, he made a special point of telling us that Mary Anne was at Mayo's for four-weeks of treatments and was so happy he'd been invited to have a little fun for a change.

"I told her I'd stay and help look after her, but she insisted," he insisted.

Patty provided the buffer.

Every now and then she or the Scotsman would point out a special flower or plant or tree or bird, but otherwise talking was kept to a minimum as we adjusted to the rapidly changing altitude and correspondingly changing flora.

All day we progressed, either climbing or descending, nothing was flat or easy. It was terribly hard work. I'd thought I was in good shape, but I was completely unprepared for the toll the higher altitude would take and for the masses of insects that swarmed constantly in the drenching humidity at the lower levels, energized by the impending monsoon. I never in my life thought I would be bitten by a leech. You cannot imagine the pain and nauseating horror of having a blood-sucking worm attached to your leg. They drill right through the skin in

240

search of veins, which they seem to be able to locate in record time, and then they start pumping the blood right out of you, growing fat and oily right before your eyes. It's terrifying, and even though I'd known all along they were a possibility, when it actually happened, I could scarcely control my panic. My heart began to pound and I was too frightened to breathe or make a sound; all I could do was open and close my mouth, point to my leg, and squeak like a bird.

Thank God for Patty. She was right there on the spot with a tube of the white ointment that sends the leech and the victim into mutually excruciating pain. Fatal for the leech. And I'll tell you, you're pretty sure it's going to be fatal for you, too. She smothered the worm with the cream and it began to wriggle and wither and curl up and die right before my eyes. Then it fell off and a gusher of blood spurted from my leg. It was hell stopping the bleeding, too. Finally, one of my pressure bandages did the trick. We all got bitten—we had to take one off Madam's neck and she was much more stoic about it than I was, but mine had been the first. She had the advantage of seeing that I was going to live.

By late afternoon, although we'd only walked for maybe a total of five hours, I was certainly feeling the effects. I had such a terrific headache I thought my brains were being crushed by a vise and my eyes felt like they were going to pop out of my head.

"Here we are," Patty announced unexpectedly as we emerged from the forest onto a flat hillside clearing. The camp had already been erected and the other members of the party, Eva and James King, waited to welcome us, offering mugs of sweet tea. The Kings were extremely fit; they were all sinewy legs and arms, bony hands, sun-wrinkled skin, and smiling, friendly faces.

"How was your hike?" Eva asked. "Baptism by leeches?"

"Gross," Madam answered, accepting the tea. "Thanks," she said. "I need this badly." She sat down on a large flat rock with a whump, pulled a Snickers bar out of her pack and devoured it and the tea without another word.

The rest of us, Ryder included, sort of circled and circled until we finally just collapsed on the ground from exhaustion and stared stupidly into space while the porters worked around us.

The camp was much more comfortable than I had expected, since my attitude toward camping had always been that it was something I'd do only as a last resort in the event of, say, a nuclear war. But here on the Himalayan plateau, we each had our own tent equipped with a cot, a small collapsible table, and a metal basin. My sleeping bag, pillows, and fresh towels were already laid out. There was a tented latrine, which also wasn't nearly as bad as I'd imagined, especially because someone had told me everyone just relieved themselves by crouching behind the nearest rock or behind their umbrella.

Shortly after we arrived, shucked our rain slickers and hats and washed up in hot water brought to our tents by the porters, we darted across the clearing through the rain and ducked under the big tent where camp stools had been set up around a large candlelit table that folded up into a tidy package for traveling. Patty offered us cocktails—scotch, gin, vodka, rum or brandy—and afterward we were served a hugely satisfying dinner of roasted barley and savory stew, during which we pretended there were not two dead elephants lying in the middle of the floor: We pretended Madam hadn't gotten publicly dumped by Armand and he was actually going to appear sometime the next day, and we pretended Madam and Ryder were friends. The tension between them, sexual and otherwise, intensified by the cocktails, was so thick you could cut it with a knife.

"What is this?" Madam asked. "It's delicious."

"Kid," Patty answered. "What do you think of it?"

"Kid, as in baby goat?"

Patty grinned. "What did you think I meant? Child?" She had a cockeyed kind of face, almost like an Irish cop. All her features were oversized. Her nose was big, but not unattractively so and it had a bump in the middle, as if it had been broken a couple of times. She had crooked teeth, and light blue eyes as big as walnut shells.

"I think it's much better than I would've thought goat stew would be. But I have to tell you, I'm sorry I asked."

"It's considered somewhat of a delicacy here, as are all meats and poultry, since they aren't raised to slaughter but to produce milk, eggs, et cetera. Be sure to tell the cook you liked it."

Patty had gotten the best of what her family had to offer, and not only that, she'd made the best of it, gotten out of Dodge while the getting was good, and made a life for herself, divorced from the shenanigans of her father and siblings. She was physically big and strong, but not at all overweight. Her body was taut and well-muscled, obviously ac-customed to long hauls over hostile terrain. Her hair was gray-blond and close-cropped, and her suntanned, wind-wrinkled face was alive with good spirits, her expression always engaged and warm. She obviously loved what she did and loved Nepal. She had slipped herself into this life as easily as duck slid into a calm pond, without a ripple, and wanted to share every possible speck of knowledge about it. Each question was met with enthusiasm, appreciation, and a gentle, self-deprecating, al-most shy, humor. She was solicitous of and involved with her crew of porters; they were well and warmly dressed. Although they had their own cook and food, they ate as nutritiously as we did.

"There are a number of trekkers and outfitters who come to Nepal and don't look after their porters," Patty explained as dessert was being served: paper-thin slices of Linzer torte that were so weighty with dark chocolate you could use them as doorstops. Despite her years away from the United States, Patty had never lost the Texas swing to her accent. "They don't clothe or feed or accommodate them properly and then they can't understand why the porters are so slow to get going in the morning, although maybe it's been five below overnight and the fellows were sleeping in only their clothes and had nothing but a little dried yak jerky for dinner and sweet tea for breakfast. The trekkers are more concerned about the care taken of the yaks or ponies than of their human beasts of burden. It's criminal. The number of porters who freeze to death or fall to their deaths because they are malnourished and exhausted would as-tonish you. And it's all because of thoughtlessness.

"I outfit my porters completely every expedition, get them medical checkups before we leave, and make sure they take their vitamins while we're on the trail. And I hope they take back a little of what I've given them to their villages and it improves the lives of their families. It's part of what you pay for to trek with me and make a gift to my foundation." She smiled brightly.

A little later, after Ava and Jim King had excused themselves to go to bed and Ryder had stumbled off to the bathroom, Patty spoke bluntly to Madam. "I know about you and Ryder, Jackie. I know you have a long history, and I know it ended badly between you and you gave him a bro-ken nose and had to throw him out in a blizzard. And I apologize if his being here makes you uncomfortable."

"Not a bit," Madam said lightly, glad that at least one elephant was being addressed. "Ancient history."

"When Armand and I discussed this trip, he initially told me he was coming alone, and then he said he was bringing this gal from Paris he travels with occasionally, Nicole. Then, a couple of weeks ago, he told me he was bringing you instead, but it was too late to uninvite Ryder, not that I would have anyway, but I've made it clear to him, in no uncertain terms, that if he wants to keep me as his sweetheart, I won't tolerate anything less than civilized harmony on my trek."

Madam smiled at her. "That's very nice of you, Patty." She started laughing in spite of herself. "We don't even know each other, but you're seeing me at my absolute worst—my life with my men. It's a total disaster. You could write a soap opera about my love affairs."

"Get in line," Patty said. "I'm hoping this one sticks. We seem to be hitting it off pretty well."

"From what I've seen so far, if anyone can handle him, it's you. You seem to have a big enough whip."

"Figuratively and literally," Patty answered and then cracked-up at her own joke.

"What's so funny?" Ryder asked, appearing from the dark.

"Just girl talk, honey," Patty told him.

"No really."

"I *said*," her voice had the sort of warning tone a mother bear uses just before she whaps her cub on his head, "*just girl talk*. That's all you need to know. Now you come on in here with me," she held open the flap on her tent, "and we'll make some boy-and-girl talk."

"*Nicole?*" Madam said after they were gone. "Nicole who?"

"A *couple* of weeks ago?" I added. We'd been in training for six weeks.

"She's got it all wrong," William answered weakly. I could tell he was lying. "I swear to God."

"Give it up, William," Madam said. "The man is indefensible."

I slept restlessly. My head ached, my back and legs ached. I couldn't get comfortable on the cot and the cold drizzle kept falling until just before dawn.

46

*P*lease speak to him, Madam," William crouched behind her and whispered in her ear, offering over the phone.

It was on the tip of her tongue to say no, tell him to go to hell, but then she noticed Ryder smirking and holding his hand over his forehead, his fingers in the shape of the letter L for loser. She mouthed a profanity at him, got to her feet and took the set from William's outstretched hand.

"Armand, darling," she said gaily, loud enough for everyone to hear, as she walked to the edge of the clearing. "What's your excuse for today?"

It was the morning of the third day and we were sitting on our stools in the big tent, sipping cups of tea that steamed in the ice-cold morning. The damp had become downright bone-chilling. The cook stirred a bubbling pot of porridge on the propane stove.

Madam kept her voice low for the balance of her conversation and when she returned, the color was high in her face but there was no sign of tears.

"When is our benefactor *du jour,* Mr. Wonderful, going to make an appearance?" Ryder asked.

Madam didn't respond.

"Knock it off," Patty said. "I'm not going to warn you again."

Patty seemed to have the right personality to manage Ryder. She was not only as mentally tough as Mary Anne, she was physically stronger than any of us. She could kick Ryder around the block without breaking a sweat, and he knew it. And, as some of us knew, he would like it.

"Sorry," Ryder mumbled, pouring a little brandy into his tea. "I really mean it, Jackie. That was out of line."

"Apology accepted," Madam responded, but it didn't sound any more genuine than Ryder's apology.

Patty looked back and forth between the two of them. I didn't think she would hesitate for one second to heave Madam or Ryder off a cliff if either one of them got any ideas. It didn't take a genius to figure out there was some sparring going on. "Here's the program for today," Patty announced. "We're going to continue on up the trail past Ringmo . . ."

As she spoke, I managed to catch Madam's eye and she shook her head ever so slightly, an indication that she had final confirmation that Armand would not be joining the trek at all. She was mildly humiliated, but not unexpectedly so. Last night she told me she knew he wouldn't come. Well, we all knew the affair was over, didn't we, when we'd heard that until as recently as two weeks ago, he was planning to bring someone else. I guess we probably even knew it back there in Kathmandu, which now seemed a hundred years and a million miles ago. Maybe Madam even knew it in Washington when he told us to fly ahead.

It no longer mattered whether Armand showed up or not. She and William and I were on the trip of a lifetime, at Armand's expense, and it was only ten days long, with three of those days already gone. And Madam had Ryder clearly in focus. For her, the break had turned out to be clean. He was the one with the relationship problem.

"What exactly did Mr. Weil say?" I asked her as we set out.

"Standard bullshit. He said he loved me more than anyone he'd ever known but he realized he couldn't go through with it. The thought of commitment scared him to death and he was ashamed of himself and hoped I could forgive him. It was just a bunch of third-grade crapola. Boy, I can sure pick 'em, can't I?" She pulled ahead of me, her long legs taking goddess—fifty times stronger than a giant—steps.

The hike that morning was spectacular. We entered the National Park and Patty handed the park ranger our visas, a sheaf of paperwork that precisely outlined our intended route, the letters giving us permission to enter the sacred Buddhist region beyond the lake, permits to circumnavigate the lake itself, and receipts proving we had each paid two thousand U.S. dollars in cash over and above the standard seven hundred dollar fee, to follow our route.

Just to make certain we did what we said we were going to, a government liaison officer would accompany us every step of the way.

"A few last minute reminders," Patty gathered us for an impromptu meeting once we'd passed the check point. Our caravan—we'd traded porters for yaks as our altitude increased—accompanied by Scottie, lumbered out of sight up the narrow trail. "Don't worry about getting lost," she explained. "Scottie will always be in front, and I will always be at the rear with the medical pack. Watch your step, it's very easy to take a tumble, and, as you've already discovered, the trail is slick in some places and downright precarious in others. Until you're completely accustomed to carrying your packs, they can throw you off-balance quickly. If you have to go to the bathroom, step off the trail and try to find some privacy, but from now on, it may not always be possible. Stick your used toilet paper into your re-sealable plastic trash bag. If you see any trash on the ground, even if it was left by someone else, pick it up. Finally, enjoy yourselves. Any questions? Yes, Nigel."

"Will there be any more leeches?"

"No, we've left them behind. See you at dinner."

Late that afternoon, as I hiked through meadows, past a chorten at the entrance to a tiny village with its spinning prayer wheels, past pilgrims on their own treks to the holy lake and monastery, past lines of red-eyed, angry-looking yaks, and along the narrow walls of a dark canyon where a fat, green snake crossed my path but was gone so quickly I didn't have time to react, I heard the unmistakable sound of my goal ahead: the echoing roar of Nepal's largest waterfall. At a point some miles south of the lake was the junction of two rivers. Millions of gallons of water a second tumbled across thousands of feet of rock, churning up thick mist and deafening noise.

The bridge crossing the torrent below this wonderfully gigantic cascade puts you squarely in the hands of God. I kid you not. This was one of the tests the trip was all about, and after I'd taken quite a lot of time to study the span of poles that connected organized piles of rocks on either bank, and had a couple of cigarettes to calm my nerves, I set out. I looked only at my feet—knowing they would not betray me—never at the maelstrom below, and when I reached the other side, I was so proud of myself I thought I'd burst. Oh, how I wished I could tell my mum what I'd done. She'd never believe it. William and Madam had done it, too, because they were way ahead, and we'd all be proud for each other, but no one can be as proud as a mum. Instead of making me cry, it made me laugh out loud. As a matter of fact, I whooped with delight and sat there on the ground just giggling to myself for longer than I should have, because I caught sight of Patty and Ryder arguing on the opposite bank. It occurred to me that this particular spot would be a terrific place to murder someone. I mean, who in the hell would go down there and look for a body in that mess?

Not me.

If I were Ryder, I'd be on my *very* best behavior.

47

*P*hoksumdo Tal is a lake of an almost unearthly blue. At an altitude of more than eleven-thousand feet, set deep in a ring of rocky peaks, the color of the water changes constantly from azure to turquoise to lapis, depending on the sun and clouds. A large red monastery, now abandoned except for a lone caretaker, hundreds of brightly colored prayer flags streaming from its roof, sits on its bank. This is where the majority of trekkers turn back, because there is virtually nothing but hard-edged, bleak wilderness beyond. This invisible boundary not only keeps the area isolated for religious purposes, but also protects the unique, nomadic culture of Dolpo, which extends a long way north to the Tibetan border. Dolpo is considered to have the last-remaining, most unspoiled, unadulterated Tibetan culture—since China destroyed the real thing—and the Tibetans who live in Dolpo keep it that way, not through any organized effort, but because the land is so vast and barren and because it is their karma.

"Scottie will leave a marker on the trail to point the way to camp," Patty had said at our briefing before we ventured forth. "It's about four steady hours, but you don't need to be there until six o'clock. Anyone who isn't there by six will be considered lost or injured and we will send someone to find you. And we really don't want to do that. I always think it's a good rule of thumb to try to get to camp by four-thirty. Please be extremely careful. Anyone who is injured jeopardizes the whole trek. Watch where you put your feet."

As we passed through the vale, we each spun the monastery's prayer wheels and embarked on our odyssey.

By now we were accustomed to our packs, each of which carried about twenty pounds of gear: bottles of water, weatherproof jackets and sweaters, lunch, phones, binoculars, and minor medical supplies. Patty remained at the end of the line with the medical pack, which weighed-in at about fifty pounds, but fifty pounds to her was like ten pounds to the rest of us. In addition to the necessities, we each carried a few extra personal items: Madam had a small camera and a sketch pad. I had a handsome Moroccan leather-bound journal in which, I'd decided, if I kept enough notes, I could begin to write stories about the Himalayas to rival Wilbur Smith's heart-stopping African adventures. William had insisted on keeping his cumbersome Hasselblad and tripod, which weighed him down and made him slow. Ryder had a bird book and powerful little Leica binoculars for spotting, although a limited number of species made the trip to this altitude. He wouldn't know an eagle from a buzzard anyway. Birding was his latest affectation, adopted for Patty's benefit.

I moved rapidly onto the trail, speeding ahead of Madam and William, and climbed the steep rock steps carved into the mountainside. The mountains plunged directly into the lake, falling hundreds of feet straight down from the very narrow twisting path, which is less than shoulder-wide in places.

With the exception of the clearing at the south end of the lake, there was not even the semblance of a beach or shore, and I had the impression that the cliffs continued their fall beneath the glacial water uninterrupted all the way to China, or whatever was opposite Nepal. I knew the Sherpas, the yaks, Scottie, Jim, and Eva were ahead of me, but I was so alone, they might as well have fallen off the face of the earth. Except for the wind, which blew in freezing gusts up from the water, the underlying silence was deafening.

In some spots, the trail was in good condition, having been reinforced by stones. In others, rickety wooden slats supported by unsteady poles thrust into the mountainside and topped with rock slabs crossed dizzying ravines and trembled with my every step. I had gotten the nerve to cross two of these spans, but when I rounded a blind corner and came upon one whose distance was twice that of the others, I completely froze. The teetering slabs were so unstable, I felt it could not be more daunting to cross from one World Trade Center tower to the other via a single bouncing wooden plank. I felt like screaming. All I would have to do was get even the slightest bit off balance, and my pack would supply the momentum to pull me off. Backwards. I pictured myself standing there on the bouncing slab, nothing but air below, my arms windmilling, one boot in the air, and then, just when it looked as if I would right myself, the wind would gust and catch me and that would be all she wrote. I would fall, and fall, and fall. Oh, God. The longer I stared at the crossing, the more panicky I became.

"Come on, Nigel, move it," Madam said, and I jumped ten feet in the air.

"I didn't hear you coming."

"Let's go."

"Right."

I had to do it. If Madam had caught up to me, that meant William couldn't be far behind, and he would tease me unmercifully if he found me still on the south side of the northbound climb. My throat and mouth were completely dry, and if I had a heart condition, I would say I was suffering from an acute attack of angina.

What choice did I have? None. I couldn't stand there and indulge my neuroses all day because at the end of it I would still be required to go forward or back. And I'd still be in the middle of nowhere.

"All right," I announced. "If the yaks can do it, I can do it. Here I go." I stuck my arms straight out, and, keeping my eyes on my feet, crossed the plank.

As the day went on, it became the most rewarding of my life. We leap-frogged each other on the trail. I passed Madam, perched on a rock doing a quick sketch, and shortly afterward came upon William, who had completely blocked the path and set up like a photographer from 1910 to take a large-format picture.

"You'd better hope a yak caravan doesn't come past," I said, "or you and your fancy camera will be taking pictures of the bottom of the lake."

"I'm keeping my eyes and ears open. You can see them coming if you pay attention."

"Smell them coming is more like it."

"Go stand over there and let me get you in this shot. You can put it on your Christmas card."

I did as instructed and then, when he'd gotten through all the machinations of reloading the camera, we switched places and I took his picture. I liked looking at William. He kept his wiry body in good shape and his auction room pallor had been colored-up by the strong high-altitude sun.

We had lunch together.

"What do you plan to do with all those notes you're scribbling all the time?" he asked.

"My idea is to write a book. A sort of adventure story."

"What makes you think you can do that? I mean, do you have any writing experience?"

I shook my head. "No, but I thought this trip would make a good book. Don't you?"

"Not so far." He leaned back against a rock and put his hands behind his head.

"Well, I'd fill in a story around it. It's something I've always wanted to do, and frankly, this is the most exciting, dangerous thing I've ever done. And I know it is for you, too."

"I *thought* it would be exciting and dangerous, but it's turning out to be merely interesting," William said.

"You are such a cynic, William." I clapped my journal closed and tucked it into my pack. "I'll see you at dinner," I said. I felt a burst of literary brilliance coming on and wanted to get it down. I found a beautiful overlook on the trail where I could sit and write, but mostly I just looked at the view and tried to organize my thoughts. Every now and then I had to scramble up the rocks and hold on for dear life while a yak caravan thundered past, the men in colorful orange and red jackets, right arm always free to drive the yaks, and the women, equally colorful in their dress, faces black from the smoke of the cooking fires, pungent from the lack of hygiene and the rancid yak butter they used to dress their hair. They rumbled by as if the trail were as wide as a freeway. Their dogs, enormous woolly black Tibetan mastiffs, had the heavy chains that were used to stake them out on guard duty at night wrapped around their bodies. Every beast carried his weight.

Mid-afternoon, I climbed up and sat on a precarious ledge next to Madam. "Do you mind?"

She shook her head. She was sketching one of the Tibetan women she'd seen pass. The woman's hair was stiff with butter, and her face was dark. She was smiling broadly, showing very white and very strong teeth. Her eyes were almost invisible—upside-down smiles in a sea of deep wrinkles. Madam tucked her pencil behind her ear and looked out at the distant mountains. "Know what I've been thinking?"

"Not a clue."

"I've been thinking we really don't need much more than this. We thrash around trying to make a living, always in a state of hysteria over money, and look at these people. They have nothing that we would consider anything, and yet they're always smiling. They're happy. I'm thinking about not going home."

"Really," I said.

"What do you think?"

"I think you could go maybe one more week without a proper shampoo and bath. Maybe two more weeks without a proper bed. Maybe even three weeks without a manicure. But then . . ."

"Then what?"

"Then I think you'd hit the wall. I think the lice would drive you home. And I really don't think you want to carry your used toilet paper around in a zip-lock bag for the rest of your life."

"You're right," she laughed. "And the lice are disgusting. Not to mention the leeches. It's just that sitting here in this majestic setting, it all seems so silly, so superficial. It sure puts Miss Collier and the IRS in proportion, doesn't it?"

"Only if you don't go back." I couldn't help it. The reality of our situation had not left me for one second of this bliss-filled trip. I worried constantly about what would become of us when we got home. "Armand never was going to send the money, was he?"

"No. Always right around the corner." She took up the pencil again. "I don't want to talk about it anymore. I'll see you in a while."

A little later, I heard the crack of ice and the roar of an avalanche on the face of Kanji Roba, a massive wall of rock, and it reminded me of how tiny I was. Just a speck of a speck. I wrote that down.

48

Late in the afternoon, I spotted the camp marker—Scottie's scarf wrapped around a rock like a hobo's bundle—and turned up the steep slope, then descended at an equally steep pitch through a stand of trees. The meadow Scottie had selected was beautiful and green, gently undulating, and the views of Kanji Roba's walls were spectacular. There was even a creek where we could wash in freezing, clean water. Such a simple pleasure taken so for granted. This would be our home for three nights.

After my bath, I dressed in warm clothes, lay down on the closely cropped grass, and fell into a deep sleep. I was so exhausted by the exercise, even the altitude had stopped bothering me.

William woke me up, fear in his eyes.

"What?" I sat up instantly.

"Armand's been arrested."

"What?"

"I just talked to the office. Interpol came and arrested him yesterday afternoon."

"You can't be serious."

"The secretary said they're waiting for me, too. In Kathmandu. They have a warrant for my arrest." William sat down heavily next to me. "I don't know what to do."

"Where's Madam?" I asked.

William motioned over his shoulder, and I spotted her lounging next to Patty, eating a Snickers bar, at least her fifth of the day. They were talking at the same time like ladies at a beauty parlor. "Don't tell her, Nigel. I don't want her to know."

"Why not?"

"I just don't."

But it was too late. She'd seen that something was up.

"Oh, man," she whistled after he'd broken the news. I prayed she wouldn't add "bad karma," or "bummer," because I think William probably would have punched her. "What was he arrested for?"

"Grand theft. The Gardner works."

"What are you going to do?" she asked.

"I don't know. Armand didn't steal the Gardner works, but now they'll start digging. Our entire business will fall like a house of cards."

The three of us discussed his options, which were few. William was a master of disguise, but his passport was his passport, and where and how could he go about getting false papers in Nepal? It took him under ten minutes to bite all his fingernails to the quick.

"Don't worry, William," Madam said, getting to her feet. "We'll think of something."

"I think she turned us in," he said after she was out of earshot.

"Who?"

"Jackie. I think she turned Armand and me in to Interpol."

"She would never do that."

He looked at me like I was stupid.

"She wouldn't," I insisted, but deep down, I had a sinking feeling she had.

"I'd rather die than go to prison."

Dinner that night was a subdued affair. Everyone was tired from the day's exertions, our legs were like jelly, and something had gone wrong between Patty and Ryder, which made the already strained atmosphere even more uncomfortable. William took his plate and ate by himself outside the main tent, rebuffing all my efforts to draw him out and discuss the situation. After dinner, Patty and Madam sat and talked late into the evening.

The next morning we bid farewell to Jim and Eva King, who were going to cross deeper into Dolpo. We watched them, with eight yaks, four Sherpas, and a band of porters disappear into the fog on the other side of the pass, and then we all retreated into our own worlds. The group was silent and reflective. William was unreachable as he sat on the ground and fiddled with his camera, carefully sliding the heavy photographic plates into their individual pockets in his pack.

"William," Madam said. "I'd like to talk to you."

His face was a mask.

"I promise you, I did not turn in you and Armand. I would never do such a thing."

"How did they find out?" His voice was hard and accusatory. "We've been in business for thirty years with no problems. Then we let you in on the process, and all of a sudden, we're caught. I've lived a hard life, I've done time, and I'll tell you, I don't intend to do more. I resent the fact that you've turned me into a fugitive. You could have at least waited until I had a few more options instead of blowing the whistle when we're at the end of the earth."

"I didn't do it."

"I should have killed you when I had the chance." He turned back to his plates. The conversation was over.

The next morning, not long after breakfast, the five of us set out, seemingly in five different directions.

I made it a point not to see anyone that day. We'd be back in the real world soon enough. I was up and down the cliffs like a mountain goat and was the first to the camp that afternoon. Madam wandered in not

long after I did, and after a bath in the creek, modestly concealed behind a portable screen, she retired to her tent for a nap. As before, I
bathed and then napped in the afternoon sun. About an hour later, I
awoke to see Ryder leaning comfortably against a rock, reading a book
and pouring brandy into his tea. The only sound was the snuffling of the
yaks. It was idyllic. I fell back to sleep.

49

It was almost dark, the deepest part of twilight, when the sun is gone and the shadows have become impenetrable, when I was jerked awake by Scottie shaking my shoulder. "What is it?" I asked. "Is everything all right?"

"They aren't back," he said. "We're going to find them. Get your headlamp."

"Who isn't back?"

"Jackie, Patty, and William."

"But Madam was here," I said. "I saw her."

"She went out again to take some sunset photos."

We searched for over an hour in the growing darkness until finally I heard the faint sound of yelling in the distance. Scottie and the Sherpas were way ahead of Ryder and me, and when we finally reached them, my heart almost stopped. Madam was lying on the trail, blocking it completely, crying uncontrollably. Her leg was turned unnaturally from her knee at a terrifying angle. I crouched close to her head as Scottie hugged the cliff almost superhumanly to get beyond her. "This has everything you need." I tossed him my pack. He dug through it for a morphine syringe. The trail was no wider than twenty inches. The lake, now an invisible sheet of black steel, was hundreds of feet below.

"Oh, Nigel. Nigel." She clung to my arm and sobbed hysterically, gasping for breath. "They fell. Oh, God. It was horrible."

Scottie pushed up the sleeve of her sweater and sank the needle expertly into her vein.

"Who?" I asked stupidly. "Who fell?"

"Patty," she wailed. "And William. I was out sketching and I saw them in the distance and they looked like they were arguing and then they were suddenly over the edge. Just over the edge. They fell forever. Oh, God."

"What do you mean, 'arguing?' " Scottie asked.

"I don't know. It seemed like that's what they were doing. She had her hand on his arm, I think. They were a long way away. They just fell, and fell, and fell. I never heard a sound." She covered her face with her hands. "I didn't call and turn Armand in. I swear to God I didn't."

"I believe you, Madam. Try to stay calm. Let the morphine work so we can fix your leg."

But she was jittery and shocky and didn't hear me. "It was like he was trying to jerk his arm away and lost his balance and fell. And Patty still had hold of him and he pulled her over with him," she babbled. "I was running for help but I tripped and hurt my leg. I'm so glad you're here." Her words began to slur. "Can you go down and get them?"

The powerful drug was beginning to take effect.

"Shhh," I told her.

"I didn't call," she muttered again before the morphine dulled her mind and senses. "I swear it."

Scottie and I rolled her gently onto her back and he straightened the leg and tied it firmly to the collapsible splints. "Now listen to me, Jackie," he said. "The path is very narrow here, but the Sherpas have lots of experience with accidents like this, and what they're going to do is they're going to sit you up very carefully and then lift you by your arms and carry you, hang you between them just like a bag of grain, to get you back to camp. I've given you enough painkiller so that you should have a pretty comfortable ride. It's not far, just a couple of minutes. Do you understand?"

Madam giggled.

"Okay," Scottie continued. "Are you ready?"

"Ready," she answered.

It was quite a sight to watch those two little men, both a good three-quarters of a foot shorter than Madam but twice as strong, kneel down and sit her up, and—with the lead man facing into the cliff, and the second man facing outward—lay one of her arms over each of their shoulders and slowly rise until she was suspended between them. The procedure had been smooth and uninterrupted, but nevertheless, the pain made her howl. My heart thudded and a chill ran down my spine. How's this for exciting? I wanted to say to William.

"Listen to me, Jackie." Scottie's voice was commanding, immediately instilling confidence in all of us. "That's the worst of it. Now we'll just get you back to your bed. All right? Just a couple of minutes."

"Okay," she answered meekly, a trusting, weeping child.

A third Sherpa, equipped with a headlamp and a strong flashlight, led the way. It was slow going, maneuvering along the trail in the dark. Scottie, Ryder, and I brought up the rear, and we reached the camp after almost an hour, with Madam crying and babbling much of the way, wanting to be sure Scottie had gone down to rescue Patty and William.

"Are they okay?" she asked a number of times.

"Everything's fine," Scottie reassured her.

But of course, nothing was fine. We were in the midst of a nightmare.

The Sherpas brought Madam's cot into the main tent and laid her down on it as gently as they could. By now she was shivering uncontrollably, not only from shock but from the frigid nighttime temperatures associated with life at twelve thousand feet. We tucked blankets around her, elevated her feet, and tried to comfort her as best we could. I gave her another injection and after a few minutes she drifted into oblivion.

Scottie was immediately on the phone.

I think that night was the longest of any of our lives. We huddled together in the big tent, listening to him arrange for the evacuation helicopter to come to the clearing at the south end of the lake, and praying Patty and William would miraculously walk in. I don't think it had completely dawned on any of us—not to Ryder or me, at any rate—exactly what had happened. We were in shock.

The Sherpas continued searching all night. The temperature fell further, and the cook brought in more blankets and endless cups of sweetened tea, to which we added small doses of brandy. Whenever Madam began to regain consciousness, I gave her a fresh injection of morphine and stuck a couple of Arnica Montana tablets under her tongue to contain the bruising and trauma to the fracture. Scottie had done a thoroughly professional job of setting her leg, it was straight and well-protected. The fact was, except for an x-ray, even if we were in a hospital, there wasn't much else that could be done.

"What can I do to help?" Ryder asked, when Scottie was off the phone.

He shook his head. "Nothing for me. But both of you make sure all your gear is organized. Put everything you need to get you home in your backpack. I'll send the rest of your kit later. God willing, the helicopter'll be at the lake by eight o'clock. We'll leave here before sunup and, with any luck, get down in time for it to fly you back to Kathmandu. It has to be back in the air by nine."

"How far is it?" I asked.

"Under regular circumstances, at a steady pace, the walk would take only an hour and a half or so. I'm hoping we can do it in three."

"Don't you want us to help search, just in case?"

Scottie shook his head. "With all due respect, Ryder, you'd just get in the way."

"But I'd really like to stay. I'd like to stay for Patty. One way or the other. Maybe Jackie's got it wrong, maybe they're just lost. But if they did fall, I'd at least like to help get their bodies home."

Scottie studied him, seemingly weighing his words. Then he drew in a deep breath. "There's no retrieving them. There's no way to get to the lake except at the south end."

"What about a boat?" Madam asked foggily. "We could go out in a boat."

Scottie was working against his own stress and fatigue and his clients' inexperience, and he made a concerted effort not to sound impatient. "There aren't any boats, Jackie."

"Are you sure?" Ryder asked. "That sounds like a good idea."

"Phoksumdo Tal is a holy lake." Scottie's eyes were hard and flinty as rocks. "You don't swim in it, you don't bathe in it, you don't boat on it, you don't touch it. If something falls into it, it stays. There are no boats, no police divers, no search and rescue teams."

"I'd still like to stay," she murmured.

"So would I," said Ryder.

"I know you don't mean to be selfish, but if we have to worry about you, we can't worry about them."

I didn't say a word, but I agreed with him completely. I just wanted to get the hell out of here. It was all I could do not to jump up and run down the trail in the dark to the landing site as fast as I could. I had no interest in being a hero.

When dawn began to color the sky deep blue, we set out. Through binoculars, Scottie spotted William's and Patty's green canvas hats floating on the lake four hundred feet below. They looked like miniature lily pads. William's camera, tripod, and pack were stacked neatly on a rock shelf. There were rocks missing from the edge of the trail. The drop to the water was precipitous, unbroken.

The Sherpas carried Madam as they had the night before, like a bag of grain sandwiched between them, and three hours later, she, Ryder, and I were lifted off the ground in an uninsulated, rusted, Russian-made cargo helicopter with no seats except the ones up front for the captain and the non-existent co-pilot. We huddled on the floor and prayed with all our might as the engine shuddered and screamed and fought its way into the air. There were no windows, but in a couple of spots, the metal fuselage had corroded away and I could see mountainsides perilously close. I put my pack against a metal support rib and leaned against it as I held Madam's hand. Thankfully, it was too noisy to talk. I was full of so many terrible, terrifying thoughts, I don't know if I could have kept them to myself.

Ryder sat on the other side. He and I looked at each other from time to time in the murky hold. His glass eye looked as dead as it was, and his good eye could only hold my gaze for a few seconds before he had to turn away. After a while, he began to cry. I envied him. I didn't feel anything but anxious to get out of this horrible place. I was glad Armand had been arrested, and before you get any ideas, I want you to know I was not the one who turned him in, either. But this venture had proved Armand to be as great a manipulator as Ryder, if not greater. Two people were dead because of his self-indulgence, one of them a remarkable, talented, generous woman. What a complete waste.

And William. William. I gazed out over the Himalayan walls. What about William? William was wonderful, funny, fun to be with, weak, untrustworthy, and lacking in integrity. He was damaged goods with emotions as deep as a comic book. While I should be feeling pain and sorrow, I didn't feel much of anything but emptiness. I'd already mourned for "Fernando" back there off the Florida coast. Now, all I could do was resent him for yanking Patty hundreds of feet to the water, where she sank like a block of cement, weighted down with the medical pack. He should have died in Florida, it would have been better for everyone.

The trip was agonizing for Madam. It seemed that no amount of morphine could adequately blunt the excruciating pain, or ease her intermittent crying. "I'm so sorry," she apologized over and over again. "If I'd just been faster, I could have saved them."

Sometimes I believe in karma, too. It doesn't make any difference what you do about anything because you're never really going to get anywhere. How ironic it was that Madam, whose life had been so negatively shaped by Ryder, who had finally found the gumption to unglue herself from his control, was bound together with him again. There were some differences, though. Madam had been dependent on Ryder before. Now she'd grown a shell and he kept his distance, minded his own business. He was no longer Mr. Big Guy in our lives. He was Mr. Nobody.

When we landed at Kathmandu, an ambulance waited on the tarmac to take us to the hospital, and once her leg had been x-rayed and properly set, we went to the Yellow Flame Hotel.

"I am so sorry," the manager wept as he showed us to our rooms. "All of Nepal is crying for Patty."

Madam and I left for home early the next morning. We got the last two first class seats. Ryder saw us off.

50

MIDDLEBURG

The sound of the little silver bell tinkled down the stairway. "Nigel!" Madam yelled. "Can you come up here, please?"

We'd gotten home two days before and as far as we knew, no one knew we were there, since I wasn't answering the phone, letting voice mail pick up all the calls. There were a lot of them, too. Mostly reporters wanting information about the accident. The only person she'd talked to was Junior, but I hadn't been in on the conversation.

When I got up to her room, Madam was just where I'd left her: in bed, casted leg resting on a pillow, reading the *Washington Post* and having her breakfast, the dogs curled along her hip. I'd been up and down the stairs at least a dozen times, and it was only seven-thirty. A pair of crutches leaned against her bed table within easy reach, but other than using them to get back and forth to the bathroom, she had found it was much handier to have me do everything.

God, how I love my routines. How ecstatically happy I am to be home. How much I want everything to be the same as it was before we went on that doomed expedition to the opposite side of the earth—when Madam and Armand were so in love, and life was full of promise and excitement. When every day a new gift arrived from Armand with a new excuse as to why he wasn't delivering it in person, excuses we were only too happy to believe. What naive babes we'd been. Well, the scales were off now, weren't they? We'd had more than our fill of excitement and now we were farther behind the eight-ball than ever. Madam seemed anesthetized by the experience, and I felt changed. Not happily so. I preferred the way I was before: polite, deferential, living in my own little world, where I was content to work the surface. Now I saw how much I loved life, how rich, and fine, and *temporary* it could be, and that knowledge had stripped away a layer of my servitude, given me a feeling of independence—a capricious and cavalier attitude for someone in service.

The fact was, I was in danger of becoming my own man. I was like the camel who stuck his nose under the tent, and we all know, once that happens, pretty soon he'll be all the way in and you'll never get him out again.

"Look at this." She handed over a folded section of newspaper. It was the obituary page. Daddy Rex Hammond, Junior's father, had died the day before of a stroke at the family ranch outside of Dallas.

All I could do was shake my head. I wasn't surprised there'd been more bad news for the Hammonds. Except for Patty, they were a bad news bunch.

"That family is as jinxed as the Kennedys," she observed.

I did not add the obvious, that their bad luck had contaminated us as well. Our life had been on a downward spiral ever since we'd come into contact with them.

"See if you can get Junior on the phone."

His office said he was in the air, en route from Los Angeles to New York. I left a message.

"Tell me again how it happened," Junior said. He was sitting on a small chair next to her bed, holding her hand. He'd diverted his plane to Washington and come straight from the airport. His jowls drooped and his eyes bulged more unhealthily than ever. His belly lay over his belt like cinched-up whale blubber, and a faint stench of body odor floated on the air around him. He reminded me of a picture I'd once seen of a Chicago shoe salesman who'd just gotten fired and was slumped on a downtown bus stop bench in the middle of August. Bereft and sweating.

"I can't, Junior." Madam's voice was listless. "It's too painful. I'm trying to forget Patty's death, not keep reliving it. It's a constant nightmare to me, awake and asleep. And you can't keep hearing about it. You should see yourself. Between your father and Patty, you're so exhausted you're about to fall off your chair. Why don't you let Nigel take you to the guest room so you can get some sleep?"

Junior shook his head slowly. He pulled a caked handkerchief from his pocket and blew his nose and wiped his eyes. "I've got too much to do."

"No, you don't," she said. "You don't have anything to do that has to be done today. Your family's all dead. And your business can wait. You need to take care of yourself for a change. Nigel, take him down and give him an Ambien and tuck him in. I'll see you at dinner, Junior. We can talk about it then."

"Come along, sir."

Like the rest of the house, the guest rooms had Madam's slightly off-beam stamp. The downstairs one was what she called David Hockney's room, because a Hockney painting (Do I have to tell you it's a copy? That the original was sold three years ago to raise "operating funds"?) dominated one of the smooth white plaster walls. It was a spare, clean, California room. She had decorated the upstairs one during an affair with an English nobleman who had provided the antiques—an English Colonial mahogany bed so Victorian the mattress was four feet from the floor, the headboard reached to the ceiling, and the footboard was as tall as I was; a frayed zebra-skin rug; and dark-stained English Colonial bamboo furniture with leopard skin cushions. This room was seldom used, and I was always a little surprised when I entered it, because it was so unlike our life today, and we hadn't had a houseguest for years. Not that a woman would be uncomfortable in there, but the room was a lion's den and made a man feel like a man, full of testosterone and just-try-that-again muscles.

Even Junior. He'd followed me down the hall like a whipped, belly-dragging basset hound, but once he'd gone into the dramatic bathroom with its black fixtures, black marble floor and countertops, mirrored walls, and multi-nozzle shower, he was transformed. He dropped his clothes on the floor as he pulled them off and jammed his chubby arms into a white terry robe, which scarcely closed in front.

"Don't be oglin' my pecker," he barked. "Gettin' any of your ideas."

"Oh, for heaven's sake, Mr. Hammond. Do you honestly think if I were going to go about "ogling peckers," as you so grossly put it, I would start with one as old and small as yours? Go to bed."

"You'd better watch your mouth, boy. Where do you think you're goin'? You aren't gonna leave my clothes on the floor like that. Hang 'em up."

"Hang 'em up yourself, sir."

"I'm gonna get you fired, you little fairy."

I laughed out loud and turned off the light. "You don't scare me, Mr. Hammond."

"You've got a dangerous mouth on you, Nigel." He slid his rotting hulk beneath the crisp Irish linen sheets, which cost approximately two-hundred and fifty dollars each, and fell sound asleep.

"I don't know if that old bed can handle so much weight," I reported to Madam. Junior's snores boomed down the hall like cannonballs rolling back and forth across a hollow, abandoned deck.

"If we hear a big crash, we'll know."

Mid-afternoon. Madam was napping, Junior was still unconscious from the sleeping pill, Effie had gone to the market, and I was at my little butler's pantry desk, triaging the household accounts, when I heard the unmistakable sound of hooves on the gravel and looked out to see Ryder on his chestnut with a bouquet of red roses tucked in the crook of his arm. He dismounted and knocked on the front door.

"How's Jackie?" he asked. In his hunt uniform of jodhpurs, black two-button jacket, snow-white shirt, red fox tie, and shiny black boots, he appeared to be fully recovered from our terrors in Dolpo. His deep love and dedication to Patty had apparently vanished and sunk along with her, into the blue, blue depths of Phoksumdo Tal.

"Well as can be expected," I answered.

"May I see her?"

"I'll inquire."

"You do that, Nigel."

"Don't push me, Ryder. You aren't the only one with jet lag."

"Sure, send him up," she told me. She was awake and reading *Vanity Fair*.

"Don't get any ideas," I warned him as I let him go upstairs. "Nobody's taking any steps backward here."

"You think I don't know that? I just want to see how she is."

"When did you get home?" Madam asked.

"Last night. Hell of a long way, isn't it? Is there anything I can get for you? Do for you?" He sat down next to her bed and took her hand, which he held between both of his for a moment before she withdrew it.

"Nothing, thanks. Nigel is taking excellent care of me."

Ryder looked over his shoulder at me and smiled. "Pretty amazing, what we've been through, isn't it? I mean, can you believe where we were just three days ago? Four days ago? Hell, it's so far away, hard to say when it was. Nothing looks like it's changed, but it has, hasn't it? We're all changed."

Oh, thank you, Dr. Freud. You deep-thinking putz.

"What do you want, Ryder?" Madam asked. In her current, slightly catatonic state, she was the most changed of all of us. I think the helplessness of seeing those two bodies fall silently, hundreds of feet to the water, had locked-up something inside her. She was remote and extremely vague, brooding, and pensive. Traumatized by what she'd seen, I suppose, would be the best description. Horrified by her inability to stop it. "I want to change everything about my life," she'd said on the way home. "What do you mean?" I'd asked. "I'm not sure," she'd answered. "But don't worry, Nigel, it won't be in Nepal."

"I want you to come back to me," Ryder was saying. "I've realized how essential you are to me and how badly I treated you and how much I took you for granted. I want you to give me another chance."

Get the bucket.

Madam dropped her eyes and shook her head, stroking the dogs, who stretched in their sleep and wagged their tails. "I'm sorry, but the answer's no. I don't love you anymore, if I ever did. I'm not sure exactly what I'm looking for, Ryder, but I know it's not you, and I know I'm going to find it. And if I don't? Well, that's okay, too. I'll find it next time around."

Ryder half-smiled. "One day, it'll happen for us—I'm completely committed to that notion. I don't know if you know this, but Mary Anne's in very bad shape. Mayo's essentially sent her home to die."

"I'm sorry," Madam said.

"I've been responsible for a lot of her unhappiness," Ryder waxed reflectively. His voice was so melodramatically earnest and sincere, it was like listening to Dudley Do-Right. "And I promised myself on the plane that I'd try to make it up to her. I'm going to see her through to the end because I want to, and I owe her that. I'm not here to make any wild promises to you, Jackie, the way I did before, about leaving her and marrying you. But when it's over, I'm going to prove to you that I'm worth having."

I snapped my ostrich plume feather duster along the top of Madam's dressing table mirrors like a whip.

"Let's just be happy to be friends and neighbors," Madam said. She was bored.

"Whatever you say. By the way, isn't that Junior's car out there?"

"Yes. He's asleep. He showed up here like a zombie and Nigel gave him a sleeping pill and put him to bed. Did you know his father died yesterday?"

"Saw it in the *Journal* this morning. Tell him I was by and how sorry I am about Patty and his dad. I was going to call him this afternoon anyway to see when we could get together. Tell him to give me a ring when he wakes up." Ryder paused. "There isn't anything going on between you two, is there?"

"Go home, Ryder." Madam picked up her magazine. "Get a life."

"What did you have for breakfast?" I asked as I saw him out the front door. "Jesus pills?"

51

front had pushed through in the afternoon, blowing away all the haze and humidity, making it cool enough for dinner outdoors. I set the round glass table on the terrace, choosing woven mats, bright blue linen napkins, and blue-colored Mexican wine glasses, whose rustic appearance added to the casual, summery nature of the setting. I surrounded the three hurricane lamps in the center of the table with heaps of lemons and limes set on a bed of fresh lemon leaves. Effie was busy in the kitchen, seasoning and breading a pile of softshelled Eastern Shore crabs, which she laid out on parchment-lined cookie sheets ready for baking. Small gorgonzola cheese soufflé appetizers were set to go into the oven.

"Town Market says the bill has to be paid," Effie said tersely. Her false teeth clicked. "Hasn't been paid for over a month."

"You and Scully must have eaten a lot while we were gone because we haven't been here for almost a month."

"Two weeks," she snapped.

"Whatever. Tell him to keep his trousers on. He'll be paid, he always is."

I set dishes of olives and cashews on a small cocktail table down by the stone wall, got the drinks table stocked, and arranged a chaise for Madam.

Then I put on my bathing suit and went upstairs to give her her bath. I accomplished this by wrapping a large plastic trash bag over her leg and sitting her down on a stool in the shower, at which point I would turn away and she would pass her towel out through the door. The swimming trunks were in case of an emergency.

"What's for dinner?" she called over the running water. The scent of her new rosemary scrub made the air tingle deliciously.

"Effie got soft-shells. They look excellent."

"Is Junior up yet?"

"Yes, Madam. He showered a while ago and I believe he's taking a walk. I saw him down by the studio." I turned on the blender to make her espresso ice cream shake. I didn't want to talk about Junior. I had spent the entire afternoon getting myself worked into a state about Junior Hammond—Watch your mouth, boy . . . I'm going to get you fired . . . you little fairy—and felt I might lose my composure with only the slightest provocation.

"He really is a nice man, isn't he? I feel kind of sorry for him."

I kept my back to her.

"Can you hear me, Nigel? I said, he really is a nice man." She turned off the water and I handed in her towel.

"Madam, I am not normally so blunt with you, as you know. But I feel I must speak my mind. I have a very bad feeling about Junior Hammond. I think you should send him away after dinner and never see him again. I know you're as worried about the taxes as I am, but our life has been in a tailspin ever since we first came in contact with the Hammonds in December. I think you should get a tax lawyer to make some kind of deal for you with the IRS—it's done all the time—go back to work, and then you should just get on with your life."

"I know you're right. I just don't know what's wrong with me."

What could I say? I don't know what's wrong with you, either, but I'm getting tired of it?

"Let me put it into perspective for you," she said.

I poured the shake into a frosted glass and stuck in a straw.

"Maybe this will make it easier: I have not worked for over a month and, unfortunately, because of my leg, I won't be able to work for at least six more weeks, and then I'll have to start with physical therapy. My leg will be very weak, so I'll only be able to work for a couple of hours a day, and you know I can't get anywhere on two hours a day. So now we're into September. It's only June and the bank account is almost empty. Effie is having a nervous breakdown about the grocery bill and promised it would be paid—we're talking basic survival, Nigel. Food. We're getting dangerously close to the bottom of the money barrel. It's possible we can make it through the summer, but only if we budget very carefully. And you know me, I've never been on a budget in my life and I'm scared to death."

I didn't respond.

"So you tell me. What would you do?"

Junior looked much healthier when he came down to dinner. He'd put on a clean shirt and fresh tie and washed and combed his hair. While he was asleep, Effie had gone through his suitcase and steamed and pressed his clothes, so his light gabardine slacks and navy double-breasted blazer, bespoke from his London tailor, looked sharp. I could have made an entire suit for myself out of the fabric in one of his pant legs. Madam put on a black cotton shift, and if it weren't for the crutches, you would never have known there was anything wrong.

She and Junior played gin rummy and drank martinis. One thing I'll say to his credit, she was very relaxed when he was around because it was almost like having an adoring older brother—she could do no wrong.

"What's up for you this week?" He crunched up a crab. Bread crumbs covered his chin and Tabasco had splattered on his snow-white shirt front. His tie, a scarlet linen Charvet, was so full of spots it was going to be a complete write-off.

"I'm going to sell the *Andromeda*."

Madam had brass.

"You're kidding me."

Madam shook her head.

"What on earth for? That's your legacy."

"Unfortunately, I don't have any choice. I've been living it up a little too much for the last ten or fifteen years, and the IRS—which has zero sense of humor—feels they've gotten the short end of the stick. I have to pay by the end of June or the party's over."

"How short do they think they are?"

"About a million."

"You're going to sell a twenty-million-dollar-painting to settle a million dollar tax bill? By the time you've paid the IRS and the capital gains, you'll only net about eight mil out of a twenty million dollar asset. Where're you getting your advice? From your horoscope?"

"Well, I'm not actually getting any advice. Armand was going to pay the taxes, but we all know what a jerk he turned out to be."

Junior laughed. "Some of us already knew what he was. Don't say I didn't warn you. Don't even think about selling *Andromeda* to pay off Uncle Sam."

"That's easy for you to say. I have to do something."

"Yeah, but that's such a girly approach."

"Well, I am a girly," Madam laughed.

"You can say that again." Junior took his checkbook out of his pocket. "Exactly how much do you owe the government?"

Madam seemed to balk. "Well, by the end of June, with the penalties and interest, it'll come to one million, two hundred and seventy-two thousand, eight-hundred and twenty-six dollars and thirty-one cents."

He wrote out the check, payable to the IRS, tore it out of his book, and handed it to me. "Take care of it, Nigel."

"Thank you, sir."

"Now, that's the end of that subject." Junior muffled a burp with his napkin. "Are there any more crabs?"

Talk about letting the camel get its nose under the tent.

52

"When is your father's funeral?"

They were back at the edge of the terrace, Madam on her chaise, Junior sitting on the wall, talking quietly, sipping coffee. The moon hung in the sky and thin little clouds drifted by. The crickets had started singing and the sound was almost deafening. Moonlight glistened on Madam's hair and the warm night air brought out the fragrance in her gardenias.

"Isn't going to be one. Who'd go but me? As you pointed out this afternoon, the whole family's dead and it's just as well. We lived under a dark, dark cloud. Maybe now, the sun will come out."

"You aren't having a funeral for your father? I thought he was a big deal in Texas."

Junior shrugged. "I suppose he thought he was. For sure one of the richest. You've heard me on this subject before—he was the meanest son-of-a-bitch I ever knew and I'll be happy never to hear his name again. 'Daddy Rex.' Now is that a Tennessee Williams name for a Tennessee Williams existence if ever you've heard one? Tennessee could have made ten times as much money writing about our family, except nobody would've believed it. Daddy Rex made that guy in *Cat on a Hot Tin Roof* look like St. Francis of Assisi."

Madam laughed. She was laughing more tonight than she had in weeks. Maybe even more than with Armand. Maybe ever.

Junior grinned back at her. "It's true. When we were little I thought we were a normal family, but when I got older, I saw we were anything but. We grew up in a sick, violent house. Daddy Rex poisoned all of us. He used to humiliate my mama, Mama Lureen, until she finally gave up, just went to bed with a bottle until she woke up dead."

"Were you close to her?"

"Who? Mama Lureen? Hell, yes. I was her baby. Like the girls were Daddy's babies. But Mama couldn't stand up to him. He beat her down until there was nothing left. Just like he destroyed all of us.

"Look at me and my sisters. Have you ever seen a bigger bunch of losers? All you have to do is look at my size to see things aren't quite right. We grew up in a state of constant terror, so afraid we'd fail and get whipped, or worse, that none of us has ever been able to relate to anyone. Lynette bought everyone around her, never had a single friend except those stupid cats. Bianca had that obsessive/compulsive business—always had to be in complete control of everything, never could let down for one second, everything had to be perfect. All you had to do was look at her hair, all plastered into a helmet, to know she had some relaxation problems. Only Patty got away, but I didn't think she was ever really quite right in the head, going off to Nepal, living among those people."

"I liked Patty a lot," Madam said.

"Well, I'm glad. I really didn't know her very well, but I'm sure she could have used a few more friends like you. We all could. Maybe then we wouldn't have ended up with so many problems. Daddy Rex used to make fun of us and diddled my sisters until none of us could stand it. My youngest sister, Jaxeen, she got it the worst. He humiliated her so bad, she finally committed suicide when she was fifteen."

"I didn't know you had another sister," Madam said. "No one's ever talked about her."

"What's to talk about? She lived and she died. She's buried out there on the ranch. Poor thing. I think when I was growing up, Daddy Rex and I spent more time in Jaxeen's bed than we did in our own."

It took a second for his meaning to sink in. "Excuse me?" Madam asked incredulously. "Did you say you and your father were in bed with your *sister?*"

"From the time she was about eleven. He diddled all the girls, that's how they got money from him, but with Jaxeen it was different. She was by far the prettiest, right from the second she was born. Daddy Rex fell in love with her, always told her she looked just like Mama Lureen when she was a girl, before she took up the bottle and turned into a floozy, which wasn't fair, Mama never was that way. Matter of fact, Mama never left the ranch, just sat in her bed and watched television and took pills and drank. Never left her room. So, as soon as Jaxeen started to develop, she carried the load for everyone, became Daddy Rex's pet. Mine, too. I learned on her. But she was real sensitive, and after a while, she couldn't take it."

"You *learned* on her?"

Junior looked at his boots.

"What did she do?" Madam whispered. Her face was still.

Junior shrugged. "I'm not exactly sure. One day when we were at school, Daddy Rex found her dead in the field. Shot-gunned herself. Blew her own head off. I never saw her body or anything. They buried her right away and it was all hushed up. I always hoped maybe she ran away or something. But I knew she hadn't. You know what? You look a little like her."

Madam let out a breath of air as though she'd been punched. I was afraid to look at her. None of what Junior said surprised me even slightly. All you had to do was look at him, and experience his torrential racial and homophobic hatreds, his provincial bullying attitude, to know you were dealing with someone whose problems were so deep-seated they were virtually untreatable. Ambassador Franklin back there in Nepal had been right. Junior Hammond was the real thing. Genuine All-American white trash.

"Look, Jackie, I'm not proud of what I did. I don't know why I'm even telling you. Never told any of this to another soul. I told you our family was bad news. Now maybe you'll understand why I'm not throwing any big Texas-sized funeral for Daddy Rex. As a matter of fact, I told the undertaker to just stick him in the ground, the way he did with Jaxeen, and send me the bill."

Madam was too stunned to speak.

"You probably want me to leave." Junior finally broke the silence. "I wouldn't blame you if you did."

"No," she answered. "Of course not."

"Can I ask you a favor?" Junior said presently.

"I can't imagine what I could possibly do for you, but whatever it is, I'll try."

"Will you let me stay here a while? On your farm? I promise I won't try anything. It's just that your little place here feels like the first real home I've ever been in. Peaceful. Cozy. Real secure."

"Stay as long as you like."

"What could I say, Nigel?" she asked later as I helped her undress for bed. "He gave us the money for the taxes."

"You could have said, 'no.' We could find other alternatives, I don't know what, but this is wrong. I'm worried for you, Madam. Did you hear what he said? He and his father used to have sex with his sisters? The little one was *eleven,* maybe even younger, and you *remind* him of her? He *learned* on her?" I shuddered. "God save us. These people are as low as people can be. They're bottom-feeders."

"I know that." Madam sounded exasperated, defensive. "I see what he is and I probably shouldn't have invited him to stay, but I feel sorry for him. He won't be here for long, a couple of days at the most. Just try to look after him as best you can—for me, okay?"

"You know I'll do anything for you, Madam, but you have terrible judgment, especially about men."

"Except you," she teased.

"I am your friend."

"Would you believe me if I told you I have an agenda?"

"No. Unfortunately, you aren't the agenda type."

I sat on the little patio off my quarters, sipped a neat scotch and looked at the stars. They were the same cruel constellations as those in Nepal, and they gave me a chill. That afternoon, all our Nepal gear, including William's possessions, had been delivered. They were stacked in the mud room waiting to be unpacked. I had dug out my journal and flipped through the pages of my overblown prose. I'd grown up a lot in the last few weeks.

53

As June passed into July, Junior became more and more a fixture in our household. I had to admit, in many ways he changed our lives for the better. He escorted Madam to parties, he provided more than enough money for our household bills, he tried to be helpful. I treated him badly, disrespectfully. I didn't care. He threatened me occasionally, and I told him to just go ahead and do whatever he felt he had to. Naturally, his threats were empty. He had no balls. He slept in his own room and never once, to my knowledge, tried to get into Madam's. As a matter of fact, it was just the opposite. When he felt the urge to indulge his crude sexual appetites he simply went away for a few days and came back home with the lion fed.

Madam and Junior spent hours playing board games and joining other couples for afternoons and evenings of bridge. She stopped working altogether. The two of them were always in demand, totally the opposite of our previous pastoral life. The sad fact is, single women are not generally included in the larger, day-to-day social swim. The number of invitations Madam received pre-Junior could be counted on one hand. But add a man, practically any man, and the party floodgates open. As you know, I had escorted her on many occasions, always the bigger ones, but everyone knew I was her butler. It doesn't matter that I am more interesting, charming, and better looking than Junior Hammond, and unbelievably better-mannered, I am a servant. He is a multi-millionaire. And a single one at that. A catch.

We had cocktail and dinner parties, and one Sunday afternoon Junior hired the brass ensemble from the Washington Symphony Orchestra and had a concert in the field to raise money for the Farquier County volunteer fire department. There was more laughter in our house than tears, and Madam became the light of Junior's life. Nothing was too much for him to provide. We had begun to live the privileged sort of existence I'd always imagined when I'd gone into training at Lady Atchley's School. I hired extra household help and played my part to the hilt. But I knew so much more now. I knew money wasn't everything, and the price we were paying for the way we now lived was too high.

It was like the old joke about the curse of the Blotnik Diamond. "What's the curse?" someone asked Mrs. Blotnik. "Mr. Blotnik," she answered.

The most surprising development of all—although, if I'd been thinking, it probably wouldn't have taken any great brain to make the connection—was that she and Junior played bridge twice a week, Tuesday evenings and Friday afternoons, with Mary Anne and Ryder. The connection was between Mary Anne and Junior: the Tool & Die Division of Schlumbacher Oil supplied drilling equipment to Hammond Oil & Gas. Or, more precisely put, Junior was Mary Anne's biggest customer. She might have been terminally ill, but she wasn't dead yet, far from it. Her brain was completely intact and she was the consummate executive. As the summer drifted by, the four of them actually seemed to become friends. Madam and Mary Anne in particular.

Junior had increased our comfort level unimaginably, but . . . we all heard his story. We all knew where he came from, and we all knew the acorn doesn't fall far from the tree. No matter how much delicious icing you spread on a cake, if the cake's not well-baked, you can't hide it; the whole thing's a gooey mess inside, completely inedible. All summer, he heaped on the icing double-time, but it couldn't conceal the reality from our minds—at least mine, I really couldn't speak for Madam so much anymore.

There was an incident the first week of his stay that defined Junior in a nutshell:

He had insisted on wearing his silly six-shooters around, as if a bear or wild boar or bull moose were going to plow out of the woods and charge him. He was always pulling the guns out of their holsters and twirling them around over his head. In the beginning it was funny, until one evening, a few days into his visit, he whipped the pistols out and unloaded them on one of our spotted fawns and one of our rabbits. Blew them to bits.

Madam screamed as if she were the one who'd been shot. She leapt out of her chair and half-ran, half-hopped, without her crutches, across the lawn to where her precious animals had fallen, literally dead in their tracks.

Junior made no move to try to stop her. "Hell," he said, reholstering the weapons and picking up his beer, "it's only a deer and a stupid little rabbit. They're wrecking your garden. You'd think they were pets or something."

"They *are* pets, you monster!" Madam screamed. She sat on the ground between the fawn's front and rear legs, stroking the soft baby fur on its belly, the bloody rabbit cradled in her lap, and cried. She and I were completely stupefied at the carnage. It was nauseating, almost as if he'd shot the dogs, who, in fact, had taken to spending more and more time in my bedroom, as if they knew we'd taken Satan under our roof. "Get your stuff and get out of here," she said almost inaudibly. Her face was bleached with anger.

"What?" He was shocked.

She turned angry eyes on him. "I said, leave. Get out."

"You've got to be kiddin'."

"I'm not kidding at all. That kind of behavior is totally unacceptable, Junior. It's . . . it's . . . barbaric. What kind of person are you? Look what you've done. You've killed these precious animals. Just murdered them in cold blood." She was disgusted. "I don't ever want to see you again."

Junior was sincerely aghast. He could not believe what he was hearing. "I'm so sorry, Jackie. Please, don't send me away. I'm sorry. I didn't know they were there on purpose. I shot 'em 'cause they were eating the plants." Junior was close to tears. "They were wrecking your garden. Back home we'd consider them nothing but pests. Please, Jackie, I'm so sorry. I'll do anything if you'll let me stay."

She studied him as tears continued to roll down her cheeks. "I don't think I can do it."

"Oh, please," he begged. "I'll do anything. I swear to you, I didn't have any idea."

The silence seemed infinite as Madam struggled between the dead angels lying on the ground and the demons of opportunity and prosperity standing right before her. She looked at me, and there was apology in her eyes: I can always get another rabbit, they were saying, but there aren't many more Juniors out there.

"I'll give you one chance. But there's a contingency: no more guns. You have to give them to Nigel."

"I'm not giving that homo my guns."

"Listen to me," she snapped. Her voice was cold as steel, as if that could make up for the shame she felt. "If you want to stay, you'll give Nigel the guns. There's no conversation about it. He'll lock them up in the safe. And you will not call him a homo again."

"It will be more than fine with me if you choose to go," I said.

"Stop it, Nigel," Madam lashed back.

"Just 'cause you said that, I'm staying." Junior all but stuck his tongue out at me. He stood up and removed the pearl-handled revolvers from his fancy embossed leather holster belt with its fancy silver buckle, flipped them over so he was holding them by the barrels, and handed them to Madam without looking at me.

"I'm telling you, Junior," she said, taking the weapons, "you do anything like this again, and you're gone. No second chances."

"I'm sorry as hell," he said. "What do you want me to do with them?" He indicated the soft, lifeless bodies. "Do you want me to gut them?"

"*Gut* them?" I gasped.

"Don't touch them," Madam said.

"What do you mean, don't touch 'em? Meat's gotta be dressed."

"Stay away from them, Junior. They aren't roadkill. Come on, Nigel, help me up and then go get a shovel. Let's bury them. My poor little angels."

Later that night, Madam handed over the guns to me to put in the safe. But I didn't put them in it. I put them on the desk in my sitting room, and after a while they became part of the scenery.

After that episode, gagged down like a dose of bad medicine, the summer would have passed smoothly except that, in spite of their bi-weekly bridge games, Ryder was becoming more and more agitated by Junior's residency at Madam's farm. In addition to that, Mary Anne's demands on him continued to increase, and while he claimed he had turned over a new leaf, she wasn't dying as fast as he thought she would. She may even have been getting a little stronger. She wasn't winning any wheelchair races, but she'd rallied enough to attend the occasional party, and she encouraged him to attend others without her and to participate in his weekly hunt club meetings. She also required that he report every conversation, and often called her friends—right in front of Ryder—to confirm the conversations had taken place. It was like he was on probation. I will say, in his defense, he was trying harder than I'd ever seen him try, but he'd lost control of his life, to whatever extent he'd had it in the first place, and a leopard doesn't change its spots. Ryder needed someone to nettle in order to make himself feel big.

He started following Madam. Whenever she went shopping, or to the beauty parlor, or to a party, Ryder followed and concocted ways to run into her. He was not what I'd call a stalker, since he didn't have the skill. And he was about as physically dangerous as a wet noodle. But he was an annoyance.

Back home, Junior tried to drive a wedge between Madam and me at every opportunity, and either she didn't, or chose not to, see it. I grew increasingly isolated and miserable.

When she got her cast off in mid-August, she and Junior took up golf. It was no surprise to me when, at summer's end, he gave her an eight-carat cushion-cut diamond ring, her own personal Blotnik.

They announced their engagement, and I announced my resignation.

54

*Y*ou're going to *what?*" Madam yelped. She was getting dressed to go out.

"I'm giving my notice." My voice quavered slightly, but it was from nerves, not lack of conviction.

"*Why?*"

"You don't need me anymore. My duties are only half what they once were, and . . . and . . ."

"And what?"

"I miss you, Madam."

"What do you mean, you 'miss me'?" She was pretending not to understand. "We're together practically all the time."

The night she invited Junior to stay, she had asked me if I thought maybe she had an agenda, and I'd answered no, she wasn't the agenda type. But I'd misread her. She obviously was the agenda type, and this was what it was. She'd always been clear about what she wanted—to be the center of attention. To come first no matter what. To marry someone with an unlimited amount of money, surround herself with a giant billow of cash, no matter the cost. And all of a sudden, it coalesced and came true. It was the sort of occurrence we would have talked over two or three months ago, the pros and the cons, maybe even laughed about. But now, a chasm had developed between us and it was too personal a subject to broach.

I was steady as a rock. "Not the way we used to be. You don't need me anymore. You need a lady's maid to keep your things in order, but you don't need a companion. I promise you, we will never again have a quiet evening together, watch *Biography,* play gin, gossip. You don't need me to escort you to parties. When you and Junior went to New York and you didn't take me with you, I could see he'd filled your life. The handwriting was on the wall. I'm happy for you, but to tell you the truth, I'm terribly lonely." My voice cracked.

She watched me sadly. "I'm sorry," she said. "I didn't realize it was so bad."

"All the fun has gone out of my life. I'm stuck here on the farm with Effie and Scully, and I can't bear either one of them." I thrust my hands into my pockets in an effort to look more casual than I felt. Then I sat down on the edge of the chaise, put my face in my hands, and tried to hold myself together.

Madam put down her hairbrush and came to sit next to me—she smelled like a fresh breeze. She put her arm around my shoulder, the way a sister puts her arm around a brother. "I'm so sorry, Nigel." She stroked my hair. "I had no idea. Please don't leave, let me see if I can fix it."

"I have to go. I can't stand to watch what's happening, and you can't do anything to fix it except get rid of him, and I know you aren't going to do that. I absolutely loathe Junior Hammond and what he's doing to you. You know how much I love you, I'd do anything for you, but I can't, and won't, work for him."

"I know," she said sympathetically, but she didn't go any farther. She didn't offer to leave him, and why should she? She was looking at a life of financial security for the first time. We sat that way for several moments, the giant diamond on her finger taking up the space like an iceberg between us, and then she asked me when I thought I'd go.

"As soon as possible," I answered. "This is my two weeks' notice."

"You mean you'd let me get married without you? You can't, Nigel. You're my best friend. You have to stay and help me. You have to plan the wedding."

"When is it?"

"Four weeks from next Sunday."

The idea gave me a bad taste in my mouth, like rotten eggs. "All right, but then I'm off."

"Is there anything I can do to change your mind? Do you want a raise? Or I'll redecorate your rooms." What nice, empty offers. Her voice lacked conviction. It was almost as if she *wanted* me to leave.

I shook my head. "You have to do what you have to do. You have your karma and I have mine." I tried a lame smile. "But as your friend, I'm telling you for the last time, you're making a bad decision."

A cloud settled over my heart and I was glad it infected the entire household. I went about making the wedding arrangements with as much glee as if I were arranging a funeral. Here I was, with a virtually unlimited budget, and it brought me no pleasure. The irony was not lost on me. I answered a number of help wanted ads in *Country Life* magazine and placed my name with agencies in New York and London. At least now I had references.

She and Junior went to meet with Junior's Washington lawyers and she signed a prenuptial agreement, the terms of which I was not privy to and I didn't ask. I kept my mouth tightly shut.

The late-afternoon wedding would be at the farm with only seventy or eighty guests, new friends from the neighborhood, and Junior's business associates from around the world. The weather would be perfect, as it always was that time of the year, and then they would leave the next morning on Junior's BBJ for an African honeymoon. A private, six-week safari. Madam took to calling him, "Bwana-honey." Sometimes it almost sounded as though she'd picked up his Texas twang.

And I would go, where? I had some money. If you're in service and a fairly thrifty person, which I am when it comes to my own funds, you can save almost all your money. Your employer pays for basically everything: your room, your board, your uniforms, your dry cleaning and laundry, so it's possible to sock it all away, which most people in my position do. We are as much a luxury item as a personal jet; all it takes is one big dip in your employer's industry, or the economy, or a divorce in your employer's household (or a wedding), and you can suddenly find yourself out of work. I had plenty of money stashed, not to mention my account with Ryder's broker, funded with his money. Madam had asked Junior to settle one year's salary on me, which he granted because she asked. But it made him hate me all the more, and vice versa.

One day, Mary Anne called and asked Madam if she had made any arrangements for the out-of-town guests. Madam looked at me blankly. I shrugged. "What kinds of arrangements?" she asked Mary Anne.

"You know, the regular things: housing, parties, transportation. It sounds like you have about two dozen couples coming in, and you know, they need to be entertained. You can't just invite them for an afternoon wedding."

"You can't?"

"Of course not. You have to do something about them."

"I do? Like what?"

"Where are you having the rehearsal dinner? Or the bridal luncheon? Or the luncheon for the out-of-towners before the wedding? Don't tell me you don't have one of those wedding planners that lay the whole thing out."

Madam and I stared at each other. I shrugged again. I was doing the wedding. Period. As far as I was concerned, that was plenty. More than enough.

She laughed self-consciously. "I guess not."

"That's what I was afraid of. You'd better come over and we'll discuss it. There's not much time."

After that, they consulted at least twice a day, on flowers, clothes, guest lists, seating—all activities Mary Anne could handle from her bed or wheelchair without leaving home, and then hand off to a staff member for implementation. Mary Anne McCormick became Madam's surrogate mother, and, to tell you the truth—and I swear to you, I mean it—I was happy for both of them.

And how was Madam during all this? Well, she had distanced herself even more. If I didn't know any better, I would have said she was heavily sedated, as though she were taking regular doses of Valium. She was going through the motions and declined to discuss much of anything with me. I thought the prenuptial agreement was at the bottom of it all. I was dying to know what it said.

But by then I was just going through the motions myself, drinking more single malt than I should have at night and, I admit, during the day, too. I had come across a new brand of vodka, which I kept in the freezer in my sitting room, and every now and then, when things got too tedious or stressful, I'd sneak back and take a quick, short, icy shot. I also used it as a reward system: Every time I could have told Junior where to get off and didn't, I got a shot. It was a delicious way to stay anesthetized during the daytime, and then the scotch provided the knock-out punch at night. I knew I was playing with fire, but I also didn't care, because I knew it would all be over soon, and I could sober up on the beach at St. Tropez or wherever I ended up.

I might have been in a state of thick-woolly-headedness, but by her wedding day, Madam was catatonic, and you and I both know why: the wedding night. She knew as well as she knew her own name that Junior intended to consummate their marriage, mostly because that had become all he could talk about. "I'm going to give you some Texas-sized lovin' you won't even believe," he boasted. He'd expect something in return for his investment, but, luckily, it wasn't my problem.

The ceremony was at five-thirty.

"It's five-twenty-five, Madam."

"I know, I know." She brushed on her lipstick and then lit another cigarette.

Guests had been arriving steadily for the last twenty minutes, we could hear them driving up. The sound of their footsteps on the gravel echoed emptily through the open bedroom windows, and the disembodied sounds of their voices floated up indistinctly. Car doors closed with muffled thuds as the parking valets pulled Range Rovers, Bentleys, Jaguars, and Mercedes Benzes into the field to park.

"There's still time to back out." I pinned the flowers in her hair for the last time.

She had smoked an entire pack of cigarettes since lunch. She shook her head and downed another glass of champagne. "I'm not going to back out. It's going to be fine."

We looked into each other's eyes in the mirror.

"You know I think you've lost your mind," I told her. "He's not worth it. The taxes are paid. You can go back to work."

"I'm going to miss you so much, Nigel. I can't believe you're really going."

I poured a second glass for myself and sipped it. "I can't either. You've been my whole life for more than ten years. But it's time for both of us to make a change. It's probably going to be healthy."

"Have you made up your mind what you're going to do?"

"Beyond flying to France tomorrow? No. I'll think of something when I get there." I unbuttoned her sleeveless white chiffon gown, removed it from the padded satin hanger, and held it open for her to step into.

She smiled and took my hand. "Make sure you let me know how to get hold of you. Are you sure you don't want to come to Africa with us?"

"More sure than I've ever been of anything in my life." We both laughed. "Nepal was enough excitement for me. You know, practically every disease on the planet comes from Africa."

"I know," she laughed. "I promise I won't kiss any monkeys."

I fastened a torsade of shell pink pearls around her neck—Junior's wedding gift. It had a porcupine-like diamond cluster closure and the coil of pearls was so thick it looked like an underwater trans-Atlantic cable—probably cost as much as one, too.

She picked up her bouquet, a mass of gardenias and trailing orchids. "Here's to you, Madam." I raised my glass. "You are the most beautiful bride I've ever seen."

The gown was as simple as could be, which made her look more elegant than ever. Her eyes, on the other hand, looked like solid black glass. She was completely drunk.

"Please don't lose track of me, Nigel." She kissed me and stroked my cheek.

"Good luck, Madam."

She walked herself down the stairs, out through the sunroom into the garden, and up the aisle to where Junior waited to take her hand.

Twenty minutes later, it was over.

Mr. and Mrs. Rex "Junior" Hammond, Jr. greeted their friends. Beauty and the Beast. Let the party begin.

55

The last of the guests left at ten-thirty. The caterers were gone by eleven, as were Effie and Scully, giggly and tipsy, gone to their cottage. Madam and Junior retired upstairs with a bottle of champagne. They were both very drunk. Staggeringly drunk.

I, for a change, was not. I was ready for the next part of my life to begin. It was my last night in my room. I couldn't believe it. All my possessions were packed into the set of canvas and bridle leather Hermès luggage Madam had handed down to me from Armand. Everything was ready to go except for my overnight kit and the photograph William had taken of me at Phoksumdo Tal. Me, the new Nigel, smiling into the camera. I sipped a light scotch and petted the dogs, running my hand over their silky little bodies. I tried not to think about how much I loved them and would miss them, and I tried not to think about what was going on upstairs.

I tucked the photo into the side pocket of my carry-on, got into bed, and tried to lose myself in *Monsoon,* Wilbur's latest. My literary ambitions abandoned, I now thought maybe I'd move to the South of France and become a painter, or study Provençal furniture and fabrics. Maybe I'd write a book about Fortuny. Whatever, it would be a nice way to spend the autumn. The crickets were getting stirred up outdoors, but except for them, the countryside was silent. That was when Madam started screaming bloody murder. The most blood-curdling screams I'd ever heard in my life. And then they stopped.

My reflexes were instantaneous. I tossed the book aside, leapt out of bed, and tore through my sitting room and out the door. I was halfway up the stairs when I remembered, and ran back and grabbed the two silver six-shooters that had been sitting on my desk gathering dust for weeks. I raced back up, three steps at a time, and burst into her room. The bed lamps were on and I could see the wide, white, shaking hairy mass of Junior's back and buttocks. He had buckled the empty holsters around his waist and was straddling her. Then I saw that he had tied a bullwhip around her neck and was strangling her. And raping her. Her face was dark, and her mouth gaped in a silent scream as she frantically dug her fingers into her own throat trying to get them under the noose to loosen it.

"Stop! Stop!" I screamed. "Let her go or I'll kill you."

"What the hell . . ." He turned, still on his knees, and saw me with both barrels leveled at his swollen, sweating face. It was enough of an interruption to make him drop the whip, and Madam escaped, falling to the floor. She scrambled to her feet and stumbled across the room, coughing and gasping for breath. The woven leather of the cat o' nine tails had been wrapped twice around her neck and had cut deeply into it.

"Where in the hell d'you come from?" Junior growled.

"I didn't think you'd ever get here," she choked.

"Put your hands up, you sick bastard," I answered, and cocked the guns. My voice had risen several octaves. Junior did as I ordered.

"Put those guns down, you goddamn fool!" he yelped. "You could hurt someone."

Madam hid behind me. "Shoot him, Nigel. Shoot him."

"Don't shoot me!" Junior screamed, his arms straight in the air. "She *asked* me to do it. I wasn't hurting her. She *liked* it."

"That's not true. He's lying. Shoot him," she begged me. "He was trying to *kill* me, Nigel. If you don't shoot him, I will. Give me the guns."

"No, no!" Junior screamed. "Don't. She wanted me to do it." He lost control of his bowels.

That was it. I was so blind with rage and so filled with adrenaline, I saw every millisecond with extreme clarity. I pulled one trigger. Then the other. The bullets ripped into his chest. They seemed to explode him from the inside out and he sank into his own filth, a look of shock on his face.

56

I dropped the revolvers where I stood and rushed to Madam, who had curled into a tight ball on the chaise. Her hair fell across her clasped arms and hid her face. The malevolent cat o' nine tails, still looped around her neck, lay across her legs like a snake poised to strike again.

"Madam, Madam, can you hear me?" I pulled off my pajama top and covered her. "Can you hear me? I'm going to call 911."

She reached up and grabbed me with almost superhuman strength. It was as if a vise had locked around my forearm. Her eyes were wide and shining with a ghastly glow. "No. Stay here. Don't leave."

"It's just on the other side of the room. I'll be right back." I pulled my arm free, grabbed a small wool throw, and tucked it around her to stop her shivering. "One second."

The central emergency number at the sheriff's office answered on the first ring, and when I heard that calm, affirming voice on the other end of the line, I started shaking, too. What was I going to say? I've just murdered a man in cold blood? A man about whom my feelings were well known? Well known to whom? Madam. Junior. Junior was dead and Madam wouldn't tell. Who else? Who else? My mind spun in a panic. William? No. William was dead. Ryder? No. No one else.

"Nine-one-one. What is your emergency?" the voice said again. "Are you there?"

"Yes," I began tremulously, then got my breath. "There's been a shooting at Miss di Fidelio's farm, eighty-four-hundred Old Norfolk Road."

"Eighty-four-hundred Old Norfolk Road? The Plains?"

"Yes."

"Are there injuries?"

"Well, yes. Mrs. Hammond is dead. I mean, *Mr.* Hammond is dead. He was raping Mrs. Hammond and trying to strangle her and I shot him." It was the truth.

"What is your name?"

"Nigel Smythe. I mean, Nigel Weatherby-Smythe." I was getting all confused. I was freezing to death and covered with goosebumps. I had shot Junior Hammond in cold blood. I could have chosen not to. And not only that, I shot him twice. Once would have been plenty. I *wanted* him dead. Oh, my God. My mother was right, my temper had gotten me into trouble. A crazy, giddy joy flooded my mouth like a dissolving Alka Seltzer tablet and burst out uncontrollably. It sounded like a sob.

"Are you all right, Nigel? Are there other injuries?"

"Yes. Madam's neck is almost broken and she's been raped." She'd drawn herself up to a sitting position and pulled my pajama top around her. She was gently probing her neck where the whip had cut into it. Deep bruises were already beginning to appear. Hematomas, I expect. "I shot him. When will you be here?"

"We're on our way now, Nigel. Stay on the line with me. Is there any chance Mr. Hammond is alive?"

I looked over at the mountain that had been Rex Hammond, Jr. His head was propped against the headboard and he was staring straight at me over his hairy belly with wide-open eyes. His mouth hung open, too, and his pink tongue came right to the edge of his bottom lip, filling the floor of his mouth. I watched him, fascinated. My God, *was* he alive? I stared at him. He stared at me. I squinted and leaned slightly forward. "Mr. Hammond, sir," I said. "Are you there?"

"Nigel, are you there?"

It was the 911 lady.

I almost jumped out of my skin. "Yes. I'm here."

"Is there any chance Mr. Hammond is alive?"

"I don't think so. I shot him."

"We're on our way. Stay on the phone with me, Nigel," she repeated.

Madam had gone into the bathroom. I've watched enough episodes of *Law & Order* to know that if she washed herself, any defense I'd have would go straight down the drain. I dashed after her and found her, hands on the counter, leaning forward and staring into the mirror at the savage bruises that now emerged not only on her throat but also across her thighs and on her shoulders, where his fingers and teeth had dug into her skin. He had actually bitten her in a number of places and drawn blood. The patterns were grotesque. Her face had gone as white as a sheet, virtually drained of color, except around her eyes, which were ringed with a raccoon mask of red bruises. Her hair, unpinned and stiff with hairspray, stood out like a corona of glossy black feathers.

"Are you there, Nigel?" The voice came through the phone, tinny and disconnected.

"Yes, I'm here. I don't know what else to say. I wish you'd hurry. Hold on a minute." I put the phone down and took Madam's terry cloth robe from its hook next to the shower. I handed it to her, and she returned my pajama top. We looked at each other and at that moment, with no words spoken, I knew we understood one another perfectly. I picked up the phone. "I'm here," I said again, suddenly filled with calm.

I took Madam's hand and guided her out of the bedroom and down the stairs to the kitchen, where I pulled out a chair at the breakfast table and sat her down. She was edgy as a wet cat, ready to explode, and she drummed her fingernails incessantly on the tin top of the old-fashioned kitchen table, making a sound like hail on a windowpane. Then she reached for Effie's grocery pad and, while I put water on for tea and continued to reassure the 911 lady I was still there, Madam scrawled pages of notes, ripping them off and handing them to me one sheet at a time. Once I'd read them, I held them in the flame under the pot until they were nothing but ash, threw them in the sink, and washed them down the drain. I went into my quarters and dressed, and was just stepping into my shoes when the flashing emergency lights shone through the trees and bounced down the drive.

"I see some cars," I said to the 911 lady.

"Yes, we're on the scene. Deputy Sheriff March will be at the door any second."

They took Madam—who had by then managed to work herself into a complete state of hysteria—off in the ambulance and after I described the events leading up to the shooting in detail, what seemed like a hundred times for the deputy whom I knew well, I was placed under arrest for murder. I knew by then they'd sent someone to question Madam. I knew we would tell the same story.

It was humiliating being handcuffed and shoved into the back of a police car, but not unfamiliar, and no one was there to see me. It also helped that the deputy apologized to me a number of times. When I arrived at the county jail in Warrenton, I called one of the many attorneys who had been at the wedding the night before, and she called a well-known Washington-based criminal defense lawyer, Leonard Slater, who spent weekends on his Virginia farm and who showed up at the jailhouse about six o'clock, looking like he'd just come from posing in a *Gentlemen's Quarterly* fashion spread. I'd seen his picture in the papers and watched him on television hundreds of times, standing at the top of various of the nation's courthouse steps, addressing the media condescendingly, as if they were ignorant students. In person, he was much bigger. He was tremendously imposing, with physical stature, persona, presence, and power. He was brilliant and intimidating and immediately took charge. He'd already been to see Madam, seen her condition, and heard her story.

"Was she conscious or unconscious when you got there?" he asked me.

"Completely *un*conscious," I answered. "I thought she was dead."

"Was she breathing?"

"I'm not a doctor, but I don't think so. I've taken lots of CPR courses."

"Yet he was continuing to strangle and rape her?"

I nodded. "It was the most disgusting thing I've ever seen. He was wearing the holsters—it was so degenerate I couldn't believe it. It was like a cheap porno movie."

"What happened next?"

"I grabbed the guns off the desk and yelled at him to stop, but I don't think he heard me. He was too involved in what he was doing. It was like he was on drugs or something. I told him again to stop or I'd shoot, but he didn't. He told me to go to hell, to mind my own business, and then I shot him. He didn't give me any choice—he was killing her. And then I dragged her out from under him and did CPR. Is she going to be all right?"

"You saved her life."

"Thank God."

"I'm going to have them keep her in the hospital for a few days. He pretty much ripped her up, deep bite marks all over the place. Her neck was almost broken."

"Oh, poor Madam," I started to cry.

"Do you realize you shot him twice?"

"What?" I said. "Twice?"

My arraignment before the general district court judge was at ten. I plead not-guilty to a charge of third-degree murder. Mr. Slater showed the judge Polaroids taken of Madam when she arrived at the hospital and argued persuasively there was no question I had saved the life of my employer, just in the nick of time, according to the paramedics on the scene. The emergency room doctor confirmed what they said: Another thirty seconds would have been too late. I was released on my own recognizance, pending a medical examiner's report.

"What happens next?" I asked my attorney as he meticulously reassembled his papers and placed them in his slim, black kid Bottega briefcase.

"There will be a preliminary hearing in a few weeks, then, based on that and the autopsy report, a grand jury will decide. Do you want a ride home?"

I shook my head. "I'll take a taxi, thanks."

"Come on, I'll walk you out."

"That's not necessary, sir. I know you have a busy schedule."

"Not a problem," he said comfortingly, and escorted me through the courthouse doors. The media were there, a mob of them. Leonard was one of their biggest stars. They'd tried hundreds of cases for him in the public arena, on television and in the newspapers, and now he was presenting mine. He stopped on the stairs to answer their questions, basking in their camera lights, eyes flashing with his trademark contempt and defiance, his shirt collar and teeth white as snow. I don't know how long it was before he or anyone else noticed I wasn't there anymore.

As far as I could tell, no one followed me home, and then I discovered why: No one needed to. Trucks from two Washington television stations and CNN, and a parking lot full of cars sat at the entrance to our driveway. The sheriff's department had stationed an officer there to keep them off the property, and after a lengthy two-way radio conversation with his headquarters, he let me through, but the wait had been excruciating. Television lights and flashbulbs burned through the taxi windows at me, as the reporters screamed their questions.

"Is it true you shot Junior Hammond?"

"Is it true he tried to murder Jacqueline di Fidelio and you saved her life?"

"Are you having an affair with Jacqueline di Fidelio?"

"Was there a prenuptial agreement? Will she inherit Hammond Oil even though they were married only a few hours?"

I sank lower in my seat and sought to get in touch with my inner self.

I unplugged all the phones and used my cell phone to communicate with Mr. Slater. Two days later, when I left to fetch Madam at the hospital back in Warrenton, I used Effie's little Honda wagon and went out the back entrance. Fortunately, the media hadn't found it yet, but I supposed it was just a matter of time. We had become the epicenter of a gigantic circus and based on my experience watching high-visibility cases on television, I knew our problems were just beginning.

"How are you?"

"Sore." Thin strips of tape on her shoulder covered ghoulish lines of stitches where Junior had bitten into her particularly deeply. She pulled on her leggings, grimacing as the tight Lycra skimmed her bruised hips. "And exhausted. All I want to do is get out of here," she said. "Are you all right?"

"Me?" I said. "I'm fine. A little anxious perhaps. You won't believe the newspaper and television people. They're all over the place."

"I know, I've been watching it on TV. I can't believe some of the stuff they're digging up about me. And you. You really were some kind of juvenile delinquent, weren't you?" She groaned as she reached behind her head to try and gather her hair.

"Let me do that." I pulled a ponytail together and fixed it with a rubber band. I handed her her dark glasses.

"Let's go."

For the first couple of miles neither one of us spoke, and then she began.

"Thank you, Nigel."

"Yes," I answered. "You're welcome."

"You saved my life."

"Yes. I did." The complexity of the situation dawned on me more every day, and the bigger the picture grew—the knowledge that she and I had concocted a story that paralleled the truth, but wasn't—the more overwhelmed I became at our audacity. I couldn't shake the feeling that I was back on that narrow, unsteady span of slab-rock at Phoksumdo Tal, just short of halfway across—too far to go back, too far to go forward, and way too far to let go and fall. "I'm very nervous about my future."

"It's going to turn out fine, Nigel. Leonard Slater is the best. There won't even be a trial."

"I hope you're right."

"Trust me. I know what I'm talking about. Will you forgive me, Nigel?" she asked. "Will you stay?"

I glanced over at her and for that second, when we looked into each other's eyes, besides the vulnerability of our complicity, I saw affection and relief. I saw the possibility that now things could go back to being the way they were. "Of course I'll stay."

The countryside passed, giant oak and ash trees heavy with changing leaves shading the way, the remains of summertime field flowers along the stone walls, sheaves of corn husks and piles of pumpkins arranged decoratively at farm gates, miles of black fencing lining the road. It was all so normal. The physical world around us was unaffected by our cataclysm.

Madam started to laugh. Then I started. And finally we were both laughing so hard I had to pull off to the side of the road.

Her bedroom, on the other hand, was no laughing matter. Junior's body had been removed, but the rest of the crime scene detritus remained. The air was foul, in spite of the wide-open windows. Chalk marks on the rug outlined where I'd dropped the guns. Every surface was black with fingerprint dust, eating into the veneer.

"I want the whole room gutted." Madam gagged from the smell.

"I'll take care of it. I've already collected a number of your personal things and moved them downstairs."

She stood in the shower for what seemed like an hour, and then pulled her work clothes on. I watched out the kitchen window as she went down the path to the studio. She moved somewhat carefully, but otherwise she appeared unchanged. The crisp, oversized white cotton shirt hid the wounds, and her clean hair was pulled into a smooth ball at her neck.

The caterer had done such a good job of cleaning up, you'd never know dozens of guests had filled our garden three days before. You might never know from looking at any of us that anything had happened.

I realized I'd been washing the same glass over and over. I put it on the drain board, went to the library, and got the bottle of Special Reserve Glenlivet from the liquor cabinet. I returned to the kitchen, poured myself a good four fingers of the soft honey-colored whiskey, sat down at the kitchen table, and lit a cigarette, all with the intention of contemplating the ramifications of being a murderer. I didn't have to shoot Junior. I could have held him at gunpoint until he was arrested for rape and assault. His hands were in the air. He was completely naked. He begged me not to shoot. I pulled the trigger. The triggers. I didn't need to pull both of them. One would have done it. I pulled them both. I chose to shoot him, no two ways about it, and furthermore, I was glad I'd done it. I needed to consider what that meant about my personality, my future.

This will sound crazy, but the longer I sat there, and the more I drank, all I could think about was that we now had a jet. We had a Boeing Business Jet. Do you know what that means? It's like having your own 737. I was more than halfway through the bottle when Effie came in to start dinner and sent me to bed.

57

We should have lived happily ever after. But there hadn't been a murder this big for years. Not to imply that Loudon and Farquier Counties were any strangers to scandal: the most recent being when the Cummings twin shot her polo-player lover to death and was sentenced to sixty days for voluntary manslaughter because he'd been beating her up, stealing all her money, and manipulating her until she was little more than a slave. But ours was a scandal of major international proportions, involving two super-luminaries and one trusty butler. Madam was world-famous for her portraits and her crazy mother, and Junior for his excesses. It was the stuff movies-of-the-week were made of—spoiled people, tons of money, sick sex, violent crime, international locales, loyal servants gone amok.

Mr. Slater had hired a security company to protect the farm, and us, from the media, but it seemed nothing could stop them from climbing trees across the meadow and taking our pictures with menacing tele-photo lenses as big as umbrella stands.

Madam and I treated each other with complete deference. There was no silly chatter, no letting down of appearances. I kept my time around her to a minimum and spoke only when required, since—in spite of the fact the house was swept every day for listening devices and none were found—we operated on the assumption that every word we said inside our walls was heard, the phones tapped, the house bugged. It was torture. We kept all the blinds drawn, and whenever one of us went outside—to the studio or the garden—we felt we had to run, almost as if we were criminals trying to escape from jail, to avoid the hidden cameras lurking in the woods. We started to scoot everywhere, hunched like crabs. It was exhausting.

Madam spent most of her days on the phone with Junior's lawyers, working out his estate. Other than lawyers, nobody phoned, nobody came to call. We were in our own dimension, as untouchable and unde-sirable as voodoo spirits.

"They're making me feel as if I were the one who did something wrong," Madam complained. *"I'm the victim. This is crazy."*

She had an uncanny knack for talking herself into things.

"Good news," Leonard Slater informed me over the phone. "The district court schedule is working in our favor. Your preliminary hearing is scheduled for next week."

It was only ten days after the shooting. And by now, we were so accustomed to the flashbulbs neither Madam nor I even blinked when we ran their gamut into the courthouse to testify. The bruises around her neck had come fully into their own, and she dressed so they were visible, like a tattooed necklace of angry, black barbed-wire.

As it turned out, a number of things worked in my favor: the bruises themselves, the photographs of the extensive damage done to the rest of her body, the medical examiner's report, which stated that not only had Junior's blood alcohol level been at three-point-one—practically off the charts—but evidence of cocaine in his blood had also been found, meaning he had rendered himself dangerous and irrational. The coup de grace was Leonard Slater's closing argument that the 911 tape was inadmissible *and* I had not been properly informed of my rights since the deputy was an acquaintance and had simply said, "You know I'm going to have to take you in."

"Your honor," Mr. Slater urged. "Nigel Weatherby-Smythe should be recognized as a hero, not a killer. He shot Junior Hammond to prevent him from killing Mrs. Hammond. He fired both those guns from fear and passion, not malice. We should all be lucky enough to have someone as quick-thinking and loyal in our employ."

The charges were reduced to involuntary manslaughter and I was placed on six weeks' probation. There would be no trial. While Mr. Slater addressed the press, a deputy escorted us out the back of the courthouse and we went straight home.

It took almost a week for the media to clear out, leaving the countryside completely trampled and trashed with McDonald's and Burger King and Seven-Eleven coffee, hamburger, and french fry containers. If this were Nepal, they'd be fined.

But inside our little house, we were finally at peace. That night, Effie brought us dinner in the library, small grilled filets and sliced tomatoes, and we ate from TV tables and watched a biography of the Captain and Tenille. I would say we were both basically brain-dead. It was the first quiet night we'd had since Junior Hammond appeared on our doorstep in June.

"Madam," I asked during a commercial. "May I ask you a question?"

"Sure."

"What was in your prenuptial agreement? I mean, is there any chance they could take the money away?"

"No. Not a chance. I fulfilled the terms."

That wasn't enough. She had to tell me and she knew it. I just stared at her until she started talking again.

"All right. There were three conditions: One, that I be lawfully and legally married to him. Well, we had a proper license and the ceremony was officiated by Judge Ruxton. Two, that I take his name, which I did, and which I will continue to do. And three, that the marriage be consummated. Which, as you well know, it was. In spite of the manner in which it was accomplished, his semen was present. Inside." She made a wretching face.

"What if I hadn't come up when I did? You'd be dead."

Madam nodded. "It was a big gamble, but I knew you wouldn't let me down."

"What do you mean, 'a big gamble'? You had this all planned?"

"Well." She tapped her fork on the edge of her plate as she considered. "That would be somewhat of an overstatement. But, I admit, it had occurred to me." Her expression was wry.

Wow. I thought about it, how, back in June, she'd insisted he stay for a few days, and how she'd taken away his guns and given them to me after he shot the fawn and the rabbit, instead of making him leave. Her insistence that I stay through the wedding. The whip around her neck. His protestation that she'd wanted him to do it, and now the realization that she must have told him that was what she wanted. She had egged him on. Because she was certain of my love and dedication to her, and my enmity for him. She was certain I would rescue her.

"You mean you orchestrated the whole thing?"

Madam glanced at me sheepishly. "Not in the beginning. I really thought there was some hope for him, but as the summer went on, I realized he was beyond salvation. I set him up. It was the only way I knew to get my hands on some money. I was sick of being broke and used."

I sipped my wine and, a few moments later, asked, "Exactly how much money is there?"

"Close to eight hundred million dollars."

"Lovely." She had been his wife for less than seven hours. That had turned out to be very expensive sex for Junior Hammond—$115 million an hour, to be exact. At the next commercial I asked her what she had planned for the future.

"I think we both deserve a vacation."

"What do you propose?"

"How about a few days in Paris and then a week at the Splendido?"

"Sounds like an excellent plan. Let's call the pilot and tell him to gas up the jet."

"Let's give it a few days to let the dust settle," she admonished. "Then we can do whatever we want."

We banged our glasses together and laughed like the hyenas we were.

58

Hammond residence," I answered. While I'd originally bridled at Madam's insistence I answer that way, I now understood how important it was. It was eight hundred million dollars worth of important. I was Hammonding up a storm. I'd just hung up from talking to the director of the Hammond Oil Aviation Department—didn't that have a nice ring to it?—and telling him that Mrs. Hammond would like to leave the following day for Paris. Nine a.m. sharp. No more of this having to leave late in the afternoon and fly all night to arrive bleary-eyed the next morning and stagger through the day. Better to fly all day, land at night, take a sleeping pill and get up bright and early, all ready to go and time-zone-adjusted, the next morning. Oh, my, I was starting to have fun.

"Oh, hello, Nigel. It's Mary Anne. Is your madam around?"

"She's down in the studio. Let me have her call you."

"She doesn't need to. I'd like her to come to tea this afternoon at about three. Do you think she's available?"

"I think she's always available for you. If she's not, I'll ring you back."

"One other thing," Mary Anne said. "It's Lionel's day off, and Sissy's got a bum hand, so she can't do much. Could I impose on you to serve? It's just tea for the two of us by the pond."

"It would be my distinct honor, Mrs. McCormick."

"Thank you. I'll see you at three."

Since the charges against me had been all but dropped, and Madam was now as rich as Mary Anne McCormick, Ryder was in constant motion between his house and ours, trying to stay on Madam's, and my, good side. He saw us as his future. Mary Anne's death, which seemed more and more imminent, would not make him a rich man. Rumors had it he would be extremely well, but minimally provided for compared to what he'd gotten used to. The bulk of her estate would go into her charitable foundation and as bequests to various institutions. The sicker she got, the more he turned into nothing but a handsome and desperate old fag.

He started dropping in every afternoon at about two-thirty to see how we were, and to ask if he could do anything to help us, or sometimes just to keep us up-to-date on his activities. To see if Madam wanted to play a hand of gin, or go for a ride, or play a round of golf. The answer was always no. She was just trying to lay low until she took off for Europe.

"And what scintillating function are you off to today?" Madam asked him, as if she didn't know. He had on his fancy hunt clothes.

"Hunt club." He tried to sound bored, but he had always been so impressed he was in the hunt club he could hardly stand it. "What are you up to?"

"Actually, we're going to your house for tea," she answered.

" 'We'?"

"Mary Anne asked Nigel to serve since Lionel's off and Sissy did something to her hand."

Ryder picked at an invisible snag on his sleeve. "Huh." He was jealous. He'd been purposefully left out by his wife. She'd known he'd be at a club meeting when she invited Madam. "Sounds boring to me," he said. "Can I talk to you in private, Jackie? Without Mr. Big Ears around?"

Madam laughed. "Sure, come on in the library."

They left me standing at the front door. My neck was crimson, and I'd just like to go on record as saying I do *not* have big ears. My ears are perfectly proportioned and have even been admired for their compactness and tightness to my head.

Whatever he wanted to talk about didn't take long and ended badly, because he stormed out of the library, slamming the door behind him, and swept past me.

"Have a lovely meeting, sir," I said blandly, but he didn't answer.

He settled his hard hat firmly, picked up his reins, jerked his horse into a fast turn, and swacked it with his quirt, sending the big gelding into a shotgun start. They galloped off to join his chums for rounds of gin rickeys while they talked about the new owners over near Outerville and who knew them and would they be receptive or resistant to allowing the Hunt to cross their property. After all, the former owners did, but that was no assurance the new people would see it the same way. It was an ongoing challenge to the Hunt, all these new people.

"What was that all about?" I asked Madam.

"Same old bullshit."

The day was magnificent, so instead of driving, Madam and I walked through the gate in the fence and crossed the freshly mowed field to the McCormicks' where Mary Anne greeted us on the terrace off the living room. I hadn't seen her since the wedding and was shocked at her deteriorating condition. She was so thin and tiny in her wheelchair, she looked like a skeleton. And lacking the substance of any underlying tissue or muscle, the skin on her face hung like wet Kleenex, showing every sharp edge and nuance of bone, making her eyes huge and luminous. She had on a quilted white satin robe, tied with a ribbon at her neck. A white cashmere blanket covered her lap and legs.

"I'm so glad you could come." Her voice was still strong. She took Madam's hand and raised her face to kiss her cheek. "Do you mind pushing me down to the pond? And Nigel, the tea tray's ready in the kitchen, if you'll bring it."

"My pleasure," I answered. "I'll be down directly."

Mary Anne's tea service and tray were right out of Buckingham Palace. The Queen could not possibly have anything finer—the tea and water pots, sugar and tongs, creamer and spoons, were Edwardian sterling, perfectly balanced and engraved with Mary Anne's monogram. The china was Royal Worchester, the linens Irish. The tiered cookie plate was arranged with finger sandwiches of salmon and cream cheese on brown bread, and watercress, radish, and butter on white bread with the crusts trimmed off; tiny cherry tarts in flaky crusts, and homemade butter cookies that melted in your mouth before you could even bite into them. I know, I tried a couple. The cart was Edwardian as well, with large quiet wheels in back and smaller ones in front. The silver tray fit perfectly onto the top.

By the time I got to the dock, Madam and Mary Anne, shaded by the umbrella, were huddled close together, talking quietly. I began to prepare the service. They held hands and ignored me.

". . . I have so little time left," Mary Anne was saying. "The doctor was here this morning and the hospice nurse starts tomorrow."

"Oh, Mary Anne," Madam said. "I'm so sorry."

"Don't be. I can't take the pain any longer. You can't imagine what agony the last year has been. The only distraction was your wedding and getting to know you. I'm sorry it took us so long to become friends, and that it's been for such a short time. You've become almost like a daughter to me."

"I wish you had been my mother. My life wouldn't have been the mess it's turned out to be."

"There's no way of knowing." She put her hand beneath her blanket and withdrew a large, flat, dark velvet case. "These were my mother's and I can't think of anyone I'd rather have them than you. They were made by Louis Cartier himself, for Czarina Alexandra."

Madam accepted the case and slowly opened it. Inside was a diamond and pearl suite—a choker, stomacher, and earrings—unlike anything I'd ever seen except in photographs of long-dead royals. All Madam could do was stare.

"It takes someone with real physical stature, like you, to wear them. I've never been able to carry them off; I just take them out and admire them sometimes. Wheelchairs don't provide much presence." Mary Anne laughed, but tears streamed down her cheeks. "I'm so happy to give them to you."

"Mary Anne," Madam said. "I can't accept these. They should be in a museum."

"Living things go to museums and die—furniture, clothes, jewelry. I insist you accept them. I have a reason. They come with strings. I need a favor, and I don't think you're going to like it much."

"Name it."

"I'd like you to look after Ryder when I'm gone."

"All right."

"I've left him enough money so he'll be comfortable, but he's such a child; if there's no one in charge of him, God knows what he'll get up to. As you know, he needs a firm hand."

Madam made a move to speak, but Mary Anne stopped her.

"Don't let's waste our time. I've always known everything about you and your mother and Ryder. I also know how much he loves you. I'm not asking you to keep daily tabs on him, and you don't have to love him back, but please, don't lose sight of him, either."

"I promise."

"I think I'd like to rest now."

While Madam told her goodbye and promised to visit every day until it was over, I took the tea things back to the house, thinking that just when things were getting good, Ryder would get them all screwed up again. When I returned from the kitchen, Madam was waiting for me on the terrace.

"She's asleep," she said. "Just quiet in her chair with the sprites and swans on the water."

We left through the front. I heard what sounded like a backfire, but didn't think anything about it.

59

"What can I do for you, deputy? Here to collect for the policeman's ball?" I joked.

It was early evening, not yet quite dark.

Deputy Sheriff March was the snappy young man who'd arrested me for Junior's murder. He was squared-away in his fawn-colored Farquier County uniform, shiny visor shading his eyes, making them invisible. His boss, the Farquier County Sheriff, accompanied him. "May we come in?" he asked. His voice and manner were professional.

"Please."

"Is Mrs. Hammond here?" the sheriff asked.

"Yes, she's down in the studio. Let me call her."

"No, we'll go to her. Will you show the way?"

"All right."

I led them down the path to the studio where Madam was sitting on the front porch, sketching the final light of day coming through the trees. It was the first time I'd seen her pick up a piece of charcoal in months.

"Mrs. Hammond?"

"Good evening, Sheriff. What are you doing here?"

"Mrs. Hammond," his voice stayed formal, "I'm placing you under arrest for the murder of Mary Anne McCormick and for grand theft. You have the right to remain silent. You have the right to an attorney. Anything you say can and will be used against you."

"Excuse me?" Madam laughed. "What are you talking about? Wait a minute. What are you doing?"

As the sheriff spoke, informing her of her rights, the young deputy took her arm and pulled her to her feet. The sketch pad fell to the porch, but she was unable to stoop and pick it up because he had already pulled her hands behind her back and efficiently handcuffed her.

"What in the hell are you doing?" she asked. "Let go of me."

"Please watch your step," the sheriff said as they guided her toward the house. "We also have a search warrant. Do you want to save us the time and tell us where you put it?"

"Put what? Wait a minute. What are you doing?" She struggled to break his grasp but he had a firm hold. The charcoal fell from her fingers. Her voice was panicked and she looked at me. "Nigel, do something."

"What?" I asked, stupidly. I felt as if I'd been kicked in the stomach. "I don't know what to do."

"Call Leonard."

"The jewelry, Mrs. Hammond. Mr. McCormick said some jewelry was missing, and you can save us all a lot of time if you'll just tell me where it is."

"You mean the necklace and earrings? They were a *gift*. Mrs. McCormick gave them to me this afternoon."

"You have any documentation to back that up?" the sheriff asked.

"No, of course not. It was a gift."

They took the velvet case and stuffed Madam into the back seat of their cruiser, throwing rocks all over the place as the patrol car, lights flashing, spun down the drive.

60

As I told you at the beginning of my story, the trial ended disastrously. People came out of the woodwork to testify against Madam. It was incredible. And why? To get on the bandwagon? To make her pay for being rich? People she scarcely knew couldn't wait to be called upon to tell about how badly she'd treated them. And then, how gentle, kind and gracious, Mary Anne had been to Madam—treating her like a daughter, and Madam had murdered her to steal her jewelry and her husband. Blew her head off at point-blank range and threw her in the pond. Madam, who already had everything once her butler had conveniently murdered her husband. A butler who'd gotten off with nothing more than a slap on the wrist. Well, Madam would pay for that.

The trial went on for months, a televised battle between two larger-than-life attorneys.

"We'd both become afraid of Jackie," Ryder mewled from the stand.

He had worn the same clothes to court every day—a rumpled sport coat with a buttoned cardigan vest and a knit tie. The sight almost made me laugh out loud. Ryder McCormick, the biggest sartorial snob on the face of the earth, in a cardigan vest and a knit tie? Please. "She was stalking us. My wife was terrified, and I know the fear intensified her illness. The doctor said she had only weeks, maybe days, to live. And then, to come home and find her floating in the lake, a bullet in her head, her wheelchair overturned on the dock. She was as frail as a dove. Oh, God, my beloved, beloved Mary Anne." Then Ryder fell apart. It went beyond losing his composure, he just flat out burst into tears and blubbered like a big baby. And the judge called a recess. What absolute crap.

Any idiot with half a brain could figure out she had committed suicide.

No one stood up for Madam at the trial, or at the sentencing hearing. No one. No one but me, and who am I? No one but the butler, with a record of my own and a complete absence of credibility. Ryder had worn an eye-patch throughout the entire, three-month ordeal, lest one single juror forget for one single moment that he was half blind. A half blind man who had cared for his invalid and dying wife. Not just any dying wife, mind you, but Mary Anne Schlumbacher McCormick, a delightful, wealthy, brilliant—and let me say it again—*invalid* who had little time to live, anyway.

The prosecution claimed my Madam, wild with jealousy, had cold-bloodedly and maliciously shot Mrs. McCormick in the head and dumped her out of her wheelchair into the lake. Her fingerprints were on the wheelchair handles, and she'd conveniently wiped them off the gun before she threw it in the water. Madam and I knew it was a lie. It was obvious she'd committed suicide, but no one would believe it. I had served them tea that afternoon out on the dock, and Madam and I had left together. I'd been with her the whole time. Well, almost the whole time. There were those few minutes when I took the tray back to the kitchen, but remember when I said I'd heard a backfire? That was *after* we left. That must have been when she put the gun to her own head.

Madam was sentenced to death.

In Virginia you have a choice between electrocution and lethal injection. I'll bet you didn't know that.

She would be incarcerated in the Fluvanna Correctional Center for Women near Charlottesville, where I could visit her whenever I liked, including a monthly contact—not conjugal—visit.

Four days before her execution, she would be transported down to Greensville, near the North Carolina state line.

61

THREE YEARS LATER

I visited her weekly until every possible avenue of appeal was exhausted and the execution date was set. A couple of months before the sentence was to be carried out, Ryder wrote to Madam, requesting and receiving permission to meet with her.

"I want to meet with Jackie," he explained on *Larry King Live,* "because I want to grant her forgiveness for murdering my wife. It's the Christian thing to do, and as the husband of the victim, I need it, psychically, in order to lay down my animosities."

That stupid bastard.

"How did it go?" I asked her after his visit. We had become as relaxed as possible, given the circumstances. We both had cigarettes and sat back in our chairs, talking to each other as if we were having a chat over the phone. Which, for all intents and purposes, we were. I brought her pictures of the dogs.

"You won't believe it," she told me. "Ryder said he would come up with Mary Anne's suicide note if I'd marry him."

"So what did you say?"

"I told him, sure. You come up with the note, I'll marry you. He made me promise on a stack of bibles. What will he do when I'm gone and he has no one left to torture?"

"I think he is the sickest person I've ever known in my life," I said through the glass. "He may even be sicker than Junior."

"I don't think I'd go that far," she laughed.

I told her about Ryder and me. About our former relationship. About how he liked his sex. How he liked to dress up in her mother's clothes. We both laughed until we were completely hysterical.

Two months later, we weren't laughing anymore. The four-day countdown had begun. She was transported to Greensville.

I moved into a Hampton Inn in nearby Emporia and drove to see her every day.

On the last day of Madam's life, as the sun turned hot outside, the door of the visiting room opened with a slow click and she shuffled in in her orange jumpsuit and white Keds scuffs, her wrists caught at her waist with a heavy shackle belt that rubbed them raw, her ankles encircled with bruising steel cuffs that were joined with a short link of chain. The light shone off her hair as off wet coal, and her hooded dark blue eyes gazed at me peacefully. She held a thick manila envelope in her hands and waited patiently while one of the burly female guards removed the shackles. Then she sat down across the table and lit a cigarette. "How are the dogs?"

"Fine, Madam. As naughty as ever." My jaunty answer was hollow. I struggled not to cry.

She smiled and handed the envelope to the heavy-girthed matron, who outweighed me two-to-one. Her only weapon, beyond arms and legs as thick as tree trunks, was a small solar-powered microphone clipped to her shirt collar. She opened the envelope and riffled through the pages, looking for contraband, before putting them back in and passing the packet to me.

"You don't need to look at those now, Nigel," Madam said. "Just some last minute papers. But listen to me, my darling friend . . ." She gave me a look so drenched in love and kindness, I could feel my heart begin to swell with tears. My chest tightened and I couldn't breathe. Her voice was calm. "That envelope also contains my will, and I've left every thing to you. You'll be able to live very comfortably."

What fun was the money without her? The brown paper felt like ashes in my hands.

"Do you promise you'll come tonight?"

I nodded.

"You'll bury me at the farm?"

"Yes, Madam," I whispered.

"You'll stay at the farm forever?"

"I promise."

She stood and ground out her cigarette and focused her eyes on mine. The matron re-hitched the chains.

"I love you, Nigel."

"I love you with all my heart, Madam."

62

I went back to the hotel, but I couldn't stay in my room. It was small and hot and I wanted to run and scream and cry. There was no release, no salvation. I went for a walk. I went to a bar and ordered a whiskey, and for a few minutes I stared blindly at the wrestling matches on ESPN. I opened the envelope and began to read.

Dearest Nigel—

Her letter began. It was several pages, maybe a dozen, all written in her illegible handwriting—illegible to everyone but me.

> *I don't want you to be afraid for me, and I want you to know how all right it is that I am paying for this crime you and I both*

know I didn't commit, because the ones I have committed are so much worse than the one I'm accused of. You have no idea.

The day after my mother died, I was looking for cash and discovered her girlhood diary behind a wallboard in the Paris studio. What it said made the hair stand out on my neck. Do you remember when Junior told us about his little sister, Jaxeen? The one he "learned" on who committed suicide? Well, she didn't. She was my mother, Constanza di Fidelio. She'd gotten pregnant by the gardener, and Daddy Rex had thrown her out. That unknown Mexican gardener is my father—there was never any polo-playing, South American playboy, Rubirosa di Fidelio. According to the diary, she worked her way across the country and ended up in New Orleans, where she became the mistress (pregnant) of a Frenchman who ended up taking her home to Paris and setting her up in Place Vauban, where she learned to paint.

You would not believe the stories about what her father and brother and sisters did to her. They were depraved beyond anyone's imagination, and when I read the journal that day after she died, all the lights came on. Why she acted the way she did, why she was crazy, where all her cruelty came from. And I made her a promise I'd get even. It sounds so dramatic to say I'd avenge her life. I didn't even like her. But all of a sudden, I loved her. I felt so sorry for her. And that first day the IRS came to the farm and offered me the choice to spy on Armand or turn over everything, it was the opening I'd been searching for. His relationship with the Hammonds was well known.

I ordered another whiskey.

I don't have time to describe to you all the gyrations I went through, but the afternoon of the party on the Kiss-Kiss, while you were packing and everyone else was sleeping, and I told you I was going to work out? Remember? I went to the engine room and taped a bomb to the fuel tank. It was simple to make. I learned how to do it off the Internet. It was rigged-up to look like a natural gas explosion.

And while you were in Paris, bringing back the Gemini? That

was a ruse to get you out of town for a few days so I could fly to Japan and buy a fugu. You wouldn't even believe what I went through to get that done. The day you got home, and Junior was there and we were eating tuna fish sandwiches on the floor and playing Scrabble? Well, the tuna was the only way I could think of to cover the smell of the fugu. I'd chopped it up that morning and turned it into sushi. I put the sushi in the freezer and then stuck it in my purse before we left for the party at the museum. I'm the one who fed it to Bianca.

Patty is the only one I really feel very badly about. And William. But they both had to go because I sensed William knew what I was up to. There was just something about him that made me think he knew I'd placed that bomb on the boat. He never said anything, but I always had the feeling he had seen me in the engine room that afternoon. And, of course, Patty was a Hammond. It was a lot easier than I thought it would be. I found William around a blind corner on the trail. He'd unloaded all his camera equipment and was totally concentrated on taking a picture. I just sneaked up behind him and gave him a little push. And then I waited until Patty came around the same corner and gave her a shove. The medical pack made her sink like a stone. Breaking my leg was a complete accident, but it certainly absolved me of any suspicion.

The one thing I've never been able to figure out is, who called and squealed on Armand?

I smiled and lit a cigarette.

Junior? You know that story. My only regret is that Daddy Rex died before I had a chance to get to him myself. I had some very special things planned for his demise.

Here's how I feel, Nigel, my only friend: I deserve to die. Not only for what I've done, but to clear the earth of Hammonds. Because I am one, myself. And although I don't feel as if I'm as awful as they were—maybe it's the gentleness of my father the gardener in me—I probably am. Lots of innocent people are dead because of me.

Thank you for making my life so whole, for being my friend.
Have a ball with the money. You deserve it.

I love you,
Your Madam

"I'll be goddamned," I said, and had another whiskey.

Two hours later, as I was preparing to go to the prison, a local news bulletin came on the television, interrupting the Monday Night Football Pre-Game show.

"The Governor has issued a stay of execution for Jackie Hammond, who was scheduled to die tonight at nine o'clock. Apparently evidence has been uncovered that casts reasonable doubt on her guilt. We'll bring you more on this story as it develops."

The next three days were agony. I couldn't get any information from anyone, until finally Leonard Slater called. By now they had moved Madam back to Fluvanna.

"They've finished all the tests, and it looks like it's real," he said.

"Looks as if *what's* real?" I blurted.

"The suicide note. It absolves Jackie of everything, including the gift of the jewelry. Come to the prison at three o'clock, they're going to release her."

I was escorted to the warden's office. It was filled with people— Leonard, Madam, a number of people I didn't know, and . . . Ryder Mc-Cormick.

"I'm so sorry," Ryder was saying. "I was so shocked that day when I got home and saw Mary Anne like that in the pond, I never thought about anything but that she had been murdered. I grabbed all her papers from the table, ran back to the house, and called the police. And then I saw the safe was open. She never left it open, but I guess by then, she didn't want to use the extra strength to close it."

I was afraid to look at Madam.

"It was only a few days ago," Ryder continued his apologia, or whatever the hell it was, "when I was going through her things, knowing that the end was coming, that Jackie would pay for what she'd done, and I could put that part of my life behind me, really say goodbye and start over, that I found the note." He looked at Madam. His eyes looked like he was crying out of both of them. "I hope someday you'll be able to forgive me."

That miserable goddamn bastard. He knew what he was doing all along. "If I find the suicide note, will you marry me?" Remember when he asked her that? He had this whole thing planned.

The range of emotions should have been note-worthy, but in fact, it was a single blanket of numbness that settled over the car as I drove us home that evening after Madam had signed a stack of documents and reclaimed the suit she'd worn to her sentencing hearing three years before.

"Did you read my letter?" she asked after a while.

"Yes, Madam."

Neither one of us said anymore. I think we were both too exhausted.

When we got home she went directly into the library and poured herself a large drink.

Moments later, there was a loud knocking on the door. It was Ryder. He brushed past me into the library and helped himself to a neat whiskey. Then he turned to Madam and raised his glass.

"Got you," he said, and tossed it off.

Madam and I looked at each other and smiled.

Now, it was just a matter of time, and we had all the time in the world. He was a dead duck.

The End

ACKNOWLEDGMENTS

Many friends and colleagues, old and new, opened their doors and assisted with the writing of *Insatiable*, and I am pleased to be able to thank them publicly:

The idea for *Insatiable* was born in a phone call with my former agent Nick Ellison, and I am extremely grateful to him for his creative guidance and support. Nigel was born in a subsequent editorial meeting with Judy Kern at Doubleday, and Nita Taublib and Kate Miciak at Bantam, and grew beyond anyone's imaginings.

Our accountant, Lois E. Hookham CPA, CFP, in Virginia Beach, provided the scary numbers on how fast interest and penalties can grow on past-due federal taxes.

John B. Hightower, President and CEO of The Mariners' Museum in Newport News, Virginia, past president and CEO of the Museum of

Modern Art in New York City, and one of America's most dashing gentlemen, put me in touch with two of the country's leading portrait artists: Thomas Buechner and Aaron Shikler, who provided me with insights into the working life of a portrait artist.

Denver Post columnist, Bill Husted, gave me the inside scoop on what's hot and what's not in Aspen; Tina Smith and Charles Pitchford at Gorsuch, Ltd. in Aspen assembled Madam's ultimate ski wardrobe.

Writing about Nepal was a tremendous challenge because, like Madam, I have a policy not to travel anywhere that isn't more comfortable than our home. However, I love to read about and talk to adventurers—I admire their ability to set aside their personal comfort for the sake of venturing into the unknown. Denver mountaineer, Sue Bickert, treks regularly in Nepal and gave me great understanding about trekking from a woman's point of view. I selected the Dolpo region of Nepal because it is seldom visited, extremely remote, very hard-going, and unlike any other place in the world. I read every thing I could find. Our friends Marcy and Bruce Benson put me in touch with Honorable Leon J. Weil, who served as ambassador to Nepal for President George Bush. Ambassador Weil, (who is no relation to the book's Armand Weil—this was sheer coincidence), kindly answered my questions and put me in touch with Frederick P. Selby, a member of The Explorers Club, headquartered in New York City. Mr. Selby had just returned from a trek in Dolpo and generously shared his adventures with me. There are unquestionably errors in my Nepal section—the errors are completely mine and I apologize for and take full responsibility for them. I have made every attempt to stay true to the wonderful people and grandeur of that magical tiny kingdom that sits on top of the world.

Larry Traylor, Director of Communications at the Virginia Department of Corrections, provided me with women's prison and execution procedures in Virginia, including the fact that in Virginia an inmate on death row can choose between lethal injection and the electric chair. The Farquier County Sheriff's Department led me through 911 and arrest procedures in that beautiful part of Virginia where they're no strangers to high-visibility cases.

At Doubleday, I want to thank William Thomas, editor-in-chief, who stood strongly behind *Insatiable,* and editors Deborah Cowell and Judith Kern for their thoughtful and sensitive editing; copy editors Harold Grabau and Lisa Yanofsky; art director Amy King and designer Dana Treglia for *Insatiable's* elegant look; and publicists Gail Brussels and Beth Dickey. What a great team of professionals—I am very, very lucky to have their support and expertise. Nita Taublib and Kate Miciak at Bantam have been equally supportive, and I am grateful for an opportunity to thank them publicly.

My friends' generosity and patience seem to know no limits—Mary and Richard Schaefer for at least one dinner a week (two if I am especially wily); Delores and Stephen Wolf for their open door policy and unflagging enthusiasm; Mary Lou Paulsen, Pam and Bill Wall, and the Bensons for being so generally excellent; Mia Hamel, Operations Manager at The Kellogg Organization, Inc. for her constantly cool, efficient, and steady Wyoming head. She keeps us on track against all odds.

Finally, my family—my brothers, John and Drew Davis, have been tolerant and forthcoming as my key research assistants. Unfortunately, they have upgraded their tastes and will no longer accept 6:00 A.M. phone calls in exchange for burritos and margaritas. They now demand ribeyes and Jordan red, but they're worth it. My parents, God love them, still get vapors over and apologize for my language, but I know they're very proud of me. Peto, Hunter, Courtney, Duncan, and Delaney bring us pride and joy we never imagined possible. And most of all, Peter, my excellent husband, whose patience and generosity of spirit and love make all good things in my life possible.

Thanks to all of you. I hope you have as much fun reading *Insatiable* as I did writing it.

Marne Davis Kellogg
Denver, Colorado
August 2000